iii

FOR SUCH A TIME, THE STORY OF JARRETT ROSS

BY ANNE GREENE

Endorsements

For Such A Time is a thrilling story that shares an unfamiliar side of the Civil War, a side fought by Cherokees. This well-researched story will keep you on the edge of your seat. You will pull for Jarrett and Delight as they navigate the dangers of war, and you will mourn as Jarrett is forced to take a side in the bloody killing. But God's message is woven throughout as you see how his care for his children never wanes. Anne Greene has created a gripping tale. Well done, Ms. Greene.
—**Paula Peckham**, author, The San Antonio Series

Kudos on this sequel to *Trail of Tears*. Anne Greene has done a superlative job of helping the reader identify with the struggles of Native Americans in the Oklahoma Territory. Readers will also sympathize with Jarrett Ross's conflict during a war he feels is not his, yet he must join the conflict against his will. With nonstop action, the story will keep you reading from the first to the last page.
—**Linda Wood Rondeau**, author of *Ghosts of Trumball Mansion*

In *For Such a Time*, author Anne Greene has crafted a memorable, well-researched story of historical fiction capturing the hardship, pathos, and courageous spirit of the people of the Cherokee Nation in the Oklahoma Territory just before and during the American Civil War. In the broad scope of these troubled times, the author introduces the reader to the close-knit Ross family and their friends, neighbors, and Cherokee rivals. In particular, the story of

young Jarrett Ross becomes a metaphor for the turbulent changes and struggles inflicted by a cataclysmic war. While Delight Flint becomes at once both an alluring and a dangerous romantic attraction for Jarrett, his transformation into a young man thrusts him into life-threatening service in the Pony Express and in desperate combat during the war. How Jarrett, Delight, and the other endearing characters of *For Such a Time* persevere, remain faithful, and grow in stature tell us much about the intensity of the period and the noble character of so many of our ancestors.
—James Yarbrough, author of *Killer App*

Anne Greene's saga of Jarrett Ross will sweep you up, not only in the love story between him and Delight Flint but also with little-known facts of our nation's early years. You will experience the life of the Cherokee, the arduous journey of the riders of the Pony Express, and how a pacifist survives his conscription into the Civil War. Meticulously researched and brilliantly written, you won't want to miss this story.
—Carol McClain, author of *Tangled Lives*

Anne Greene transports readers into a troubling time in history with an emotionally charged and captivating story of faith and hope. After the illegal 1835 Treaty of New Echota removed the Cherokee people from their land, Jarrett Ross and his family make the best of life in the Indian Territory, despite enemies both white and brown.
Jarrett's life in Oklahoma Territory while living among the Indians includes love, buffalo hunts, his time in the Pony Express, and the Civil War. All this makes intense

drama. Anne weaves fact and fiction into a story that makes you experience love, joy, anger, sadness, and compassion.

Though I taught this piece of history, I learned a lot and gained a new respect for the people involved. If you enjoy page-turning history, this book's for you.

—**Susan G Mathis**, award-winning author of *Thousand Islands Gilded Age*

Ms. Greene has done it again. *For Such a Time: The Story of Jarrett Ross*, accurately portrays the Civil War as fought in the West as a time of brutality, hatred, and hardship that dismantled two countries—a young United States and a highly successful Cherokee nation. The war not only divided a homeland but shattered relations as well. Then add a family feud to the rising tempest. How will twenty-year-old Jarrett Ross, a Pony Express hero, marry the love of his life, who is on the opposite side of the war and the feud? Anne Greene always brings history to life with facts and strong characters, plus romance to make the story real and memorable. An adventure you don't want to miss!

—**Lana Newman Kruse**, author of *Just Call Me Scrumptious*

For Such a Time is a moving story of Jarrett Ross's journey into adulthood. From the restlessness of a young man itching to get away from the family farm, to his work at the Pony Express, to having to make the most difficult decisions regarding fighting in the Civil War, Jarrett lives out his Christian and cultural convictions. I felt the desperation of his daily dangerous travels across the desert and his hope when he sought to find his true love after the ravages of war. What a great story!

—**Karen H. Richardson**, author of *Curtains for Maggie*

Dedication

I dedicate this book to my wonderful husband, Larry. Thank you for our love story. Thank you for supporting me in this great adventure of being an author. You are a gift from heaven.

And to my dear Lord Jesus Christ who gave his life so I might live.

And to you, my readers, I pray you will love this book.

Acknowledgments
Thank you so much for the help of my dedicated critique partners and dear friends: James Yarborough, and Lana Kruse. And my dear husband for his final edit.

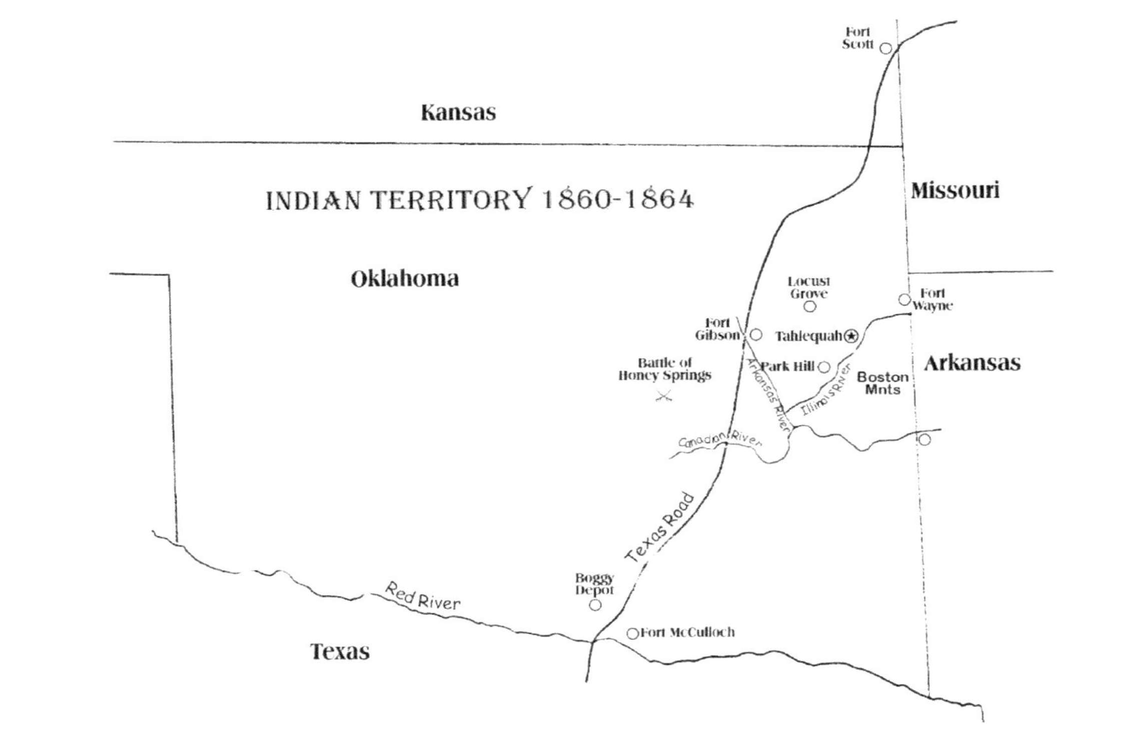

INDIAN TERRITORY 1860-1864
Kansas
Missouri
Oklahoma
Arkansas
Texas
Fort Scott
Fort Wayne
Locust Grove
Fort Gibson
Tahlequah
Park Hill
Boston Mnts
Battle of Honey Springs
Arkansas River
Illinois River
Canadian River
Texas Road
Boggy Depot
Fort McCulloch
Red River

Preface

In 1838, when the US seized Cherokee land, the Cherokee Nation split into two factions.

The Ross Faction, headed by Chief John R. Ross, labored to keep Cherokee Appalachian land and fought the federal government using legal methods and passive resistance to retain the ancient Cherokee homeland.

The Ridge-Boudinot Faction, led by Major Ridge, his son John Ridge, Elias Boudinot, and Stand Watie, reasoned the future of the Cherokee lay in the removal of the Nation to Indian Territory, now Oklahoma. So, the Ridge-Boudinot Faction signed the illegal Treaty of New Echota in 1835, allowing the government to remove the people from their land. This faction represented only a tiny portion of the Cherokee people. The majority considered the treaty treason.

The Cherokee people assassinated Major Ridge, John Ridge, and Elias Boudinot for signing the Treaty of New Echota. Stand Watie escaped the vigilante execution. He appears in this book, *For Such A Time: The Story of Jarrett Ross,* the sequel to *Trail of Tears: The Story of John Ross.* The first book tells the story of the Cherokee removal.

For Such A Time: The Story of Jarrett Ross continues the

Ross family saga and portrays Jarrett Ross, John Ross's second-born son, and his life in the Indian Territory.

Bitter feelings continued between both factions during the long lives of both Chief Ross and Stand Watie. The rift resulted in great suffering for all the Cherokee. Ironically, both Chief Ross and Stand Watie claimed to be Christians.

With the exception of Chief John R. Ross, General Stand Watie, and Saladin Watie, all other characters in this book are fictitious.

This book begins with Jarrett's new life in Oklahoma Territory living among less civilized Indians, his time in the Pony Express, and continues through the little-known drama of the Civil War as fought in the western states.

CHAPTER 1

*November 1859—Tahlequah, (Tah-la-quaw) capital of the
Cherokee Nation in Indian Territory.*

Jarrett Ross slammed the ax into the tree. The trunk bent,
and he used his foot to topple the sapling.

The rhythmic beat of hooves grew distinct. He
dropped the razor-sharp ax and jumped. The blade missed
his foot by a miracle. He raced to the split-rail fence and
stared up the dirt road. At the crest of the hill, an Indian
astride a piebald horse thundered into view.

With a rush of wind and a splatter of dirt clods, the horse
swooped toward Jarrett. The Indian pressed both fists against
his temples, forefingers curled forward to simulate curved
horns, then galloped past and out of sight around the bend.

Jarrett raced to the back door of the two-story log cabin.
"Buffalo sign! Runninghorse just gave the buffalo sign!"
Before his foot touched the stone step, the latch lifted from
inside, and his younger sister's elfin face peeked out.

"I wish you weren't going." Ten-year-old Jerusha
swiped her long, blonde hair out of her sky-blue eyes and
turned up a woebegone expression. "It's dangerous."

Jarrett pulled his sister outside and tossed her into the air.

She squealed. He slid her to the ground and charged into the house. "Mother, the Osage scout is back! Runninghorse found buffalo!"

His mother stooped near the open fireplace stirring venison soup bubbling inside a black kettle suspended over glowing coals. The delicious aroma set Jarrett's stomach grumbling.

She straightened, smoothed her red-gold hair, and adjusted her apron over her long calico skirt. "You're like a thunderstorm sweeping across the prairie. Calm down." As she smiled, dimples dented her cheeks. "I think the weather's getting too cold for you to go."

Jarrett laughed. "Takes more than bad weather to stop me." He grabbed her slender waist, lifted her feet off the plank floor, and whirled her around the room.

"Cold hands off, please. You're giving me a chill." Pink colored her clear skin, and her green eyes twinkled.

Jarrett strode across the room, boots thudding on the wide wooden boards, and shoved his hands near the fire. "I've got to get away. Find excitement. See what's happening in the world. I can bring back enough buffalo steaks to feed us for months."

Hoofbeats and buggy tires rattled on the dirt road.

"There's your father."

Drawn by a high-stepping brown mare, the buggy clattered past the living room window and continued toward the barn.

"I'll go unhitch …" Jarrett sped across the room and banged out the front door.

Dark followed him when he strode back into the cabin from the cold. He shed his mackinaw and rubbed his chilled hands. Granddad Worchester, Mother, Dad, and Jerusha waited around the table set with white cloth and pewter. Bayberry candles lit the room.

A frown puckered Jerusha's usually sunny face. "Hurry, Jarrett. Supper's ready, and I'm hungry."

Splashing cold water from the oak bucket, Jarrett scrubbed off the smell of leather, horse, and oats, then slid into his chair.

Granddad prayed.

Conversation flowed around Jarrett in a warm, gentle stream. He perched on the edge of his ladder-back chair, one foot hung over a rung, the other tapping the floor, and spooned stew into his mouth. But the savory food didn't calm his rocky insides.

He listened as Dad recounted his day of medical rounds and whose baby he'd delivered. He'd let Dad eat, then tell him. He'd planned this for weeks. Dad had to agree.

Finally, Dad pushed aside his empty plate, pulled his coffee cup toward him, and settled back into his chair. "What's on your mind, Jarrett? You have a run-in with the wrong end of a porcupine? You've been pulling out splinters since I came home."

"Sir." Beneath the tablecloth, Jarrett gripped his hands together and tried to stop jiggling his leg. "I need to leave tonight. Right now." He couldn't keep his words from tumbling over each other. "The Buffalo Dance has started." He scooted back his chair, jumped up, and paced the room.

Dad unbuttoned his brown frock coat and sipped coffee. His gray-streaked blond hair shone like silk in the candlelight. "Not a good idea. Hunting those beasts is dangerous. Plus, the buffalo range is on Pawnee land. They kill Osage hunters." His face held a mixture of pride and reluctance. "You remind me of my father. He had your spirit of adventure." Dad shook his head.

Jarrett stopped midstride. "We need the meat to get us through the winter."

Granddad Worchester laughed his low, rumbling laugh. "Well, John, you can't expect to keep your colt tied when he's ready to run. Won't do him any harm seeing the way of the Osage. He's a good Christian lad." Granddad's faded green eyes twinkled behind rimless glasses. "A hunt's dangerous, but Jarrett can handle the challenge. He won't get another chance to bring us steaks before he heads east to college." He shook his white head. "Maybe never again."

Dad shoved his chair back from the table. "I don't know if your mother can manage without you, Jarrett." Dad glanced at Mother.

Before they could collaborate against him, Jarrett fired all his shots. "I've split more than enough wood to last a month, and I'll only be away two weeks." He faced his father squarely. "Fences are mended, corn's in the silo, pig's butchered and hanging in the smokehouse, cows are in the barn, manure's shoveled out, and the cabin's chinked for winter." His words jerked together as they would do when he was excited. "Work's all done. I drove in a wagonload of supplies from Tahlequah last week."

"I don't like your being gone so long. With Jordan at college, me on the road most days, and you chasing buffalo, your mother's—"

"I'm here with Hope, John." Granddad Worchester adjusted his spectacles. "And I've prayed about this. I think God wants Jarrett to go."

Jarrett laid a hand on the slightly stooped shoulder. "Thanks, Granddad."

Dad stood and threw up his hands, a resigned expression crossed his face. At six feet two, he towered three inches above Jarrett. "Then God bless you and take care of you. Don't bring shame to the Ross name."

Jarrett grinned. "Trust me, Dad." He took the stairs three at a time to the loft he shared with Jordan when his brother was home.

The fragrance of drying herbs hanging from the rafters filled the room. Moonlight filtered through the window illuminating bunches of sweet basil, bloodroot, St. John's Wort, and dill that Mother gathered from time to time.

Jarrett inhaled the pleasant aroma as he pulled off his flannel shirt, yanked on his leather hunting shirt, shoved his pistol into his belt, and snatched his saddlebags. He clattered downstairs, cheek-kissed everyone, and headed for the front door. He grabbed his mackinaw from the door peg then bolted outside.

Moonlight transformed the small farm into a world of shadows and patchy light—eerie and exhilarating. He inhaled the crisp scent of frosted leaves and packed earth, lifted his arms, and stifled a hoot and holler. He was free. No chores for two weeks, and—he'd go to places he'd never been. The thought of danger made him grin.

He jogged down the path to the barn, his exhaled breath visible in the air. The sturdy wooden building welcomed him with its sweet scent of timothy hay, blue-stem grass, manure, and the soft breathing of horses.

"Hello, Sampson. Good boy. Ready for a run?" He saddled his horse, then with a creak of leather and a clatter of hooves on frozen ground, he galloped for the Osage village.

The position of Orion announced the time to be close to midnight when he pulled Sampson to a stop at the edge of the village. Ghostly in the moonlight, grotesque shadows flitted between tepees.

He leaned across his saddle horn, breath coming fast, and gazed at the confused bustle. Laughter, songs, and loud noises floated through the darkness. Unfamiliar aromas rose from campfires tended by ethereal women.

He stood in his stirrups as adrenaline surged through his body and left him tingling. Tapping his heels against Sampson's ribs, he trotted forward among the tepees. Where was Horse? Pungent smells and odors assaulted Jarrett's nostrils. This was a different world. A multitude of dogs rushed his pony's hooves, nipping and snarling.

Sampson kicked the dogs away.

Jarrett circled Sampson around a large tepee where three women stood at the door flap arguing like witches over a cauldron.

Jarrett pressed his knees in Sampson's side, gazing over the array of tepees. He caught sight of his new friend talking with a group of braves.

Bells tinkled on Horse's moccasins. He sported a leather shirt and leggings and wore a buffalo robe draped over his shoulders. When he moved, a necklace of bear claws and teeth swayed around his muscular neck. Rings dangled from brown ears, and two eagle feathers stuck out of his long, black hair. Firelight flashed on something at Horse's waist.

Goose bumps shivered Jarrett's arms. Horse carried a war hatchet. Nerves tightened along the base of Jarrett's neck. The deep shadows, a new arrogant expression, and the ax transformed his friend into someone more savage.

He waited for Horse to notice him.

His friend looked wild. His black eyes gleamed in his bronzed face. He yelled in his own language to his friends and brandished his war hatchet. Then his gaze focused on Jarrett. Tossing his head like a wild animal, he shouted the short barking yips of the Osage victory cry.

The Indian rushed over, kicked the dogs snarling around Jarrett's stirrups, and grasped Jarrett's arm. "At last, you come."

"Pleasure to be here." Jarrett dismounted, his heart thudding.

"Come, friend. You late. Ceremony begun."

Jarrett tied Sampson to a tree behind a large tepee. He raced after Horse toward a blazing fire spewing thick smoke to the inky sky. Black clouds moved in, hiding the moonlight. Everything outside the fire's light disappeared into darkness.

"Buffalo great medicine. Good you come."

Jarrett shrugged. "Yeah." Maybe not. Horse seemed a stranger with his hawk nose painted red and tossing his war hatchet from one hand to the other.

A wide grin spread over Horse's features. "Careful. Maidens think you make good husband. Think you look soft. Think you no wallop with tent pole when she bad!"

"Don't talk crazy!" Jarrett poked his friend on the shoulder. "Who wants a wife?"

They skirted behind a large circle of seated men until they found an opening. Jarrett followed Horse's lead and dropped to sit cross-legged beside him facing the fire.

Women in colorful dress danced around the mammoth blaze, their long skirts whisking close to the shooting flames and exposing trim ankles. This wasn't bad. He liked to watch the ladies, and four or five were young and pretty.

Beneath Horse's hooked nose, his mouth thinned. "Strict rules for dance. Horse no look good in Osage eyes if Woodcarver no act well."

Jarrett nodded.

Horse pointed to poles planted at four corners around the circle. "Punishment poles. If Woodcarver no act well, move at wrong time or get up, guards tie you to pole, much high, much hurt, until sun rise. Much bad medicine."

Jarrett stiffened his spine and straightened his leather shirt. "No worries. Trust me."

Horse frowned and sat ramrod straight, face impassive, black eyes fixed on the fire.

Women quit dancing.

Fifteen braves assembled before the mystery lodge. Each wore the head and horns of a buffalo, had a buffalo robe draped over his shoulders, and carried a bow and a lance. In a single line, the men circled the fire. Each one imitated a buffalo, lowering and raising its massive head and bellowing. Other Indians hunched cross-legged around the fire's perimeter, beating drums. The wild drumming quickened Jarrett's pulse.

Without turning, Horse murmured, "Brother Buffalo Great Medicine. After dance end, Brother Buffalo say he give him life to Osage Brother. Buffalo keep Osage from starving through winter." With his erect, impassive posture, Horse seemed unaffected by the crazy rhythm and wild dancing.

Jarrett's blood thrummed with the drums and the dancers' silhouetted forms leaping about the flames. The bounding animal-like figures danced and chanted, tossing their horned heads to the hammering cadence.

Horse leaned close and whispered, "Drumbeats are breath of Great Spirit. Osage in tune with Great Spirit. Let Great Medicine enter self."

The chanting and drumbeats crept into Jarrett's nervous system. Heat ignited his body. He was one with the night, one with the dancers, one with the buffalo.

Hours later, the thwacking noise morphed into a throbbing headache. Cold from the frozen ground seeped into his feet and spread through his body. He shivered. His leather hunting shirt was no match for the cold. He rubbed circulation into his legs and leaned toward Horse so his whisper could be heard above the pounding drums. "How about taking a stretch?"

"No move in circle. Give offense."

Jarrett stiffened his back. This rivaled a fourteen-hour day behind a lonely plow.

"Soon Horse dance. Watch, that one tired." Horse nodded toward a dancer.

The man bent lower and lower. Another brave jumped up, drew his bow, and hit the sinking Indian's buffalo robe with blunt arrows that thudded against the leather with a hollow sound. The brave fell to the ground like a wounded buffalo.

Indian women hovering outside the ring rushed to the fallen brave, grabbed him by his heels and dragged the exhausted brave into the night. The drums never missed a beat.

Women danced about the fallen buffalo brave, brandishing knives and making motions of skinning and cutting. Beaded buffalo and doe skin, flashing necklaces and earrings, and bright feathers gave the women festive beauty. They chanted, their voices blending in a low moaning note and rising to a piercing crescendo.

Jarrett folded his chilly hands under his arms to stave off the cold creeping into his bones and examined the seated Indians. All were Osage men wearing paint on their faces. Many carried war hatchets, and all sat incredibly still. Only their black eyes moved, watching the dancers.

Out of the corner of his eye, Jarrett noticed the only other white man there sitting between Horse and a big Indian. A trader, by the looks of his clothes. The fellow appeared to be about thirty, stocky built and unshaven, with the muscular arms and shoulders of a blacksmith.

"Who's the white guy next to you?" Jarrett whispered.

Horse scowled, eyes fixed on the dancers. "Plenty bad man. No should be here. Sneak into dance. Osage no want."

"Why?"

"Him smuggle whiskey. Make trouble for Osage." Horse leaped to his feet and joined the dancers, shooting his arrows at a tired man-buffalo.

A sharp poke in his ribs jerked Jarrett's attention to the trader, who had scooted closer. Though the trader sat cross-legged, he towered head and shoulders over Jarrett.

"Have a snort." Saliva trickled from the corner of his mouth.

Jarrett shook his head.

The massive elbow poked him again. The man reeked of whiskey and dirty socks. "Come on, kid, have a nip. It'll warm you up."

"I don't want any." Jarrett clinched his fists.

"Thash no way to talk to a man's trying to be friendly."

The women's rising song covered the trader's loud voice.

"No." As Jarrett answered, the crescendo fell to a low chant. Every eye in the circle of immobile men turned his direction and glared. Bronze hands tightened around war hatchets. Horse missed several steps.

Jarrett's face heated. He rotated his shoulder from the sour-smelling bully. At five feet ten in his boots and weighing one hundred sixty-five pounds soaking wet, Jarrett attracted every rowdy looking for a fight. He sighed.

"You'll thank me for this." A brawny arm enveloped Jarrett in a bear hug. With his other arm the trader lifted a jug, shoved the lip to Jarrett's mouth, forced the jug against his teeth so hard, he had to open his mouth or lose teeth.

He struggled in the giant's grasp. Like a rushing stream, liquid flowed into his mouth. He gagged. No choice but to swallow. And swallow again. The liquor burned all the way down his throat into his chest. Some sloshed down his chin and over his shirt front. He choked, gasped, and sputtered. His eyes watered, and liquid dripped from his nose.

Jarrett twisted and turned, fighting the iron grip.

CHAPTER 2

Jarrett pitted all his strength against the smuggler's grip and shoved aside the half-empty jug.

The drums hammered on like so many blows to his brain. Shuffling moccasins increased in force and tempo. Black eyes glared in his direction.

Heat flooded Jarrett from his chest to his toes. He clenched his jaw and curled his hand into fists. He couldn't let the drunk get away with his bullying, but he'd given his word to Runninghorse not to disturb the dance. Blast! He'd learned years ago the only way to stop a tormentor was to confront him so—

Runninghorse rushed from the dancers, threw his robe over Jarrett's shoulders, and jammed the buffalo head over Jarrett's. He pulled Jarrett to his feet and shoved him into the circle of dancers.

Jarrett's insides burned. The robe smelled of Runninghorse, and the buffalo head suffocated him. His hands and feet tingled, and his head felt peculiar—dizzy. But Horse counted on him. The dance couldn't be hard. He shuffled his feet, but the ground tilted. He lurched and stiffened his legs, but his feet tangled. He tossed and lowered his head. *Yahola.* Big mistake! He clamped his mouth and clutched his stomach.

Immediately a brave entered the ring and shot arrows which thudded against Jarrett's buffalo robe. The ground rose to meet him. He staggered. His hands banged the frozen earth and broke his fall.

Vague shadows rushed in, rolled him over, and dragged him from the ring by his heels. Someone stripped off the hot buffalo head. A wave of cold air hit his face, and moonlight glimmered through heavy clouds.

A gaggle of women bent over him. Their giggles, whispers, and laughter sounded from a long distance. He rolled onto his stomach and shielded his ears. Hands grasped his wrists and ankles, and he swayed and bumped through the air. Women carried him inside a tepee and dropped him near a fire. A shuffle of moccasins and then silence.

Jarrett hunched to a more comfortable position.

Runninghorse entered the tepee. The Indian had a presence. "Had Woodcarver been Osage, him would be dreamer of dreams, seer of visions, interpreter of wampum. Shaman," the bass voice rumbled. "But him jaw have look of warrior."

Jarrett blinked.

"Woodcarver act well when bad man make trouble. Trader no cause war between Osage and blue-eyed Cherokee. Him sell more whiskey if Osage take war path."

Ah, so that was the trader's motivation. Jarrett smiled and fell asleep.

***

A hand shook Jarrett so roughly his head bounced on the blanket-covered ground. "Take it easy." He shoved at the hand.

"Come!" Runninghorse's voice sounded loud.

Jarrett slit one eye open. Through the tepee flap, ribbons of color lit the eastern sky. "Go away. Let me sleep."

Runninghorse shook Jarrett's shoulder.

Nails of pain drove into his brain. He squinted in the dim light. "It's dark. Go to bed."

"Hunt starts!"

Jarrett yawned and rubbed his stinging eyes. He pushed into a sitting position and cradled his throbbing head in both hands.

"If rule broke, penalty must pay. Village depend on each man keep rules."

Jarrett flexed his cramped back and arms and jacked himself to his feet. Why was he inside this tepee? Like a fog lifting, grogginess eased, and last night's events came into focus. He twisted his lips into a grimace.

"Come."

Jarrett groaned, then bent and followed Horse out of the tepee.

Morning village smells curdled Jarrett's stomach. The sweet tobacco from the ceremonial pipe, hot tallow wafting from cooking pots, and the musky smell of the Indians' bodies forced him to swallow against the bitter taste rising in his throat.

"Now we talk with Great Spirit." Runninghorse accepted a long, large-bowled, pipe from an Indian with yellowed teeth. Horse inhaled, then puffed, facing first north, then south, then east and finally west. He passed the pipe to Jarrett.

Jarrett stared at the well-chewed stem, wet from contact with hundreds of mouths. His stomach flipped. But he thrust the putrid pipestem into his mouth and inhaled. Coughing shook him. His eyes watered. The sweet scent deceived. The tobacco tasted strong, pungent, and unpleasant. He forced himself to repeat the ritual three times. Then he pulled fresh air into his lungs.

"You want eat?"

Sweat broke out on Jarrett's forehead. "Uh, no thanks."

"Then we ride." Runninghorse jogged to the meadow where horses waited.

Jarrett followed. Every step jostled his head and thrust daggers into his brain. In the pasture, he knelt beside a stream and plunged his hands into frigid water, splashing his face. Face dripping, he approached the horses, his boots thudding over the frozen ground. He whistled for Sampson.

His mustang raised his head, pricked his ears, trotted over, and nuzzled Jarrett's hand.

He stroked Sampson's velvet nose and shaggy mane.

Runninghorse snapped his reins against his thigh as he waited for Jarrett to saddle his mustang. "That only horse you bring?"

"Sampson's the only horse I own. But he's fast."

Horse leaped on his piebald's blanketed back. The mustang danced, excited, eager to run with the other horses galloping toward the prairie. Runninghorse reined him in. "This Horse's buffalo pony. Horse ride him and no other to hunt buffalo. He fastest pony in tribe."

Jarrett couldn't resist. "Race you to the front!" He vaulted into his saddle and ignored his pounding head. He caught up with Horse, and they raced, hooves clattering on frozen turf, hair flying in the wind, weaving in, out, and around the moving Indians.

Dogs harnessed to travois yapped and children squealed. Mothers scolded and men dodged in and out of the melee. Maidens wearing beaded doeskin walked their horses, keeping an alluring eye on the braves.

Runninghorse threw back his head and yelled.

Jarrett echoed his shout, stood in his stirrups, and urged Sampson on.

Many female eyes gazed at him.

He grinned at them all.

Indians sang and laughed. Soon they would eat meat.

Jarrett glanced behind him. Like a living carpet, the people crept over the hills toward the prairies.

Horse passed him and surged ahead.

"Come on, Sampson. We can't let Horse beat us. Let's go." He touched his heels to Sampson's sides.

The mustang flattened his body and galloped full-out.

Jarrett leaned along his neck, urging him faster. They broke into the open, in front of the moving caravan.

Runninghorse pulled his piebald up so short, he rose on his hind legs, his forefeet pawing air.

Sampson skidded into a three-point stop behind him.

"No look down in heart, friend. You horse much fast. Saddle slow Woodcarver. Why no leave saddle with women?"

Jarrett shifted in the saddle, making the leather creak. "I'm not crazy. Picture me riding bareback, caught off balance and falling beneath stampeding buffalo." He raised an eyebrow. "Besides, if I did, you wouldn't have the fastest horse."

He and Horse sat at the crest of a rise, watching the people travel toward them. Morning sun glinted in Jarrett's eyes. He inhaled the crisp air, scented with late autumn, fallen leaves, and drying grass. Even with the shattering pain in his head, he was glad he'd come. "What's next? Do we wait for them?" He pointed toward the moving village.

"No. We scout. Too dangerous go far. Run into Pawnee. You horse fast. We outrun Pawnee if we find."

"I'm ready for anything."

They kneed their mounts into a mile-devouring trot. Jarrett pushed his pistol further into his belt. If he met any Pawnee, he would not be caught off guard.

"Watch for holes!" Runninghorse called. "Elk or deer sleep there." He pointed to a spot where the bushes flattened, and the frozen ground had gotten mushy.

They entered a ravine so steep the mustangs put their feet together to slide down and arrived at bottomland near a river. On the sandbank, tracks of wolves, turkeys, and waterfowl etched the soft mud.

Woods thinned into a few scattered trees dotting the hills, then into bushes and shrubs.

Runninghorse cut his mount toward a clump of willows. "War party camp here. Pawnee. No wigwams, no women. See open spot tramped? Ashes? Mean war dance."

Jarrett shivered. "This close?"

"Pawnee watch us. Now we hunt buffalo. Scouting party made war dance." He held up two hands, all fingers lifted. "No hide tracks. No care we see."

"How can you tell how many?"

"See twig broken here and here?" Runninghorse pointed out sign. "See grass bruised there, so wide." He pulled down a piece of bark hanging from a sapling that swayed above his head. "Bark-talk say three more war parties."

Jarrett stopped Sampson beside the tall Indian's mustang.

Runninghorse touched the picture of a saddled horse whose rider carried no bow. "Here you."

Jarrett stared. "What are these symbols? Must be twenty or thirty of them." He fingered the left corner of the bark.

"Scalps. Pawnee want scalps and horses. Also want six-shooter." Horse reached over to touch the worn handle of the old pistol protruding from Jarrett's belt.

Hair rose on the nape of Jarrett's neck. He glanced around the clearing. "How far away are they?"

"Ride to hill. We see."

Near the top of the hill, they dismounted, dropped their reins, then fell to their bellies and crawled to the summit. Hidden in tall, yellowed grass, they commanded a panoramic view. The hills decreased in size, intersected with straggling stands of black-jack and post oaks that could hide four Pawnee war parties.

"That's the most barren land I've ever seen," Jarrett whispered. "Like a graveyard with no headstones. Just you and me out here alone gives me goosebumps."

Runninghorse's lips curled, and he shrugged.

"How far to the prairie?"

"Two moons. Many stops rest women, children. Not worry, much good. Woodcarver see—Osage play games." The Indian's black eyes gleamed.

Jarrett grinned. He'd never backed down from a challenge. "Right, games."

Runninghorse grunted, his gaze on the land laid out in front of them. "No see Pawnee, but Pawnee there. We go back."

Long before they sighted the moving camp, Jarrett heard shouts, the sound of hooves, an occasional yipping cry, and dogs barking. With the village stopped for lunch, children collected wood. Women set cooking pots on tripods, and men hobbled horses in a meadow of wild pea vines near a stream.

Horse rode off to alert the chief about the Pawnee war party.

Jarrett dismounted and ran to help a woman carry two heavy pails of water. The woman scowled, scolded him in Osage, and refused to let him help.

"Cooking woman work. Brave, scout, hunt, make war, show son how live. All else woman work." Horse's copper features showed amusement. He dismounted, pulled his blanket off his pony, and stretched full-length on the cover, eyes closed.

Jarrett rubbed his chin. Osage were sure different. He sauntered over to Sampson and rummaged in his smallest saddlebag. His hand closed over a smooth piece of seasoned wood. Jerking the leather bag wider, he pulled out his flannel-wrapped tools and strode to where Runninghorse dozed. Jarrett dropped to slouch against a tree, moving his shoulder blades against the rough bark until he felt comfortable.

He studied the cherry grain, then opened his packet and laid out his tools. The wood felt alive in his hand. He stropped the three pocketknife blades on the leather strop hanging from his belt. Then severed a blond hair on his wrist. Making his first incision, he whittled in line with the grain. He inhaled the wood scent as shavings curled from his knife.

"Again, Woodcarver work."

Jarrett startled and almost cut his thumb. "You awake?" He pulled a scrap of paper from his shirt pocket and spread it across his leg. "Want to learn? First, I draw the shape to keep the image in my mind." Light wind ruffled the paper.

"That good drawing. Show strength. How you make look so real?"

Jarrett's shoulder touched the Indian hunkered beside him. "Bone structure. Especially here where the bones lie near the surface" He pointed to different parts of his drawing. "Here, the skull, for instance, and the shoulders. The spine must be kept flexible. The skeleton gives form to the statue."

Jarrett folded his drawing as carefully as a love letter and returned the paper to the pocket of his leather shirt.

Horse shook his head.

Jarrett frowned. How could he explain better? "You know how you recognize a person when he is far away by his walk? I capture the things that make a person or an animal unique. Like the way he holds his head and how he balances and moves."

Horse nodded.

Jarrett picked up his gouge, pushed and twisted the tool, working out the design. "Carving's slow work, but the job gives me time to think."

"Dream. Woodcarver dream. Get far look on face, eyes stare out at nothing. Horse watch. Horse see."

"Aw, just when the work's not too delicate."

"Or when Woodcarver head hurt from drink." Runninghorse kicked Jarrett's thigh with his moccasined foot.

"Huh." Jarrett wiped the largest blade on his pants. "You

only use your black mustang for buffalo hunts. I only use this pocketknife for whittling. If I used it for cutting anything else, the edge wouldn't be keen enough."

"Why you no shoot pistol at whiskey man?"

Jarrett tightened his jaw. "I don't believe in killing."

"No if he try kill Woodcarver?"

"I hope I never find out." Jarrett's eyes strayed to the war hatchet hanging from Runninghorse's waist.

In the distance, feminine voices yelled Osage words.

"Women say come, eat."

Jarrett wrapped his tools inside the packet and packed it and his unfinished carving inside a square of wool, then thrust everything inside his saddlebag, and followed his friend to where the people sat in a circle on the grass.

Mimicking the Osage, Jarrett ate with his fingers, picking hot meat from the iron kettle, wiping his hands on his trousers, then dipping brown Indian bread into the stew. He settled in the tall grass, enjoying the pungent food, the warm sunlight, and the chattering people.

After the males finished, the women and children ate. Then they were on the move again. All day they rode, braves showing off, flashing in and out among moving hordes of people. Jarrett's thighs burned, his back ached, and his rear felt glued to the saddle.

He'd never ridden so many miles from home.

Braves showed their riding skill, leaping astride ponies as they galloped by or sliding onto one side of their pony, only a moccasin toe visible.

I will learn that trick," Jarrett mumbled.

The sun glared on the western horizon. Jarrett's shoulders drooped. When the command to make camp came, he slid a stiff leg over the saddle and lowered himself to the ground.

Women prepared the food. Campfires cast splashes of light across the meadow. Spits rotated meat above fires, juices sizzling in the flames below. Delicious scents filled the area.

Horse rode up. "Good life, always it was so. Buffalo Great Medicine. Osage no could live without buffalo. Big brother buffalo sacred. He give meat, hide for tepee, hide for boat, hide for robe. Buffalo give pemmican, bone for soup, shoulder blade for war club. Buffalo give Osage all things need to live."

Jarrett grinned. "No waste."

"Now meet father." Runninghorse flicked his glossy black braids. "He much old. Mother number four wife. She favorite. Old wives quarrel."

"Which are your brothers and sisters?"

"All. All in tepee one father. Mother has Horse and Mist Over The Water." Runninghorse pointed to a pretty girl standing near, staring at Jarrett. She laughed saucily when her brother pointed to her.

"Horse take wife soon."

Jarrett grunted. "You want a wife?"

Runninghorse shrugged. "Have ponies, want woman, want son. What is scout without son?"

Jarrett followed his friend to a huge tepee. A tall Indian, his thinning braids gray, his skin wrinkled like a piece of old parchment, held out his gnarled hands.

"Him get sore bones from sleep on ground all life," Runninghorse whispered.

The old Indian peered at Jarrett through clouded eyes and

mumbled.

Runninghorse translated.

The ancient man's stern face softened. He placed his crippled hands on Jarrett's shoulders. "Welcome. May your time with Osage be a warm day in coldest winter."

Jarrett shook the man's hand. "Thank you, sir."

Horse slapped Jarrett's on the back. "Now we go to games."

Jarrett's backside ached, and his head still pounded. But he followed Runninghorse toward a knot of braves gathered in the light of a large fire.

The circle surrounded two men lying on their stomachs, right arms extended, arm wrestling. Craning his neck to see around the welter of dark heads, the musky smell of Indians strong in his nostrils, Jarrett saw one of the Indians pinned. Howls of triumph lauded the winner and jeering laughter the loser.

Horse confronted Jarrett. "Runninghorse put down Woodcarver!"

Jarrett's toes curled. He should fade into the darkness, yet something inside wouldn't let him back down. "Why not? I owe you for making a buffalo of me last night."

Lying on the cold ground, elbow embedded in the earth, hand gripped in the Osage's brawny paw, Jarrett sensed impending disaster. He set his jaw.

"Runninghorse is buffalo playing with deer," an onlooker's deep voice rumbled.

Others jeered in Osage, but the tone was unmistakable.

At the signal, Jarrett strained mightily, and their arms remained locked vertically. Sweat broke out over his face and torso. He grunted and struggled.

The circle quieted and the crackling of the fire grew loud. Cords bulged in Jarrett's neck. He clamped his teeth. His breath came in gasps.

Horse squinted. His mouth grimaced. His face clenched.

Imperceptibly, Jarrett forced Runninghorse's hand toward the ground.

Indians howled, encouraging their champion.

Jarrett's face twisted. He splayed his knee to gain leverage. Eyes shut, he concentrated his entire energies on his right hand and arm. Perspiration blinded him. Using every ounce of strength, with a final surge, he pinned Runninghorse's wrist.

Jarrett flopped flat on his back, gasping, waiting for the stars to stop whirling.

Indians cheered. There were no jeers for the loser.

Horse leaned over Jarrett. "Woodcarver strong in mind." He tapped his forehead. "Horse no lose face when lose to Woodcarver."

Through a fog of whirling stars, Jarret hoisted himself to a sitting position. "You're getting weak in your old age."

Runninghorse laughed. "We see who weak. Come, more games."

Jarrett massaged his numb hand. "I'm wiped."

But his friend towed him toward the racecourse.

All around camp, men sprang to their feet and headed across the meadow to a series of blazing bonfires.

Jarrett ached from his head to the tip of his boots. The village had been awake the preceding night. Did the Osage never sleep?

"Big race life training." Runninghorse motioned, "Race run in dark."

The moon concealed itself behind clouds as more clouds scuttled to hide the evening stars. Away from the campfires the night loomed inky.

Horse pointed into the inky darkness. "Old men hide. Trip runners. If Woodcarver fall, must get up, run. Much bad medicine if race no finish. At halfway point stop. Kiss Mother Earth. Run to finish." Horse motioned toward the line of fires burning beside the camp. "Race dangerous. Hole in ground. Root. Trippers."

"I'll pass. A guy could break a leg. You win this one, Horse."

"All who hunt buffalo race." Runninghorse waved his war hatchet. "Eyee! Must show Father, Horse beat Woodcarver."

Jarrett shook his head. "I've had enough for one day."

"Village think you afraid. Woodcarver lose respect."

"Not my idea to race." Jarrett turned and walked toward the teepees.

"Father lose two horse you no race."

"Yahola!" Jarrett knuckled tired eyes. He shoved his hands into the pockets of his denims, pivoted, and strode to the starting line.

Posed into a sprinter's crouch, when the starting arrow whizzed overhead, Jarrett sprang into the lead. For fifty yards, he outdistanced the other runners, with Runninghorse close to his heels. As light from the line of fires grew dimmer and darkness closed in, Jarrett slowed.

Runninghorse sped past.

Jarrett dashed blindly into the darkness, reckless in the hot blaze of competition. Racing past Runninghorse, he dodged, barely avoiding running headlong into a tree.

Labored breathing and another racer's footsteps thudding behind him spurred him forward.

He retained the lead, conserving energy for a burst of speed at the finish. Once, he caught a foot in a tree root, but he regained his balance and remained the leader.

Behind him a heavy thump sounded as a body struck the ground.

Jarrett passed the lances marking the halfway point and crashed into a double line of watching women. Grabbing one, he used the startled lady as a pivot. Then he whirled, knelt, and kissed Mother Earth, still clinging to the Indian woman for balance. Springing up amid ear-shattering cheers, he sprinted for the finish.

CHAPTER 3

Jarrett kept his breathing deep and controlled. He must participate in the buffalo hunt. His parents needed that meat. He could do this.

The closer he got to the finish line of fires, the rockier the terrain appeared. Light from leaping flames caused gigantic shadows to jump at him like banshees from the nether world. Ghostly shapes on the ground had to be boulders. He vaulted the obstacles, but his feet landed on even terrain. Not stones, shadows.

Behind him, Horse's moccasins pounded nearer.

Jarrett groaned. Not good.

Another Indian's heavy breathing close to Jarrett's heels forced him to sprint full-out.

A hand gripped his ankle.

Jarrett fell to his knees, his body jolting on the ground. Instinct curled him into a ball and tumbled him into a cartwheel. He landed hard against a tree, struggled to his feet, and raced on.

An iron grip jerked both ankles.

His knee hit frozen earth. He fell backward, his ankle twisted beneath his weight. Pain shot up his leg.

Runninghorse dashed past, the certain winner. Other

runners followed, some limping, some cradling arms or nursing backs, but running.

Jarrett wobbled to his feet. Pain shot up his leg, but he clenched his teeth and limped to the finish line.

Runninghorse met him. "Much bad race. Leg no so bad no can run. If Pawnee chase, Woodcarver be dead."

Jarrett dropped to the ground and tugged at his boot, but his foot and ankle were so swollen he threw up his hands. "There weren't any Pawnee chasing me. Help me get this boot off." Anger roughened his voice.

"No Pawnee in race, but race train Osage keep run, even hurt bad. That way, no die." Runninghorse squatted and jerked on Jarrett's boot.

"Ow! Hold on! Stop!" Jarrett cradled his injured ankle and rocked back and forth.

Horse ignored him, worked the boot off, then pulled strips of deer hide from his shirt pocket and wrapped Jarrett's ankle.

Jarrett tried not to wince.

Once Horse had the ankle bandaged, the lithe Indian plopped cross-legged facing Jarrett.

"I can't get my boot back on. How am I going to hunt buffalo?"

Horse spoke Osage to a friend who lurked nearby. The Indian ran into the darkness and soon returned with a moccasin he slipped over Jarrett's bandaged foot.

"Now we wrestle." Runninghorse stood and pulled Jarrett's arm.

"Count me out. I'm not moving."

"Tomorrow when moon shine, you wrestle."

"Sure, maybe. If I can walk."

"You sit with women?"

"Yeah, that's me. The guy who sits with women." Jarrett shivered. Even this near the fire, the wind whipped through him.

An Indian girl, watching from the other side of the blaze, rose and ran into the darkness. When she returned, she carried a buffalo robe.

As soon as the heavy garment covered his shoulders, cutting out the wind and wrapping him inside a cocoon of warmth, he recognized Mist Over The Water's silhouette against the fire.

She spoke to him softly in Osage.

"Thanks. Thanks a lot. Didn't your brother teach you any English?"

Kneeling beside him, the pretty girl shook her head. Her hands smoothed the robe around him.

Jarrett inhaled her sweet breath. Her black eyes looked large and her mouth rosy and full. Her nose was delicate. She was lovely.

Jarrett's whole body alerted. He pulled the buffalo robe tighter. She was so near her body heat warmed his face. He shifted away. "You should go sit by your mother." He motioned toward the group of women reclining nearby.

Hurt shadowed Mist's face, then she smiled as though she understood. She rose and hurried away, her moccasins making no sound.

He closed his eyes.

She returned and handed him a small bowl with steam rising into the cold air.

He took the container and drank. The hot broth ran down his throat and warmed his insides.

She sat nearby and set the empty bowl beside her. Trying not to look at Mist Over The Water, he forced himself to concentrate on the stars. From where he lay, he picked out the constellations. His eyelids grew heavy, and he drowsed. Game noises subsided.

"Woodcarver." Runninghorse shook his shoulder.

Jarrett jerked awake. He pushed himself up on one elbow. He and Horse were alone.

"Where Woodcarver find strength win arm wrestle? Why no find strength run good race?"

Jarrett shook hair out of his eyes and yawned.

Runninghorse squatted beside him.

Jarrett pushed himself to a sitting position, accidentally knocking his ankle against the ground. Pain radiated up his leg. "You're asking the secret of my life." He stretched, yawned, and ran his hand through his hair. Cold air blew the fog from his mind. He sucked in a deep breath. "My God uses the weak person to confound the strong. I know I looked like a pushover to you." Jarrett shrugged. "That's where God likes to show his power. I entered that match realizing you were the stronger, but I prayed God would give me the strength to win."

"White God give strong medicine. Runninghorse respect. Why no race better?"

Jarrett ducked his head and gazed at the ground. He reached into his jeans pocket, tugged out his penknife, and tossed the sheathed blade from hand to hand. "I can run faster than you, right?"

"Right." Runninghorse swelled his chest, looking proud of his new response.

"I figured I had a good chance to win that race." Jarrett

kept slapping the knife from one palm to another.

"Right."

"So, I didn't need any help, did I?"

Runninghorse laughed until his body shook. "You need help, but you no know."

"Right."

~

The following day, Horse and he left the village behind to scout.

Jarrett caught his first sight of the prairie, which stretched a billowing sea of grass swaying in the wind as far as he could see. The trackless, wide land had no landmarks. As he gazed at the vast, empty expanse, loneliness so deep it felt like pain hit him.

The wind blew endlessly, reddening his cheeks and bringing moisture to his eyes. "Makes a person feel small." Jarrett reached behind his saddle and tugged out his mackinaw.

Runninghorse chuckled. "White man get lost. Red man find way on prairie." He beckoned. "Come, we find buffalo."

Jarrett nudged Samson until the two of them rode side by side into buffalo grass which reached above their ponies' knees and swished against their feet. Jarrett's nape prickled. He palmed his pistol and checked the paper cartridges.

Runninghorse fingered his bow and resettled his quiver on his back.

Jarrett followed Horse to the edge of a pool hidden by tall grass. As Jarrett's mustang splashed across, wood ducks quacked, flying from their swim, water cascading from their feathers.

"When Father young, buffalo thick. Osage no need go prairie. Buffalo everywhere. North wind chase buffalo to Osage. Always it was so. Now Osage need travel prairie find buffalo."

Jarrett shrugged. "Plenty of buffalo for everyone." Sampson lowered his head and drank from the water rippling around his hooves.

Runninghorse splashed his mustang through the pond and up the sandbank. He slid off, knelt, and a grin spread across his face. He pressed his ear to the ground. A second later, he sprang up and shouted, "Buffalo come!" He pointed. Then leaped astride his pony and galloped off.

Jarrett tapped his heels into Sampson's flanks.

He caught up and rode neck and neck with his friend, buffalo grass switching his ankles.

At the top of a small summit, he pulled Sampson to a standstill beside Horse. A thrill tingled Jarrett's hairline and flashed through his torso.

Beneath them, like a slithering snake, a single column of buffalo advanced. Another column, miles from the first, hove into view. A third column appeared, also miles distant from the other two.

Jarrett's jaw dropped. "I had no idea buffalo traveled with each herd following a leader in single file. I thought they mingled like cattle."

"Father say many moons past buffalo travel in small herd. One herd and leader. Always it was so. Now, buffalo travel with other herd for keep safe." Horse's voice lowered. "When white hunter kill all buffalo, what Osage do?"

Jarrett had no answer.

On the plain beneath, spreading as far as he could see, hundreds and hundreds of buffalo lumbered toward them. Each followed his leader in single file. The columns grew thicker and thicker until the landscape crawled with massive shaggy creatures moving south. As the single lines merged, the less apparent it became that many herds traveled together, until the buffalo appeared as one vast herd. The ground trembled beneath their weight. Buffalo grass parted before them like the Red Sea.

"Buffalo no smart. If leader killed, other no know what do. Stand and look at dead leader and get killed. White man kill many buffalo, take tongue, leave rest on prairie for bird. Not Osage. Osage kill and use all buffalo."

Jarrett nodded, hypnotized by the sight. "What's that rasping noise?"

"Buffalo eat grass. No sound same on Mother Earth."

Buffalo breath rose in the cold air, wafting over the herd like fog over a river. Heavy breathing and the thud of their muscular bodies bumping together, their bellowing and snorting grew loud.

Each buffalo sported a rich brown winter coat. They stood from hoof to shoulder well over six feet and were at least ten feet from great black nose to short, scruffy tail. Each magnificent head wore a thick frontlet, and each muzzle grew a bushy beard. A short, black horn curved out of the shaggy hair on either side of the frontlet.

Jarrett rubbed his tight neck. He and Sampson would be no match against those two thousand pounds of fur-coated muscle. Yet the beast's eyes appeared gentle.

Sampson danced and reared, wanting to bolt.

Wolves prowled the edges of the herd.

"Wolves wait for old, sick, young." Horse signaled. "We go."

Jarret raced after him, back toward the Indian camp.

Horse reported the buffalo location to the hunt leader.

Despite wind-whipped cold air buffeting them, braves stripped to breechclouts and moccasins, slung quivers across their backs or strapped on pistols, and mounted horses.

Runninghorse spoke to his mount. "No fear brother buffalo, little pony. Run well, take care no be gored."

Jarrett wiped sweaty palms on his jeans. His mouth went dry.

Runninghorse hurried through the hunt regulations. "You no move or shoot before signal. Herd spook. Then stampede. Then village go hungry."

"What's the signal?"

"Hand signal. Then ride fast. Choose buffalo, ride to side, shoot arrow between hip and rib. You no ride until Horse ride. You no break rules!"

"Right."

The hunt leader tossed a white eagle feather into the sky. Every eye followed its erratic descent. The biting wind obviously blew from the north.

At a hand signal from the hunt leader, braves lined up, single file behind him. Horse, as head scout, rode in the privileged second place. Jarrett urged Sampson in beside his friend. At a hard, eye-watering gallop, he and the braves thundered toward the prairie where the buffalo churned the grass.

The sentinel bull sniffed the air and began pawing the ground. He turned in a circle, sniffing and snorting. He stopped to gaze at their approaching horses.

White-knuckled, Jarrett gripped Sampson's reins, his body stiff.

Sampson trembled, ears pricked forward.

In front, Horse's bare muscular back tensed. He unslung his bow, slid an arrow from his quiver, aimed, and directed his mustang with his knees.

What a woodcarving Runninghorse and his pony would make! Jarrett etched the picture in his memory.

Sampson's skittish dancing jolted him. He jerked the old pistol from his belt and checked the six cylinders again. His hand shook.

CHAPTER 4

Jarrett reined Sampson behind the line of braves waiting just yards from the noble beasts. He wrinkled his nose at the rank odor.

The agitated sentinel buffalo grew more and more alarmed. He tossed his head trying to adjust his nearsighted eyes. With a hoarse bellow, he galloped into the wind. Instantly the entire herd stampeded, tails in the air like black flags.

The hunt leader signaled.

Sampson broke into a gallop.

Ahead, Horse raced beside a buffalo. He swayed on his mustang, and his bowstring twanged. The animal fell, the arrow so embedded in its hairy side that only feathers protruded. Runninghorse's mustang pivoted and chased another buffalo.

Sampson reared and pawed the air, almost unseating Jarrett. Jarrett struggled to control his bucking horse. All around him, horses crossed and recrossed from every direction. Shots and arrows whizzed by.

Sampson squealed, ears skinned back.

A wounded bull wheeled. Angry, bloodshot eyes glared into Jarrett's. The bull lowered his massive head. Snorting and bellowing, with pain from an arrow near his hindquarters, the buffalo galloped toward them.

Sampson reared, snapping Jarrett's gun arm, fouling his aim. The buffalo's long tongue hung from the corner of its mouth, dripping saliva.

Jarrett sighted and fired.

The round struck the bull in his great hairy chest. The beast staggered and bellowed. Blood spurted from a hole in his chest. Still, he attacked.

Sampson bolted, almost smacking into another horse and rider.

Jarrett turned in his saddle and shot the bull again, opening a bloody hole just behind the right shoulder. The beast stared at Jarrett, his eyes wild, his beard touching the earth. Blood streamed from the buffalo's nostrils. He stumbled to a halt—slowly his legs doubled beneath him. The giant lunged forward onto his side, his legs stiffened.

Jarrett's stomach knotted. His throat tightened. A sense of loss shuddered through him. He murmured, "Buffalo, please pardon me for taking your life." He stuck his heated pistol in his belt. He would kill no more. One buffalo would provide enough meat to sustain his family through winter. He choked bile down from his throat.

Pounding hooves shook the ground. Dying animals bellowed. Indians whooped. Gunshots cracked. He yelped when a wild arrow ripped through his jeans, grazed his thigh, and zinged into his saddle. He hugged Sampson's neck.

Great humps dotted the churned prairie. The stench of blood churned his sick stomach. Vultures circled overhead, their great black wings beating the air.

Runninghorse trotted over, a grin lit his face. He lifted

two fingers.

Jarrett raised one.

Women ran up, brandishing knives. No longer clad in beads and bracelets, but dressed in worn deerskin, four women bent over each buffalo. With quick strokes of a long knife, each hacked away hide or chopped out bloody flesh.

Jarrett trotted up beside his friend. "How can you tell which ones you killed?" He waved a hand toward the lifeless forms.

"Easy. See feather on arrow. No Osage have same feather. Arrow like name. My woman skin." He slid off his mustang and jogged toward a motionless hump.

Jarrett rode to the bull he had shot. He dismounted, circled the animal, and unsheathed his hunting knife.

On every side, groups of women bent over each carcass, knives flashing.

He dropped beside the still-warm body. His first incision sliced thick fur from glistening pink flesh. He rocked back on his thighs.

Mist rushed up, followed by three women who seemed to be either friends or family. She knelt beside him, grabbed his bloody knife, wiped the blade on the grass, and motioned for him to sheath it. Then she signed that she and the other ladies would butcher his kill.

Jarrett touched her arm, leaving bloodstains on her worn buckskin. "Thanks." His voice came out hoarse. Using what little he knew of sign language, he signed his gratitude.

Mist smiled and nodded, her black eyes flashing. The sun shimmered on her long braids. Her smooth skin, stretched delicately over her bones, glowed pale copper like a new penny.

Jarrett jumped to his feet.

She pulled on his arm, speaking Osage.

Jarrett shook his head.

She signed, "Stay."

Jarrett dropped to sit cross-legged on the ground near the ladies kneeling around his kill. He wiped his bloody hands on the grass.

Mist sliced an incision into the buffalo's side, reached both slender hands inside the body, grasped something, pulled hard, and offered him a large, slippery organ.

Jarrett stared at the brown hunk of bloody liver quivering in the girl's outstretched hands.

Eyes bright, lips parted, she gazed at him.

Jarrett swallowed, cleared his throat, and shook his head. "No thanks. You keep that."

Mist's mouth drooped. "Give strength," she signed.

"Thanks, but no." He turned, leaped on Sampson, and galloped toward the meadow, away from the killing field.

Toward dark, he rode back.

Many of the buffaloes were butchered. Women gathered buffalo hearts and arranged the bloody organs in a massive pile. Offer appeasement to the dead animal Runninghorse had said.

Mist had fashioned a pouch from a buffalo's stomach. She hung the contraption from a tripod and threw in bits of meat, bones, and fat. The mixture boiled, popping and sputtering, wafting a tempting aroma, not unlike Mother's beef stew.

Other women cut meat into strips, then wound the flesh about sticks. Mist hung the sticks to smoke over a smoldering fire.

Jarrett's mouth watered. He'd not eaten since breakfast. He loved pemmican.

With time on his hands and Runninghorse nowhere to be seen, Jarrett retrieved his tools and wood from his saddlebags. He honed his blades, then snapped open the largest and began to carve. He ignored the lengthening shadows.

Women drifted to the camp of tepees they had erected while the men hunted. Only a few Indians remained.

Mist wandered over to stand beside him. She sat on the ground across from him, her knees almost touching his. "Mist butcher you buffalo. Pack on pony. You good hunter," she signed.

She had changed into a white doeskin dress and wore bracelets that tinkled with each movement. "You come back for robe."

Jarrett grinned. "Right."

"Right," she mimicked, her voice throaty.

Jarrett returned to carving, but he cut deeper than he intended. "Yahola!" He dropped the wood on the ground. "You make me feel like I'm going to jump out of my skin. I've never been around girls."

Her black eyes held a world of knowledge, maybe she did understand English? Her smile sent a stream of warmth from his head to his toes. She offered both her hands, cupping something inside. She tilted her head, her expression bright.

Jarrett slowly extended his palm. "I hope you don't have another surprise like the last one."

She folded his fingers in both her warm brown ones and held them. When she withdrew her hands, a beautiful, polished buffalo horn lay in his palm.

"Big medicine," she signed.

Jarrett grinned. A leather strap hung from the horn. He touched the colorful symbols.

"Right?" Mist's voice softened.

"Right!" Jarrett almost sang.

She bent so close he inhaled her clean scent while she hung the pendant around his neck, smoothed the medallion over his hunting shirt, and patted his chest.

His whole body tingled.

Horse appeared, towering above them, hands on his hips, his legs spread apart. With a chunk of raw liver in one hand, tallow in the other, and a broad grin on his face, he offered the slimy organ to Jarrett.

Jarrett shook his head. "No thanks. I've played this scene before. You can have the strength of the buffalo, and you can have his poor eyesight, and his underabundance of brains."

"You no longer pork-eater." Horse's eyes sparkled.

"Pork-eater? Oh, like being a tenderfoot. Right. No more pork-eater." Jarrett stood and stretched.

"Come, tepee women fix you. We stay four moons." Horse leaped on his mustang and motioned him to follow.

They rode to a small tepee sheltered in a triangle of leafless trees on the edge of the village.

Runninghorse pulled a brush and a pouch of red paint from a strap tied around his waist and painted symbols on the tepee's skin. With strong strokes he portrayed a white man on his mustang as he shot a bison.

They laughed and talked until dusk.

Back inside Horse's tepee, they devoured soup and buffalo steaks like hungry wolves.

His friend darted knowing looks at Jarrett.

What was Horse up to?

Jarrett yawned. After the heavy meal and three nights with little sleep, he was whipped. He rubbed his eyes.

"Go tepee." Runninghorse winked.

Huh? What happened to wrestling? His ankle ached, but with the Osage's stoic attitude toward pain, this was a surprise.

Something was up.

CHAPTER 5

Limping toward his borrowed teepee, Jarrett smiled. Couldn't wait to wrap up in a warm buffalo robe.

Smoke puffed through the hole in the top of the new teepee, leaving a hickory scent lingering in the cold night air. Who laid the fire?

Jarrett lifted his arms and stretched tired muscles, stooped to open the flap, and stepped inside. A breath of warm air caressed his face. The teepee looked cozy. Shadows cast by the rosy light of the small fire burning in the center slithered over the creamy walls. The flap closed behind him. He straightened. And froze.

Mist Over The Water sat on a pile of robes, watching him.

Jarrett stared, his body still. The girl's long black hair hung loose to her knees, cascading in masses over her white deerskin dress. Her clean scent and another subtle musky odor wafted to him.

She rose and stepped close. Her breath warmed his cold cheek.

"Uh. Hello, Mist." Every nerve in his body tingled. Heat spread over his face. "Do you need something?" He sounded like a bullfrog. His scattered senses warned she didn't understand English, but his scrambled thoughts couldn't remember how to communicate with hand signals.

She raised graceful fingers to unfasten the lacing holding the bodice of her dress, and a sweet smile showed a glimpse of white teeth.

Jarrett stared at the slender brown hand threading open the ties, his feet rooted to the ground. "Uh …" He turned, ducked out of the tepee, and ran. Not until he arrived at Horse's teepee did he notice the sharp pain in his ankle. "Horse!"

As he emerged from the tepee, the muscular Indian pulled a robe around his bare shoulders. "Problem, little brother?"

"You set me up! You knew your sister was waiting inside my tepee. Why didn't you warn me?" Jarrett's words jerked. He ran hot fingers through his hair.

"No need fear Mist. She maiden. No have disease." Horse laid a heavy hand on Jarrett's shoulder.

Jarrett shrugged Horse's hand off. "That's not the problem. Why is she inside my tepee?" He rubbed both hands over his face. Thoughts whirled through his mind like a tornado through a forest.

"Mist chose you. Many brave bring horse to Father. She no want. She make choice."

"But I … I … don't want a wife!" Jarrett forced the words through his tight throat.

Runninghorse spoke as though to a slow-learning child. "You strange, little brother. When Mist come tepee, no need buy for wife. She give happiness."

"But Horse, she is your *sister*!" Jarrett squared off in front of the big Indian, fists doubled. "She's not an animal to be bought, or a … a … dog to lie down with anyone she wants. She's a woman!"

"This way of Osage. Osage share women. Always it was so. Is it not so with your people?"

"Share her…with me?" Jarrett choked.

Runninghorse pounded him on the back.

"No! It is *not* so with my people!" Jarrett paced a short path in front of the teepee, hands clinched behind his back. "Yahola. Yahola." Muscles twitched in his jaws. "Come with me. I have to explain to her."

"No need talk. Carver left tepee. Mist know you no want."

Jarrett smacked his fist into his open palm. "Please come, Horse. I need to tell her why I left. I don't want to hurt her." Jarrett hauled on the muscular Indian's arm, urging him toward the tepee.

Runninghorse shrugged, allowing himself to be propelled through the darkness.

Mist stood inside the tepee where he left her, shoulders drooping. When she saw him, she turned away and hid her face in her hands.

He had never meant to hurt her. What should he do? He exchanged glances with his friend, then touched the trembling girl's shoulder. "Please let me explain, Mist." Jarrett swallowed, but the hoarseness only got worse.

Horse translated.

Why was Horse taking so long? Was he adding other words? Changing his meaning?

Mist faced him. But her shoulders remained slumped, and her mouth trembled.

Jarrett paced the small tepee. The girl had been kind, and

he'd humiliated her. He admired her beauty, but what had he done to make her think he wanted her? Not that he didn't. Perspiration dripped between his shoulder blades. He wiped wet palms on his denims. Sweat slid down his temples. He took a deep breath and tried to slow his words so Horse could translate.

"Your people have ceremonies and dances to show your devotion for the Great Spirit. My people, those who are Christians, show reverence for our Father God, by the way we live. We don't have many ceremonies, but we try to live in a way that our Father approves." While he waited for Horse to translate, Jarrett shifted from one foot to another. If only he was better at explaining.

Mist stood looking down at her hands, her form as dejected as a wilted flower crushed under his boot.

"My God gave me life that will never end, and because of this I want to please him." Jarrett's voice rasped in his dry throat. "He is my God. I belong to him." Groping for words, he ran his hand through his hair and down the back of his neck. "My God expects me to live a life that is … umm … useful to him."

Mist's eyes met his for the first time.

Runninghorse continued to translate.

"Do you understand?" Jarrett spread his hands wide. If only he were not so inadequate.

Mist shook her head.

Jarrett stared into the embers left by the fire. He shoved his fists into his pockets.

"My life code is something like the rules of the buffalo hunt. If rules are broken, people get hurt. Look, I hate seeing you look so sad and knowing your unhappiness is my fault.

You are …" Jarrett hesitated, a warm flush oozed from his scalp to his toes. "You are beautiful. Any man would be crazy not to want … I mean …" His ears burned and sweat bathed his neck.

He cleared his throat. "My rules are more important to me. My Holy God demands I be set apart to follow his way and not my own path." He wiped his forehead with a sweaty palm. He glanced at Runninghorse, but the Indian's face was shadowed.

A trembling smile flitted across Mist's lips. "What are these rules?"

Horse translated her Osage.

"My Bible—you call my book Talking Leaves—tells me to run from…" Jarrett faltered, glanced at Runninghorse, found no help there, and faced Mist. "From…women outside of marriage." Jarrett swallowed and rushed on. "If I reject this teaching, I reject God."

As Horse translated, Mist smiled and straightened. She wiped traces of tears from her face. "Mist know God more important than this." She waved toward the buffalo robes waiting cozily beside the fire. "God center of life. All else like flowers in meadow, like beads on moccasin, pretty but not necessary."

Jarrett nodded. He turned toward the tepee flap. He had to get fresh air.

"Tell me how Woodcarver serve God." Mist flashed a sweet smile that made her face look angelic.

Jarrett sighed and dropped down to sprawl by the fire. He stirred the embers and tumbled on more wood.

Runninghorse pivoted toward the teepee flap, but Jarrett grabbed his friend's ankle.

"Don't go," he hissed. "I need you to translate. And don't leave me alone with your sister. I'm not made of iron."

Horse frowned, but folded down by the fire, his face twisting. He tapped his knee with an ever-speeding cadence.

Mist, her pretty face composed and interest sparking her dark eyes, signed, "Tell more."

Jarrett gazed across the fire at the shadows dancing on the tepee's skin, His hand touched the leather strop hanging from his belt. He reached into his jeans pocket and took out his two pocketknives.

"This pocketknife," Jarrett flicked open the three blades. Illuminated by the flames, each reflected a smooth, razor-sharp edge. "Is set apart for one purpose. I use this knife only for whittling. If I used this for other things, the blade would grow dull, and the edges notched. This is a special knife to me, and I don't let anyone else use my tool."

Jarrett flicked open his other pocketknife. Firelight shone on a duller surface. "See these tiny notches?" He pointed to almost imperceptible notches on the cutting edge. "If I used this knife, these notches would mar any figure I carved."

Two glossy black heads bent over the knife.

After translating, Horse pointed to the everyday knife. "See, dry blood, from brother buffalo."

"Right, Horse. I cleaned my knife too. But sometimes cleaning an instrument is difficult. It's not important that this knife be perfectly clean. This one's not set apart for a specific purpose. I use this old knife for everything." Jarrett turned the knife in his hand. "Except whittling."

Mist smiled prettily. "Set apart." She touched the whittling knife.

"Yes. Christians are like my whittling knife, set apart for a specific purpose—living a life that pleases God. God wants to carve me into a person like his Son. That's why I try to keep his rules."

Her brother finished translating.

The corners of Mist's lips lifted. "Woodcarver strange." Her smile lit her exotic face. "Strange as sun strange to mole."

"Yes." Runninghorse finished translating and nodded. "Woodcarver has found knowledge. His mother's father Spirit teacher. He read Talking Leaves. Perhaps if Osage had Talking Leaves, Osage have knowledge."

Mist tilted her head and spoke Osage. "Is possible husband treat wife better after Osage read Talking Leaves from their God?"

After Horse translated, Jarrett grinned and nodded. "Absolutely. No sharing wife. Or beating."

~

That night, though he didn't want to leave the buffalo hunt, he had to go. Mist was too tempting. Jarrett gave her his specially painted tepee as thanks for the work she'd done dressing the buffalo he'd killed.

Saddlebags bulging with buffalo meat, he and Runninghorse rode across the prairie under cover of darkness until they had no further need of secrecy to elude Pawnee or Comanche raiding parties.

As Jarrett entered the relative safety of Osage land, he and his friend halted their mounts. Dawn glimmered in the east, with lines of red appearing on the horizon. The two of them, their horses huddled side by side, their breath steaming in the cold air, faced each other.

"Runninghorse bring hides and pemmican to you when Osage return from hunt."

Jarrett's saddle creaked as he leaned across to wrap an arm around Horse's shoulder. "My family will eat well this winter."

"Is good."

Jarrett fumbled inside his shirt, pulled his jacket closed again, and shoved a polished buffalo carving into Horse's muscular hand. "This is the only way I can thank you for inviting me on this hunt."

Horse lifted the carving to the light. The powerful brown buffalo head rose majestically, the lordly body caught in a noble pose. The expression of the bull sentinel, alert but not yet sensing danger.

"This good. Runninghorse keep."

"And I'll keep these memories. See you again, my friend."

Horse clasped Jarrett's hand, then turned toward the prairies, kneed his mount, and thundered toward his people.

Jarrett wheeled Sampson's head east toward Tahlequah and home. With a little luck and no rest, he would arrive by late afternoon. The sky had turned threatening, so despite his fatigue, he urged Sampson into a mile-devouring trot.

As the temperature dropped, Jarrett tugged his collar up over his ears. He didn't stop for lunch but pressed on. With frigid weather blowing in, he pulled the sleeves of his mackinaw as far down over his bare hands as possible.

The wind howled, whipping his hair around his face. He thrust the reins in his teeth and stuffed his stinging hands inside his jacket pocket. Hunching his shoulders against the cold, he urged Sampson into a faster trot.

Shortly after midday, a strange blue dusk descended, and a wet drop landed on the tip of his nose. Then another on his ear. Large, cottony flakes blew from the north. Thicker and thicker they fell, covering bushes and hills. Sampson's hooves no longer tapped on the frozen ground. The heavy flakes muffled sound. Silence surrounded him.

Despite repeated shakes, snow settled in his hair and on his shoulders. Soon Sampson wore a white mantle covering his mane. Steam from the trotting horse wafted in the frigid air. Dense snow mounded on the limbs of trees, dressing the branches.

The day grew darker. Huge flakes fell so thick that Jarrett saw only a few feet ahead. He must travel in a straight line or risk getting lost. He spotted trees and bushes.

Unease crawled up his spine. Few people had settled in this part of the country and cabins were rare. His head began to ache, and his ankle throbbed. He sighed. Shouldn't he be nearing home?

He blinked snow off his lashes, and shook snow from his legs, but his denims were soaked. For hours he and Sampson labored on, the only moving objects in the heavy snow. As the wind picked up, anxiety spiked his stomach.

"Buck up, Sampson. Tahlequah must be close now. We'll be home soon." Jarrett spoke aloud to encourage himself as much as his tired horse. "You'll be safe in the stable with warm mash to eat." He pushed on.

Snow drifted deep into hollows and ravines and swirled in whirlpools of whiteness. Sampson slowed to a walk. Only Sampson's heavy breathing and the wind howling broke the eerie silence. Jarrett could see only as far as his horse's laid-back ears. There was no place to seek shelter. He must keep going.

Jarrett's hands, feet, ears, and legs were numb. Cold crept into his brain. Thick white flakes lashed his face and curtained his view. He wound the reins around the saddle horn, blew on his hands to warm his stiffened fingers, then stuffed them into his mackinaw pockets. Where was he? Was he lost? He'd have to follow the golden rule of the prairie. Trust his horse. He dropped the reins and gave Sampson his head.

Sampson floundered through drift after drift, up to his hocks.

Jarrett flicked snow from mounds on his eyebrows and staring into the swirling white, saw nothing. His teeth chattered. "I can't tell north from south in this storm," he muttered. A fit of shivering hit so hard his honing strop thudded against his belt. "Whoa, Sampson," he yelled above the wind.

He dismounted, his legs stiff as an old man's. Maybe he'd get warmer if he walked. He floundered, forcing one foot after the other through thigh-high snow. Rest. He needed to lie down. But if he did, he'd never move again. How long had he been in this storm? Time was as trackless as the landscape.

Sampson snorted, and Jarrett stopped in the lee of a large oak. The mustang stood head down, drooping tail to the wind while the merciless whiteness sought to bury them. Jarrett leaned against Sampson's neck and draped his arm around the horse's shoulder, breathing heavily. Easy to stop. Give up.

He straightened. No more thinking like that. Got to keep going. Better to go on than die here. Isn't that what the Osage race taught him? Even in extreme pain, you keep moving. And he wasn't in pain. His sprained ankle didn't even hurt. Nothing hurt except the breath he forced through his lungs.

The sky loomed an ominous black. *Oh Father, God.* A terrifying lump sank to his stomach. That was the same tree he passed almost an hour ago. He'd been walking in circles! Wild laughter rose in his throat, but wind smothered the sound and threw it back to his ears.

God, help me. He set his jaw and plunged in the direction he hoped was east, wallowing in a drift that soaked him to his waist. He plodded on, slipping and falling, his body wet and numb with cold. Darkness descended. Where was Tahlequah?

"Oh please, God, help me."

Howling wind seized his voice and carried the sound away as if it had never been.

CHAPTER 6

Someone pounded on the front door.

Delight Flint started. Who could be out in this blizzard? Daddy and Clairmont had surely stayed in Tahlequah at the Grand Hotel when the storm worsened.

The urgent pounding continued.

She crossed the rug and pressed her ear to the door. "Who's there?"

A faint male voice seeped through the door. "Please let me in. I'm freezing."

Delight glanced around the large front room with its thick rug and striped wallpaper. No weapon here. She ran to the kitchen, lifted a heavy iron skillet from the stovetop and hurried to the door. With her weapon raised for action, she slid the bolt and pulled the front door open.

She stepped aside as a snowy avalanche tumbled inside.

The mountain of snow shook itself and cascaded icy balls around the entry. Cold wind whistled in rattling the row of copper utensils hanging above the fireplace. A gust crashed the door against the wall. Delight slammed the door shut.

A shivering, ice-crusted young man struggled to stand, then brushed white crystals from his face and rubbed red hands together. "Where's the barn? I need to get my horse out of the blizzard."

The man's teeth chattered so fiercely that Delight could barely understand his words. "Come in." She led him to the blazing living room fire.

He left a trail of snowy boot prints on the rug.

She glanced at his desperate face, then laid the iron skillet on the entry table. "You must get out of that wet coat." Hands on her hips, she surveyed him from his sopping hair to his dripping boots. Tiny ice mounds clung to his eyebrows and chapped skin. Melted snow matted his thick tawny hair. The firm set to his jaw and his intense eyes shadowed with weariness awakened strange feelings in the pit of her stomach. Her toes tingled.

"I've got to get my horse sheltered."

Who was he? She shook herself. "I'll see to your horse, but first I'll find some of my brother's clothes for you. You look absolutely done in. How long have you been out in the blizzard?"

"Since it started." The stench of wet wool warmed by heat filled the living room.

She scurried down the hall and into Claremont's bedroom, then chose a flannel shirt and jeans from his clothespress. When she rushed back to the living room, the stranger stood in front of the fire, rubbing his hands close to the flames.

"Sit down. I'll pull off your boots. You're lucky you found our ranch. There's not another within a ten-mile circle." Delight brushed at the wet stain his boots left on her dress after she tugged them off. His stockinged feet, like blocks of ice, chilled her hands.

"You'll catch your death of cold if you don't take off those wet things." She handed him Claremont's clothes. Though the young man resembled a drowned spaniel, he looked honest.

He glanced about the room, his back close to the fire. "Where's your family?"

"Out." Best not to tell a stranger the whole truth. "The storm must have delayed them. I'll stable your horse while you change. When I return, I'll fix you something warm to eat." Delight wrapped a heavy woolen shawl around her shoulders and knotted a smaller shawl over her hair.

He struggled to remove his coat and fumbled with the buttons of his hunting shirt. His hands trembled.

She longed to assist him but decided from his independent attitude that he wouldn't want her help. So, she scampered to the front door and, using the rope attached from house to barn, fought her way into the storm.

She found his horse, head down, legs splayed, near the porch. She grasped the reins and led him behind the house to the stable.

Inside, out of the gale, he lifted his head and whinnied.

She offered the horse hay, oats, and water, then wiped his wet coat until she had him dry. "Good boy, you'll be fine now." She patted his muzzle.

She stepped out of the barn into the blizzard. Worst one she'd ever experienced. She lunged through the high-drifted snow to the house, then fought the wind to close the back door behind her.

Then peeked into the living room.

The stranger wore Claremont's clothes. Her brother was six foot two, and the shirt sleeves rolled to this man's wrist were inches too long. But the too-long jeans turned up at the ankles couldn't hide his look of wiry strength.

"I'm J … J … Jarrett R … R … Ross."

Ross! She clamped her mouth to still a gasp.

"Thanks for seeing to my horse." Teeth chattering, he managed a smile that lodged itself right inside her heart. He shoved a wing-back chair close to the fire.

"Nice name." She ran into her bedroom, brought her handmade quilt, and tucked the thick cover around Jarrett. She smiled as she smoothed the material under his chin, liking the cleft. He had a beautiful, straight nose.

"Thanks for taking me in."

"Only neighborly thing to do." She picked up her skillet, scurried into the kitchen, shoved another stick of wood inside the cook stove, and smiled as she dished up a bowl of the soup she kept simmering during winter. Cutting two healthy slices of her own home-baked bread, she buttered them, carried the food from the kitchen on a tray, and set the meal on his lap.

He took a deep whiff. "Smells great." He bowed his head, closed his eyes, and his lips moved silently. Though his hand still shook, he dove into the food as if he hadn't eaten in a week.

A blush heated her from the top of her head to the tingle in her toes. He was a Christian. How nice. She pulled a chair to sit across from him, curled into a comfortable position, cupped her chin in her hands, and watched him. "My name is Delight."

Jarrett glanced at her with a quick smile but continued to eat, his attention on the food and the fire.

So, Delight felt free to stare at him. He was handsome,

but unlike a few other men she'd met, appeared unaware of his masculine attractiveness. All her life, she'd heard every one of the Rosses were exceptionally attractive folks. Father said their looks were the only acceptable thing about them. But as soon as she'd gazed into Jarrett's blue eyes with those thick sooty lashes, she knew for certain she had nothing to fear from this stranger. His face looked quite serious until he smiled, then his entire expression changed.

He was charming with his polite manners and concern for his horse when he was in such bad shape himself. Father had warned that all the Rosses—from the father, John, and the mother, Hope, to the children, Jordan, Jarrett, and Jerusha—could charm a rattlesnake out of its rattles. She guessed Jarrett to be somewhere around nineteen. His lips were full and well-shaped. As his hair dried, its color resembled warm honey. His hands were nice, strong—not a farmer's hands, though they looked callused. She considered hands important, revealing a man's character.

He raked his fingers through his tousled hair. Sandy wisps of hair curled on his wrists where they emerged from Claremont's long-sleeved shirt.

She shivered and hugged herself.

Too bad he was a Ross. He was dangerous for her to know, and she must not allow herself to like him. How unfair! But how fortunate Papa wasn't here. He'd have kicked this man back out into the blizzard to freeze.

When embers shifted in the fireplace, Delight jumped, shook her head, and laid on more logs.

Jarrett stopped shivering, but he slumped in the chair, his hand barely grasping the spoon, like a little boy up long past his bedtime.

"Do you want to rest?" Delight pointed. "You're welcome to use my brother's room."

Jarrett nodded, his eyelids drooping. "Thanks, Delight." Blue circles shadowed his eyes.

She led him to the bedroom. "Go ahead and lie down while I build a fire in the fireplace and warm a brick for your feet."

Before the brick was ready, even breathing sounded from the four-poster bed.

"How strange to meet one of the dreadful Rosses like this." She snugged the brick near his icy feet. Fortunately, he'd be gone long before her family made their way through the drifts to come home.

~

When Jarrett woke, sun streamed in the windows. He frowned. Where was he? He glanced around the unfamiliar room with its brown striped wallpaper and massive four-poster bed. His eyes strayed to the huge, well-stocked gun cabinet. Some place owned by rich folks. Cheerful singing from the next room brought a rush of memory. God had brought him through the storm. He was blessed to be alive.

He groaned. Blessed, but his chest felt as heavy as if a log lay across it and pushed him into the feather mattress. He shoved aside the quilts. He was hot. Burning up. His head ached and every bone in his body throbbed. He closed his eyes. If only he were still asleep.

"The girl didn't tell me her full name. What was her first name? Some strange sounding one. one. Desire? No...Delight. Yes, that was what she called herself,

Delight." Jarrett wiped a hand over his brow and found the skin hot. Maybe he'd dreamed her.

As though summoned by his words, she—uhm, Delight—knocked at the open door and entered, carrying a tray. The girl wasn't as young as he'd thought last night, maybe seventeen or eighteen. Small, but definitely not a wisp. Her eyes, enormous and blue-violet, looked wiser than seventeen. But she wore her shimmering white-blond hair in long braids.

When she smiled, his thoughts scattered.

"So, you're awake. I thought you might be hungry again. I'll keep you company while you eat."

"Thanks." Talking rasped his sore throat. He sipped the hot tea and pushed the scrambled eggs around on the China plate. Strange, he wasn't hungry.

"How high did the snow drift?" He had to make Delight stop staring at him.

"Pretty high. We're snowed in. I expect my family will return tomorrow or the next day." She smiled as if being snowbound were an exciting adventure.

He sighed. Not fun. Just harder to ride home.

"Look out the window. This is a magic day. With the sun beaming down like that, the snow sparkles like sugar. Our yard resembles a sugar plum forest." Her face reflected the sunshine pouring in the window. "This special day celebrates our new friendship."

Friendship, not even close. If he felt up to the challenge, he'd jump up and kiss her. "Why did your family leave you here alone?" He pushed the tray aside.

"I wasn't eager to travel to Tahlequah. They went to a political rally. I don't like being near so many armed men, and I'm tired of hearing about secession, states' rights, and slave rights." She gave him a brilliant smile. "So, I begged off. Providential for you."

"Yeah, if I hadn't seen your light …" Jarrett didn't want to think about how close he'd come to freezing.

"Would you like me to read to you, or would you rather I sing?"

"I'd like more tea." Jarrett leaned back against the pillows and tapped his fingers on the tray. Being sick was a chore. The more cheerful she was, the more irritable he felt.

Delight moved the tray to a nearby table. "Father likes me to sing to him when he's ill." She began to hum, a haunting melody in a minor key. After a few minutes she left the room, but soon returned with a fresh cup of tea. Still humming, she stood by the edge of the bed and felt his forehead.

He closed his eyes. Her cool hand moved from his forehead to his cheek, then fell away.

"You have a temperature. I think you best stay in bed the rest of the day."

Jarrett opened his eyes.

She frowned but started to sing in a lovely alto.

Her voice reached inside his pounding head and loosened taut nerves.

She sang in Cherokee.

He recognized a few words but didn't speak the language. The soothing cadence evoked pictures of open meadows, woodland animals, sun shining over cascading waterfalls … he dozed, then drifted into sleep.

When he opened his eyes, she had gone, but he heard her stirring in the front parlor and then in the kitchen, moving pots and pans.

Long shadows filled the room and darkness crept into the corners. He'd slept through the day. And he did feel better, not so hot. He lay on the featherbed listening to the soft rustle of her movements.

Suddenly, he tired of being alone. "Delight!"

She strolled in, bringing light with her. "Hello, sleepyhead. Hungry?" Her hair shimmered a silver-blond halo in the kerosene lamplight.

"No, just lonely. Where am I? You didn't tell me your last name." He pushed himself up into a sitting position.

"So, you're finally curious."

Her smile looked impish. Two dimples appeared as if loving fingers compressed her cheek.

"Flint."

Jarrett stiffened. "Yahola. Why didn't you tell me? I've got to get out of here. When will your family be home?" He thrust his legs over the side of the bed. A wave of blackness hit him. He eased down onto the pillows.

Delight pressed a hand against his chest. "You can't go anywhere yet. You're sick. My father wouldn't kick a sick man out of our house. Not even a Ross." She stuck a finger against her chin and smiled. "At least, I don't think he would." She flirted with him, her silky brown brows arched. "He wouldn't like your being here with me alone. He insists you can't trust a Ross further than you can throw him. But he won't make you leave. Not while you're sick."

"I'm feeling better. I should go."

"No. I won't hear of it. Besides, it's dark and awfully cold outside." She lowered her voice and gazed into the shadowy corners of the room. "I might become frightened, alone."

Jarrett grinned. "You should be scared having a big, bad Ross in your house. On the other hand, how do I know I'm safe with a Flint?"

They laughed.

He settled the covers over his chest. "That storm blew me way off course. I missed Tahlequah completely. Your ranch is fifteen miles south. You're right—this day is magical. For the first time since that illegal treaty, a Ross and Flint meet without a shot being fired."

"It's just like the Capulets and the Montagues."

"Who?"

"Romeo and Juliet. The star-crossed lovers." She giggled. "And, who said no shot's been fired? There's more than one way to vanquish an enemy." Delight's blue-violet eyes gleamed mischief.

She was definitely old enough to flirt—judging by the way her glance made his heart beat faster— and he'd best let her comment pass unanswered.

"Come into the parlor. You must be tired of the bedroom."

Jarrett swallowed. Girls had to be born flirting. The message in her eyes sent tingles darting through him. Time to depart. But when he stood, his bones were water. He grabbed the bedpost with both hands until the swirling in his head cleared. He glanced out the window at the gathering darkness. Could he ride to Tahlequah? Not tonight. He'd leave in the morning at first light.

He walked to the living room, settled in the yellow wing chair in front of a robust fire, wrapped a convenient quilt around his legs, and watched through the archway as Delight bustled in the kitchen preparing a tray of food and hot tea.

Hungry this time, he ate. They laughed and talked, and with her quick wit, he found her good company. Flames in the fireplace made the room glow with color and warmth. Outside, the wind howled, and darkness grew.

"This is quite—"

The front door burst open. Frigid air blasted inside.

Jarrett startled.

Delight yelped. She glanced at Jarrett. Then she jumped up and dashed across the living room to embrace the older of the two heavy-coated men who had entered.

"Daddy! Claremont! I didn't expect you back until tomorrow!"

"Mother insisted we return tonight, Bunny. She was afraid something might happen to her little angel, so here we are."

The big man shot a questioning glance at Jarrett, then smiled as he shrugged off his coat, wet boots, holsters, and guns. "Ah. I see we have a guest. Caught in the storm, were you?" He crossed the room and held his hands out to the fire. "I'm Peter Flint."

"Yes, sir." Jarrett stood, the quilt falling about his stocking feet, took a step forward, and stretched out his hand to Flint.

Delight gathered the guns and coats and hurried from the room.

"Guests are always welcome at the Flint fireside. What brought you out in the storm? Looking for me?" Flint's muscular hand crunched his.

Claremont approached more slowly, his deep blue gaze piercing Jarrett before he extended his hand.

"I was buffalo hunting with the Osage. I got caught in the blizzard on the way home, saw your light, and came knocking at your door. Your daughter was kind enough to offer me shelter."

Claremont was at least four inches taller than the elder Flint. The younger man's hair was the same silver-blond as Delight's. He was slim, with muscular shoulders. Above a military-style mustache, eyes the shade of his sister's held a cold, suspicious glint. His clenched hands said loud and clear that he didn't like finding Jarrett alone in the house with his sister, and Jarrett better have a good reason for being there.

Jarrett swallowed. He didn't relish being found here either.

Mr. Flint was Jarrett's height, strong, built solid, with dark eyes and hair. The older man nodded from time to time as Jarrett explained his riding in circles and almost freezing.

"Sit back down." Peter Flint draped himself into a chair opposite the wingback. "Delight, we'll take dinner in here by the fire. Dang cold outside. We need to thaw out." He glanced at Claremont and motioned for his son to relax.

Jarrett gave him details of the hunt and told of the buffalo he shot.

Delight brought cups of tea, hot soup, and homemade bread for the two men, but she spilled tea and slopped some soup onto the tray. She darted anxious glances from her brother to Jarrett.

Claremont didn't eat. A tight line grew between his brows.

"That's quite a story. Brings back memories. Always planned to take Claremont buffalo hunting. Never got around to that with all these political meetings to keep tabs on. Can't let the Abolitionists have it all their own way, can we?" He laughed, giving Jarrett a look of shared conspiracy.

"I don't think you mentioned your name." Claremont's bass voice sounded as arctic as the long icicles hanging outside the windows.

Delight's dropped teacup clanged into the saucer.

Jarrett worked up a tight-lipped smile. He faced Flint and squared his jaw. "Name's Jarrett Ross, sir. My family lives about eight miles to the east of Tahlequah. My father is the doctor."

Silence became a living barrier, walling the four of them into separate compartments.

Peter Flint broke the blockade. "Ross!" Flint's jovial features hardened into a mask. "Did you say Ross?"

Jarrett tensed.

With a lightning hand, Peter Flint drew for his gun, but his fingers fumbled, and he scowled when he realized his gun belt was missing. His flashing eyes skewered Jarrett.

Without question, had Flint had access to his gun, Jarrett would have a bullet in his chest.

Claremont lunged for Jarrett. Gripping him by the shirt collar, he smashed a fist into his face.

Jarrett crashed down across the supper dishes on the low table. Hot soup burned his legs and spread in a pool over the carpet. The metallic taste of blood seemed unreal. He shook his head, but his vision blurred.

Claremont leaped on him, his heavy weight crushing Jarrett's back to the floor.

Delight screamed.

Jarrett deflected the blow Claremont intended for his nose and countered with a hard left fist that struck Claremont on the side of his head. Flint rolled off-balance, and Jarrett struggled from beneath him.

He leaped to his feet with his back to the fireplace, facing both Flints. Hot blood trickled from the corner of his mouth. Legs spread, arms raised, fists ready, he waited for either or both men to make a move.

"Daddy, stop! Please, Claremont. What's the matter with you two?" Delight tried to block Claremont's lunge as he struggled to his feet. She clung to one arm, trying to hold him back. He freed himself like a large dog brushing off a kitten. She landed on the horsehair sofa.

Flint glanced at his daughter as if just realizing she was present. The hate faded from his expression.

Claremont pounced and gripped Jarrett by the throat.

Jarrett tried to break his grip, but he gasped for air.

"Claremont." The stern voice stopped the young giant. He released his hold on Jarrett's throat.

In the suddenly silent room, heavy breathing and Delight's ragged sobs rasped.

"Ross," Peter Flint spat, "Out! Leave this house. If I see you on my premises again …" Flint spoke each syllable like rocks sinking into deep water. "… I shall kill you."

This can't be real. Jarrett braced against the brick fireplace to steady his knees, forcing himself to face the hate distorting Flint's features.

Claremont stood poised as if he itched for another punch. Such intense emotion was as out of place in this richly decorated parlor as the soup puddled on the carpet.

"Father, you call yourself a Christian," Delight's horrified voice cut into Jarrett's dazed mind. With the back of his hand, he wiped blood from his mouth.

"Some things tempt even a Christian too far. The Rosses are responsible for Caldwell's death. I'm part of the treaty party, not him. They had no cause to gun down my oldest son." Harsh lines molded his face into granite." A life for a life, a tooth for a tooth, a son for a son—the Good Book says."

"My family had nothing to do with whoever killed your son. My father's a doctor. He saves lives." Jarrett hated that his voice broke as it had not done since adolescence. "We've never murdered anyone."

Loathing filled Flint's eyes, pinning Jarrett against the fireplace as effectively as a weapon. "I call that justice, with a capitol J. My son avenged by the death of Ross's son. Who, according to his word," Flint's voice oozed contempt, "was not involved in the Ross Party."

Jarrett stiffened.

"Claremont, fetch my gun." Flint's razor-edged voice slashed through the room.

"I call what you're planning 'murder!'" Jarrett burst out. "Silence."

Instead of going for the gun, Claremont grasped Jarrett's arms and backed him against the wall.

Flint turned to his daughter. "Delight, you would have done your father a great service had you kept Mr. Ross outside during the storm with my complete expectation of his freezing to death. Now, I must let him live since I have no wish to involve you in his death. Do not be mistaken though, Ross. Should I find you on my premises again, I shall not hesitate to kill you. Get out!"

Claremont released his grip.

Jarrett stumbled toward the door. Yet something deep

inside rebelled. He faced the Flints. "No Ross gunned down your son. You've got—"

"Claremont, take Ross outside and shut his mouth with the thrashing of his life."

Claremont leaped at Jarrett, slamming him against the door.

"Daddy, Mr. Ross is sick. Beating him would be unmanly." Delight wedged herself between Jarrett and Claremont, a hand braced against both their chests as if she could separate them.

"Hold it, son. Delight is right. We leave unmanliness to the likes of the Rosses. Hightail it out of here, boy. Be grateful the Flints have honor, or you'd be a dead man."

Claremont threw Jarrett's boots at him.

Jarrett hauled a damp boot onto a stockinged foot. Crouching in the hall, he hopped on one foot and fought to pull on the other boot. "Mr. Flint, you don't have your facts straight." His words came in jerks as he tugged at his boot. "My great-uncle Ross had nothing to do with shooting the men who signed that illegal treaty." Jarrett met Flint's stony gaze. "Chief Ross was out of the country when the shootings occurred. An investigation never found evidence he had anything to do with any murders."

Peter Flint threw the door open, his gun pressing against Jarrett's temple, and shoved him out the door.

Bitter cold bit into Jarrett.

"No one can find evidence against a Ross. They have lily-white alibis. We know Chief Ross ordered Major Ridge, John Ridge, and Elias Boudinot killed for following the dictates of their consciences. Not satisfied with those murders, he killed my son."

"Yes," Claremont mocked. "They would have shot Dad too. Except he was out of the territory. So, instead they murdered Caldwell."

Jarrett picked up his pistol from where the weapon lay on his Mackinaw and shoved it into his belt.

"How about it, Ross. We can rectify this matter right now!" Claremont grabbed Jarrett's arm.

Jarrett made a sudden, sharp movement, freeing his arm. "Not my fight. That treaty was signed before I was born." Jarrett's words jerked against each other. "This feud has caused enough bloodshed."

"True to the Ross tradition. Talk yourself out of difficulties and don't face your enemies in an open fight. You Rosses are yellow, stinking …"

Jarrett glimpsed Delight hovering behind her father, her enormous blue-violet eyes shining with sympathy and something more, something indefinable, something almost like a promise.

Jarrett slammed the door shut between them. Cold wind whipped his face and hands, slashed through his jeans, and burned his ears. The weather was nothing compared to the hate of the Flint men. He strode into the darkness.

Claremont's scornful voice, carried by the rising wind, followed him to the barn. "Cowardly, gutless, unmanly …"

CHAPTER 7

Jarrett walked into the cabin, hot with pneumonia, just a week after leaving for the buffalo hunt. Mother, Father, and Jerusha smothered him with love and the best medical care. As he recovered, they spent hours listening to him recount his experiences.

Grandfather Worchester nodded. "Grew up a bit, didn't you, boy? Sometimes it's a good thing to get off the farm."

Father ruffled Jarrett's hair. "That was a dangerous reaction the Flints had when they discovered you in their home. That daughter of theirs seems to have more sense than either of the men. God was looking after you."

Jarrett nodded. She had good sense … and a lot more than that. "Yes, sir."

Grandfather settled his glasses more securely on the bridge of his nose. "No one knows how the Flint boy got killed. My speculation is the lad was probably in the wrong place at the wrong time. Rumors flew like crows descending on a cornfield. But this is the first time I've heard anyone try to pin Caldwell Flint's death on your father. Or your great-uncle for that matter."

The lines in Father's face grew heavier. "I'd like you to

steer clear of the Flint Ranch, Jarrett. Who's to say what those men are likely to do now that you've stirred up that hornet's nest again."

Jarrett grunted. As if he needed to be warned to stay away from the Flints.

For another couple of days, he lay in bed recovering, but with regained health came restlessness.

Even the exhausting physical labor of endless chores failed to ease his driving dissatisfaction. Confined to the farm he felt trapped, with woodcarving providing his only release. In the evenings, cross-legged in front of the fire, he sculpted a set of chessmen for his father.

Those finished, more long, lonely winter months loomed ahead, so he carved another piece he kept hidden in his chifforobe. He fashioned the new work from yellow beech. He captured Runninghorse, stripped to breechclouts and moccasins, bow raised in his left hand, arrows ready in his right, guiding his mustang with his knees as he galloped after buffalo. Jarrett polished the light wood with beeswax for days until he was satisfied.

Days and nights dragged on. He'd experienced dissatisfaction before, but this year's discontent itched like the measles. Afternoons when gloom descended like a heavy hand on his heart, he gazed, mouth drooping, at shadows fingering the frozen earth. This slow death stole his enthusiasm. He had no relief from the tedium, no faces to see except family, no excitement to experience other than the bull breaking out of the pasture. Even with Mother and Dad, he was edgy, impatient, unsettled.

Early one frosty morning, he rode Sampson to visit the Osage village.

Horse nodded to a young girl who looked about fourteen and then to another who appeared even younger. "These Runninghorse two wife. Happy to share little brother. Which you want?"

Both girls stood with lowered heads, glossy long hair hiding most of their faces, but peeking up at him with smiles. Both were lovely and might be sisters.

"No, thanks. You are too generous." Jarrett backed out from Horse's tepee into the cold.

"You strange, Woodcarver."

"Sharing wives is not our … Cherokee … way. Nor my way as a Christian." Appeared he'd have to put their friendship on hold … much as his life was on hold this winter. How much more boredom could he handle?

On the way home, he rode past the Flint ranch, as he had done at least once a week since he'd been able to ride again. But he never caught a glimpse of Delight's face. Knowing people inside that magnificent house hated him held a special fascination. Yet, he took care not to be seen … nor to set foot on the property.

With spring came added work—plowing, seeding, and tilling.

Before Jordan left for college, his brother had preached that this season brought pleasure to a true farmer. Jordan loved farming.

But Jarrett hated the whole kit and kaboodle of farming. Spring for him meant *time to walk softly, Mother Earth was pregnant.* A time to study the rebirth of growing things, newborn wildlife, to feel the fuzzy brown hair of a calf, smell the sweet scent of the air, experience the exhilaration of a storm, ride the land carpeted with tiny flowers, and sit in the yellow glow when sunlight was like warm syrup, and he could dream.

He clipped a newspaper article from *The Cherokee Advocate*. He had to leave. But how should he approach Mother and Dad? He'd bide his time, get the crops planted, and when Jordan returned home for summer vacation … Jarrett expelled a long breath … he *would* go. He tugged the worn paper from his denim pocket and read what he'd already memorized.

Wanted: young, skinny, wiry fellows, not over 140 pounds, under 18. Must be expert riders, willing to risk death daily. Orphans preferred. Wages $25.00 a week.
Pony Express Riders.

He refolded the article and slipped the creased paper back into his jeans pocket.

As irresistibly as rock candy attracted a child, the job lured him. He must find a reason to offer his parents for leaving the farm.

He would minimize the risk and play up the wages— money to help with his college tuition. Twenty-five dollars had to be more than Dad made in a month. An average doctor call amounted to one dollar, and that included the time Dad spent traveling to and from the patient. And many patients couldn't afford to pay, so Dad accepted whatever they offered—eggs, pork, butter, even quilts.

Today's events were the last straw. He jerked off his jacket and lifted his face to the setting sun. He had to leave. Since sunrise, he'd sweated in the lower field. For fourteen solid hours he pleaded with those two stubborn mules, cajoling them to furrow the unwilling sod. A more obstinate pair he'd never met.

Jarrett bent and rubbed his calves. Leg cramps hurt like the dickens, and his shoulders, neck, and arms screamed weariness. His throat ached from yelling. Jordan liked to plow, and those two mules liked Jordie behind the plow … they worked as a team for Jordie.

Jarrett stretched his back.

Both mules gazed at him, tails switching, mouths open, big teeth bared. They laughed at him.

He slammed the barn door.

~

Inside their cozy kitchen with its calico curtains and homemade furniture, Jarrett laid down his fork and wiped his mouth with his napkin.

As Jerusha cleared the dishes, she leaned over and kissed his cheek, leaving a wet place on his skin.

The front door opened, and Dad's tall figure entered.

"Daddy!" Jerusha set her dishes on the sideboard with a clatter and ran into his arms to be swept high in a bear hug.

Mother rushed to Dad's side and kissed him. Her face glowed as he pulled her into the circle of his arms.

Granddad Worchester cleared his throat.

Jarrett stood.

Mother reached for her apron and tied the gingham in place. "John! I never once expected you for dinner, or I would have kept your food warm. I'll heat soup, toast some bread, and fry a slice of buffalo. I'll have hot coffee for you in a jiffy." She measured coffee beans into the grinder, her eyes snapping with vitality. "How are the diphtheria patients? At my count, you've been with them three nights running."

"Over at last. That is, unless fresh cases develop. I'm exhausted. Haven't slept a wink. Hope, don't fix me anything to eat. I want to shuck these boots and slip into bed."

Dad's face was lined with weariness. His claw-hammer coat was rumpled, and a lock of his graying blond hair hung over his scholarly forehead. With a sigh, he slid into the rocker.

Jerusha knelt and tugged off Dad's boots.

"Thanks, sweetheart." He leaned back in the rocker. "Father Worchester, Jarrett, how's the farm fared since I left?"

Jarrett nodded to Granddad to take the privilege of answering, stretched out on the floor at Dad's feet, and eased his aching back onto the bare boards.

Granddad brushed a hand through his white hair. "The way I see it …"

Jarrett nudged Grandad to stop.

Dad's closed eyes, measured breathing, and relaxed frame spoke loudly in the room, even before the first snore.

Grandfather Worchester rose and placed a pillow beneath Dad's drooping head. "John always could sleep just about anywhere. I remember on the Trail of Tears when the army disciplined him for slipping away from the guards, he had to sleep in a supply wagon, draped over boxes, barrels and what-not. Yes, sirree, John always could sleep anywhere. One way he stays healthy."

"Granddad, tell us about that time," Jerusha begged.

Jarrett grimaced. If only he had Dad's ability. Jarrett squirmed his back into a more comfortable position. He had trouble sleeping lately—no matter how tired he was, he couldn't relax.

Granddad stumped across the room and lowered his body into a rocker on the other side of the fireplace. He removed his rimless glasses and polished them on his handkerchief.

Before he could speak, someone pounded on the door.

Jerusha bounded over to answer.

"Oh no, not tonight. John's exhausted," Mother whispered.

Jerusha opened the door.

"Can the doctor come? My father's been shot! There's lots of blood. And we can't get it to stop bleeding, we just can't! And besides that, he hit his head when he fell down. Did it sound awful, just like a ripe watermelon cracking on the ground."

Mother hurried to the door, her finger on her lips. "Shush." She glanced toward Dad.

Too late, Dad opened his bloodshot eyes.

"Come on in, Robert. You live about an hour ride from here and over an hour from Honey Springs, don't you?"

The boy nodded, hopping from one foot to another.

"You must be hungry. Hope, fix Robert a bite of dinner, will you?" Dad turned. "Jarrett, put Robert's horse in the barn. The boy will stay the night. No need to wear out him or his horse." He put a hand on Robert's shoulder. "And Jarrett, hitch the old mare. The gelding's tired." Dad shook himself, yawned, and motioned to Jerusha. "Bring me some clean socks, will you, Bunny?" He caressed her dark curls.

Jerusha ran to Dad's bedroom.

Mother ushered Robert to the table. Grandfather Worchester trailed them.

Jarrett struggled up from the floor. "Wouldn't you know somebody would need help tonight." He limped to the door and rushed into the darkness toward the barn. He hitched Maresy to the buggy, then rubbed her warm nose. "At least one of us is fresh. You're ready to step out." He rubbed her ears. "You'll be worn out when you get home, though. Lucky *you* don't have to work tomorrow."

When Jarrett stepped back into the kitchen, Jerusha sat at the table across from Robert Etowah.

She looked up. "We're settled in to enjoy a good gossip."

Jarrett nodded. There'd been a time when a talk with a neighbor eased his need to be social … but nothing so simple worked these days. He had to find some excitement. "I'll drive you over to the Etowahs, Dad. You can sleep in the buggy on the way." Jarrett grabbed a slice of toast from the plate Mother had brought for Dad to take with him.

"Good, Jarrett. I was hoping you'd offer." Dad rose from the rocker, picked up his black medical bag, kissed Mother and Jerusha absently, as if his mind were already fixed on the man who needed his help. "We'll be back sometime tomorrow, Hope," he called over his shoulder.

Jarrett opened the door, and the two of them left the cabin.

Mother waved goodbye. "Take care of your father, Jarrett. Do make certain he eats and sleeps. Don't let him stop for anyone else unless it's life-threatening, or he'll be a medical case himself."

Jarrett jumped into the driver's seat, and a moment later the carriage sagged as Dad climbed aboard. The candlelight at the door illuminated Mother, Granddad, and Jerusha.

Dad settled on the buggy seat, squirming to find a comfortable position for his long legs.

Jarrett clucked the old mare to start.

The evening was fine and warm for spring with a star-lit canopy. Trotting down the dirt road under a brilliant moon, Jarrett whistled the old mare into a canter. Ahead, once off the main road, they'd hit rough trail. Now was the time to make tracks.

Jarrett's spirits lifted. Tomorrow, chances were, he wouldn't be behind the heavy plow following those blasted headstrong mules. He had a day's reprieve! He leaned against the leather cushion and relaxed. He sucked in a deep breath, tingling as the air filled his lungs. His nostrils flared to catch the fragrance of lilacs and honeysuckle.

The rhythmic drum of the mare's hooves on the dirt road blended with the croaking of frogs and the chirping of a million insects. The shimmering moonlight lit Dad's sleeping face as he slouched on the seat, his head swaying with the buggy's motion.

Jarrett guided the carriage between the biggest ruts and potholes. He stayed on the main road for half an hour before turning the old mare at a fork jutting toward the Illinois River.

The old girl slowed to a walk. Trees shut out the moonlight, obscuring the trail.

Jarrett had little choice but to give Maresy her head as she picked her way over the rock-strewn road.

The buggy's bounce and sway failed to awaken Dad. His face remained peaceful as he slid from side to side on the cushioned seat.

Jarrett's back and shoulders screamed from the long day at the plow and driving the buggy, so he halted the carriage and stepped down to stretch.

After another half hour of bruising riding, he sighted the double log cabin with a dog-trot in the middle.

Hound dog baying fractured the still night air announcing their arrival.

Dad yawned. "Are we there?"

Jarrett pulled the old horse to a standstill. "Yep."

The door burst open, spilling shadowy forms carrying lanterns.

Dad reached for his bag and stepped from the buggy. The flickering lantern cast light and dark shadows.

"My man's in the kitchen, Doc. His breathing's bad, rapid-like, and then slow, like he cain't hardly take another breath. We thought you'd never get here."

At the accusation in the rough voice, a flicker of annoyance bit Jarrett.

Another woman's voice ordered from the porch, "Jesse, you take care of Doc's horse. Put her in the barn and rub her down good and feed her,"

"Come in, Jarrett. You can assist me." Dad's face betrayed no irritation, just kind and smooth, as if he were smiling. Same as always.

"That's what I was afraid of," Jarrett muttered. Jumping from the buggy, he strode the dark path to the cabin.

Inside, Dad unbuttoned his claw-hammer frockcoat, then leaned over the man lying on a mattress-like pallet in one corner of the kitchen.

Jarrett took the coat and folded it across one of the straight-backed, homemade wooden chairs.

"We'll fix you up in no time, Bob." Dad laid his hand on the middle-aged man's arm as the injured fellow looked up with tight-pursed lips.

Dad's voice assumed a commanding tone. "I'll need clean sheets spread on the table, boiling water, and all the lighted lamps you can bring."

Jarrett glanced at the family gathered around the injured man. Dad was different from most doctors in the way he insisted on things being clean. But Dad's patients usually got well.

People scattered to fetch the items. Footsteps thudded on the wooden floor, doors banged, and then everyone hurried back.

Dad motioned to Jarrett. He and Dad lifted the groaning man onto the sheet-covered kitchen table.

Dad opened his surgical case.

Inside, each instrument was tucked into its own pocket. Jarrett's gaze darted over a tourniquet, dental extractor, two orthopedic bone saws, four foreign-body removers, and a pouch full of vials.

A large pot and a dishpan of steaming water arrived.

Dad laid his instruments inside the dishpan. He and Jarrett scrubbed their hands. He cut off the patient's bloody shirt, then nodded. "Now, Jarrett."

Jarrett noticed a small wound on the back of the man's head, then avoided looking at the patient lying on the table. He kept his gaze on his father and his mind on the job he had to do. Taking a folded piece of white flannel, he pried open a flask and dripped ether onto the flannel. He calculated the correct amount, then laid the wet square over the man's nose and mouth.

"More, Jarrett, you don't need to work so slowly. There, that's right. Keep checking his pulse. Tell me if the speed changes."

"Okay, Dad." Jarrett ground his teeth. If only he guessed correctly. "Bob's unconscious now."

Using a pair of tongs, his dad selected an instrument from the dishpan, then probed the bloody hole.

The man groaned.

Jarrett dripped more ether onto the flannel lying over the patient's nose and mouth. The rising fumes made him feel lightheaded.

A heavy body thudded to the kitchen floor.

Jarrett glanced up.

The eldest son lay sprawled on the floor, his arms spread, his eyes closed.

Jarrett shrugged.

Another son retrieved the lantern. The lamp chimney had rolled next to his feet, and the flame had gone out. The boy replaced the chimney, relit the lantern, and held the light high, while Jarrett dripped ether.

The mother leaned over and helped the son who fainted climb to his feet. Head down, the son vacated the kitchen for parts unknown.

Jarrett switched his concentration back to his dad.

Dad used artery forceps to hold open the jagged hole in the man's shoulder. He probed deeper.

The entire family, from wife to humpbacked granny, stood lined up around the table holding lighted lanterns, mouths hanging agape as they watched Dad dig into the hole.

His father exulted, "Got the bullet."

Jarrett glanced at the injured shoulder. His insides

churned. With his stomach knotting, he refocused on the man's faltering pulse.

Long, slender fingers moving with expert skill, Dad pulled the jagged pieces of tissue together and held them in place with crossed artery forceps. Using smaller forceps to hold the needle, he stitched the wound with catgut.

Myriad eyes followed the needle's progress.

Dad glanced up from his stitching. "Someone run out to the barn and fetch me a good straight piece of lumber. I'll be needing another sheet as well."

One of the lantern bearers scampered off, returning moments later with a board.

Dad rummaged in his bag and lifted out his saw.

A gasp swept around the table.

"I'm not going to amputate his arm." Instead, Dad sawed the lumber into the desired length, bandaged the shoulder, then made a splint with the board and strips of sheet. Dad finished by tucking the unconscious man's arm into a sling.

Then Dad turned his attention to the head wound, bathing it with iodine.

Bob squirmed and moaned.

Dad frowned. "Hold his head, Jarrett."

Jarrett laid the ether bottle beside the light and, using both hands, grasped Bob's head.

Dad sewed the ragged edges of the small wound together. He used two fingers on the man's carotid artery to count his pulse, looked him over, and used his stethoscope to hear his heartbeat. He grinned. "Hazel, your husband should mend now. I'll stay here until he wakes. Cover him and keep him warm."

The family brought a handmade stool for Dad.

Jarrett shifted his tired feet. "Mrs. Etowah, my father's been up for three nights running with diphtheria cases. If you have a pallet he can use, I'll sit here with your husband."

Jarrett perched on the hard stool, his back complaining, until dawn, sponging the unconscious man's forehead and, from time to time, checking his pulse.

One by one, members of the family stole off to wherever they slept.

Jarrett paced the small kitchen, empty now except for him and Bob. Had he given too much ether? Why didn't the man wake?

As light rose in the east, Bob Etowah stirred, muttered something, closed his eyes again, and fell asleep.

Jarrett released a deep breath and nestled his head on his arm, inches from Bob's.

A rooster crowed.

Jarrett raised his heavy head.

Mrs. Etowah stood at the cookstove, frying bacon.

Dad stirred on the pallet, jumped up, and checked the sleeping patient. He nodded and joined Jarrett at the table.

Jarrett took a sip of coffee. "Your patient woke at about one and then went to sleep."

"You did a good job, Jarrett. You'd make a fine doctor."

"No thanks, Dad, that's not a profession I'd like to follow."

Dad frowned but said nothing.

Jarrett's mouth watered until the good lady placed heaping dishes of bacon, eggs, and fried mush in front of them. Sometime during breakfast, Dad started looking fresher. After two cups of black coffee, Jarrett didn't feel too exhausted from his all-night vigil.

Mrs. Etowah refilled Dad's coffee cup as Dad pushed aside his empty plate. "How'd your husband get shot?"

"You know, Dr. Ross, that Stand Watie has forty or more armed men he keeps around his house. For protection, he says. Protection from what, I'd like to know. Anyways, my husband was out looking for stray cows like he does every spring. End of April, first of May, he goes out looking for strays. They always get over that north split rail fence. Don't seem to matter how many times we mend that fence, they always get over." Mrs. Etowah heaped more fried mush on Jarrett's plate and passed him the sorghum, her plump figure jiggling with effort.

"My oldest son Vern, he was out with Bob. Thank the good Lord. Vern's the one what fainted when you was operating on Bob. Vern swore they was three bushwhackers. Vern, he said they was Stand Watie's men." She poured hot coffee for Jarrett, her round face creased between the brows.

She lowered her voice and glanced out the single window. "Must be 'cause Bob just joined up with the Keetowahs. Don't you think?"

Dad sipped coffee. "Since the patient is sleeping and has no fever, Jarrett and I will take our leave." He rose and picked up his medical bag.

"Well, we do thank you so much, Doc. We don't have any cash money now, but after the crops come in, we'll be sure to get you your pay, and I'll send along a fresh pie."

"No hurry. Whenever you have money on hand, flag me. The charge is one dollar." Dad buttoned his claw-hammer coat.

Outside, the dogs set up another ruckus and swarmed their feet as Jarrett climbed into the driver's seat. "I'll drive.

You can catch up on more sleep, Dad."

"No, let's talk. We don't get this opportunity often."

Jarrett slapped the reins on the mare's shoulder. Was this a good time to approach Dad?

Dad checked his medical bag to make certain he'd not forgotten anything, then set the black case at his feet.

No, not a good time. Maybe later. "I don't know much about what's going on, Dad. Who are the Keetoowahs?"

"They're a new society some New England Missionary originated." Dad's voice jerked as the buggy jounced over the rock-strewn road. "Supposedly, Keetoowah was organized to preserve ancient tribal tradition. Mostly full-bloods joined, but ..." Dad lifted an eyebrow. "Like many organizations, the original purpose has been superseded by a more urgent one."

Jarrett concentrated on his driving. "And?"

"Some folk say the Keetoowahs agitate for the rights of slaves. New Englanders are rigidly against a man's owning slaves."

Jarrett nodded. Grandfather Worchester was a staunch New Englander. Many conversations at the dining table centered on slave problems.

"Quite a few people think the Keetoowahs organized to unite people who support the North in event of war."

"Do you think there will be a war, Dad?"

"I'm afraid so."

"What will happen to our people if war does come?"

"Your great-uncle John is seventy. A man that old wants peace. Wherever he goes, he speaks of 'holding one hand out to the North and holding the other hand out to the South.' This is not our war, Jarrett. Here in Indian territory, we have the right to remain neutral."

"But you don't think we will?"

"No. I don't think we'll be left alone here any more than we were in Georgia. Look at the situation this way. Stand Watie's treaty party is pro-South. Some still own slaves." Dad frowned. "The Ross party is pro-North. Our nation is split down the middle."

Jarrett guided Maresy between two deep potholes.

As the buggy swung round a corner onto the main road leading to Tahlequah, Jarrett urged the old mare into a trot. They drove past the trail that forked off toward the Flint ranch.

His heart grew heavy. If only they could drive by Delight's ranch.

Dad nudged Jarrett's arm. "Let's stop by the Female Seminary this morning. Today is May first. May Day. We should arrive in time."

Jarrett nodded and sat forward on the bouncing seat. He urged Maresy into a gallop.

"Not so fast, son!"

Jarrett slowed the mare back into a sedate trot.

The road wandered through grazing land, fenced with herds of cattle. Farms nestled closer to one another as they neared Tahlequah. Fathers and sons worked together, plowing and planting corn, cotton, or wheat. They shouted and waved as he and Dad rattled past.

"Is our plowing finished, Jarrett?"

Jarrett shrugged. "No, sir. I still have that lower field left. The wheat's in and the corn—and the garden, of course. I could have had that plowed if those two mules weren't so obstinate!"

Dad's lips tightened.

As they passed, barnyards filled with hogs, chickens, and turkeys spread their distinctive odor into the warm spring air. Farmhouses with apple, peach, and cherry orchards were flowered in white and pink, scenting the air with sweetness.

"Jarrett, I've never put my roots down quite as deeply as they were in Georgia before the government took away our plantation. Nothing material has been as valuable to me since, because I learned the hard way that everything can be snatched away." Dad motioned with a long, muscular arm toward the farm. "Houses, lands, and possessions are not the important things in life. Our relationships with God and with people are the lasting values. These can be damaged if we don't protect them."

Jarrett nodded. So good to have his father's unexpected gift of time spent together.

"There's the Park Hill public school. We're here."

Jarrett slowed Maresy to a walk. Visiting the small village a few miles south of Tahlequah was always fun. He drove under stately trees that canopied the dirt avenue. Park Hill had been built when the Cherokee arrived in 1839. That had been twenty-five years ago—before he was born.

Fashionable brownstone and red brick homes with extensive yards lined both sides of the street. Horses grazed in pastures behind the homes.

Two women strolled along the brick sidewalk, long skirts swishing, their umbrellas unfurled, protecting them from the sun. They waved white-gloved hands.

"Morning ladies, lovely morning." Dad tipped his tall beaver hat.

They smiled and trilled, "Yes, isn't it? Are you attending

the ceremonies?"

Dad turned in his seat to answer. "Yes, we will see you there."

A few blocks later they passed the Murrells' three-story white frame mansion with its twelve-foot ceilings and hand-hewn stone fireplaces.

"The Murrells entertained dignitaries such as Zack Taylor and Jeff Davis when those men were stationed at Fort Gibson."

Jarrett clicked Maresy to a faster pace. "Impressive."

They passed the brick Presbyterian Church just as the bell hanging in the fourteen-foot spire chimed ten mellow peals.

The college was still a mile north of Park Hill, but buggies, carts, wagons, and horses were hitched in every conceivable spot. Jarrett threaded through vehicles, searching for an opening in which to swing the buggy. They approached the three-storied brick and stone seminary building with massive columns on three sides. People streamed toward the college from all directions.

A good distance beyond the college, he found a small grassy area, pulled a quick rein, and the old mare swung the carriage into the spot.

Dad squeezed his eyes shut. "Jarrett! Don't drive so recklessly."

Jarrett leaped out and tied the horse to a tree, leaving her sufficient rein for grazing. He smoothed his hands through his hair, brushed dust from his shirt and denims, and matched Dad's long-legged stride toward the seminary.

The military band from Fort Gibson, resplendent in bright red uniforms and plumed hats stood in formation on the manicured lawn in front of the veranda, their instruments flashing in the sun.

He and Dad joined the crowd, climbing the broad steps into the entry hall.

Inside, rows of chairs faced a stage on which a bower entwined with vines and flowers waited. Long oval windows on both sides opened to a cool breeze.

Formally dressed men and women crowded inside.

"Wish I'd had time for a bath this morning." Jarrett smoothed his work shirt. He walked to stand at the back, leaving the few remaining chairs for the ladies, and craned his head, searching for a familiar face. Nope. Most of the young men his age must be where he should have been … plowing. The room overflowed with women and a sprinkling of old men dressed in green or mulberry frock coats and velvet vests. Young officers from Fort Gibson swelled the crowd.

"Some easy way to make a living," Jarrett murmured, eyeing the officers clustered in small groups with chests stuck out and arms gesturing, acting important.

Band music drifting in from the open windows changed tunes, and with a roll of drums rattled into a march. From the far end of the room, a door opened. A group of young ladies cascaded into the room like a rainbow over a waterfall, wearing dresses of pale yellows, pinks, and blues.

The beauties sang as they glided up the aisles and around the center dais. Fourteen pretty girls gathered around the throne, carrying bouquets of flowers, with fluttering ribbons wound in their long hair.

With a crescendo of music, the Honor Maid entered carrying a crown of yellow rosebuds. She was tall and willowy with glossy black hair curling around a pale, oval face. Her large hazel eyes shone as she stepped up on the dais, into the bower, and waited beside the throne to crown the May Queen.

"You remember Jill Adair, Dad. Jordie escorted her home from church last year. He should see her now!"

Dad nodded.

Another crescendo of music, and the queen entered wearing a white gown. Jill slipped the ringlet of rosebuds on the May Queen's head.

Along with the rest of the audience, Jarrett rose to his feet and clapped.

After more singing, the girls braided colorful ribbons about the maypole. A few speeches ended the ceremony. The double line of girls spilled out onto the lawn.

"They'll have a picnic lunch."

"Sounds like fun."

"Probably pair off with a young man and dance to the music of the military band." Dad squeezed Jarrett's arm. "We should be on our way. Mother needs you to finish that plowing. If I don't get any more calls, I'll give you a hand."

"Yahola." Jarrett's shoulders slumped. He had so little time to be with young people his own age.

"All right." Dad tapped him on the back. "We'll eat the lunch the Etowahs packed. But we can't stay long. There's a fellow over there I need to talk with." He pointed to a family settling on the hilltop above them. I'll meet you back at the buggy."

"Yes, sir." Jarrett wended his way back to their buggy and had almost reached their spot when he saw Delight Flint.

His world lurched. His senses leaped to life. His knees

went weak.

The air around her charged with energy.

His heart thumped. Blood surged from his fingertips to his toes.

94

CHAPTER 8

J arrett stared.

Delight helped an older lady spread a quilt beneath the trees. By the family resemblance, her mother.

Would Delight's mother catch him gawking? He ducked behind a buggy.

Silvery blonde hair fell in ringlets around her face and cascaded to her waist. The sun gleamed on the strands, spinning her hair into gold. Her oval face, enormous eyes framed in dark lashes, and her rounded lips set his heart leaping. His blood pounded.

She must have felt his stare because she gazed straight at him, and her eyes changed, deepening to lavender. A rush of pink tinted her cheeks and dimples appeared.

An intense aura of attraction grew more tangible with each breath he took.

She was so lovely a man would do his utmost for her, so adorable he wanted to …

Delight winked.

What? What? What? He struggled to recover his ability to think. Then motioned for her to meet him in the forest on his side of the buggy. Taking deep breaths to slow his rapidly beating heart, he sauntered into the woods. Would she follow? He trod further into the deep forest, located a secluded spot, and waited. If Flint found them alone together, his life wouldn't be worth a plugged nickel.

She appeared, slipping between the trees closer with each step.

Her eyes radiated intrigue, her smile conspiratorial and vivacious. Dimples played on her face. "I prayed you would make your way home safely. I'm sorry my family acted rudely. I've never seen my father so angry or Claremont so eager for a fight. You must excuse them for me." She laid a soft hand on his arm.

His arm tingled from fingertip to elbow. He raked his fingers through his hair and tucked his shirt into his jeans. If only he'd changed clothes last night after sweating in the sun all day. He jammed one thumb into his belt. Where was his voice? He shifted from one foot to the other. With her so close, under the cool solitude of the trees, he yearned to gather her into his arms.

"Apology accepted," he mumbled. The breeze wafted her sweet scent to his nose. He couldn't think straight.

She whispered, "I've thought of you often since last winter."

Jarrett swallowed. Waves of excitement raced through him. He resisted a tremendous urge to finger a loose curl on her cheek, to touch the silk of her skin, to hold her in his arms. Instead, he sprawled on the spring-scented earth, plucked a blade of grass, and formed it into a whistle.

Delight folded her long skirt and settled beside him.

The scent of fresh apples drifted to him. Her dress, blue with tiny white flowers, fell across his knee. She reminded him of a porcelain figure he'd seen in the Murrell home. "Is that your mother with you?" Stupid question.

"Yes, of course." She smiled. "We don't have much time. Mother will be calling me for lunch." Delight plucked a blade of grass, then tore it into sections. Dropping the pieces, she reached out and laced his fingers with her own.

Sparks streaked up his hands.

"We'll be friends, won't we, Jarrett? I mean, there's no reason we can't be the first Flint and Ross to become friends." Her blue-violet eyes glowed.

Jarrett centered his gaze on the ground, hiding his eagerness. He pretended to search for another piece of grass, muffling his voice with his drooping head. "Sure, we can be friends. If we don't stop this feud, who's going to?" He glanced up and smiled.

The crease between her brows smoothed and dimples charmed her cheeks. Like a rising sun, a smile illuminated her face. "How can we be friends if we never see each other?" She gently disengaged their hands.

She liked him!! She wanted to be with him! To disguise his excitement, he flopped onto his back and, folding his hands beneath his head, tried to look casual. He controlled his words, but his voice trembled. She was leading him into extreme danger. He knew it. "We'll know we are friends. We're bound to run into each other now and then. Like today." He smiled a lazy smile, turning up the corners of his lips. But his hands felt ice cold.

Her entire face beamed.

She loved this secret meeting! He felt reckless, able to overcome any obstacle that hindered their being together. Did he dare kiss her?

"My father didn't forbid us from seeing each other. He

said you're not to come onto his property." She tented her hands into a prayer position. "Please ride over soon, and I'll meet you in the woods by the stream. That's not our land, but the place is close enough and hidden, so I can meet you there."

A warning bell clanged deep inside Jarrett's brain. Hold on, her plan could lead to a wagon load of trouble. The Flints weren't joshing. If they discovered them meeting secretly … his heart jolted.

Jarrett's grim thoughts must have reflected on his face.

Delight's blue gaze swam with tears.

He couldn't stand to see those tears overflow. Okay, if necessary, he **would** die. Regardless, he had to see her again. Somehow, he would make a way. A cautious way. Not immediately. But he would win this girl's heart and make her his. But first he had to tell her.

"I'm leaving home this summer." He pushed himself up to sit cross-legged, heat flushing his skin. "I'm joining the Pony Express! Don't tell anyone. My folks don't know yet." But I'd like you to wait for me." Blast—that jumped out before he knew it.

She blinked, stared at him a second, then watched a butterfly flit across the meadow, as if the insect were a rare species she needed for a collection. A tear slid down her cheek.

Jarrett's throat dried. Heaviness pulsed through him, twisting his stomach into a lump.

She seemed intent on the butterfly, but whispered, with a tiny catch in her voice, "Oh, I wish you weren't leaving just when we are getting to know each other." She sighed, a whisper of sorrow. Her teeth nipped her lower lip.

Yahola, this is risky. "I can ride out before I leave. But how will you know I'm at your ranch?" Could he deny this girl anything in his power to give ... no matter how dangerous? Everything inside him cried out for her.

She unwound a blue ribbon from her long hair. "Tie this to our gatepost. If anyone else sees it fluttering, they'll assume I lost my ribbon. The blue on the post will be our signal that you're waiting in the woods." A shadow belied her sunny smile, darkening her blue-violet eyes.

"I'll meet you before I leave." He reached for the ribbon and tucked the bright signal into his shirt pocket.

"Thank you. I'll be watching for you." Delight touched the pendant hanging around his neck. "I've been wanting to ask you since last winter—what is that?"

Jarrett's mind still explored the possibilities of what would happen if Flint discovered he secretly met Delight, so he answered without thinking, "A buffalo horn. A friend gave it to me."

Delight turned the polished buffalo tip over and over in her hand.

Jarrett loved her being near ... loved the way she made his heart sing. Made him think he was capable of anything. Even winning Delight.

"What are the little figures painted there?"

"I don't know. The pendant's big medicine for the Osage. I wear it because I like the design, and the horn reminds me of my friend."

"Is your friend a girl?"

His cheeks burned. "Yes. Her name is Mist Over the Water. She and her brother are my friends."

"Oh." Delight looked down, her dark lashes touched her

cheeks. "I wish you had something of mine so you would think about me."

"I don't need anything to remind me of you. I think of you all the time," he blurted, then bit his tongue. "I mean, meeting you here today … this moment with you in the woods has changed my life … I want—"

An exasperated voice called, "Delight, where are you, child? Delight!"

She crinkled her forehead.

"Delight Flint. Come at once. Your father is waiting!"

Jarrett frowned and jumped to his feet. "You'd best go. I don't want your father to find us."

"I have nothing to give you. Please come and see me. I'll look for you every day. Don't forget!"

"As if I could." The naked sadness in her eyes had to be erased. He reached out and folded her into his embrace. His lips lowered until he found her uplifted ones. He kissed her. Her response sent every nerve, every sense afire.

The voice screamed, "Delight. This instant!"

He breathed in her delightful essence, then released her. "I'd like for you to wait for me. I'll return for you."

She gazed up, her violet eyes wide.

Twigs snapped and the sound of people thrashing through the woods toward them.

She blinked, then raced through the trees, her long skirt toppling bluebells, glancing twice over her shoulder and waving. In her wake, the grass and flowers sprang up leaving no trace of her path.

He heard her meet her people and leave with them the way they came.

Long after the bluebells straightened, Jarrett stared after

her. He eased down on the grass. Had she heard him ask her to wait? No matter. Before he left, he would ride over and make his intentions clear. He grinned. Life had become such a pleasure. Warm happiness glowed inside his chest. Beautiful sun in the sky, cool shade overhead, grassy meadow, bluebells wild among the grass … and the most daring girl in the territory waiting for him. Her eyes **had** promised. He lolled on the ground. Mr. Goldfinch twittered in a branch overhead trying to distract his attention, but his mind spun a shining dream. Dreams could be good. And this one was very good.

~

Rumbling in his stomach nudged him into action. Leaving from the opposite direction Delight had taken, he zigzagged and circled back through the trees until he arrived at Dad's buggy. He stroked Maresy, who flicked her tail, then he rummaged in the carriage and hauled the picnic basket from beneath the leather seat. Dad was nowhere in sight, so he sneaked behind Dad's buggy to spy on the Flints.

Surrounded by a company of armed men, a sprinkling of matronly women sat on a patchwork quilt beneath an ancient, gnarled oak. Delight's fair hair shone in the middle of the somber group, pinpointing her as the only young person.

Peter Flint wore a double set of revolvers holstered around his waist and tied above his knees. He had the look of a man most men would avoid tangling with. Evidently, even on this peaceful college campus, the Flints' politics segregated Delight from other young people.

A thrill filtered through him that he and Delight had met. And they'd not been detected. Yet he best not get brash. Who was he kidding? He'd wacked at the hornet's nest. He'd kissed Delight. He'd asked her to wait for him. A chill spiraled down his backbone.

One gaze into those soulful violet eyes and he'd lost all brain power. He shook his head. He was a nut. Crazy! Reckless! Totally mindless!

Yet he wouldn't have missed that kiss for a million lives.

Dad walked up to the buggy. "What have you been up to? You look like you're sitting on top of a mountain."

"Just looking around, sir. Just looking around."

As they ate lunch, Jarrett shared his excitement in meeting Delight and hinted at the strong feelings he felt for her, but he didn't tell Dad everything. Not be a long shot.

"You're treading a dangerous path, Jarrett." Dad's face grew deep wrinkles. "I won't forbid you meeting the Flint girl, but I strongly urge you to forget any future encounter."

"I didn't tell you I planned to see her again."

"You didn't have to. I ascertained from your buoyant mood that you made plans. Hear me, Jarrett. Don't get involved."

~

As Jarrett drove their buggy toward Tahlequah, an open carriage with a liveried driver and a uniformed black boy perched on the box clattered in the opposite direction.

Dad called to the elderly man with white hair and bushy white eyebrows wearing a tall beaver hat seated beside a young woman. "Morning, Uncle John."

The pair seated in the carriage nodded and smiled. "Morning, nephew. Sorry, I can't stop and chat. You must come and see us soon." The vehicle clattered on down the street.

"My great uncle must be headed to important business to miss the May Queen crowning." Jarrett snapped the reins to urge their mare to trot faster.

"Yes. You should see him, Jarrett, when he goes into an outlying town. I've watched him ride in, tie his horse to a post in the square, and become immediately surrounded by people. They stand in line for hours to take Chief Ross by the hand."

"The Treaty Party and the Flints are a small faction, aren't they, sir?"

"Yes, just a few thousand who follow Stand Watie. There are a few of us neutralists who believe mistakes have been made on both sides. Everyone else worships Uncle John, certain he will lead the nation along the right trail."

The buggy rattled over a bridge as they approached the outskirts of Tahlequah.

Jarrett yawned and rubbed his eyes. With a full stomach, hot sunshine, and the lengthening of the day, losing last night's sleep caught up with him.

They clip-clopped past the gristmill and salt works with a glance and a wave to the burly workmen sweating in the heat.

In front of the smithy, muscles bulging, the blacksmith pounded glowing hot metal on the anvil. Then he plunged a horseshoe into a trough of water where the metal hissed and steamed. He glanced up, nodded a greeting, and lifted the cooled shoe from the water.

"Lots of folks around here are happy with a fenced farm, barn full of crops, pens full of hogs, a fast horse on a racetrack, and a comfortable home. But that's not the life that suits you, is it, son?"

"No, sir. That doesn't appeal to me."

"What do you want from life, Jarrett?"

He couldn't tell Dad he wanted to marry the only girl in Tahlequah he couldn't have. But he could share his other dreams. "Excitement. Sometimes I feel trapped in a cage and can't escape. I'd like to travel—go to California and see if there's any gold left—or down into Mexico or Texas. I'd like to trap in the Sierras or ride shotgun on the stage or … or ride Pony Express."

"But after you've had your adventure, what then?"

"I don't know. I only know what I don't want." Jarrett hunched in his seat, frowning at the road unfolding before their dependable horse. Dad would never agree to his courting Delight.

Dad gripped the rail in front of the seat with a white-knuckled fist. "What don't you want to do?"

"I don't want to farm! Or be a doctor or a circuit rider. I don't want to spend my life here in the same place, doing the same hard work. I've … I've *got* to try something different."

"You'd better be thinking about your future, Son. What are you going to study this fall at college?"

Jarrett sighed. "I'll have to give that more thought." He slouched in the seat, turning from his father. College sounded as dull as farm work. He had other plans. Plans that suddenly included an adorable girl who apparently liked his kiss. He smiled. More than liked. Enjoyed.

They entered Tahlequah with the dirt road broadening

into a brick street lined on both sides with houses. Driving to the square, they passed the elegant Grand Hotel, which dwarfed the two-storied Cherokee Supreme Court building next door. In the lazy afternoon heat, old-timers, waving palm fans, rocked in the shade of the hotel veranda.

At the corner of the square, they passed the wheelwright shop. Across the street the post office door stood open to admit any straggling breeze. At this hour of the day, he and Dad had the town to themselves, except for a few lethargic dogs.

As they left Tahlequah, Jarrett urged Maresy faster, past farms stretched widely apart. He yawned harder and blinked heavy eyes. The hot sun and the bouncing buggy mesmerized him. The surrounding landscape receded, and Jarrett dreamed. He was back in the secluded woods with Delight.

Dad stretched and leaned back against the buggy seat. "I'm going to take a snooze."

Soon, a snore drifted from Dad's side of the buggy.

Jarrett's thoughts returned to Delight, the reins lax in his hands, no longer aware of the buggy, the road, or the hot sunshine.

A big hound dog leaped at Maresy, barking and nipping at the old mare's legs.

She shied and broke into a gallop.

Jarrett caught at the reins, but they slipped between his fingers to drag on the ground close to Maresy's flashing back hooves. "Yahola!"

Dad woke and gripped the buggy's side rail.

The dog outdistanced Maresy and leaped for her nose.

Maresy bolted from the road and galloped into an

unfenced field, the dog's teeth still trying for her tender nose.

The buggy jolted and lurched, threatening to overturn as they headed straight for a tree. The mare swerved, missing the tree by inches. The wheel on the driver's side slammed into the tree, smashing the carriage onto its side. The buggy hooked on the tree and yanked the old mare to a stop.

Jarrett catapulted through the air to splat on the ground near the mare's front hooves. Dazed, he lay there as nausea swirled in his stomach. He worked his way to his feet, wincing when he moved his left shoulder. When he turned to face the buggy, dizziness muddled his brain.

"Are you injured, sir?" Jarrett stumbled across the tangled buggy tack and extended his right hand to help his father out of the broken buggy.

"Just shook up. Banged both knees. You hurt?"

Jarrett hauled his father to his feet. "No, sir." He rubbed his aching shoulder. "Looks like the buggy's a total loss. I'm sorry, Dad, I didn't see that mutt."

Dad's eyebrows bristled above a furrowed forehead. Flashing eyes, deepening from vivid blue to black, sparked. "What is it about you, Son, that trouble follows you like a shadow? I've been driving that buggy for ten years, and this is the first time I've had an accident. You draw trouble like a magnet."

Jarrett winced. Was this a sign to leave?

CHAPTER 9

As Jarrett expected, the storm broke across the supper table.

Dad's normally mild eyes narrowed and darkened. "Your carelessly demolishing our buggy puts us in a tight spot. That hour we spent walking home hasn't sweetened my temper."

Jarrett tightened his jaw. *Seize the opportunity.* "I'd like to leave home this summer to work for the Pony Express. With what they pay, I can buy a new carriage. Since the accident was my fault, it's only right I replace the buggy."

He avoided looking at Mother as she stood, spoon raised to heap steaming New England boiled dinner onto his plate.

Wide-eyed as a startled cat, Jerusha stared at Dad. With her hands folded in prayer, she begged, "Daddy, please don't let Jarrett leave."

Dad's anger blew stronger. "Jarrett, even when Jordan returns home, you're needed for weeding and harvesting, and for the hundred other things that require work during summer."

Jarrett's throat constricted. He sounded like a

melancholy foghorn. "I have most of the crops planted. Last year, when Jordie left early for the University, I managed the haying alone. Jordie can handle the crops this summer." He pushed his food aside and clutched the arms of his chair.

Between bites shoved into his mouth, Dad ranted. "That job's dangerous. Your mother needs you. You're bound to get into trouble."

Mother squeezed Jarrett's hand. "I know why you're angry, John, but how else are you to replace the buggy? You rode a horse the first ten years of medical practice before we saved enough money for a carriage, and you're not as young as you used to be." She wound her arms around Jarrett's shoulders and kissed his cheek. "Our son has to leave home sometime."

Dad sighed and rubbed the back of his neck. "Don't remind me I'm getting old. I don't need that, too."

Grandfather Worchester's deep voice rumbled through the tension like a mountain stream over rocks. "John, please don't make the same mistake I made with Jeremy. Don't keep your colt tied up when he's strong enough to run."

The old man's lively eyes twinkled over the top of rimless glasses. His white hair gleamed in the lamplight above his weather-beaten face and white whiskers. "Even with our small acreage, it's obvious Jarrett's not cut out to be a farmer. Not that he doesn't do the work well enough, but his heart's not in tilling the soil."

~

Two weeks later, events had fallen into place, and Jarrett packed to leave. The emotional goodbyes were difficult, so

Jarrett kept them short.

Early morning sun sparkled on dew-covered meadows, transforming them into fields of diamonds. A blue jay, chattering like an old friend, flew from tree to tree following him as he rode. In a golden daze, frequently humming, he trotted toward his dream.

He nudged aside his feeling of having broken something warm and precious yet smothering. Leaving home was more painful than he'd anticipated. Freedom had better be worth this price.

When the trail forked past the Flint Ranch, he detoured. Fumbling in his shirt pocket, he touched the blue ribbon.

The dew had lifted by the time he trotted to the long rail fence surrounding Delight's home. His insides coiled into a hard lump.

The ranch boiled with turmoil. Jarrett counted thirty-two men, armed with rifles and pistols, milling around the ranch building. All strangers, the men appeared to be waiting for someone or something. They eyed him with frowns and stares.

Thirty-two men! Impossible to meet Delight today. He trotted past the long avenue of fence, his heart a lead weight.

The armed guards glared as he rode away.

As the Flint ranch disappeared behind him, he forced himself not to look back. He set his mind toward his future and to the latest article he'd read in the *Cherokee Advocate*. The news had been over a month old when the paper reached his hands.

The Pony Express operation opened April 1st. People from the St. Joseph area celebrated the start-up with five bands. Crowds congregated to give the initial Pony Express rider a hearty sendoff. The inaugural journey from St. Joseph to Sacramento took nine days and twenty-three hours. Until modern times, mail delivery had taken three months between those two cities.

Jarrett blew out a breath. Incredible, those pony riders made that journey from east to west so quickly. He had to get to St. Joseph before all the jobs were spoken for.

He scarcely noticed the familiar countryside he passed.

~

Days later, with darkness closing in, trail weary and blanketed with dust, Jarrett rode into St. Joseph, Missouri. He reined in Sampson in front of the Pony Express office, a single-story, unpainted frame building on the outskirts of town. He shrugged off disappointment. Not much to look at.

He had spent his last nickel on the ferry crossing over the Missouri. If the Express Office were closed, he would have to spend another hungry night under the stars.

Early in the week, Sampson had pulled a tendon, so the trip had been slower than planned. He paid the last of his money to a horse doctor and didn't have two cents in his jeans pocket.

Throwing a stiff leg over the saddle, he dismounted, tied Sampson to the hitching post, then walked a few steps to restore feeling to his numb legs and sore backside.

Fifty feet from where he stood, the railroad tracks ended. He stretched, rubbed his back, and stared at the tracks. They sure looked strange, ending that way in a bed of grass. From this point, the tracks only headed east. He spoke aloud. "Reckon this is what they call the end of the line. Odd. But it fits in with the seedy part of St. Joe I just rode through."

How could a town as well-known as St. Joseph have unpainted buildings, dirt roads, and farm wagons parked haphazardly on vacant lots? Not what he'd expected.

Unsavory characters loitered on the boardwalk.

Jarrett patted the pistol ducked in his belt. But no one heeded him. Not even a friendly nod. Big city coldness. He straightened his shoulders, beat trail dust from his chest and legs, shined his boots on the backs of his calves, and ran a hand through his disheveled hair. He lifted his chin as if daring someone to confront him, then turned toward the office.

The unimposing, one-story building next to the railroad tracks boasted a false second floor front and sagged like an empty bag. A chipped sign hung from rusty hinges proclaimed *Russell, Majors & Waddell*. Another sign tacked below stated *Pony Express*.

"Looks like a mule could kick that whole place into firewood," Jarrett mumbled. He stepped up on the boardwalk, gripped the loose doorknob in an unsteady hand, and entered.

Inside the office littered with piles of papers, newspapers, and horse tack, a youngish man with a tired face and baggy gray eyes looked up from behind a desk buried under more papers and various pieces of leather and horse bits.

"Come in. I'm Cliff Hansen, Mr. Waddell's assistant." Hansen's curious stare took in Jarrett from head to foot.

Jarrett brushed more dust from his butternut shirt. He

should have stopped to wash in the river.

"So, you want to be a *pony rider*." Hansen spoke a statement, not a question. "We use eighty lightweight riders and four hundred fast horses. We maintain eighty relay stations. From St. Joseph, the route runs over the prairies, up the Platte and Sweetwater Rivers to South Pass, across the Rockies to Salt Lake City, across the Nevada Desert, and over the Sierra Nevada Mountains into California. It's rugged country all the way. What section are you interested in?" Like the city, Hansen's voice sounded cold, impersonal, and tired.

"I'm from Tahlequah, Indian Territory. I'll take any opening."

Hansen sat straighter, his tone grew more personal, and his gaze more intense. "Indian Territory, huh? Never had one of you Indians apply before. Yep. We have one opening. It's in Western Utah, a few miles the other side of Salt Lake City." He stood to face Jarrett. "I'll give it to you straight. Bart Riles died at Cold Springs a few days past. Just got word. Paiute war parties prowl all over that area. You want the job?" His shrewd eyes probed.

Jarrett nodded.

Hansen gripped Jarrett's shoulder. "I think by the time a new rider gets out there most of the Injin fuss will have died down. Bart's the only rider who's been killed, and we don't want to expose any more men to danger." He shook Jarrett's shoulder. "Don't make a hasty decision. Tell you what, we'll put you up at the Patee House for the night and you can sleep on your decision."

"Sounds good."

The recruiter dropped into his wooden swivel chair and

leaned back, a satisfied expression on his face. He flicked a thick hand toward a wooden seat. "Sit down. I'll explain our operation."

With a soft groan, Jarrett lowered himself joint by joint into the chair, leaned back, and jiggled his trail-weary legs.

While Hansen talked, darkness crept inside the office. Hansen lit the kerosene lamp and leaned toward Jarrett. The oily smell of kerosene hung in the room until the lamp burned away the fumes.

"The Hannibal and St. Joseph Railroad delivers mail from the East, which our riders carry west. I can tell you're no southern sympathizer by the cut of your clothes and the sound of your voice." Hansen gave Jarrett a superior look, with which he was intended to agree—that the two of them knew more than any southern cracker.

Lips compressed, Jarrett stared at Hansen.

Hansen shook his head. "Seeing as how I can't influence you with that kind of talk, I'll tell you our mail delivery is keeping the great state of California inside the Union." He leaned forward and pounded his fists on the scarred desk. "After we made our first Express run, California declared itself a *free-soil state*, all slavery abolished. Rumors of that great state becoming a separate country, isolated from the United States, ceased. The Express welded California to the Union." Hansen's face grew animated—the fanatic look stamped him a visionary.

Probably what made the man good at his job. He believed what he preached. Jarrett's pulse quickened. He forgot his fatigue and inched forward on his chair.

"All across this great West of ours, a string of eighty young men on fast horses traverse this land, taking communication from east to west and from west to east. Much from California is addressed to the War Department, the Congress, and even to President Buchanan. Men pay as much as $25.00 a letter to have their voice heard in Washington. That mail can change the destiny of our nation. If Lincoln is elected president this November, let me tell you, war will come!" Hansen pounded a fist on his armchair.

"If war comes, we need the men and the gold that California can provide. Keeping communication with California open is a dangerous task, calling for the utmost courage, stamina, and dedication from our riders. Russell, Majors, and Waddell lose $15.00 on each letter delivered, because our government does not underwrite us." Hansen scowled.

Hansen's voice was as inspiring as any general leading soldiers into battle. "The Pony Express needs men with heroic endurance, nerves of steel and reflexes of lightning." Hansen's tenor rang to every crevice of the small, dimly lit room.

The man was a motivator. Jarrett didn't need the talk, but he liked the new reasons to uphold his decision to join the Pony Express. He ruffled a hand through his hair. "None of this means much to me since I live in Indian Territory outside the boundaries of the United States and am governed by Cherokee tribal law."

But Hansen had planted a vision of the glory that was the United States of America in Jarrett's mind. Hansen's fervor aroused feelings Jarrett had not suspected existed—loyalty, dedication, selflessness. He sat forward in his chair, hands flexed on his knees. If necessary, he would ride to California to deliver the mail alone.

Hansen nodded. "In the difficult days ahead, you will need to reflect on why you do this job." He leaned back and steepled his fingers, a slight smile on his lips.

"Okay, Mr. Hansen. I'm your new rider. When do I start?"

"Fine. I knew you were the young man we sought the minute you stepped into this office. A few formalities, and you can sign a contract. First, we've planned for each horse to carry no more than 185 pounds. That gives us 20 pounds for the mail, 25 pounds for your equipment, and 140 pounds for you. How much do you weigh?"

Jarrett frowned. "I'm not sure. A little more than that I think."

"No problem. We have a scale right over here. Step on." Hansen fiddled with the weights on the scale while Jarrett stood, shoulders tense, watching the man's stubby fingers adjust the weights.

"One hundred fifty pounds." Jarrett groaned.

Hansen looked him over. "You're taller than most of our riders. About five foot ten, aren't you?"

"Right."

"I can't expect you to lose any weight. Far as I can see, you don't have any excess." Hansen's eyes twinkled. "You've got a good build, though, broad enough in the shoulders, and lean, hard muscle." He poked Jarrett's shoulder. "We'll have to lighten your equipment."

Jarrett shifted from one foot to the other. Just what equipment would he be missing?

"This is a mochila." Hansen handed him a leather pouch on which the words *Overland Pony Express* were lettered. "The mochila fits over your saddle and can be thrown on and pulled off quickly." Hansen pointed to a lock in each corner of the pouch. "See these locks. We store the keys in St. Joseph, Salt Lake City, and Sacramento for safekeeping." He laid the pouch on top of a short filing cabinet.

"We provide you with fast mustangs for the rough desert country of Western Utah. You'll ride over one hundred miles a day, with a relay station every ten miles where you'll switch to a fresh horse. We allow two minutes for a change of horse. All your boarding and living expenses will be paid, and you'll receive $100 per month, which we will deposit in your name at the St. Joseph Security Bank here in Missouri."

Hansen retreated to a closet in the back of the room and returned carrying guns.

He handed Jarrett a lightweight repeating rifle and a Colt revolver and holster. "These are yours. On no account are you to use these weapons except in self-defense."

Jarrett examined his new weapons. They looked to be high quality. Buckling the holster around his hips, he swaggered across the room, enjoying the feel of the new revolver swinging with the movement of his body.

"Tie the two strings at the holster's bottom around your thigh so the weapon won't bounce when you gallop. A bruised leg won't be good for you or your revolver."

Jarrett's face heated. He nodded.

Hansen smiled as he reached for a large black Bible. "Raise your right hand and swear before God the following pledge." Hansen placed the Bible under Jarrett's left palm.

With solemn face and steady gaze, Jarrett pledged after Hansen, "I swear by the great and living God, while an employee of the Pony Express, I will not use profane language, will drink no intoxicating liquors, will not fight, and will conduct myself honestly and faithfully in all my duties. So help me God."

The recruiter bent down and opened a desk drawer and removed some clothes. Hansen's face glowed as he handed them to Jarrett. "These are the official Pony Express riders' working uniform."

Jarrett accepted the gaudy red shirt and bright blue trousers.

The agent placed a Bible in Jarrett's hand. "Russell, Majors, and Waddell want God-fearing men as their riders."

"Yes, sir. I am that." Jarrett stood straighter.

"Oh. And go over to the General Store and buy yourself one of those new broad-brimmed hats with the high crown. They are just the thing for riding in arid country. Have them send us the bill."

"Thank you, sir. I'll do that!"

"One last command. Keep away from that English gent staying at the Patee House. He's with the *London Illustrated News*. He's writing articles on the Overland Pony Express. You'll recognize him easily enough. He wears a chimney-pot hat and carries a silk umbrella. Name's Burton, Richard Burton. *I'll* tell him what I want him to know about the Express."

Jarrett raised his forehead in a salute. "Got it."

"Run on over to the Patee House and get yourself a hot bath, have your supper, and get a good night's sleep. Report back at seven o'clock tomorrow morning. Tell the people at the livery to send the bill for your horse to us. Same to the Patee House."

"Thank you, sir. I'll return first thing in the morning." Jarrett shook Hansen's hand and walked out of the shabby building, certain he floated in midair, and that his boots never touched the boardwalk.

CHAPTER 10

During the days as Jarrett rode the desolate, sparsely settled country to Salt Lake City, he hungered for the green meadows, trees, and flowing rivers of home. The desert seemed dead. Stark and barren, cold and empty at night, hot and empty during the day. He talked to Sampson more each hour, but Sampson had no sense of humor. And seldom answered.

The final morning, with the sun heating his back to the sweating point, he arrived at his home station on Dry Creek. He dismounted on shaky legs and wiped a clammy arm over his face, only to find his arm smeared with dirt. He swiped grime from his shirt and stomped his feet to dislodge dust from his trousers and boots.

He leaned against the lone hitching post and gazed at the station. Ramshackle place looked to have been thrown together in a hurry. He walked inside through the open door. Tiny with a dirt floor and no windows. Four bunks built into one wall, no furniture except three boxes the men probably used for chairs. No people.

He trudged outside and stared around. The station,

perched on the desert floor with only a few cactuses and sagebrush to relieve the flat barrenness, looked desolate except for a small corral and a horse shed. Probably the horses were inside out of the hot sun.

Jarrett sagged against the cabin's rough wood. "So, this is Dry Creek. Some adventure," he mumbled, using his hand to shade his eyes from the glaring sun. "A relay station."

Back in St. Joseph, Hansen had explained, "Relay stations are ten miles apart for the horses' stamina. Each station houses two attendants to care for the horses."

The shed door opened.

Jarrett straightened.

Two men moseyed toward him. Silhouetted against the sun, they loomed tall, muscular, and bearded, wearing jeans and long-sleeved shirts that looked slept in.

"Howdy. Guess you're the new rider. My name's Jim." He spat on an arid thistle-like plant, that, considering the brown splotches splattered around it, seemed a usual repository. "Drop your roll inside and come meet the horses." Jim jerked a thumb toward the corral.

"My name's John." The other man so resembled Jim under the bushy whiskers and long hair, they might be brothers. "We been in the barn shoeing a new horse."

Jarrett held out his hand. "I'm Jarrett Ross. Glad to meet you."

Both men nodded, turned back to the shed, and started strolling as if the sun beat them down so hard, they couldn't move any faster.

Jarrett dropped his arm. Right. Taciturn desert fellows. He stepped into the cabin, slung his pack roll onto a lower bunk, fled the grim hovel, and rejoined the attendants outside the corral, now filled with horses.

Jarrett eyed the spirited animals milling inside the large, oval pen. "The horses look half-wild."

"Green broke." Jim propped a foot on the bottom log of the corral. "Wild, but you can't wear 'em out."

Jim lassoed a mustang's hoof and staked it to the ground before the dancing animal could pull loose. Sweat poured down both men's sunburned faces and necks, drenching their shirts before they managed to stake each hoof of the screaming, biting mustang.

John wrestled the pony's head, holding the writhing animal still, while Jim trimmed the hoof and replaced the shoe. The blazing sun outlined their movements with incredible distinctness in the huge, empty land.

"Ever ride a horse like this?" John punctuated his question with a juicy splat of tobacco targeted on the single blade of grass growing bravely in the cracked sandy earth.

"No, sir." Jarrett's dry tongue felt fuzzy in his mouth. The shimmering heat burned his nostrils. Which was worse, the wild horses, the crazy attendants, or the awful heat?

He led Sampson into the barn and gave him water and feed, then rubbed him down. With Sampson comfortable, he returned to the corral and leaned against the fence.

After the men finished shoeing the pony, Jim glanced at the sky. "We got time 'afore dark. I'll show you the route you'll ride."

Jim lassoed one of the saner-looking ponies for Jarrett and another for himself. They saddled and mounted.

Jim led the way over the route. "This'll get as familiar as your own boot print. You'll call to mind each boulder, each clump of mesquite and sagebrush, each pinion tree, arroyo, and canyon. You gotta know where an ambush is most like to happen. The river floods bad. This here's one place to ford when the water's up. 'Cept sometime you cain't get across a'tall."

"You're joking." Jarrett gazed at Dry Creek, little more than a depression in the sunbaked sand. He licked his lips, already cracked from the harsh desert heat.

"Ain't you never heard of a flash flood?" Jim laughed. "I gotta tell ya, you look greener than the kid the Injins murdered."

"Looks can be deceptive." Beneath his saturated shirt, Jarrett squared his shoulders.

Jim led him past sandstone cliffs beyond which low mountains, miles out on the plateau, sprouted like islands from a desert sea.

"You ride ten relay stations, each ten miles apart. At each stop, you get yourself a fresh horse."

When they stopped at the fifth station to spend the night, Jarrett swayed in the saddle. "I'm bone-weary." He followed Jim into the tiny cabin already crowded with the two attendants fixing dinner on a camp stove. Content to eat in silence with the men, he rolled into one of the bunks as soon as he laid down his fork.

One lesson he'd learned—men didn't talk much out here because they were just too tired. Jarrett's thoughts trailed into a fuzzy stupor, then he fell into a deep sleep.

Next morning, he continued to follow Jim. "Riding's getting rougher with all these boulders and rocks cluttering the trail."

"Yep."

Their horses jumped steep depressions crisscrossing the

dry earth like wrinkles that creased the skin of his new cohorts. Both Jim and John were tough, dark men, their skin like old leather acquired from their years wrestling with the extreme climate.

Jarrett wedged his broad-brimmed hat more firmly on his head.

Around noon, at the westernmost tip of his route, Jarrett's final station wavered against the horizon like a mirage. Across the desert, through the swirling dust from their horses' hooves, the Stars and Stripes flew jauntily over Fort Ruby. Civilization at last.

Or. Maybe not. One small cavalry unit billeted here. A dilapidated post office, general store, and a single cannon warded off the emptiness of the vast land. The officers' quarters were much the same as their cabin in Dry Creek. Enlisted men roughed it in tents. A stockade surrounding the buildings and parade grounds offered some feeling of security.

Jim jerked his hat off and slapped the shapeless felt against his knee, spiraling dust. "No females ever set foot inside this fort."

"Not surprising," Jarrett muttered.

"Here's where you bunk." Jim motioned to the tiny windowless cabin perched next to the corral as though it had been built as an afterthought and didn't plan to stay. "You git here to the Fort twice't a week. It's darn near four hundern' miles of fast, hard ridin' each week. Most like you'll jist eat and sleep. Ain't much else to do here."

Jim entered the cabin and threw his roll on the bottom bunk. "When the rider gits here from eas'n Nevada, you'll high tail it to Dry Creek. And vice versa when you lug the mail from Dry Creek back here." Jim smiled broadly. "It's a hundern' miles each way, four times a week. Jist amounts to a Sunday Walk for a young squirt like you." He laughed, tickled at his own humor.

"Huh." Jarrett flopped down on one of the three boxes and swiped his arm over the sweat on his forehead.

"The rider from Nevada is due at the Dry Creek Station day after tomorrow at four p.m. In the meantime, you and me gotta get back to our station. You'll catch a few hours shut-eye a'fore you start yer first run."

~

At 3:40 on the appointed day, Jarrett stood at the open doorway of the Dry Creek Station. Heavy rain deluged the arid ground, turning the entire area into a quagmire.

To lighten his load, Hanson had not issued the regulation rain poncho. Jarrett, soaked to the skin within minutes of leaving the cabin, watched his new shirt bleed red trickles onto his new blue trousers. At least the hat's broad brim sheltered his face from the slashing downpour. His boots were twin plows sloshing through ankle deep mud, furrowing his path to the corral.

Both Jim and John clutched one skittish mustang's halter.

Jarrett crawled into the saddle.

The instant the horse felt weight in the saddle, he bucked straight up, all four hooves off the ground.

Jarrett's mucky boots slipped in the stirrups. As the mustang's hooves slapped the slick earth, Jarrett hung on. The hard jolt snapped his neck.

The mustang jumped, landed, jerked his head, and bucked.

Jarrett pushed deep in the wet saddle,

The horse twirled wildly, shook his bit, and hopped sideways, darting angry looks backwards.

Jarrett kept a firm seat, clutched the reins with both hands, and murmured in the horse's pinned back ear.

The mustang calmed to an excited prance.

"Owe you five." Jim's disgruntled voice was almost inaudible beneath the pounding rain.

Jarrett lifted his face and laughed into the rain. So, Jim had bet he would land on his backside in the mud.

"Well, the rain'll keep the dust down, anyways." John held out his hand to Jim. "Hand it over."

"Yep, and they ain't much fear of Injin attack during this storm. You watch now for that Dry Creek. It's sure to be flooded." Jim squeezed Jarrett's wet leg.

A sound, muffled beneath the steady drumming of rain, grew louder until hoofbeats reverberated through the gloom.

"Here he comes!" shouted Jim.

Splashing through the rain, great sprays kicked up by his mustang's hooves, the express rider arrived at top speed. With a practiced swing, he transferred the mochila from his own saddle onto Jarrett's.

Jarrett swung his horse around. The downpour blocked his view as great drops slashed down from the gloomy sky. Needles of rain pricked his body, diverted only from his face by the broad-brimmed hat.

Racing his mustang toward the first relay station, exultation grew and multiplied until Jarrett's body warmed from the burning in his heart. He rode for the Pony Express!

Exactly forty-five minutes later he splashed to his first change of horse. Both attendants stood waiting, each hanging onto the bridle of a spirited mustang. The horse had kicked thick goo on the two men until they looked like giant mud balls. In the dusky light as they smiled, their teeth gleamed under the sludge.

One, two, three—counting seconds, Jarrett flipped the mochila onto the fresh pony and vaulted aboard. Keeping his seat, he managed to subdue the half-trained animal. Two minutes. On schedule.

At the next several relays Jarrett could barely see the muddy attendants holding a fresh horse. The wild night stormed dark as the inside of a rifle barrel.

At the latest station he shouted above the roaring wind. "Does this horse know the way?"

"Yep! This be the mustang what brought in the mail alone when poor Bart got his."

The answer, distorted by the snarling wind, echoed in Jarrett's ears. "Great," he yelled as he galloped away, "because I can't see beyond this animal's ears, let alone the trail."

An uneasy, out-of-control feeling enveloped him, as he galloped in the slashing rain with darkness shutting out his sight as effectively as a blindfold. He had to depend on the horse's knowledge.

This ride is like my life. I don't know what the future has in store for me, but I have faith that God knows the trail ahead, even though I can't see my way. He leads me, and I'm as dependent on him as I am on this mustang. God knows what is best for my life, and nothing will happen to me that God does not plan.

Suddenly the pony balked, almost hurtling Jarrett over his head. The sound of rushing water thrashed louder than the storm. Straining into the darkness, he saw nothing. He took a deep breath and dismounted, gripping the reins. His boots submerged into a current that threatened to pull him off his feet.

"What now, horse?" Jarrett leaped back into the saddle. A vision of the dry creek bed that had looked so innocent when he and Jim had ridden across flashed into his mind. He wriggled wet toes inside waterlogged boots.

"This mail's sure to be late now. Yahola! Why does the weather play Noah and the ark the first time I ride?" Jarrett urged his mount into the water. The mustang refused. Kicking the animal's ribs, Jarrett gave the horse his head. "Come on boy, find a way to cross."

The mustang headed upstream.

"Horse, I hope you know what you're doing. Right now, I'm just wet baggage. I'm depending on you to get us to the next station across that river," Jarrett yelled, leaning against the mustang's matted mane.

The sturdy mustang picked his way upstream, sometimes slipping so badly Jarrett slid sidewise in the saddle and imagined the raging waters sweeping them away.

Twenty tense minutes later, the horse entered the creek. Every few steps he stopped, gazed over the water, ears pricked forward. He turned his head toward Jarrett, as if seeking guidance.

"Don't look at me. I don't know what's out there," Jarrett grumbled. "You're supposed to be the homing pigeon."

The water boiled around the animal's legs. Then rose higher. The frigid water engulfed him to his waist. Jarrett yelped. The current grabbed them like a giant hand almost tearing him from his saddle. A low moaning came from deep inside the horse's throat.

Jarrett locked his arms around the slippery neck. Panic paralyzed his thoughts.

CHAPTER 11

As the current sought to pry him loose, Jarrett fought to keep his seat. The mailbag loosened and floated over the mustang's shoulder. He grabbed for the heavy mochila and hung on.

The mustang swam, hooves churning, trying to thrust his head above water foaming around his nose. The flood pulled them downstream.

If this horse thought this was a good place to cross Dry Creek, what was the trail crossing like? *Maybe my mount doesn't know anything. Maybe we'll both drown.*

Water slapped his shoulders, spraying his face. He gasped for air. The mail bag slithered from his cold fingers. He dropped the reins and grabbed the bag.

The gelding snorted and blew as water thundered around them.

Waves slapped his head. Hair plastered in his face, he struggled to breathe. With one arm wrapped around the mochila, his other hand gripping the saddle horn, he felt himself sliding from the saddle.

The horse's hooves struck something solid. He surged forward and scrambled out of the roaring waters. His horse, flanks heaving, stood on the bank, four legs spread, and head lowered.

Panting like a steam engine, Jarrett settled the mochila across the mustang's shoulders and slumped over the horse's neck until both their breathing slowed. Muscles trembling, Jarrett murmured to the screaming wind. "So, that's a flash flood. Thank you, Lord, for saving our lives."

Without direction, the wiry animal picked his way toward the next station.

When they arrived at the relay, the attendant stepped from the barn, lantern held high in one hand, leading a fresh mount with the other. "What kept you?"

"Creek's up. Had to find a different ford." Jarrett dismounted and dragged the heavy, dripping mochila onto the fresh horse.

His spent mustang stood, head and tail drooping, as though unable to lift a hoof.

Jarrett felt much the same way. He braced for the struggle to command the fresh mount, hauled his foot into the stirrup, and, seconds later, kicked the new horse into a gallop.

Soon after the lantern glow behind him faded, Jarrett's throat tightened. He must be lost. Had to be! The ground beneath his mustang's hooves felt too rough to be on the trail. The horse slowed to a walk, then turned in one direction then another.

"Night's as black as the inside of a kettle. Yahola! I can't see anything."

The rain slackened, but that made little difference. Water sloshed inside his boots, dripped down his back, and slithered in his saddle. An hour later, he still wandered, searching for something familiar. Ready to fall from the saddle, he noticed that the horse pricked his ears forward and at last seemed certain of his direction.

"There's a limestone bluff I recognize. We're on the right trail." Jarrett patted the horse's wet neck.

Twice more Jarrett lost his way before arriving at his destination. Inside the fort, not a light gleamed. But a single lantern flickered by the corral. He flipped the mochila to the waiting rider and dismounted, his movements as slow as if he were seventy rather than twenty.

The attendant's voice sounded grouchy. "It's four a.m. The mail's three hours late. We'd 'bout given you up. Come on in. I'll fix us both a hot drink."

Inside the cabin, Jarrett surveyed himself. He was a soggy, dirty mountain of mud. He stripped, wrung the worst of the water out of his clothes, and hung them over a crate where they dripped rivulets of sludge onto the dirt floor. The soaked brim of the big hat drooped. Setting the hat on top of a box, he blocked the shapeless mass into a caricature of its former appearance. "Hat will never be white again. Forget the hot drink, Tom. Good night." Jarrett flopped onto the nearest bunk.

~

Days slipped by as Jarrett acclimated to the bone-wracking ride, every other day. He was sure the hundred-mile stretch west of Salt Lake City was the roughest riding Pony Riders endured—broken, twisted mountains, dead-end canyons, and a critical lack of water. He carried the only dependable water in his canteen. The route passed through Paiute Country, and their mood was hostile.

He kept alert for sign of Indians or outlaws. His fast horse, his pistol, and his intimate knowledge of the trail were his only defenses. He remained hair-trigger alert—scowling if a bush ahead of him moved. Any motion could betray an animal or an Indian waiting with bow strung. His experience with the Osage had taught him Indians didn't warn of their presence with clouds of dust or hoof beats but sneaked up or lay in ambush. He remained vigilant while riding at a dead gallop.

The days he didn't ride, he mostly slept. At times, he practiced fast-draw and target shooting with his Colt. He easily bested both Jim and John.

At Dry Creek, the two attendants proved to be interesting companions. Evenings they lounged in front of the cabin, drinking coffee under a star-speckled sky and filling Jarrett's ears with tales of outsmarting Indians, throwing in an occasional tale when the reverse was true.

Jarrett used his spare time to teach Jim to use his gnarled hands for something other than work. He shared his wood carving skills, and Jim turned out a credible likeness of a desert owl. He and the two men spent hours together whittling and talking while basking in the hot sunshine or by the light of flickering fires.

The vast, empty land wove a spell over Jarrett. He was content. And yet his last thought at night and first thought in the morning centered on the sunny disposition and dimpled smile of the girl that family and distance kept from him. He played their time together over and over in his mind.

What was she doing right now?

During his times at the fort, he discovered the troopers envied *his* job. Who could believe it? The soldiers pointed out he earned a great deal more money than they. Hearing the troopers complain about army regimentation, the poor quality of their food, and how they resented their officers, Jarrett decided military life was not for him.

The solitude, broken by a few growing friendships, caused several months to pass before he realized.

On a day off from riding his route, he lounged against the corral at the Fort Ruby Station.

Tom, one of his fellow riders, strode toward him, grinning, the space between his teeth making the grin appear even bigger. "Ross, someone back east is a cogitatin' on you. You got yourself a letter!"

Jarrett's heart sped up, but he ambled around the corral to meet Tom as if receiving mail was not an important occurrence.

Tom's eyes widened and his eager expression creased into a mischievous grin.

"Hand it over." Jarrett slid the envelope from between Tom's clenched fingers and inserted the letter into his breast pocket. "Not so hot today." He wouldn't give the man the satisfaction of seeing how anxious he was to read the letter.

"Ain't you gonna read that?"

Jarrett smothered the chuckle rising in his throat. "Sure. But first I plan to get away from the smell of these horses and find a *quiet* spot."

"Oh, don't mind me. I'll trail along with you and if you got bad news, why then, I'll be right here for you." Tom followed Jarrett like an eager puppy chasing a stick.

"This won't be bad news. This little gem is an answer to a letter I sent about a month and a half ago." Jarrett grinned. "Have a heart, Tom, I don't get mail every day. I want to be alone."

"Only if you tell me who sent that expensive letter."

"You're worse than a wolf howling at the moon. Go on, get out of here!"

"Fine, fine, don't get huffy. You'd think a guy'd share the only letter that's come to the station since I been here, wouldn't you?"

Jarrett sauntered through the fort's gate, walked a quarter mile to a gnarled old tree, and slid down to sit in its shade.

The handwriting, neat and pretty as an engraved invitation, quickened his heartbeat until it thumped against his rib cage. He pictured how she looked at that May Day picnic, how the sun spun her long hair into gold, and how he longed to touch her.

He thought of their kiss. Remembered every sensation. Could almost feel the warm pillow of her lips.

He rubbed a crease between his brows. "Was that her first kiss?" Jarrett glanced around. "Hope no one heard that." His fingers trembled as he opened the flap. Then he hesitated. Would this letter end his dreams?

Even if she did, he'd never forget her sweet scent and her smile like warm sunshine. When her lips turned up, her cheekbones rounded, and those dimples showed up. He would do anything to coax a smile, to see her dimples flash, then hide, then flash again. And her lips …

He pulled in a deep breath, squared his shoulders, and slipped the letter from its envelope.

Dear Friend,

I watched for the ribbon until the day I received your letter. I'm glad you did not forget me entirely.

As if he could.

I'm happy that you enjoy your career and your freedom. How I envy you. I wish I were a man and could leave home.

Tahlequah is very tense. I fail to understand why Indian Territory must become involved in a war over the Union of the United States. I believe Chief Ross is correct in speaking for the Cherokee to remain neutral. I, of course, don't voice my thoughts to my father.

But men are so passionate. Last Sabbath Day, after the pastor delivered a political message, my father stalked out of church with Mother and me trailing behind like Indian squaws. I was quite embarrassed.

Almost daily, strange, heavily armed men visit our home. They frighten me with their stern faces and cold eyes. I wonder what my father is up to. Of course, he doesn't tell me. Mother goes about her duties with a pale, strained look, while Claremont rushes about like a foolish colt, as though the situation is a delightful game.

Jarrett gripped the letter tighter and frowned.

Perhaps it is good you are not here. When we arrive in Tahlequah, men with northern sympathies cross the street to avoid encountering my father and his cohorts. I expect fighting will explode in our town soon.

Our home has become a meeting place for southern sympathizers. Groups of men have recently arrived in Tahlequah with southern accents so thick one can scarcely tell what they are saying. The men agitate the home folk.

From what I understand, Indian Territory seems to be in a crucial position. The Confederacy thinks we should furnish them with food for the troops. I think that no matter who is elected president in November, war is unavoidable. The Confederacy courts all the tribes in Indian Territory to gain allegiance.

Jarrett lowered the letter and frowned. She's surrounded by men. *Dear God, please don't let her father encourage her to keep company with one of those southern men.* He raised the letter again.

I hope we can remain friends even though I know all you Rosses prefer maintaining the Union, even though you believe we Cherokees should stay out of this war.

Nope. He'd do something stupid if he were back home. Get himself killed trying to see her. No way that gorgeous girl and he would remain merely friends. His feelings had gone way to far for that.

The men in this house make no secret they think women have no mind for politics. I am vexed with Claremont and his superior attitude—but I won't burden you with my feelings.

I wasn't planning to write this, but I feel this issue so strongly I shall. Often, I sympathize with our blacks. I believe southern men have little more regard for the intelligence of women than they do of the blacks. Perhaps we are both more clever than they suspect.

Jarrett smiled. Delight was intelligent. Of that, he had no doubt.

Life is not totally dismal here. I amuse myself with the

piano. My family appreciates my playing, congratulating each other on how talented I am. I have no such delusions, although I sing in church, and I love to serve in this small way.

I think about you more often than I should. Do you ever think of me?

He grinned. Only every time he had a moment alone. Only last thing at night and first thought in the morning.

I've written much more than I planned, but I feel almost like I am talking to you, and so I don't want to stop.

I read in the newspapers of the exploits of the Pony Express riders and am <u>most fearful</u> for my friend. You may be certain I pray for you each night. Do please write me again.

Delight

Jarrett sat a long time beneath the tree, folding and unfolding her letter. She had said nothing about their kiss. Or if she would wait for his return.

~

An unbearably hot August sizzled hotter. Jarrett had hoped for a cooler September. Nope, the days grew sizzling.

With the sun scorching the earth, and the rocks and sky reflecting the blistering heat, riding felt akin to a journey into hades.

The debilitating temperatures didn't bother Jim and John.

Jim encouraged, "You get used to it, Ross."

John slapped him on the back. "You'll get acclimated."

"Doesn't help." Jarrett drank water like a camel.

Despite constantly wearing his broad-brimmed hat, the sun burned his skin a deep, coppery brown and streaked his hair white. The alkali dust worked the worst hardship. Jarrett tied his handkerchief over his nose and mouth to keep from breathing the poisonous dust. When he galloped into his home station at the end of each circuit, so much alkali grit powdered his clothes and hair that he resembled a baker who had fallen into a barrel of flour. So, he stripped and ducked his head into a water barrel.

His friends nicknamed him *Ghost Rider,* and the nickname spread to all the stations. He alone rode the route through this alkali desert.

A few evenings later, he relaxed on the step outside the cabin, shirt off, trying to catch the slight breeze. "I discovered in the *Salt Lake City Times* before I handed the newspaper off, that as more and more immigrants push west, Indians are attacking the wagon trains."

"Yep." John sprinkled tobacco into a thin twist of paper and rolled a homemade cigarette between brown-stained fingers.

"So, troops from the fort patrol the trail—to keep the Indians from the wagon trains."

Jim perched on the door step a few yards away. "Yeah, well the cavalry cain't be ever' where. You gotta look out, son. The law of the Paiute, *death to intruders,* meaning all the immigrants swarmin' in, is hard for the Indians to carry through. So, watch out—a lone man racin' from relay station to relay station is a easy target."

Jarrett stretched his arms above his head and yawned. "Understood. I'm going to bed. Long ride tomorrow."

~

Blistering sand burned through Jarrett's boots. He tapped the Fort Ruby thermometer, but the temperature line stuck at 115 in the shade.

The Express rider galloped in from the west, his face pale, his body drooping. "Tough ride. Hotter than blue blazes."

Jarrett nodded, hopped onto his horse, accepted the mochila, and rode out his mustang's wild bucks until the bay gelding plunged into an obedient gallop toward the first relay.

Only a few minutes later, his bay's stride broke.

Jarrett reined him into an easy canter. "No need to kill you with this run, boy."

Lather foamed around the mustang's shoulders and flanks, but the slower canter buried them in a cloud of poisonous alkali.

Beyond the haze nothing moved in the shimmering heat, not even a tumbleweed. Jarrett cocked his hat lower to shield his eyes from the glaring sun, the handkerchief tied over his face heavy with dust.

What was he doing here? He rubbed a chalky hand across his forehead and swallowed a long drink from his canteen. The tepid water tantalized his dry mouth. Mirages shimmered in front of his eyes. He breathed dusty air through his mask, burning his nostrils and the back of his throat.

He reined his panting bay to a standstill and scrutinized the most treacherous two miles of his route, snaking between sheer rock. The trail narrowed so only one horse could travel the zigzagging path. One side sheer limestone wall and the other limestone fronted with sagebrush, pine trees and mesquite tall enough to hide a man astride a horse.

Was it imagination or mirage? Had that sagebrush moved without a whisper of a breeze? The rocky trail didn't show tracks. He stared at the still bushes. No sound broke the silence but his own panting breath.

He pulled his rifle from its sheath and shot into the bushes. His horse squealed. Something thrashed and churned, then deathlike silence. He reloaded and shot into two other clumps. No sound, only the echo of his weapon resounding in the empty land.

With an irritated slam, Jarrett shoved his rifle back into the saddle scabbard and directed the bay's head north. "Yahola! Today of all days, we got to detour around the zigzag trail," he muttered through gritty teeth.

A spine-chilling war cry split the air. A dozen almost-naked Indians astride horses materialized from the bushes.

Jarrett took a second to get off a shot with his revolver, then galloped for open country. For a strange instant, the twang of war bows reminded him of the buffalo hunt, but this time he was the prey! He pulled ahead of the Indians.

He fled over rough country with no trail, marveling at his bay's stamina. Still, the Paiute clung to them, well within arrow range. Jarrett pivoted for a shot with his Colt, hoping to scare them off.

The foremost Indian, a strapping man with copper muscles rippling across a broad chest, galloped so close his face gleamed wetly beneath red paint as he aimed his arrow.

Jarrett lowered his aim from the Indian's mid-section

toward his horse's head, but before he could squeeze the trigger, his own bay staggered.

Wind whistled past Jarrett's shoulder as an arrow ripped through his shirt.

Jarrett's horse faltered again and fell, an arrow protruding from his chest.

An instant before his dying bay hit the ground, Jarrett kicked free of the stirrups. He landed heavily, boots skidding, rolled, and struck his head on a boulder.

Groggy, he sprawled on the rocks.

The Paiutes dismounted and circled him. Blinding pain slammed into his temples.

An Indian grabbed his pistol. Another reached down, unbuckled his holster, and stripped the leather from his waist. Two hefty Indians jerked him to his feet.

Jarrett struggled. His shirt ripped open.

Both Indians wrestled his arms behind his back, holding them up beneath his shoulder blades.

Face twisted in pain, he quit struggling and fell to his knees.

The muscular Indian with the painted face stood above him, speaking Paiute, expecting an answer. The other Indians jabbered in the same tongue.

Jarrett groaned. Pain radiating from his head scrambled his thinking. The fast-talking, gesturing Indian standing above him had to be important. His face, chest, and bare thighs were covered with red-painted symbols. Red was sacred to all tribes, so this man had to be a mighty warrior, a medicine man, or a teller of tales.

A different Indian kicked him in the ribs.

Jarrett doubled and groaned.

The angry Indian spoke in rough grunts and growls and pointed to where Jarrett had shot into the bushes, then pointed to his own shattered quiver.

Jarrett showed as much defiance as he could, the pain in his head, arms and ribs blasting through his body.

Red-Painted Face shook his head at the angry Indian, pointed to his muscular chest, then to his horse, and finally to Jarrett's Colt revolver.

Jarrett grunted. Seemed obvious from their movements that the Indian who'd kicked him, angry at getting shot at in the bushes, wanted to kill him, while Painted Face appeared to be questioning why Jarrett had not shot him when he had the chance.

Jarrett closed his eyes. "Lord, please let Painted Face win."

Suddenly, Painted Face grabbed the buffalo horn hanging from Jarrett's neck.

Jarrett gasped, struggling to breathe against the leather cutting into his throat. Black spots darkened his vision, he choked, and dizziness weakened his knees. The throng broke and the buffalo horn fell into the Indian's hand.

As Painted Face examined the horn, Jarrett squirmed in the two Indians' grasp.

The Indian pointed to the painted figures and turned the horn over and over in his copper-colored hand. He grabbed Jarrett's hair and jerked his head up.

Yahola, he'd lose his scalp now.

With his harsh voice, Painted Face spoke, then waited for an answer.

Jarrett gulped, "Osage."

The Indians talked, words spewing from their mouths

like hot grease spattering from a skillet.

Jarrett shook his head. What were they saying?

Painted Face pointed toward the sky and then down to himself, signifying in universal sign language he was a chief.

The two Indians freed Jarrett's arms.

He sprawled in the rocks, then hoisted himself to his feet to face the chief.

An Indian strode to Jarrett's dead mustang, jerked his rifle from the pouch in front of the saddle, and raised the weapon in the air, uttering a shrill cry.

Jarrett forced himself to gaze into the chief's glittering black eyes. Would he be shot with his own rifle?

CHAPTER 12

Jarrett waited, his heartbeat clogging his throat. What was the sign language he'd learned from John and Jim?

Using Hand Talk, the chief signed. "Thunderbird, giver of life, say to Chief Horned Owl, that Man Who Rides Trail Never Stopping did not harm Horned Owl, but turned gun toward horse. Braves want to kill Man Who Rides Trail. Chief listen to Thunderbird and Osage and let Man Who Rides Trail live. Paiute take guns, boots, bag."

Jarrett signed with clumsy fingers, "Man Who Rides Trail thanks Chief. Let Chief give Man Who Rides Trail bag which carries words to white men and not harm to Paiute."

"Because Man Who Rides Trail wears the Osage amulet from Thunderbird, Chief give talking words." The chief motioned for a brave to remove the mail bag from the dead horse.

The Indian kicked the saddle, took the bay's bridle and blanket, and tossed the mochila to Jarrett.

Chief Horned Owl signed for Jarrett to strip off his boots, belt, and red neckerchief. One brave knocked Jarrett's big hat flying from his head, then strutted the sand with the hat perched atop his own long-haired head. Another grabbed Jarrett's canteen. The chief kept Jarrett's buffalo horn.

A belligerent Indian stripped off Jarrett's uniform shirt and flung the garment around his own broad shoulders like a bright red flag. A swaggering teen relieved Jarrett of his uniform pants.

At some secret signal, the Indians leaped on their horses and galloped away.

Jarrett stood naked under the blistering sun and watched the Paiute disappear into the empty land. "Thank you, Father, they let me live." He licked his dry lips. "But they took my canteen."

With the dust settling behind the vanished Indians, the adrenalin surging through Jarrett faded. He dropped to sit on his haunches and rested his head on his arms. Despite the hammering in his temples, he closed his eyes and fortified himself. It was a long hike to the relay station.

His tongue, thick and cottony, clung to the roof of his mouth. He stood, slung the mochila over his bare shoulder, glanced at the vultures already circling his dead bay, and started walking.

The sun cracked his lips and blistered his body. Rocks and cactus stems pierced his naked feet. Dizziness threatened his balance.

Words he had learned as a boy kept him going. *I can do all things through Christ who strengthens me.*

Hours later, sunburned, and feet bleeding, he limped to the relay compound, reached the cabin, pushed the heavy door open, and fell inside. He blew out a breath as the mud floor cooled his skin.

If he'd been a quitter, he would have resigned. But he wasn't. He'd learned that lesson with the Osage

~

Exactly two months later, Jarrett received his next letter. He stretched out on the bottom bunk and slid the papers from the envelope.

Dear Friend,

I do thank you for writing. The summer has been long, hot, and frightening. There has been talk of nothing but war, which states will secede, which ones will stay firm in the Union, and the value of slaves. It seems life in Tahlequah would be barest survival if one had no slaves. I do not understand this since many farmers live well without slaves.

Time hangs heavy on my hands, and I think of you more often than I should admit.

"Thank you, God, she cares about me."

I'm certain your rides are not as routine as you write. I suspect you fear to worry me. I am greatly concerned for your safety, my good friend, so you see, you must tell me what really happens on those rides. My imagination pictures your life worse than you admit.

Jarrett frowned and shook his head. Nope, wouldn't share that last encounter with her. The sooner he forgot that confrontation with the Paiute and that devilish walk to the relay, the better. He turned back to her letter.

None of us were surprised that Lincoln was elected. From his pictures in the newspaper, he looks a melancholy man. But his homespun humor is a relief after Buchanan's solemnity. Even if Lincoln is a northerner, I like him.

Jarrett smiled.

Yes, I am interested in politics, though my father doesn't let me express my views. My father expects to be Stand Watie's deputy chief if Watie is elected principal chief in place of John Ross. Chief Ross and Watie have different philosophies as to what is best for our Cherokee Nation, and each thinks his path is right. I wish they could resolve their differences in a Christian way and unite for the peace of the Cherokee and harmony between our families.

My mother nags me unbearably about your letters. I cannot keep them from her, so please be careful not to reveal your identity. She browbeats me to discover who "my secret friend" is. I must post my letters to you covertly because she forbade me write until I tell her your name. I used all my savings to send this letter so Mama wouldn't know. You see how much trouble I have taken? I do miss you so. And think of you much more often than you would believe.

Jarrett pulled in a deep breath. He felt like shouting halleluiah but didn't want any of the curious troopers lounging close to the cabin to suspect how this letter moved him. His hand trembled as he smoothed the letter on his knee.

You asked me if I am a Christian. Yes, I thank you for your concern. I am. I am well acquainted with the Rosses' history. How can you know so little of the Flints' history? My parents are pillars of the Presbyterian Church at Tahlequah, and our entire family is active there. I realize my church is more liberal than your staunch New England beliefs. I know your family, unlike mine, came to Indian Territory over the "Trail of Tears," and your Grandfather Worchester accompanied them as a missionary to the Indians. You attend the small Circuit Rider's Church near Park Hill, where your Uncle Jeremy Worchester preaches once every month, when he is not on circuit. I know your grandfather preaches there the other weeks.

I've often begged to visit your church, but of course, family feuds keep me away. Someday I shall visit there on my own. I shall not have my world narrowed because of old animosities. But at present, I'm under armed guard.

Jarrett straightened so fast he hit his head on the top bunk. Guards! They best keep their hands off Delight. Wouldn't put the idea past her father to insist one of his men court Delight. Jarrett counted to ten, took a few deep breaths, and smoothed the treasured letter over his raised knee.

Quite by chance last fall, I met your Uncle Jeremy. He is a most dashing figure. He must be at least forty, but all the young ladies and those few old maids of thirty find him most eligible. Will he ever marry, I wonder?

Mother and I were shopping in Tahlequah and rode past a temperance meeting he was holding. They met in the first week of September under a great apple tree. Most of the group were young people, and many belong to the Cherokee Temperance Society. Mother relented to my pleas to attend, and we tied the horse and buggy and joined the people.

The young people urged newcomers to sign a pledge to abstain from intoxicating liquor. I was inclined to add my signature, but Mother intervened. I am not permitted to drink liquor, of course, but my mother felt signing a pledge unnecessary. Whether I drink or not is between me and the Lord. She abhors rules and regulations. Of course, here in Indian Territory, temperance societies are a great help. There is so much pressure on people to drink. The trading posts and forts, not to mention whiskey peddlers, cater to young people, so forming a society to fight back seems a common-sense approach.

But I digress. There was a stir under the trees when Pastor Jeremy walked over to stand in front of the crowd. His black frock coat and stovepipe hat looked somber among the flowery dresses and bright shirts. I shall never see another black frock coat without thinking how much better the clothes would look if the wearer had the same red hair as your Uncle Jeremy. His face looked genial and not at all stern like most preachers. And he has an aura. It's difficult to explain, but I knew I was in the presence of a man of God. My mother, however, recognized him and whisked me away from the meeting. How I longed to stay.

I do have some relief from boredom. The fort is full of soldiers now. Most of our own young men have enlisted. Every fortnight, the officers provide a dance, and my parents let me attend. There are far more soldiers than girls, so I seldom sit out a dance. The men look most handsome in their uniforms.

Jarrett gritted his teeth so hard his jaw made a cracking sound.

I must close now. Mother is calling, and she mustn't find

this letter.

I remain your very dear friend. Your dearest friend,
Delight

Jarrett clenched his hands into fists. Pain stabbed his heart as he gazed across the bunkroom. The November warmth, despite the sunshine spilling through the open door, didn't reach the dark corners of his soul. After folding the neatly written sheets, he returned the paper to the weather-beaten envelope.

He leaned against the pillow and closed his eyes. He pictured Delight surrounded by admiring soldiers. She accepted a tall, black-haired soldier's invitation to dance. He took her in his arms and held her close. She smiled, her beautiful cheeks grew pinker, and dimples played around her parted lips. The soldier bent his mouth near her golden hair and whispered in her ear.

Jarrett dropped his chin to his chest. Yahola … he missed home … and Delight. Longing tightened his throat. Perhaps woodcarving would calm his mood. He searched the box beside the bunk for a half-finished carving and his special knife. He sliced into wood that bore the resemblance of a weathered old sea captain who was, in reality, a faithful preacher of the gospel. He lopped off the old captain's head. "Yahola! Got to get my feelings straight about that girl. She could get me killed."

Tom stepped inside. "Bad news in your letter? Did someone die?"

Jarrett grabbed the severed head and body in his left hand and snapped his knife closed with his right. "Nope. I just realized I'll never be the same person I was when I left home.

Things change. People change. Opportunities change."

"Homesick." Tom jerked a thumb toward the open door. "Come on, let's vamoose to the back of the corral for some target practice and fast-draw. That'll cheer you up."

~

The Paiute had been peaceful for several months while winter settled in with the hush of snow, muffling the usual rowdy sounds around Fort Ruby.

On a cold, brittle Thursday, snow gleamed whitely in the weak afternoon sunlight.

"Sure you're up to riding today?" Tom matched steps with Jarrett. "I'll take your route if you want."

"Thanks for the offer, but you've got work to do here. I can't ask you to ride my route." To his clogged ears, his own voice sounded hoarse and nasal, yet he slogged toward the corral.

At 8:00 p.m., he forced his sluggish body to jump into the saddle to start his return ride to Dry Creek. His sheepskin jacket failed to keep the chill from penetrating, so he turned up the collar and watched his breath funnel in the air before it wafted to the dark sky.

Hoofbeats sounded far out to the west and grew louder. Jarrett fought the desire to head back to the bunkhouse, dive into bed, and nurse his cold.

With a thunder of hooves, a tired paint horse slid to a stop alongside him. The rider switched the mochila to Jarrett's mount.

"How's the route?"

Bill threw his leg over the saddle and jumped to the

ground. "One or two inches of snow on the trail, not too bad. I saw a group of Indians traveling this way from up north."

"How big?"

"Couldn't tell."

Jarrett nodded, turned his horse, and galloped east. As he rode over the snow-crusted trail, with fever-racked bones and aching head, he set his mind on the hot drink and bunk waiting for him when he reached the Dry Creek Station.

Nine hours later, as he galloped close to the Chollas Cactus relay, even with his nose thick with cold, he smelled the acrid odor of smoke. He pulled his mount to a standstill. Where were the cabin and the corral? He circled his mustang in the dim predawn light, straining to see. No fresh horse and rider waited. No horses stood inside the empty corral. As a breeze blew glowing embers into the darkness, a shudder racked him.

"Hal! Buzz!" Jarrett leaped off his mount. Stumbling on numbed legs, he searched through smoking debris. Where were the attendants?

His mustang nuzzled a dark pile on the snow near the corral. Jarrett knelt, poking the mound with his chilled hands. His hand touched skin. His heart hammered. A body—still warm, with bare scalp and drying blood where the hair had been.

Jarrett stumbled away from the corral and toward what was left of the bunkhouse. He discovered two charred bodies buried in the ashes.

A coughing spasm shook him. He doubled over and vomited.

For a second, he froze, listening to the silence broken by the shift of burnt timbers. He shook himself, then vaulted on his tired mustang and rode into the darkness. Could he reach Dry Creek Station before the marauding Indians? Could his horse last?

Ten miles further east at Dry Creek, flames licking the timbers of the relay cabin caused shudders to shake his body. Too late! He must have missed the murdering Indians by minutes.

CHAPTER 13

Jaw clamped and mouth set, Jarrett stumbled through the darkness searching for his friends. He tripped over two mounds huddled together on the ground just outside the burning cabin. Jim and John. Too late. Like a wounded buffalo, he bellowed.

Nothing more he could do here. But he could … he jerked into the saddle and urged his tired horse toward the next station. He'd ridden less than half a mile when he came upon a lone horse grazing beside the route. He needed a fresh mount—his own horse labored just to canter. This Express gelding had somehow escaped the marauding Indians. Jarrett bowed his head. God looking out for him, really.

He made short work of shifting saddle and bridle to the fresh gelding and set his exhausted horse free. The animal would wander back to the burned-out station, and someone could come by tomorrow to get him. Jarrett hopped onto the fresh mustang.

After a savage ride through thickets and shortcuts, he expected to find flames and carnage. Instead, he pulled his horse to a standstill at the feet of the waiting attendants leading a fresh horse. "Mount up!" he yelled. "Paiutes on the warpath. Likely they'll be here any minute."

Jarrett vaulted onto the fresh, saddled animal.

"Marauding Indians?" Both attendants raced through the corral and opened the barn stalls, freeing all but two of the other horses, then jumped on them bareback.

At a top gallop, Jarrett led the way on the trail to the next relay.

Behind him, a war whoop split the night. He glanced back. A dozen dark forms thundered toward the corral. In a flash, flames lit the sky outlining Indians storming through the station, setting the buildings afire.

He and the two attendants outdistanced the marauders and arrived at the next station. He alerted the two attendants there. The five of them hunkered in defensive positions with guns leveled.

But the band of Indians didn't appear.

~

His muscles stiff and burning, his eyes gritty, his chest hot with anger, Jarrett leaned against the side of the relay cabin and shook his head. He tried to smooth the frown creasing his brow. He had lgazed evil square in the face, and he would never be the same.

But in the uncertainty and chaos, one truth shone like the sun. Now, he truly understood why the one, true, perfect Son of Man had to die to atone for that evil. His perfect God could not look at evil. But God loved the world he created. So, God's perfect Son, in obedience to his Father, died to save the people living in the evil world.

Jarrett leaned lagainst the side of the cabin and shook his head. In fact, God's plan was the *only* way to overcome evil.

He wiped grime from his face. He'd accepted Jesus's sacrifice for his own sin when he was young, but now he had a deeper understanding of evil … and, even more important, of God's bottomless love.

Hardly able to shove one foot in front of the other, he stumbled inside the cabin. Nightmares kept him tossing and turning in a sweat-soaked huddle.

~

Russell, Majors, and Waddell awarded Jarrett a special hundred-dollar bonus for saving the lives of the two station attendants. Thankful for the money, he tried to duck the attention.

Jarrett tossed down a newspaper regaling the *Ghost Rider's* heroic story. He didn't feel like a hero. Rather the opposite. He'd not been able to help his friends.

Only when autumn brought cool rain could he overcome the physical effects of that night's ride. The heavy cold gripping his lungs dissolved. But the horror of his friends' murders still branded his mind. Each time he rode up to a relay station, foreboding gripped him until he saw the attendants waiting with a fresh horse.

He didn't notice the loss immediately, but his appetite for adventure seemed to evaporate with the coming winter, and he longed to return to Tahlequah. Seemed adventure had a high price.

Yet, newspapers carried urgent news of a nation dividing. The Union needed California's resources.

So, he squared his shoulders and forced himself to remain at his post.

Jarrett scanned the headlines of the December 20, 1860, *Charleston Mercury*. What he read chilled his blood.

THE UNION IS DISSOLVED
Passed unanimously, an ordinance, to dissolve the Union between the State of South Carolina and other states united with her under the compact of the United States Constitution.

Jarrett and other Pony Express riders sped the newspaper to California, along with bulletins and letters from the United States Congress and the War Department. He rushed the news of hotheaded brawls and speeches in Congress.

He carried the news that on January 9, 1861, Mississippi had withdrawn from the Union. By January 26, Florida, Alabama, Georgia, and Louisiana had all dissolved their allegiance with the United States.

When Texas seceded on February 1, Jarrett found sleep hard to get. He was needed here, but if war came, he craved to be with his family to help and protect them … and Delight.

Finally, a packet addressed in a familiar hand arrived. He tore open Delight's longed-for letter.

Dearest Friend,
The news is alarming with so many states declaring themselves apart from the United States.
Chief Ross is adamant that the Cherokee Nation remain neutral. He wrote to the surrounding tribes that we should let the whites settle their own affairs. Yet, the tribes did not heed his advice. You possibly know the Choctaws, Chickasaws, and Creeks have shifted allegiance to the

Confederacy.

We hear the Northerners want our lands, while the South will protect us.

Chief Ross has another problem remaining neutral. Texas troops occupy all the military forts in Indian Territory except Fort Gibson. So, you can see the Confederacy has cut Indian Territory off from the Union.

The Confederate, Stand Watie, organized a band of guerrillas to be ready to fight if war is declared. Do you know what this type of warrior does? I assume you do.

Are you coming home?

I am torn in my longing for you. Part of me wants you to remain in Utah, safe from the war, and another part of me wants you here. You are a special friend, and I long to see your face.

Our world crumbles around us. I fear for my father and Claremont. I tremble each week as I attend the dances at Fort Gibson. I look into the face of each soldier with whom I dance and wonder if he will be struck down. I cannot bear the thought of men dying. My face smiles, but my heart breaks.

Our Cherokee Nation is deeply divided. We must make an alliance with the South. We have no choice. So, please understand, dearest friend, why I must cast my lot with my father.

Do come home. I miss you so. Dare I say, I need you?

My father issued orders that Mother and I are not to leave the house without a large bodyguard. I am happy to have the protection. Life is very difficult. School has been let out two months early because of the danger, and no one walks alone or unarmed. No one molests your family since your father is the only doctor in the Territory.

I wish I could see you. I remember your strong arms ... and other things.

My mother has found us out. It was only a matter of time since you are the only Pony Express rider from the Territory. She read of your commendation in the Cherokee Advocate. Mother was not nearly so upset as I had expected. I think she understands your family had nothing to do with killing Caldwell. Mama agreed to keep our secret, but I had to promise her not to write you again.

Promise me <u>we</u> shall continue to be friends!!! Very good friends. Devoted friends.

This will have to be my last letter.
Your Confederate Friend,
Delight

Frowning and muttering to himself, the permanent crease between his brows deepening, Jarrett reread the letter.

"Yahola, Yahola, Yahola!" He slammed his new hat onto his head and strode out into the clean desert air, his boots crushing newly awakened yellow flowers thrusting tiny petals through crannies in the rock. Sunrise painted the sandy floor and limestone cliffs pink. He scowled at the beauty.

What business did the Cherokee have in a white man's squabble? If war came, fighting shouldn't touch the Cherokee. For sure, Watie would divide the Cherokee Nation and force old Chief Ross out of power. What would that mean for Delight?

Jarrett tried to focus his thoughts on politics, but an image of Delight plagued him like a horde of hornets defending their nest.

She forever danced with that tall, dark-haired lieutenant. He held her in his arms, splendid in his fancy uniform. He touched her golden curls falling across her cheeks, and then he kissed her soft, full lips.

Jarrett groaned and broke into a run. His deep voice reverberated in the still calm of morning. "I'm going home."

CHAPTER 14

J arrett leaned against the corral, studying the new mustang.

"There you are, Jarr. You've got to ride. Immediately! This special edition of the *Missouri Advocate* has to go out today. Now!" Breathing heavily, the attendant thrust a newspaper into Jarrett's hand.

As he read the front page, Jarrett pulled in a shuddering breath. "So, this is it."

April 15, 1861.

The United States of America Declares War.

On April 12, Brigadier General Pierre Gustave Toutant Beauregard bombarded Fort Sumter. April 14, Fort Sumter surrendered to the Confederacy.

President Lincoln today called for seventy-five thousand State Militia Volunteers to quell the rebellion against the Union. Today President Lincoln declared war on the Confederacy.

Jarrett clenched his hands into fists. No, he couldn't resign yet. He had to make an extra run each week to keep California informed of war events.

As the days passed, he had to face a new danger—outlaws. The added responsibility weighed on him, but he wouldn't quit. Daily, before his rides, he checked his rifle and his Colt to make sure the weapons remained in top working order. His part in the war was as important as that of soldiers on the battlefields.

~

By this time, the telegraph stretched across most of the Pony Express territory—almost reaching his route, linking San Francisco to Fort Churchill, Nevada. Until the link was completed, the Union needed the Pony Express to travel the long distance from Nevada to St. Joseph.

Hardly able to contain his eagerness, Jarrett champed at the bit for the new telegraph to be working. That connection would spell the termination of his duty. And he could go home.

The newspapers and letters he carried relayed dark news for the Union.

John Floyd, US Secretary of War, and Secretary of the Navy, Isaac Toucey, both joined the Confederacy.

Many army officers from southern states resigned and joined the Confederacy. Colonel Robert E. Lee declined President Lincoln's offer to appoint him Field Commander of the Union armies and instead became Commander-in-Chief of the Confederate Army of Northern Virginia.

Jarrett remained on duty in the desert.

August burned hot, dry, and heavy with alkali dust. The War Between the States seemed far away as he fought his own battle with the heat, the Indians, and the outlaws.

~

Jarrett lounged on his bunk inside the stuffy cabin. Today, he would carry an additional heavy leather pouch of gold from California.

He read the newspaper account of the Battle of Bull Run, foot tapping the mud floor, then jumped up to pace the room with a bowed head. Confederate forces at Manassas Junction had defeated Union forces.

Jarrett tossed the newspaper to the end of the bunk. Lincoln had called for another volunteer force of five hundred thousand men.

Would Jordie volunteer? His brother seemed clear-headed enough to steer clear of the war. But Delight's letters indicated men in Indian Territory were quick-tempered and trigger-happy over the issues.

He picked up the newspaper, folded it, tucked the paper under his arm, and stomped out of the cabin.

Thundering hoofbeats from the approaching mustang grew louder and louder.

He dashed to the coral where his saddled paint waited, shoved the newspaper into the mochila, and mounted.

As he rode, he gazed over the countryside. His mind raged. Should he return home, or should he volunteer to join the army? He shook his head and leaned lower to pat the racing paint's neck. *What should I do?*

Would Chief Ross be able to remain neutral? Or would

he lead the Cherokee Nation to join the Union? How could he with Confederate forces surrounding his people and land.

It's not our war! Jarrett raised a clenched fist toward the blue sky. *The United States never did anything for us. Why should we join them? They took our land in Georgia.*

But Delight had written the Confederacy promised if they win, we Cherokee keep our lands and our sovereignty.

Jarrett jerked off his hat and wiped his forehead with his arm. *But I can't fight for slavery. I believe every man is equal in the eyes of God.* His mouth twisted. *I don't want to fight. I've seen too much death.* His groan barely sounded above the pounding of hooves against the rocky earth. Is *slavery or States' rights or preserving the Union worth killing a man?* He clenched the reins so hard the mustang slowed. He relaxed his fist and urged the animal forward.

Perspiration dripped into his eyes. He knuckled them with a gritty fist. *I can't send a soul for whom Christ died into eternity ... I can't.*

A horse suddenly barricaded his path.

CHAPTER 15

Jarrett's mustang reared, pawing the air.

The two horses stood face to face, their lathered shoulders touched.

Steely eyes above a handkerchief-covered face challenged him.

Jarrett wheeled his paint.

Another horseman blocked the return route.

Jarrett streaked off the trail, over the uneven ground, across dry gulches, gullies, and washes.

The two horsemen closed in behind, their horses fresh.

Yahola! Where did they come from? I've got to keep my mind on my job. He leaned lower in the saddle.

A revolver boomed.

A jolt almost knocked him off the horse. Pain slashed his right arm, slamming him against the mustang's neck. The whine of another bullet zipped past his ear. He slipped down on the left side of his paint, only a boot hooked on the saddle.

The two robbers closed in.

Thank God Runninghorse taught him the Osage trick. *Lord, please let the outlaws think they shot me from the saddle.* With his injured arm useless, he worked the decoy money pouch loose from the saddle and flipped the satchel to the rocky ground.

The bandits pulled their horses to an abrupt stop, dismounted, and bent to grab the decoy pouch.

Jarrett urged his mustang. "Come on, boy. Run for it." They galloped hard and fast until they were out of range of the outlaws' revolvers, then he let his mount slow to a canter.

When the Stars and Stripes hanging limply on the pole above the newly built Dry Creek Relay hove into sight, he swayed in the saddle. Dizziness transformed the station into a wavering mass. His arm hung useless, pain radiating deeper with each jar of the mustang's hooves. His drenched shirt sleeve splattered a trail of blood on the ground.

Jarrett's knees were water as he stalled halfway trying to dismount.

The attendant hauled him off the horse and lugged him to the cabin.

Hank, the fresh rider, streaked off to forge a different route.

Inside the cabin, slumped on a bunk, Jarrett muttered, "Mason, you'll have to remove the bullet wedged in my upper arm."

"Right. Done this before." The attendant pulled a bowie knife from his belt, poured whiskey over the tip, and dug into Jarrett's blood-coated arm.

"Yahola!" He blacked out. The room slowly came back into focus.

"There. Got the sucker." Mason held the bullet on the tip of his knife. "Better drink this while I heat my knife." He handed Jarrett a bottle.

"Yeah. Even my … Uncle Jeremy … wouldn't fault me

for drinking." With his good arm, Jarrett swiped sweat from his face. In four gulps, he downed the fiery liquid.

"Here goes." Mason touched the hot metal to cauterize the wound.

Jarrett's flesh sizzled. "Yahola!" He whooshed out his breath, then sank into blessed darkness.

Two days later, shaky and unsteady on his feet, Jarrett rode his return trip to Fort Ruby. A secret pride that he had outwitted the outlaws and allowed no disruption in the mail schedule warmed his insides.

His injured right arm hung in a sling as he picked up a pen to write.

My dearest Delight,

My time with the Pony Express has almost ended. Soon I will return home. Please wait for me. I miss you more than I ever thought possible. I think of you every waking moment. Please wait for me.

Thoughts of your sweet beauty, with your gorgeous eyes revealing your giving heart, keep me sane in this crazy world. You are my sanctuary.

I hesitate to tell you more.

Yours,

Jarrett

~

Word spread that the Pony Express was in deep financial difficulties. Southern sympathizers had entangled Russell into an intrigue to deprive the North of its mail routes. The venture had never made a profit, and because of the

Express's pressing debt, Russell had been desperate.

Trying to obtain credit to keep the business open, he took $870,000 in bonds as securities from Secretary of War Floyd—before Floyd left his office to join the Confederacy. Floyd knew the bonds were bogus and left Russell holding the bag.

With their routes now covered by the new transcontinental telegraph, Hansen paid off all the other riders and sent them home.

The last link of the construction team raced east from Fort Churchill, Nevada, over the desert to Salt Lake City, Utah and the other crew raced west from Omaha, Nebraska, over the plains and the Rockies to Salt Lake City. Soon they would meet.

Jarrett whistled more each day.

~

On a bright, midsummer morning, Jarrett caught sight of a telegraph construction team. He galloped near the crew, waving his broad-brimmed hat.

The workers cheered and waved, grinning widely. "Hoo ray, it's one of the legendary pony riders."

As he raised clouds of dust galloping past, Jarrett counted twenty-six ox-drawn wagons. The crew worked, distributing poles, wires, and other materials along the trail.

A day later on his return trip, he glimpsed another crew laying out the line and driving stakes for the poles. As he thundered by, the workers yelled, dropped their tools, jumped up and down, and waved.

On his next trip Jarrett galloped past two additional

crews. One strung wire between the poles while the other cooked and cared for the camp. Always, they stopped working and hailed him as a hero.

The affirmations felt good.

One day, after he finished his route, he rode back to visit the crews. He chatted with them on their lunch break and swapped tales. Having someone to talk with was like returning to civilization. He'd been too long alone.

He watched the hardy, broad-shouldered men dig holes, then four or five sweating men dropped the poles into place. Once the poles were in place, another crew clambered up the post on ladders and strung wire from large reels from pole to pole.

That night, the men invited him to join them at their campfire and eat. He sat on an overturned log and ate cornbread and beans and listened as their talk turned to the war. A few men outlined their strategy on how the war should be fought.

Jarrett shifted his position on the log and stretched out his legs. How did he fit into this war?

These men were all pro-Union and planned to join the fighting if the war was not over when they finished stringing the telegraph wires.

Jarrett's insides churned as he sprawled under the silent, starry sky with the overalls-clad men and drank coffee while the campfire flickered on solemn faces, and coyotes howled in the hills.

~

He heard nothing from Delight. Nothing from Jordie.

Nothing from his family. Were things still tense in Tahlequah? Had Delight's father paired her with a Southern soldier? His insides boiled until his skin itched. Each day he measured how much further the telegraph had to go before the wires connected.

Days grew crisp. He started wearing his mackinaw. On October 22nd, the team from the west won the race to Salt Lake City and captured the prize. A scant two days later, a disappointed crew from St. Joseph reached Salt Lake City.

Jarrett spent a final night with his construction friends. They were fired up to join the war.

At last, on October 26, Hansen gave him notice that his services were no longer required. He accepted an additional one-hundred-dollar bonus and a plaque stating that Majors, Russell, and Waddell highly esteemed his months of courageous riding. They gifted him one of their best mustangs.

Hansen patted him on the back. They left the building and walked to the end of the tracks. "So, what now, Ghost Rider? Did you spend all the money you earned on booze and women?"

Jarrett chuckled. "I checked my Bank of St. Joseph bankbook. During my career as a Pony Express rider, I earned over $1,990.00."

"Woozie! You saved it all!"

"No. I sent Dad the $200.00 I owed so he could buy a new buggy. And I figured Maresy's too old to pull now, so I sent enough for a new mare."

Hansen shook his hand. "Good man. Any plans for the rest of your ill-gotten gains?"

Jarrett grinned. "You know riding that route was some of

the hardest work a man can ever face. I won't spend that money like it cost me nothing. I'll watch every penny."

"I know, kid. You did an admirable job. So, what are your plans now?"

Jarrett pushed his large-brimmed hat back from his forehead and frowned. "I've enough cash to buy a ranch, a good stallion, and some mares. After the war ends, I'll raise horses."

"Don't you blue-eyed Cherokees have enough horses already?"

"I've thought about that. With the East tethered to the West by telegraph, settlers will come. They will need horses."

"Sounds like a good plan."

"I believe in well-thought-out plans." Jarrett grunted. *So far, my plans to win Delight seem goofy and ill thought through. They always end the same way. With me facing the wrong end of a gun.*

~

A week later, astride his new Express mustang he'd named Sampson in memory of his first horse, he arrived in St. Joseph and went on a shopping spree, buying gifts for everyone.

As the general store owner wrapped his parcels in brown paper, he said, "Looks like you're the right age to join Lincoln's army."

Jarrett shook his head. "The war can't last much longer. Besides, I'm Cherokee. This isn't my war."

"Ha. We don't see many of you folks around here. Can't

say as I blame you none though. Bloody fightin'. Lots of men killed." He winked. "I see that horse you tied up outside has got the PE brand. You're that legend, *Ghost Rider*, aren't you?"

Jarrett nodded. So, word had spread. He gathered his parcels. "Keep that information under your hat, will you?"

"Hard for a man like you … a legend, not to live up to your name. Could be downright embarrassing … or worse. Not to join the fray. Don't seem manly."

"Not my fight." Jarrett slapped on his big hat. His boots thudded on the wooden floor. Face hot, he opened the door, and sped into the crisp, sunshine-filled day.

He packed the parcels in his saddlebags and vaulted aboard Sampson. The storekeeper had a point. But with any luck, no one in Tahlequah had heard of Ghost Rider. His plans did not include the war.

He had to win the Flints' friendship.

Good to know Delight's mother seemed on his side. After the war, perhaps Mr. Flint and Claremont would be more amenable. He'd track down the people responsible for Caldwell's murder. Then Flint couldn't hold that against his family and him.

When the time was right, he'd marry Delight.

Unless her father had married her off to a Confederate officer.

He jammed his broad-brimmed hat lower on his forehead. Months had passed since her last letter and although he'd written her each month, he'd been gone a long time.

And he had not told her he loved her.

CHAPTER 16

Father, Mother, Grandfather, and Jerusha welcomed him home with such fervor his heart ached. He hugged them close. "I never expected to be gone for so long or to be so far away I couldn't return for a visit."

Dad had gone grayer at the temples, and Mother had new lines shadowing her eyes. Jerusha had grown to almost shoulder-height, and he could no longer toss her into the air. Not that she would let him. She was a young lady now, and her childish awkwardness had grown into gracefulness. Grandfather Worchester seemed unchanged … perhaps bent a bit more and walking a tad slower.

"I love you all so much." Jarrett's heart raced. "And I'm home for good."

Dad nodded. "Lots for you here, son. There's no place like home."

Mother hugged him yet again. "That's music to my ears. And answers to my prayers. We are so proud of you, dear."

Jerusha bounced up to kiss his cheek. "I've got lots to tell you, big brother. There's so much news. So much is happening here. I'm absolutely elated you're finally home!"

He and his family laughed and talked until well into the night.

The next day, Dad spent almost two hours walking with him around the farm, his eyes bright.

Toward evening, a call came for Dad, and he set off in the new buggy.

Jarrett helped with dinner dishes, then patted Jerusha's backside. "Time for me to go."

"I know you'll have fun. Wish I could go."

"Next time, maybe." Jarrett folded the tea towel and headed upstairs to his old room. He changed into his new white ruffled shirt, dark fitted breeches, and mulberry frock coat. Good he'd had the foresight to purchase the new clothes while in St. Joseph.

He ran his hand over the velvet and checked the fit in his mirror. Not bad.

Nor was his hair. He'd invested in his first barber shop haircut, and his sun-bleached hair feathered against his earlobes. The barber called this cut the latest fashion. Jarrett practiced a dashing devil-may-care expression in the mirror. Grinning, he bowed to the looking-glass and invited an imaginary Delight to dance.

He frowned and shook his head. He didn't even know how to waltz.

What would he say to her? What if her father had set her up with a beau? A right-hand man he trusted. One of the men guarding her … or maybe her father had designated a young lieutenant to watch over her when she attended the weekly balls at Fort Gibson.

He grimaced at his image, flicking the ruffles on his white shirt. Women seemed to prefer men who wore uniforms. He picked up his Colt, then laid the weapon back on his dresser. "I'll take the repeating rifle. Keep it in my saddle. Should be close enough if trouble starts."

He straightened his shoulders. "Feel like I'm going into battle," he muttered. His new boots clattered on the stairs, then he slowed to enter the living room.

When Mom caught sight of him, her cheeks flushed. "Jarrett, you put me in mind of my brother, Jeremy." She stood on tiptoes to kiss his cheek. "Only you're even more handsome. That mulberry coat is perfect for your eyes and complexion." She stepped back and viewed him from top to toe. "Yes, I do think so."

He ducked his head. "Think what?"

"You're even better looking than Jordan."

"You wouldn't say that if Jordie were here." Jarrett's cheeks heated. But he couldn't help smiling.

"Jordan's taller, of course, and heavier, but you've got …" Mom cupped her warm fingers around his chin. "Should I tell you?"

"Unless you want me to tickle the words out of you."

"Right, that wouldn't be pretty, and I know you'd do just that. Since you've lived so long in your brother's shadow you should know." She kissed his cheek. "You have a magnetism that's attractive to young ladies."

Jarrett didn't squelch his rumbling laugh. He winked, twisted his expression into mock seriousness, and spoke with feigned gravity. "Perhaps this is the night when I shall meet my love."

"Oh, Mother, both my brothers are the handsomest fellows in the country. *Both* of them." Jerusha rushed over to hug him yet again.

"Strange you said *meet* my love rather than *fall in love.* Surely, you're not still thinking about that Flint girl?"

"And if I am?"

Her brows angled. "You must not go anywhere near her. Doing so is far too dangerous. Erase that thought from your mind!"

"Don't worry, Mom. Delight most likely has a beau by now."

"I pray that's true. We have enough problems with the war." She gazed straight into his eyes. "Son, you've changed. You have confidence now. You look more mature than twenty." She traced the crease between his brows. "You've grown up too fast."

He bowed and took her hand. "Come with me to the dance. I'll see that you have a good time."

Mom giggled like a young girl. "You would, too, wouldn't you? Imagine saddling yourself with your mother when all those beautiful young girls are dying to meet you. No, indeed, go. Have fun." She held up crossed fingers. "I recall what a thrill I experienced the first time I saw your father. But save your love, dear. You're off to college this fall, so we don't want you to get serious about a girl until after you graduate."

A sick feeling rose in Jarrett's throat. Way too late for that.

"You're too young to settle on one girl. Spread that charm around," Mom teased, her eyes sparkling. "I'm so happy you're finally home. You bring such vitality. How I've missed you." She stepped back and beamed up. "Here you stand, the boy who hated to dress for church. I never could induce you to wear a frock coat."

"I didn't say I was all that comfortable."

"You look ..." Mom spread her arms wide.

"Magnificent."

"Yes, you do, Jar," Jerusha hugged his middle.

"You two are biased."

"Not in the least." Mom grinned, then she shivered. "But war is too close. Already the Confederates have enlisted Jordan. Now they will lure you with arms outstretched like the prostitute in the Book of Proverbs."

Jarrett sat on the ladder-back chair and drummed his fingers on his knee. "You told me Jordie's in the First Regiment Cherokee Mounted Rifles under Captain John Drew, but I thought he joined Chief Ross's Indian Home Guard. What's this First Regiment Cherokee Mounted Rifles."

Mom walked behind him and put both hands on his shoulders. "Jordan did join the home guards. The home guard became part of the Confederate cavalry after Chief Ross signed the treaty to join the Confederacy." Mom's forehead puckered.

Jarrett covered her hands with his. "Chief Ross joined the Confederacy to keep the Cherokee Nation from splitting back into those two opposing sides, didn't he?" Jarrett shook his head. An uneasy edge pitted his stomach.

"Yes. Your great uncle had no choice."

Jarrett grunted. *Awful that Jordie serves in the Confederate Army, while I've spent the last fifteen months doing my part to defeat the Rebels.*

He loosened his cravat. *I've returned to Tahlequah to discover my family, my nation, and everyone I love, sides with the wrong cause.*

"I'm glad you weren't home for that treaty-signing business." Mom bunched her hands in her apron. "Stand

Watie brought several companies of armed men to town, hoping to overthrow your uncle and take over the Cherokee Government. Only your uncle's signing the treaty to join the Confederacy kept our nation intact. Events got so bad people were afraid to leave their homes for fear of bushwhackers."

"I hate that I wasn't here for you, Mother."

"We missed you, so, Jer." Jerusha unhooked her arms and gazed up into his face.

Mom smiled. "But your father enjoys immunity. He follows his calls as though nothing unusual was afoot. And neither side bothers him."

Jarrett squeezed her hand. "Even crossing a battlefield wouldn't deter Dad from the sick."

"Don't say that. It's true—but knowing that scares me." She sighed and traced a finger down his nose. "But since October seventh after the treaty was signed, life's quieted down. No more killings.

Jarrett took out his knife and tossed it from hand to hand, flicking the edge open and shut, running the blade across his thumb. He frowned. "And Jordie was in the thick of everything."

Mother pressed a finger against her chin, suddenly looking older. "Jarrett, do you think the war will reach us? It's so far away, and it's so meaningless for our people. If we lived in Boston, my son would be in the Union Army. But because we live in the west, my son wears the Confederate uniform. This is a strange war of geography." Mom scooted into her chair and her face firmed into a look of resolution. "Jarrett, promise me you won't join the army."

Jerusha jumped up and down as she had when as child. "Yes, Jarrett, promise!"

"That's easy. I promise. I've done a lot of thinking and know I can't kill a man."

"You will be very unpopular around here. Men will pressure you to volunteer."

"I can handle that."

Mom's expression relaxed, and she smoothed the velvet on the shoulder of his new coat.

Jarrett grinned. "No more talk about war. Tonight's my night!" He leaped to his feet and clicked his heels in midair.

"You're incorrigible. Go and have a splendid time. Don't forget you're a Christian and behave yourself. You won't dance of course, nor sample anything smuggled inside in a flask. I understand there is a lot of drinking and fighting at those balls."

Jarrett mimed an expression of mock horror, then compressed his lips. He'd been on his own for over a year and didn't need to be told how to behave. He hugged her, ruffled Jerusha's hair, and walked out the door.

"And come home at a decent hour, please. I won't sleep a wink until you return. You are armed, aren't you? It's not safe to be out alone, and certainly not without a weapon." Mom called.

Jarrett swung onto Sampson and galloped out into the night.

Once away from the cabin, he slowed Sampson to a trot until he neared Fort Gibson, then walked Sampson to keep the dust down. The fine November evening boasted a full, yellow moon hung over the peaceful road meandering through woods and meadows. Clouds flirted with the moon, plunging the world into darkness, then brightening into flickering shadows.

Jarrett inhaled clear, crisp air. Expectancy flooded him like the mellow light flooding the earth. He would soon see Delight!

"Bother the dust." He urged Sampson into a trot, then a gallop.

The trail merged onto the Texas Road. Accompanied by the rhythmic sound of Sampson's hooves on the hard-packed dirt, Jarrett took the turn-off and halted Sampson at the Fort Gibson Gate. Music floated from inside the big main building. Was it a waltz, a Virginia reel, or an old-fashioned quadrille?

If only he knew how to dance. His puritan family had forbidden such trivial things. But he'd give the steps a try. He'd watch until he got the hang of the rhythm. Then he'd have an excuse to hold Delight in his arms.

The double wooden gates swung wide, guarded on both sides by a shadowy form in a gray uniform. Fifty yards distant, the Grand River lapped across sand bars.

Jarrett rode inside the gates and shifted in the saddle. Moonlight illuminated the entire fort. Familiar tall pickets fenced the north and east sides, while two-story buildings formed the stockade on the south and west. Blockhouses loomed at the corners, with the officers' quarters, the chapel, schoolhouse, and the government store composing two sides. Whitewashed logs gleamed in the moonlight. He rode past a split-rail enclosure surrounding a burying ground with the tombstones set in haphazard rows.

Further inside, horses, some harnessed to carriages or wagons, were tied to the hitching post.

He dismounted and secured Sampson at the far end of a long string of horses. He dusted off his clothes, raked his fingers through his hair, and strode toward the large main building.

Light, music, and laughter drifted out the open door.

He clattered up the stone walk between the parade grounds and the double-story structure which housed the officers, his boots clicking on the stones.

Behind a grapevine entwined up a wooden staircase, a young couple kissed in the shadows. Jarrett glanced at them, felt an answering flutter in his heart, then entered the candlelit room.

The ballroom was large enough for dancing to the small military band he remembered from that May Day so long past. But now the band wore the gray of the new Confederacy.

Jarrett stepped inside and leaned against a wall letting his eyes adjust to the candlelight.

At the far end of the room, a table heavy with food stood beneath a barred window. Candles projected from the walls at intervals throughout the room. Shadows and brightness flickered over the scene. Beneath his feet the wood floor pulsed to the rhythm of the dancers. Jarrett tapped his foot.

He stalked the crowded room. Delight must be here somewhere. Pretty girls glanced at him, then looked again. Giggles and flirtatious looks followed him.

His neighbor, Andrew Bushyhead, clad in a new gray uniform and sporting a single stripe, approached with a girl on his arm. "Jarrett, good to see you again. I'm proud to know a hero. Guess I should call you Ghost Rider." His broad face creased into a huge grin. "I trust you'll join our company soon and change that dandy outfit you're wearing for our proud gray."

Jarrett bit back a negative answer. "Good to see you, Andy." They shook hands.

Andrew nodded. "I'd like to talk with—"

The stunning dark-haired girl, her hand on Andrew's left arm, interrupted. "Some other time, Andy, please. Remember me? Introduce us."

Andrew cleared his throat. "Sorry. Jarrett, this is Dolly Lewis. She lives in town. Her folks moved here just after you left to ride with the Pony Express." His grin weakened until he looked miserable. "Dolly's been pestering me since you walked in the door to be introduced. Dolly, Jarrett Ross."

Dolly dropped her hand from Andry's arm. Her fan fluttering, her gloved hand extended, she tilted her head and leaned toward Jarrett. "So nice to meet you. I haven't seen you here before."

"No, Miss." Jarrett cleared his throat.

"Perhaps you'd like to dance with me, Mr. Ross." Dolly arched her brow and dipped her chin.

Andrew's face melted into total angst.

Jarrett half-turned away. "Well, I'd like to, but …"

Dolly grasped his hand and led him to the dance floor.

Sweat popped out on his forehead. Was every feminine eye in the room watching? Yep, they were—some shy, some staring openly.

Dolly waited, her rounded arms extended in an invitation to waltz.

His feet were tree stumps, rooted to the polished wood. He glanced away, then centered his attention toward the ballroom where couples danced, the ladies' long dresses cascading around their partner's legs as they swayed together with the waltz. "W … w … would you rather have something to drink, miss?"

Dolly's face clouded, then her full lips pouted. "Yes, if that's what you prefer. I'll walk with you." She took his arm as they made their way toward the refreshment table.

Jarrett's ears burned and sweat dripped beneath his cravat.

A beautiful girl with red hair flowing to her shoulders approached. "Dolly, introduce me to your friend. You're not planning to keep him all to yourself, are you?"

Dolly tugged on his arm. "Sign your name on my card. Please remember I saw you first." She scratched out three names from her full dance card and handed him her card and a tiny gold quill.

What should he do with this? He let it dangle by the ribbon.

With a pouted lip, Dolly motioned to the redhead. "This is Sarah Jane McCain. She's my cousin. Our families moved to Tahlequah at the same time. Sarah Jane, this is Jarrett Ross."

Jarrett backed a pace from the girls, but Dolly and Sarah Jane stepped closer.

"I'm looking for someone." When had his throat gotten so tight? He desperately needed a drink. "Give me a few minutes to locate my gr— … my friend. I'm not certain she's here."

"First you must sign my dance card." Dolly's sugar-coated voice insisted as she wrote his name above two of the scratched-out promises.

"I don't dance."

"No problem. I can teach you. Or …" Dolly's vivacious face sparkled. "We can stroll in the garden."

"What about me?" The pretty redhead planted herself in front of him. "I claim my time now. You may get me some food and a drink."

"I really want to find my friend." Jarrett stepped away.

"A drink first and then we can search." Sarah Jane thrust her arm through his and headed on toward the refreshments.

Jarrett swallowed, but he let her tow him to the table. He needed water.

Silver goblets waited beside two immense, cut-glass punch bowls.

"We'd like the spiked punch, please." Sarah Jane accepted a full goblet from the boy attending the table and handed Jarrett the glass.

"Thanks." So, the drink had a little something added. But with no water in sight, he could handle a little alcohol. He gulped it all, and the boy placed another in his hand.

"May I help you make your selection? Would you like the chicken in pasté, the beef alamode, a few pickled walnuts, and surely some hot biscuits?" Sarah Jane piled a plate with food. "Will you sample some of the desserts? Do you prefer the floating islands, macaroons, or my favorite— the Indian-style dumplings drowning in blueberries?"

"No, thanks." He lounged against the wall, the glass of punch cooling his hand.

Sarah Jane, red curls flying, fluttered around him like a butterfly. "Enjoying yourself?"

He drank the punch and studied the room. Was Delight here or not?

Sarah Jane brought him a third drink.

"No thanks." The surroundings fuzzed pleasantly. The polished floor, reflecting the flames of scores of candles, wavered. The aroma of bayberry mingled with perfume.

He'd been too long alone in the desert. He'd never felt so relaxed.

A soldier stopped on the opposite side of the table.

Clothed in a rosy haze, Jarrett gazed at the Confederate uniform. A double-breasted gray coat, with two rows of gilt buttons. Yellow cuffs and collar. Gray trousers with a yellow stripe up the outside seam. Ankle boots and yellow spurs, saber with steel scabbard and a half-basket hitch, yellow sash tied on the right hip. The uniform transformed the plain man into a soldier a woman might find hard to resist.

Jordie in his uniform with his blond hair, blue eyes, and tall, muscular frame, must have a fine time when he's not on patrol.

"Sure, you wouldn't like another?" Sarah Jane reached for his empty goblet.

"No thanks. I must find my friend."

A soldier strode over to claim Sarah Jane.

She put her hand on the man's gray-uniformed arm and glanced back over her bare shoulder, "Nice to meet you, Jarrett."

Gone at last. Jarrett watched her sashay around the dance floor with her partner. Glimpsing Dolly heading his way, he ducked into a shadow. Coward. She was not why he'd come tonight.

Who was that? Jill Adair, looking pretty in a white, silk dress, waltzed past.

Jarrett stiffened, then jumped out of sight behind a long curtain. Claremont Flint, fully decked out in his Confederate uniform, had his arm around Jill.

Jarrett glanced out from behind the heavy curtain. *Fairly*

certain he didn't see me. He clenched his fist. Claremont. Here!

What should he do?

His frock coat stood out among the gray uniforms. Wherever he stepped, girls flirted with him. Murmurs and giggles followed him wherever he walked. He loosened the ruffles confining his throat. Hot in here.

"Yahola, where is Delight?" he muttered. "Why didn't I realize Flint would be here?"

Jarrett stiffened his jaw. He had as much right as Flint to attend this dance. He stepped back into the ballroom.

Three girls towing an older lady approached.

He frowned at them.

They slowed but continued toward him.

He pivoted and strode in the opposite direction.

Then he saw her.

She danced with a tall, dark-haired captain. They appeared unaware of anyone else in the room. She laughed, leaning back to look into his eyes, the tip of her head touching his shoulder.

The captain's eyes never left her face.

Jarrett's heart squeezed into a vise. Perspiration dripped between his shoulder blades. His chest heaved.

Delight wore her silvery-blonde hair upswept. Her silk dress matched her blue-violet eyes. White gloves reached above her elbows and a single strand of pearls reflected the ivory of her complexion.

The dance ended, and the captain touched his lips to her gloved hand.

Two soldiers elbowed their way across the floor and attempted to claim her.

The captain shook his head. Arm in arm, the couple strolled to the food table.

Jarrett inhaled ten gallons of air.

CHAPTER 17

Jarrett stepped back into the shadows, his gaze riveted on Delight and the captain. Heat flared through him, washing over ripping pain.

Sarah Jane moved in. She slipped her white-gloved hand into his. "I know you're hurt … and angry. But since Delight has already found a beau and I have not, perhaps we could become better acquainted?"

He glanced into Sarah's amber eyes. Muscles jumped along his clenched jaws. What was she babbling about?

"Delight can't fail to notice us." Sarah led him across the dance floor and out into the garden.

Crisp air startled him.

Sarah Jane tugged him into a dark alcove. He grew aware of her silk dress whispering over the dormant grass, her bare shoulders, and the red blaze of her hair. In the moonlight, her eyes gleamed from the pale oval of her face.

"You weren't aware that Delight Flint is all but engaged to Captain Drew? Of course, there is nothing official yet. But Captain Drew monopolizes her. Rumors fly that they plan to marry."

The silky purr of her voice cleared the haze from his

mind. Jarrett glared at the ballroom door where light spilled out dissolving into dusky night. His heart burned. Captain Drew. Why hadn't Delight waited for *him*?

Sarah Jane tugged his arm. "Come, let's walk. You need to cool off. You don't want to return to the ballroom and start a fight."

Jarrett shrugged off her hand and strode across the parade grounds, heading for the river.

Sarah Jane, running in high-heeled slippers, breathed hard as she struggled to keep up with him.

He stopped at the river's edge, legs spread, and fists clenched. His breath whistled through his lungs.

"I'm sorry you had to find out this way." Sarah Jane's voice rose above the rushing of the river. "If you had told me your friend is Delight Flint, I could have prepared you."

Jarrett didn't move.

"Would you like me to tell her you are here?" Sarah Jane patted his crossed arms.

He turned from her. "I'm going back inside."

"I'll go with you."

Jarrett shook his head and strode toward the ballroom, his boots hammering the rocky ground.

Before he entered, Sarah Jane, breathless and bright-cheeked, caught up and slipped her arm through his. They swept into the room together.

Heads turned. Whispers rippled through the room.

Jarrett glared around the area. Where was Delight?

Was she in the garden with Drew?

Then he spotted her. She stood in a candle-lit nook, her silvery-blonde hair incandescent, her face a pale blur. Captain Drew's body mostly shielded her from view.

Jarrett started across the dance floor, not certain what he would do, vaguely aware the music had started, and dancers whirled in his path. Then, somehow Sarah Jane was in his arms, propelling him into a clumsy waltz.

"Seeing us waltz will be good for her," Sarah Jane whispered.

Her silken dress flowed around his legs. He dropped his arms. Chill sweat dampened his palms. He lifted his chin and strode through the dancers toward Delight.

Sarah Jane followed, almost treading on his heels.

Delight's blue-violet eyes opened wide. Her cheeks grew pink. As she gazed from Jarrett to Sarah Jane and back to Jarrett, her mouth trembled.

"Delight, I believe you know my escort, Jarrett Ross." Sarah Jane's voice rose above the violins. "Jarrett, this is Captain John Drew."

The tall, muscular captain extended a gray-sleeved arm toward Jarrett.

The captain's saber rattled as Jarrett automatically shook the offered hand. His gaze never left Delight's face.

"Pleased to meet you, Ross," Drew said, his voice pleasant.

"I want to talk to you, Delight." Jarrett ripped out the words like icicles.

Captain Drew frowned and interposed his body between Jarrett and Delight. His right hand lifted to the hilt of his saber. "Ross, I don't like the tone you are using to the young lady."

"What I have to say to the young lady is private."

"Jarrett, John, please don't quarrel!" Delight stepped between him and Drew.

Captain Drew thrust out his chest. "Sir. You have no right."

Jarrett's face burned. What was wrong with him? He hadn't meant to speak so brusquely. Heat deepened into his neck and ears. The man held a possessive arm around the girl he loved.

"Drew, outside, now!" Jarrett commanded. What had he just said? He was acting like an ass.

Delight stepped from behind Drew into the candlelight. She looked so incredible. Candlelight spun her silver-gold hair into a halo. Her enormous eyes spanned the gulf between them. "No, Jarrett. If you fight, I'll never speak to you again." She spoke with a hushed voice, and with absolute certainty.

A crowd gathered around them, the dancing stopped, and the music wavered.

Jarrett stood in a circle of silence. Her words drained his anger. Left him defenseless. His legs felt heavy, bloodless, rooting him to the floor.

He nodded and stepped back.

Captain Drew pulled Delight close, put his arm around her shoulders, and walked her toward the door.

Sarah Jane slid her arm through Jarrett's and frowned at their backs.

Delight pulled free of Drew and turned toward Jarrett. She glanced at Sarah Jane, hesitated, but took tiny steps toward him. "I would like to talk with you."

The hot glare from the crowd bored into his back.

Violins picked up tempo and swung into a Virginia Reel.

Sarah Jane tossed her red hair. "Why, Delight, Jarrett is *my* escort. We are just about to leave. He is escorting me home."

Delight's head tilted, a question in her eyes.

His face burned. He slid his hand free from Sarah Jane's grasp, and sidestepped Drew. "Delight, come outside with me," he croaked. "Please."

She shook her head.

An ache jabbed his heart. He turned away.

"You forget Claremont. I'll meet you outside when he's not watching. Wait for me. I may be some time." She whispered.

He gaped at her.

She smiled ever so slightly. A dimple appeared and disappeared. With a curtsey, she turned away and glided back to a baffled-looking Captain Drew.

Jarrett pulled in a deep breath. The red haze before his eyes faded into a rainbow.

Across the room, Delight spoke to Drew.

The captain nodded, shot Jarrett a warning look, and steered Delight to the banquet table.

"Will you take me home, Jarrett?" Sugar dripped from Sarah Jane's lips. Her cat eyes sparkled, and her white-gloved hand dragged him toward the door.

"Sorry, I can't. You heard Delight."

"You're a fool!" Sarah Jane's voice rose above the music.

Heads craned in their direction.

"Delight's all but married to John Drew. Besides, you're a Ross and she's a Flint. Everyone knows your families hate each other."

"Enough."

"What if I tell Claremont Flint you're going to meet his

sister in the moonlight?"

"That's a risk I have to take."

"All right, I won't tell him. I don't want you to get hurt. But he'll suspect something. You made an awful fuss over Delight."

Jarrett scowled. Yep, he'd been stupid alright.

"If we leave together, Claremont may think you've taken me home," Sarah Jane whispered in his ear.

He shook his head. "I'd rather take my chances with Flint."

"You're impossible!" Sarah Jane stamped her foot and pouted. "Why couldn't I have met you before Delight did? At least dance with me. Claremont has friends here. I really am afraid for you, Jarrett."

"I can take care of myself."

Sarah Jane smiled a mischievous smile. "You're the only man here who doesn't want to take me home." She laughed and walked off.

Jarrett melted into the shadows to watch Delight.

She danced gracefully in the circle of Drew's gray uniformed arms until she missed a step, when her searching gaze swept across him. She apologized to Drew.

The captain lifted her gloved hand to his mouth and kissed her fingers.

Jarrett smothered the sudden urge to murder the captain. Instead, he winked wickedly at Delight.

A rosy glow warmed her complexion. She missed another step. A few more circles in the waltz, and her eyes sought him as she pirouetted on tiptoe to see over Drew's shoulder. She smiled across the room.

Jarrett's heart turned cartwheels.

Other couples danced between them.

He glanced around the ballroom. He'd best keep track of Claremont. Know your enemy. There he was, dancing with Jill Adair, his attention focused on Jill's face. The man looked besotted.

Jarrett moved toward the door. Stepping out into the cool night air, he inhaled deeply.

He passed the hitching posts, the officer's quarters, the commissary, and then rounded a corner. The center of the parade ground, bathed in moonlight, looked too conspicuous for a quiet conversation. The fort appeared deserted except for the ballroom and the dour men guarding the entrance.

Jarrett passed four rooms with barred doors. He rounded the building and discovered open ground between the rear of the calaboose and the stockade walls held enough shadow to shield a couple desiring solitude.

He stepped onto the walk beside the empty jail, leaned against the wall, and waited. He forced himself to stand quietly, willing her to hurry.

Finally, in the distance, he heard her clear voice.

"I really must have a glass of punch. Please get it for me. Also, some of those delicious desserts. Bring me one of each."

A low murmuring baritone, then her soprano rose once more, "No, I don't want to help select the food. I'm certain you can find just what I want. I must rest."

The instant the officer left, Delight slipped out the door and tiptoed down the boardwalk. The moon hid behind broken clouds.

In the darkness, the rustle of her silk dress announced her approach. She was almost beside him before he stepped out of the darkness. She gasped.

He took her hand and led her behind the jail.

The moon reappeared revealing the oval of her face and her violet eyes. His stomach felt hollow and his knees weak. The world vanished … disappeared—empty, except for the two of them. He stood arm's length from her, trying to breathe.

She shivered in the cool air.

He shrugged out of his frockcoat and draped the velvet around her bare shoulders. He could barely catch his breath. Beneath her delicate beauty he sensed a fervor as deep as the one that flooded his heart. He felt woozy with the same giddiness the whiskey had caused the night of the Buffalo Dance.

"Oh, Jarrett, I'm so glad you're back," she whispered.

Jarrett's throat tightened. "Doesn't look like you've been lonely."

Delight moved closer. "Don't be jealous. You've no reason to be."

He didn't? "What about Drew?"

"What about him? He's a friend."

"You're not promised?"

"Promised! To John Drew? Of course not." Delight 's face crinkled, then lit. "Is that what Sarah Jane told you? Is that why you were so angry?" Her laugh tinkled into the darkness mingling with music from the ballroom.

"You might say that."

"Your anger frightened me. I couldn't imagine what I had done to deserve it. I feared my father had tried to kill you. I never once dreamed you were upset because of John Drew."

Jarrett couldn't inhale enough breath. The air around her seemed electrified. The moonlight washed the ivory satin of her shoulders with a warm glimmer. "Delight." He took her hands in his.

"Yes, Jarrett."

His own hands tingled with her touch. He brought her closer and whispered into her hair, "I missed you so much. Did you miss me?"

"Yes, oh, yes. I thought you'd never come home."

Her breath fanned his face. He inhaled the intoxicating perfume of her presence. "You're so beautiful. You're an angel, a sorceress. You were with me in the desert, never far from my mind, always in my heart. I saw your face in the slashing rain, in the blazing sun, in the desert flowers, and in the glorious sunsets."

So easy to get lost in the way she looked at him. He tried to control his quick, uneven breathing. Blood coursed through his veins like a river rushing to the sea.

"And you were with me in every face I danced with, in every sunrise, in every dream I dreamed, and in every fear I felt. I was so afraid for you. Oh Jarrett, I can't believe you're here!"

He gathered her into his arms. She nestled against his chest until he lifted her chin and kissed her on the tip of her nose. Then, cupping her face in his hands, he kissed her again.

Her arms wrapped around his neck. The frock coat slipped from her shoulders to the ground.

When he released her, she raised her lips for more. He kissed her with his eyes, then his mouth molded with the soft fullness of her lips.

Their lips held the harmony of their souls, and her answering passion was wild and sweet.

Jarrett released her. He dare not kiss her again. Not here. Not now.

A boot crunched on the boardwalk. They jumped apart.

The soldier walked past their hiding place with no awareness of their presence.

"I must get back. Claremont surely will notice I'm gone and come searching for me. Oh, Jarrett, I never meant to stay out here so long," Delight whispered.

She touched his face. "Before I leave, I must know about Sarah Jane. How is it you know her?"

"She's nothing to me. I only met her tonight."

"I don't understand. You two seemed so attached. I, I felt—"

"I love *you*, Delight. You are the only woman I will ever love. Someday, somehow, regardless of your family, regardless of the war, I'm going to marry you … if you'll have me."

"Yes, oh yes. I love you. I've waited so long for you. I loved you from the first moment I saw you. I loved you when you came in wet and shivering from that wonderful snowstorm that brought you to me."

"I'll find a way. Trust me. Wait for me."

"I must go."

"Wait for me."

She ran through the moonlight toward the music inside. The soaring notes matched the music in his heart. She loved him.

Who would have believed love felt so good?

Yet a nagging thought thrust a thorn into the center of his

happiness.

Now, how do I deal with her family?

CHAPTER 18

Jarrett stood in the shadows and watched as the moonlight faded until clouds moved in, shrouding the fort in darkness. Would Delight's flushed face and bright eyes start tongues wagging?

He stood there pondering until couples drifted from the fort in buggies and on horseback. Laughter and banter hovered through the darkness and mingled with still-rollicking music.

When Delight left with her mother, a gang of armed men escorted their buggy.

Jarrett slipped on his coat, tiptoed to where he had tied Sampson, jumped aboard, and cantered through the gates. He followed the Flint buggy at a distance.

Visions of Delight, her expressions of love, and the intoxicating emotions she loosened inside him, dulled his Pony Express-sharpened senses.

He was several miles from the fort on the Texas Road when a horseman burst from the darkness of a clump of trees and blocked his path.

Samson reared.

"What the—"

The click of a hammer pulled back on a gun sounded ominous. "Hold it right there," a deadly voice ordered.

Jarrett froze. A gun barrel glinted in the inky shadows where the lone horseman barred his way. The voice struck a chord of memory. Who was it?

"Get down off that horse."

Slow and deliberate, careful to keep his hands away from his rifle, Jarrett dismounted. He stood beside Sampson, his hands in the air.

The horseman whacked Sampson on the rump. Sampson whinnied and exploded into a gallop down the empty road toward home.

"Walk to that strand of blackjack oaks on your right." The rider crowded his horse against Jarrett's side.

The animal's breath blew hot on his neck.

Walking across the rough ground away from the road toward the trees, Jarrett connected the voice with the owner. Claremont Flint.

Jarrett's mind started functioning again. *Flint probably expects me to run. Then he won't have to shoot me eyeball to eyeball. I won't run. If he's going to kill me, he'll have to do it face-to-face.*

Flint leaned over his horse's neck and pushed the cold gun barrel against Jarrett's temple. "Don't try to run."

His horse's shoulder shoved Jarrett into a stumble.

Jarrett caught his balance, turned and faced Flint. "What—"

"Shut up, Ross. You're not going to talk your way out of this! Get on over to those trees!"

Perspiration dripped into Jarrett's eyes. As he strode, he scanned the empty countryside. They were over two hundred yards from the deserted Texas road. Not a house, a barn, or even a dog was within calling distance. Flint had picked his spot well.

No ravine in which to dive for cover from a barrage of bullets, just flat ground heading toward another clump of blackjacks. His boots slipped on the rocky ground and the flinty hooves of the horse broke the silent night.

The eerie sound of an owl hooting rose above their footsteps.

"You heard the old Indian saying, Ross, 'When the owl hoots your name, you'll be dead before dawn.' That owl just hooted your name," Flint taunted.

Jarrett stopped and faced the shadowy form above him, the gun barrel near his temple. He had to stall. Figure what to do. "You're not going to—?"

"I said move!" Flint pressed the gun against Jarrett's head.

Hands in the air, Jarrett stumbled on toward the grove of blackjacks.

A few minutes later they entered the deeper darkness beneath the trees.

Jarrett's arms felt like lead.

"Stand where you are, don't wiggle a hair." Flint dismounted, tied his horse to a tree, and leveled his revolver.

Jarrett pulled in a deep breath. *Unreal. Why didn't I notice Flint following me?* He licked dry lips, swallowing hard, conscious of his Adam's apple bobbing in his throat.

Flint pressed the muzzle of the cocked gun against Jarrett's chest.

Jarrett didn't breathe.

"You thought you could sneak around with my sister,

and nobody would be the wiser. We warned you, Ross."

"Flint, you don't know—"

"Shut up!" Flint's fingers brushed Jarrett's ruffled shirt. "Why aren't you in uniform? Too lily-livered to fight? You'd rather sneak around with a man's sister than fight for your country. I know your kind. Great with the ladies, but no taste for duty."

He shoved Jarrett against a tree.

Jarrett's head snapped back and hit the rough bark. Pain stabbed his head and neck. "You talk of fighting. Shooting an unarmed man isn't—"

"Shut up. I'm not going to shoot you. I leave that to the likes of you Rosses. Perhaps you remember my brother, Caldwell?" Flint pressed the gun against Jarrett's chest. With his other hand, he unholstered his gun belt, unhooked his saber, and removed his uniform coat. He tossed everything on the ground and laid his revolver on top.

What?

Jarrett reacted too late.

A hard fist smashed his jaw. He reeled backward and landed hard on the ground.

Fast as a cougar Flint jumped him, pinned him to the rocky ground and landed smashing blows, one after the other.

Stunned, Jarrett wrestled and parried. He kneed the heavy body and delivered a tight uppercut to the chin. Claremont slid off. Jarrett staggered to his feet.

Claremont recovered and swung hard but missed.

Jarrett exchanged blow for blow with Claremont, gasping and grunting as his fists reached their marks. He fought desperately, always on the defensive, his left eye swollen shut.

Jarrett dodged Claremont's longer reach, but Flint closed in again, pounding Jarrett's face and body. Jarrett ducked in close enough to land a solid right on Claremont's nose. He grunted as pain flashed through his swollen knuckles, but a crunch beneath his fist told him he had inflicted damage.

In the darkness, Jarrett stumbled on hidden rocks. His arms grew heavy, his mind jarred into numbness, his feinting and dodging slowed. He took every blow Claremont delivered, but with dogged persistence, he kept fighting.

Flint pinned him to the ground, knee in his chest, both hands clutching his throat. A red haze diffused the blackness.

Flint's voice sounded far away. "Enough, Ross? Enough? You going to leave my sister alone?"

Jarrett smashed a fist toward the voice.

Flint lost his hold on Jarrett's neck and slid off.

Jarrett was halfway to his feet when Flint's head struck him hard in his midsection. Jarrett doubled, clutching his stomach. Flint kneed his chin. Jarrett's head snapped back. He fell. His head struck a rock, and he slipped into darkness.

A rough hand shook him. An insistent voice called his name. Pain converged over him, centering in the agonizing throb in the back of his head. The taste of blood, thick in his mouth, churned his stomach.

"Leave me alone," Jarrett muttered. Pain washed over him like waves over sand. With his tongue, he tested his teeth. All still intact.

Still, the hand shook him.

Jarrett reached out to push the annoyance away.

The hand shook him harder.

Jarrett forced open his unswollen eye. Flint knelt above

him. Jarrett groaned. He hurt all over.

"You all right?" Flint sounded as if he had a bad cold.

"Dandy." Jarrett touched the back of his head to find a large bump. "I think you fractured my skull."

"You're some fighter. I thought you Rosses were all talk."

Jarrett struggled to lean on a battered elbow. "Right. I never lose." He managed a painful grin. "Sounds like I broke your nose."

"Reckon you did. A bit hard to breathe." Flint laughed. "Look, Ross, it's seventeen miles to your farm, and your horse is long gone. You'll never make the trip home unless I take you."

"Don't do me any favors."

"No favor. I got you into this scrap, I feel responsible for getting you home."

Jarrett sat up. Pain shot through his head. White stars swirled. "What's this? First you threaten to kill me, then you dish out a beating, and now you want to take me home?"

"I've been sitting here thinking, while you slept so peacefully, and my nose hurt like you'd shoved a musket through it. You're not the kind of man I thought you were— fast-talking and good with the ladies."

Jarrett grunted.

"I've seen enough men since I've been in uniform to judge a man pretty quick. I got to know you fairly intimately a few minutes ago, and I don't think you're a bad sort. You have grit."

The moonlight picked up the glimmer of teeth. "Besides, I can't leave you out here for the coyotes to eat. Or bushwhackers to shoot. You weren't too bright, not to wear a gun. Lots of bushwhackers around, and I'm not the only Flint out looking for your hide. You top our most wanted list!"

"So now you feel responsible." Jarrett hoisted himself to his feet and patted his ribs for broken bones. "I'm feeling so lousy I'll take you up on your offer."

Claremont smoothed his long blond hair, dabbed his nose with a bloody handkerchief, and clapped his military cap on at a jaunty angle. He continued as though Jarrett had not spoken. "Then I started thinking about Delight. She's a level-headed sort, for a girl. And I commenced thinking some more. If she's got her heart set on being sweet on a Ross, well, maybe that isn't a bad idea. It's time this feud between the Rosses and the Flints ended. I can't speak for my father, but what say, Ross, want to bury the hatchet?" Claremont extended his hand.

Jarrett hesitated. *Is this real?* He stuck out his hand, wincing as Claremont gripped his bruised knuckles.

"But you will not compromise my sister. No more secret meetings."

Jarrett stared at the shadowy figure.

"If you must meet, I'll arrange a place and be present as chaperone. Too many tongues are wagging already. Give me your word."

He was more than willing. "I agree to protect Delight's reputation."

"Come on. We'll get you up on my horse and ride home double."

"Give me a minute. When you do a job, you do it thoroughly. I'm a tad shaky." Jarrett glanced at his new shirt—ripped and blood-blotched and dirty, one sleeve torn, and the ruffles pulled from his throat.

"Sorry about your shirt. You'll be in uniform soon anyway. Every man in Indian Territory has gone to the defense of his country." He brushed Jarrett's coat, flung his arm around his shoulder, and half-carried him to his horse.

Once aboard, hanging onto the back of Claremont's saddle with both hands, Jarrett's mind cleared.

His head and torso throbbed with every jolt of the horse's hooves, but he couldn't keep a smile from his swollen lips. *How did this miracle happen? Perhaps now he had a real chance with Delight. Thank you, Father God, for working this out for me.*

Yet the thought nagged. Would Claremont still be friendly when the ardent Southerner discovered he had no intention of joining Stand Watie's Confederate forces?

CHAPTER 19

June 1862.

Jarrett waved to Claremont. His new friend, good as his word, arranged for him and Delight to meet once a month where all three would not be seen. Yet Jarrett ached to be alone with her. But bulldog Claremont refused to let them out of his sight.

Jarrett ducked Claremont's friendly punch. "Your worse than any governess. A person would think you'd understand."

"And why would that be?" Claremont teased.

"Because you're in love with Jill."

Claremont winked a twinkling eye. "Am I?"

"*Her* folks approve."

Claremont gripped his arm. "They do. And Dad will come around to accepting *you*. After we win the war. Have patience."

Jarrett squared his jaw. *I'm running out of patience. Yahola, love isn't supposed to be so painful.* "I have to see Delight more often."

"Sorry, once a month is all I can arrange. Father's already asking questions about where we go."

Jarrett sighed. At least last week, after Claremont arranged the meeting, Mom, Dad, Jerusha, and Granddad all met Delight and Claremont.

Delight had charmed his folks with her frank talk and gracious ways. She made no secret of her love. He'd felt like a hero. He'd known his family would adore Delight.

He had basked in a rosy glow all week. But tonight, he chomped at the bit. Three long weeks until he could see her again.

Like a tidal wave, loneliness hit him. He ached to hold that warm, responsive girl with the scent of apples hovering around her silken hair. He longed to sit with her in the moonlight, to see himself mirrored in her eyes, to hold her close, and breathe in the perfume of her skin. He dreamed of exploring the message of her lips. He yearned to hold her hand and stroll with her beneath the stars. Her every move and word were magic—unique, and lovely. He had to see her. But he had to wait.

~

Jarrett and his family welcomed Jordie home from Fort Gibson. He had twenty-four-hours before he returned to duty. The whole family surrounded him, grinning, hugging, and patting his back.

Jarrett hunkered with them in the rear yard, elbows on the picnic table, belly filled with barbecue bison. Though Jordie, as usual, was the center of attention, joy flooded Jarrett that Jordie was home.

Darkness fell. Jarrett inhaled the sweet scent of blossoming trees and freshly cut grass. Stars dusted the sky as thick as freckles on a red-haired boy.

Jordie rose from the table and walked to stand by the crackling bonfire. The family followed like loyal puppies after a loved master.

Jarrett left the table and stretched out on his back in the grass near the fire.

Basking in the fire's glow, the family spoke in low tones, laughing occasionally.

Jordie's voice increased in volume.

Jarrett rolled over, cupped his chin in his hands, and started listening.

"Yep, old Opotheleyhola became Commander of the Creeks as well as the Seminoles, Chickasaws and a few Kickapoos, Shawnees, Delawares and Comanches who refused to join the Confederacy. They took food and livestock, loaded their families on wagons and headed north for Kansas to seek protection of Union forces there. He ended up with thirty-three hundred warriors plus their women and children."

Jordie's voice lowered.

Jarrett strained to hear over the crackling fire.

"Then on November 26th—I'll never forget that date— Colonel Cooper caught up with Opotheleyhola. As you know, I served under Captain Drew, 2nd Cherokee Mounted Rifles." Jordan stretched his hands toward the fire. He looked tired, like a man who understood his audience could not grasp the reality of his story but, nevertheless, felt compelled to relate the tale.

Six-foot tall Jordie embodied everything Jarrett thought a man should be. Jordie was the kind of man who became the center of any group. Men trusted his leadership. To

Jarrett, Jordie loomed larger than life. He respected, admired, and tried to emulate his older brother. Jordie had always overshadowed him because Jordie dazzled people. No one ever forgot Jordie.

Jarrett grunted. But this man in the gray uniform was different from the Jordie he knew and loved. War had left its mark. Jordie had lost his assurance.

Jordie backed from the fire, his face shadowed. His fingers clenched and unclenched. His voice sounded harsh. "Dad, we came across Opotheleyahola's camp on Hominy Creek just northwest of Tulsa. Before sunup the next day, half my regiment deserted. To desert goes against my grain, but I sympathized with those who left. Do you think I did the right thing, Dad?"

"Son, if you felt it was right to stay, I'm sure that was the correct choice." Dad laid his big hand on Jordie's shoulder.

"But my regiment had to fight against friends. I have no allegiance to the South. Our Nation joined the Confederacy to keep from being annihilated. I felt I must remain loyal to my captain. That day ..." Jordie covered his eyes, "... that day I fought my Indian friends."

Dad hugged Jordie. "We do what we must. This is a strange war. I've heard stories of brother fighting brother. I pray that horror won't happen to us."

"Yes!" Jordie glanced at Jarrett. "Stay out of this madness, Jarrett!"

Jarrett jumped to his feet. "No way I'm taking up arms. What happened out there?"

"Old Opotheleyhola had his camp atop a wooded hill. We fought hand-to-hand for over six hours." Jordie blew out his breath. "In the end, they abandoned their wagons, over nine hundred cattle, and two hundred fifty horses. We confiscated everything. His men fled on foot." Jordie rubbed a hand over his face. "A blizzard hit before they reached Kansas. But the warriors tried to cover the women and children's retreat. Lord, they were brave!"

"Don't swear, Jordan," Mom's soft voice broke as if she held back tears. She gripped Jordie's fidgeting hand. "We know you did what was right." Tears glistened.

Jordie pulled his hand away and paced in front of the fire.

"The whole thing makes my blood boil! I'm ashamed I fought that battle. The Indians lost everything, Dad. I think I made a mistake not deserting." Jordie dropped his head into his hands and groaned.

Why did war confuse a man so? Jordie had been so confident he knew how to handle life. Where did a man put his allegiance? Jarrett stared at his brother, knowing one thing more certain than life itself—he wanted no part of war.

"But they did escape. The battle was not decisive?" Dad put his arm around Jordie's shoulder. "Son, is there more you need to get off your chest?"

"Yes, sir. The Indians escaped because none of us had the stomach to go after them. But Captain Drew ordered my company to scout them out. So, we followed them all the way up to Kansas. We found them camped on the frozen snow with only scraps of cloth for shelter. Some help they got from the Union! An army surgeon amputated frozen arms and legs. We saw a pile of arms and legs and hands and feet." Jordie shook his head. "Awful! We didn't stick around to see any more. We hightailed it out of there before Union soldiers sighted us."

In the light of the crackling fire Jordie's eyes flashed, and his chin rose. Flickering shadows made him look half-mad.

"Before this blasted war of secession, Opotheleyhola was a rich man. Now he and his people—those who survived—are destitute. Yet, we hear they enlisted in the Union Army, and they plan to march on Indian Territory to win back their land." Jordie lowered his voice. "Which means we'll soon have fighting in our own backyard."

Mother gasped and clutched her hands together. Jerusha squealed like an injured kitten.

Jarrett clamped his lips, fearful he might lose his barbeque.

"Tell me what our nation has to do with this white man's war?" Jordie gazed at Dad.

His words reverberated between the stars and the sky and echoed across the silent hills.

At last Dad spoke. "Had Chief Ross not signed the Confederate Alliance, the Cherokee Nation would be in the same fix those Creeks are in."

The quiet words appeared to calm Jordie. He shook his mane of blond hair, dropped down cross-legged close to Mother and reached for Jerusha. "Come here, pixie. I need some hugs and kisses."

Jerusha leaped onto his lap. Giggling and laughing, she hugged Jordie.

Jarrett stood. "You were in the Battle of Pea Ridge, weren't you, Jordie? Give us an account of that."

"Yes, tell us, but don't get angry or sad." Jerusha cupped both hands on her brother's cheeks and rubbed the short, blond bristles.

Jordie wrapped Jerusha in his arms and rocked her back and forth.

Lines etched Mom's face.

Grandfather Worchester's wise eyes blinked behind rimless glasses.

Jarrett kept his gaze on Dad's peaceful face. Dad had learned to rely on God during his tragic past. And Jarrett had learned, riding for the Pony Express, the difficulty of relying on someone else's faith. Would his faith withstand fighting the war in his own neighborhood?

What was his place in the coming battles? Was he a coward? Was he unmanly not to volunteer? Should he? Somehow God would have to let him know.

Jordie hugged Jerusha and spoke over her shoulder. "The battle of Pea Ridge lasted three days. There were fourteen thousand of us Graybacks. That newspaper reporter, Horace Greeley, wrote a biting article for the eastern papers, but he didn't know the whole story. He was right in one respect. Our Indians *did* behave like savages—how else would we behave?" Jordie winked at Jarrett and ruffled Jerusha's hair.

She giggled at his joke.

"Captain Drew found it impossible to keep our Indians at the front line, so they were of no value in the battle. The tribes used their bows and arrows rather than the ancient muskets issued to them. It was my job to stop them from divesting the dead and injured Yanks of their scalps."

Jerusha shivered. "You mean the Osage and other tribes? You don't mean our Cherokees did that?"

"Yes, I mean the other tribes. Our group's a mixed bunch."

Jerusha hugged Jordie and kissed his chin. "Go on, tell us what happened."

Jordie made a wry face. "Our Indians had been promised

we would only fight on Indian soil. But now they expected us to fight in Arkansas, with our own territory left open for invasion. So, our men were not inclined to fight."

Jerusha made a face. "Course not."

Jordie hoisted her into the air, then back against his chest in a bear hug. She buried her face in his neck. "Watie's men fought three-to-one and won the only skirmish of the battle. He's the darling of the Confederates. When we were forced to retreat, he and his men covered for us. That man knows how to fight, and his men will go into the jaws of death for him."

Jordie straightened and glanced around. "After that our troops were ordered back here. If the Union gets this far, we are to burn bridges and cut off their supplies." He shrugged. "We're back where we belong. Maybe the war will be over before the Yanks get here."

Jarrett hunched his shoulders. Since he'd been home, he'd postponed going into town to avoid the taunts of soldiers because he wore no uniform. He had no loyalty to the Southern cause. Nor, with Jordie fighting for the Confederacy, would he join the Northern army.

Mom stood and turned toward the cabin. "Enough war talk. Let's go inside and have dessert. I've made your favorite, Jordan—steamed pudding with wild strawberries. I don't want to spend our precious evening together without giving you good memories to take back with you."

Jarrett doused the fire and roughhoused with Jordie on the way to the cabin.

Inside the cozy kitchen, he lit the two lanterns hanging above the kitchen table and they all sat down. He took the cup of hot chocolate Mom handed him.

Jerusha announced, "I have a secret to share."

While Mom clattered dishes at the dry sink serving dessert, Jerusha squirmed onto Jordan's lap, twisted to make certain she had his attention, and held her hand over his mouth. "No more war talk." Jerusha's green eyes widened, and her young voice rose. "You'll never guess what's wrong with Jarrett!"

Jarrett grabbed for Jerusha.

Jordie held him off with a long leg.

"You promised. You said you wouldn't tell. Give it over, Ru, be a good girl and hush your mouth." Jarrett lunged for Jerusha, but Jordie warded him off again.

"Guess, Jordie. One guess. Jarrett's done it before you!"

Jordie grinned.

Mom beamed.

Grandfather Worchester and Dad looked stern.

"Only a little clue, Baby, only a little clue. Let me solve this mystery."

Jerusha took a deep breath. "Daddy says Jarrett is making a fool of himself." She threw Jarrett a triumphant look.

"Mmmm. What's so unusual about that?" Jordie smirked. "You'll have to give me more to go on."

"Daddy gets mad when Jarrett moons around the house and sits at the kitchen table without hearing what's said. He's absent-minded and forgets to do his chores. When I can't find him, I look in the barn or in his bedroom, and there he is daydreaming." Jerusha threw her hands up with a dramatic flourish.

Jarrett's face burned. "Forget it, Jerusha. Leave off, will you?"

"So little brother's daydreaming." Jordan grinned. "Not doing his chores, that's not much of a clue. Sounds like Jarrett. What else have you got for me, Baby?"

"Well, he stands in front of the mirror a lot."

Jarrett grunted.

She nodded so emphatically her curls shook. "Yes, you do. If you're not staring off into space, you're looking into the mirror or combing your hair." She tossed her curls. "Doesn't he, Mother?"

Jerusha unbuttoned and buttoned Jordie's uniform collar. "He even asked me once if I thought he was good-looking." Jerusha giggled.

Jarrett groaned. "I thought you were *my* friend. A friend doesn't tell—"

"I'm afraid I've solved your mystery, Baby." Jordie spoke in a mock-sorrowful voice. "My little brother can only be exhibiting the symptoms of undying love. Who's the unlucky lady?"

Jarrett snorted.

Mom plunked the pudding before Jordie. "You two stop teasing Jarrett. He's serious about this girl."

"Aw, Mother, how can he be serious, he's only twenty. He'll be in and out of love five more times before he's dry enough behind the ears to be real."

Jarrett jumped to his feet. "Please excuse me." He scooted from the table, almost upsetting his chair. He clattered across the room, out the front door, and slammed it behind him. He strode across the porch and sat on the wooden steps beneath an open window.

Silence followed his departure until he heard Jordie say, "I'm sorry. Guess I was having too much fun at Jer's expense. Is he serious about a girl?"

Mom explained about Delight, about his fight with Claremont, and his desire to marry Delight.

Jordan whistled. "Some pickle, getting interested in a Flint. Jarret's gone daft."

"I'm afraid there's little hope for their relationship. Although it is satisfying that Claremont and Jarrett have become friends. But Delight warns us her father will kill Jarrett if he gets the chance. With the war, Delight's father has gone off the deep end. The band of armed desperadoes that Flint keeps around his ranch for protection … any one of those men will murder Jarrett to gain recognition from Flint. Much as I like Delight, I wish Jarrett had never met her."

Jordie's voice sounded worried. "Dad, I think you should put a stop to Jarrett's thinking about this Flint girl. Those men around Flint have been implicated in the disappearance of several key Unionists. Jarrett's not safe. Those men are known murderers."

"Jarrett's been able to meet Delight a few times at the fort, always circumspectly, and in Claremont's company. They keep their meeting secret. I can't stop him, Jordan. Jarrett knows the danger."

CHAPTER 20

Next morning, with mockingbirds cheering them on their way, Jarrett, riding beside Jordie, started for Fort Gibson.

"Sorry I upset you last night, Jarrett. Sometimes you go off the deep end, but whatever you decide about the Flint girl, I'll back you."

"Thanks, Jordie—I know you will. I don't have an inkling how I'll handle Delight's father, but God willing, I'll find a solution. Glad you don't think I'm a complete idiot."

Jordie reached across Sampson's neck and poked Jarrett's shoulder. He grinned. "Not a *complete* idiot, but I still think you've lost your sense."

"Hey, that hurts!" Jarrett rose in his stirrups. "Race you to the main road!" He squeezed his heels into Sampson's side.

The horse bolted, leaving Jordan eating dust.

Jordie caught up with him at the main road. "So, what are your plans?"

"I'll canoe down the Arkansas, pick up the supplies and a team of horses and a wagon at Fort Smith, then drive back. I have a need list from our neighbors."

"With supplies so low, that'll be dangerous. A wagon

like you'll be driving, attended by a single armed man, will provide fair game for bushwhackers. Better have some protection."

"I hope to pick up an armed escort at Fort Smith."

"Sounds good. They should have someone available."

Jarrett's horse trotted side by side with Jordie's. Jarrett wanted to make the most of this time with Jordie. Who knew when they would be together next? So, they talked about the farm, their plans, and their hopes. Thankfully, Jordie made no more mention of Delight.

A breeze stirred leaves of newly foliaged trees. Vivid red, yellow, and blue wildflowers dotted the meadows. The war seemed far away as Jarrett related his adventures riding with the Pony Express. Jordie described the drudgery and demands of life inside Fort Gibson.

They crested a hillock, and the stockade surrounding Fort Gibson glistened in the sun. They halted their horses and dismounted.

"Jarrett, your job now is to stay home, get the crops in, and take care of the folks. Don't do anything foolish like enlisting. Take my word for it, there's no glory in war, and the folks need you. I know you hate farm work, but as soon as you get back from Fort Smith, break up that lower meadow and plant corn. Some of our neighbors don't have any men left at home to plant the crops, and we can share what we harvest. It's late to plant, but we can still put in a harvest if you get to the job immediately."

Jarrett nodded. He shook Jordie's hand, then gripped his brother in a bear hug.

Jordie swallowed, his eyes turned brighter blue, and his face twisted. "Take care, Jer. You're the best brother any man could ask for. Stay away from the Flint girl. I don't want you getting killed."

"Don't worry about me. You watch out for yourself and come back in one piece!"

Jordie wiped his fist across his eyes, mounted, kicked his horse into a trot, then galloped down the hill and inside Fort Gibson's open gate.

Jarrett mounted Sampson, turned his horse in the opposite direction, and trotted off.

When would he see Jordie again?

He forced his attention to this morning's errand.

He had to paddle down the Arkansas River to Fort Smith to pick up supplies. Flour, sugar, and coffee were running low in Tahlequah and Park Hill. Only a trickle of goods squeezed through the Union blockade from the east, and nothing sneaked through from the south.

The sun rode high in the sky, well past noon, by the time Jarrett located an available canoe, procured a grizzled old man armed with two rifles and a side gun, and stabled Sampson, arranging to have him taken care of for the duration of his trip.

The old man, who called himself Clem, wasn't who Jarrett had in mind for an armed guard, but he was the only male Jarrett found not wearing a gray uniform.

Jarrett and Clem pushed the canoe into the frothy Grand River. Standing on the muddy bank, Jarrett attached tufts of white eagle feathers to the canoe's prow.

"Don't count on them feathers to keep away bushwhackers or Injins. I'm trustin' my shootin' irons." The white-whiskered old man chortled.

Jarrett grunted.

The old fellow hitched his faded gray trousers up under his protruding belly and jumped into the prow with surprising agility.

Jarrett stepped into the stern. Yahola, those baggy trousers and the dirty gray shirt looked like part of a cast-off Confederate uniform. Where had Clem gotten them?

Jarrett slid Indian fashion to his knees, and gripped the sides of the unfamiliar canoe. He glanced back at land, then raised his paddle, and pushed off into the swift current.

"Water level's running high due to our spring rains. You familiar with the Grand?"

Jarrett shook his head, in no mood for chit-chat.

"Thought not. The Grand pushes a mighty strong current. We'll run some dandy rapids." Clem's uncut white hair blew like a tattered flag in the wind. "We'll navigate us some tricky turns before this river empties into the Arkansas. But, no worries, I've piloted this water many a time."

Jarrett put his back into paddling. "Glad one of us has."

The canoe, caught in the swift current, plunged toward white water boiling over rapids.

A shiver streaked down Jarrett's spine.

"When we want to turn left, paddle on the right side. Get ready for a sharp left!" The old fellow pointed to a bunch of roiling rapids. "Turn away!"

The roar of white water all but drowned out Clem's quavering bass voice.

Jarrett strained, digging his paddle deep into the river. Water spraying from the sunken rocks drenched him from hair to bare curled toes. He shook his head like a dog, clearing spay from his eyes as the dugout skimmed through water way too close to the rapids.

"Clem, you sure you know this river?" Jarrett called over the roar of rushing water.

The old man either chose not to answer or couldn't hear. Jarrett settled at the stern, paddling first on one side and then the other.

He gave himself up to the joy of the rushing river, paddling to negotiate turns and to avoid the rapids but often letting the canoe speed down the river with the current.

Soon the river widened to flow between tall bluffs. With the plop of the paddles dipping in the water, and the cicadas and birds calling from the shores, the tension in his shoulders unwound. He became one with nature, with the now-placid river, the birds, the sun, and God.

The dugout skimmed beneath beautiful overhanging bluffs, in deep, cool shadow sheltered from the heat. At some spots, the river narrowed, so a canopy of branches from the opposite shores met overhead. At other places, the river widened, the current slowed, and Jarrett put his back into paddling.

As they glided through the water with the paddles softly splashing, the birds chirping overhead, and on shore an occasional glimpse of deer or a small animal too swift to identify, contentment warmed his chest. If only Delight sat in the bow, her silver-blonde hair shining in the sun. She would turn her laughing face toward him, her eyes mischievous, her dimples flashing, her arms outstretched and … and … the canoe would flip, and they would plunge into the water together. He would rescue her … they would lie on the warm beach together … he closed his eyes.

"Yahola," he said aloud, "I haven't seen her alone since that first night at the dance. Claremont Flint makes a danged nuisance of himself.”

The sun slanted lower in the sky, shining reflections off the water into his eyes. His knees, bruised from the unaccustomed kneeling on the rough dugout bottom, ached. His back and shoulders throbbed, so he called to old Clem. “Let’s beach the canoe and take a swim!”

Clem nodded his white head and dipped his paddle harder on the right side.

Jarrett turned the canoe and grounded the boat on a sand bar.

Stretching cramped legs, he stepped onto the sand. Without removing his sweaty shirt and pants, he splashed in the clear water. Below, maybe seven feet, he clearly saw the sandy bottom of the Grand. An occasional small fish swam by.

Jarrett plunged beneath the water, letting the fresh coolness invigorate his tired muscles.

Clem walked the sand bar, splashing his feet in the water. Grudging satisfaction crossed his wrinkled face. “I don’t hanker to get anything but my feet wet. You splashed enough water on me with your paddling to keep me from drying out,” the old man complained in a peeved voice.

Jarrett laughed. He wouldn’t give in to the old man’s bad humor.

After a few minutes, Clem climbed aboard the canoe.

Jarrett floated to the sand bar, walked across the sand, shook himself, wrung the water from his clothes, then pushed the canoe off the sand, and climbed back aboard.

Soon the Grand narrowed sharply. Rocks jutted in the raging current. Swirling strongly, the current propelled the canoe downriver. Jarrett, bruised knees pressing on the rough bottom, manipulated the dugout away from the rocks.

Didn't work.

He battled to keep the canoe upright as it swept over the rocks. The current grew stronger. Jarrett paddled furiously, first on one side of the dugout and then on the other, running the rapids. Water sprayed them, filling the bottom of the canoe. He barely negotiated one level of rapids when they faced another.

Jarrett grinned. "Exhilarating."

"You keepin' one eye out for bushwhackers? If they're out there, we're sittin' ducks."

"No time!" Jarrett panted, working hard to keep the dugout from catastrophe and the two of them from breaking themselves on rocks.

The canoe jolted on a rock. The right side scraped against another boulder and threatened to overturn.

Jarrett backpaddled with all his strength.

Out of control, the dugout turned and wallowed sideways. They sped backwards, leaning far to the left side. Scraping, sliding, and jolting, with the stern dipping under water and Jarrett half submerged, they flew back side first down the rapids.

A rock crashed into Jarrett's shoulder, numbing his arm. Another smashed his hand. He lost his paddle.

Then they were through, but water dragged the canoe into a vortex, whirling them around and around.

In the bow, Clem looked white-faced. "You sure made a mess of that. I coulda been kilt. What did ya think you was doin'?"

"Sorry, the current was too strong. You all right?"

Clem shouted above the splashing noise. "No thanks to

you. Here, grab my paddle since you was so stupid you let loose of yours. You got to get us out of this here whirlpool or we're stuck here. Dig in on the right side, and we'll try for that deep water on your left. Lost your paddle—I cain't believe it!"

Jarrett fought the whirlpool, his arms heavy with fatigue, until suddenly, they broke free to drift in deeper water. He relaxed, catching his breath, and relieving his strained muscles.

Clem growled, "What you waiting for? Let's get goin'. We only got three more hours till dark."

Jarrett sighed, lifted his paddle, dipped the blade into deep water, and the canoe spun back into the current.

They flew over more rapids, until the river widened and deepened. Jarrett's sagging arms could no longer stave off destruction.

They approached the junction with the Arkansas. A long sandbar stuck out from shore. Late afternoon sun glinted on the smooth sand.

Jarrett didn't bother telling Clem. He headed for the bar.

When the boat bumped on the sand, he slipped out into the chilly water.

The water, placid and deep, relaxed his cramped muscles. Curious fish swam by to gaze at him. He floated, feeling rejuvenated and ravenous. He dived into water over ten feet deep but so clear he saw the sandy bottom.

Maybe he and old Clem could catch a fish and have dinner over a fire on the sand bar. His mouth watered. He hadn't eaten since before sunrise. He swam up until his head broke the water's surface.

With the sun almost three quarters down in the west,

shadows lengthened on this side of shore. Must be somewhere near six-thirty. Time to eat.

Clem must have had the same idea because he stood knee deep in the water, with a bandanna spread out, attempting to snare a fish.

Jarrett swam over to help.

A voice hollered from shore, "Hold it right there. Don't move a muscle or you're dead!"

Jarrett's leg muscle cramped. Grabbing his stricken leg, he sank underwater. The hours kneeling in the canoe and the chilly water caught up to him, and his other leg cramped. Both legs fiercely contracted. He tried to massage them, but his wet clothing pulled him down.

He plummeted deeper into the clear water. Fighting to the surface, he gulped half a breath of air before the painful knotting forced him under again. His back scraped the sandy bottom. He lunged for the surface, bubbles frothing the clear water, his arms and legs churning. Hampered by the painful contractions and his wet clothing, the surface seemed far away. The sun shone above him, its rays slanting down through the water, tantalizing him with a promise of oxygen. He broke the surface and drank in the sweet air.

A strong arm gripped him around the neck, shutting off his air. Someone towed him toward shore. But he couldn't breathe, and agonizing pain cramped his legs. He tore at the arm strangling his throat.

A hard fist connected with his chin.

Darkness closed in.

Chapter 21

Next Jarrett knew, he was sprawled on the hot sand, coughing and choking, fighting for breath.

With easier breathing came return of sensation. He moved his jaw, feeling sharp pain. "What's going on?"

He opened his eyes. Jarrett lay splayed on the sand, struggling for breath. Where was Old Clem? The sandbar crawled with Union soldiers. Where had they—?

A giant crouched on his knees, gazing at Jarrett. The man extended a large hand and rested the heavy palm on Jarrett's heaving shoulder.

"Glad to see you're breathing." The giant spoke with a slight lisp.

Jarrett fingered his jaw. "I didn't need help. I could have made my way to shore. You almost smothered me." He sat up.

"Sure, you could have, son, sure you could have," the giant's tone was soothing. "And I just gave you a little tap."

Jarrett checked his teeth with his tongue. All still imbedded. He worked his jaw. Still attached. *Who is this guy?*

The giant stood. His long hair, plastered with water, glinted fiery red in a shaft of sunlight. His wet blue uniform sagged on his huge frame. Too short at cuffs and ankles, the ill-fitting clothing made him appear larger. He towered over six feet four and had massive shoulders. His freckled face, rugged features and square jaw, appeared friendly. A red handlebar mustache looked incongruous beneath his nose.

"Name's Rusty. Rusty Nolan. You got three hundred bucks on you?"

Jarrett's head felt muddled. "What?"

"Three hundred bucks. You got three hundred bucks on you?"

Three hundred dollars? Does the fool want to be paid for almost killing me? Jarrett gazed up at a circle of armed soldiers peering down at him. What was going on?

The men carried their rifles carelessly, but each was armed. Jarrett glanced inside the dugout. His own rifle and Colt were gone. So were Clem's two rifles.

"Where's Clem?" He sounded like he spoke from the bottom of a well. He rubbed his jaw. Talking hurt.

"The old man's Captain Good's prisoner. Wears Rebel trousers, so he's seen the last of this war." Rusty shook his head, spraying water in an arch.

Jarrett swallowed.

Rusty hunched beside Jarrett on the sand. "Since you ain't in uniform, you got to be a civilian. If you was a spy, you'd of been more careful. Never let us get the drop on you like you did. I figure you must be on your way to Fort Smith to get provisions, and you had that old man along to ride shotgun, or vice versa. Right?" His voice sounded friendly—confidential.

"That's right. Why take old Clem prisoner? He was going with me to get food for the folks at home." Yahola, he'd gotten the old man captured.

"Don't worry about him. Won't be any chance of his being killed in battle. He's better off where he's headed. How about you, got three hundred bucks?"

Moving slow, Jarrett sat up, ran his fingers through his dripping hair, massaged his sore calf muscles, and stalled. What was Rusty up to?

He estimated at least fifty or sixty soldiers stood on the sandbar. Some were Choctaw and Chickasaw Indians who jingled with every movement. Tiny bells and rattles decorated their arms and ankles. Their orange and green painted faces looked unfriendly. They wore buckskin hunting shirts and leggings, and they carried obsolete rifles, Indian knives, and tomahawks.

An impatient voice called, "Hurry up, Rusty. Captain Good said shake a leg. We only got two, three more days to meet up with Major Phillips."

"No, I don't have three hundred dollars." Jarrett massaged his jaw. The hundred bucks clumped in his drenched pocket didn't belong to him.

"Tough luck, son. Stand up." Rusty held out a hand.

Jarrett ignored the hand and struggled up. What now? His head whirled and his stomach gurgled, but his cramps were gone.

"If you had three hundred bucks, you could pay for your release. Captain's looking for conscripts. Looks like you're a prime target. As you probably don't know, we have authority from the federal government to conscript any male not enlisted."

Jarrett's chin dropped, shooting immediate pain into his jaw. "Wrong! I'm Cherokee." Well, a thirty-second-part

Cherokee. "I don't live in a state, my home's in Indian Territory."

Rusty's hazel eyes surveyed Jarrett like a panther his prey. "That's bad. I'll have to take you prisoner then. Indian Territory's Confederate." He leveled his Colt at Jarrett, then slowly lowered the big weapon. "Now take these Choctaws and Chickasaws. Yes, even some Cherokee and other tribes have joined the Union. And Major Phillips is coming down from Kansas with the First and Second Indian Regiments of Opotheleyhola. Who is to say you're not another Indian who's changed sides? Just where do your sympathies lie, son?"

"Don't call me son. I'm as old as you are." Jarrett frowned. "And I don't know. I've been asking myself that question for over a year now, and I'm no closer to an answer." Jarrett turned his back on the red-haired giant.

His sudden motion spurred the soldiers into a burst of movement. The rattle of rifles raised and pointed in his direction forced him to turn again and face Rusty.

Jordie had said he wished he'd deserted and taken sides with Opotheyahola. Would his situation improve if he joined the Union, or should he become a Union prisoner? He'd heard tales of men dying in prison camps. Didn't leave him much choice.

"I've no use for the Confederacy."

"What's the problem then?"

"I don't believe in killing! I couldn't kill a man," Jarrett blurted.

Rusty grinned, but his hazel eyes bored into Jarrett. "Still no problem, son. You're an Indian, even if you don't look like no Indian I ever saw."

"He's one of them blue-eyed Cherokees," a voice called.

Rusty flicked a hand as if swatting a fly. "Captain Good said he wanted me to find him another scout. He trusts my judgment." Rusty stood to his full height. "You can scout, can't you? You know the area around Fort Gibson?"

Jarrett stared. These soldiers were headed for Fort Gibson. A knot gripped his stomach. Bile gurgled up into his throat. "That's my home territory. I'm from Tahlequah."

Rusty's grin grew so big, his eyes squinted. "Raise your right hand."

Jarrett looked up at the giant, then stared into the cold eyes of the surrounding soldiers.

"Make up your mind, kid. This is the best chance you'll ever get in your life. Better grab it," a hard voice urged. The soldier who spoke wore sergeant's insignia on his sleeve and a sour expression on his face. "Life ain't got many good chances. You'd best grab this one. I've seen some of them Rebel prisoners, and they're a sorry looking bunch." The soldier whistled through a gap in his front teeth. "Yep, you best join up with us. We're cavalry."

Still Jarrett hesitated.

"You wouldn't have to kill. Just scout. And takes messages," Rusty urged. "Come on, raise your right hand."

Jarrett slowly raised his right hand. And in less than a minute, he was duly sworn in as a soldier of the Federal Army of the United States of America.

Rusty smiled, his freckles giving him a boyish look. "Cheer up, son. You'll be earning five bucks a month, plus your beans."

Jarrett gave Rusty a stony look. "I want my rifle and Colt."

Rusty nodded to two of the soldiers. "No man should be without defense. Let's go!" Rusty called.

The men slapped the weapons into Jarrett's hands.

The soldiers clambered over the sand bar and into the dense woods. Jarrett glanced back at the empty canoe beached on the deserted sandbar, then followed Rusty's long footprints in the sand.

Once inside the woods, Jarrett discovered an entire division secreted from the river's view.

"Follow me." Rusty led the way to the middle of a large camp and stopped at a larger tent with a wooden floor. A soldier slouched in a camp chair behind a make-shift desk shuffling papers.

Rusty saluted. "Cap'n Good, sir, this here's your new scout."

The spare man, around fifty, raised a strong, weathered face beneath iron-gray hair. A gray handlebar mustache bristled under a sharp jutting nose. His eyes, black as any Indian's, looked as though they belonged to a younger man. An air of authority set him apart. If ever a man were a leader, Captain Good looked to be that man.

Good's piercing eyes probed Jarrett. "Fine." He turned his large head. Quartermaster!" Good's tenor voice echoed among the trees.

"Yes, sir." A beefy middle-aged man, his bald head shining in the twilight, strode toward Good and saluted.

"Issue this new conscript the proper uniform and horse."

The Quartermaster saluted and headed toward some wagons.

Jarrett turned to follow.

"One minute, Private." Captain Good's stern voice

stopped Jarrett. "My name is Captain Jubal Good. I was duly elected captain by the men of the Tenth Kansas. From now on, when you approach your captain, you will salute and maintain proper respect."

Jarrett hesitated a long ten seconds, then he executed a fumbling imitation of the salutes he had just witnessed. "Yes, sir, Captain Good."

"What's your name?"

"Ross, sir. Jarrett Ross."

"See to it that Ross is inscribed on the roll, Rusty." Good dropped his head and studied the papers on his desk.

Jarrett pulled in a deep, uneven breath. He was in the Union Army. How had he let himself get into this mess?

How would he explain this new prison to Delight? Who would get supplies to his family? Put in the crops? Would he have to face Jordie in battle?

CHAPTER 22

Jarrett rustled through the dry grass in the direction Captain Good pointed.

A beefy form in front of a Conestoga wagon to which eight mules were hitched beckoned. "Name's Hadley. Get your tail over here."

"Good to meet you."

The bald soldier slipped carrots to his mules, rubbed their necks, and spoke into their flapping ears. "Beulah, you old she-devil. Don't you try to snitch that carrot. That's for Jocko. Now you had yours. Be a good girl."

Stamping their hooves and switching their tails, the mules' large, brown eyes followed Hadley's ponderous progress climbing up into the wagon.

Jarrett ambled over. Somehow, he had to get word to his family that he'd been forced to enlist. Mother would be upset.

Grumbling came from inside the Conestoga where the quartermaster rummaged.

Jarrett shifted from one foot to another until the man poked his chubby face through the canvas opening and tossed down some white cotton material.

Jarrett held the item at arm's length. "What are these?"

Hadley's laugh rumbled out. "That's a new article of clothing the army wants every man to wear. A bother if you ask me. But the army don't ask me, they tell me. Them're drawers. You wear 'em under your trousers."

Jarrett frowned. "Huh. Learn something new every day."

Quartermaster Hadley tossed a pair of blue woolen trousers with a scarlet stripe down the side. They landed on Jarrett's head. A pair of bright spurs, a saber, and a small flat cap with crossed sabers above the bill followed. Knee-high boots tumbled to the ground at Jarrett's feet, followed by a rubber blanket, a canteen, a haversack of rations, rounds of ammunition, and a bayonet belt.

Jarrett bent and tugged on his boots. A dark-blue woolen coat landed on his back. He fumbled with nine buttons on each breast. Others shone, one on each side of the collar, four along the flaps, and two on the hips. He brushed the epaulet strap on each shoulder.

"This uniform isn't designed for June heat here in Indian Territory." His skin broke out in prickly heat.

"All year uniform," came the terse reply.

Jarrett's neck dripped as he slipped on the leather stock. "Stiff as a dog collar."

"Makes you hold your head high."

"Umph." Jarrett scratched. The wool jacket grew damp with his perspiration. He swiped a palm across his clammy brow and ran his finger around the leather collar.

The hoarse resonance of a steam whistle shrieked.

Hadley stretched his head to gaze toward the river. "Right on time. Steamboat's a comin'. Chugging up the Arkansas from Fort Smith."

Her signal gun boomed.

Shivers of anticipation swirled through Jarrett.

Excitement swept the division.

"Mount up, men," Captain Good ordered.

Before Jarrett could move, mounted men streamed through the trees toward the steamboat.

The whistle sounded again.

"She's landed!" Hadley chortled.

Jarrett took a few steps toward the river. Obviously, the soldiers had been waiting for the steamboat. He glanced back at Hadley. "Okay if I head over?"

The man scowled, then grumbled, "Come along. You can ride the supply wagon until you get your horse."

Jarrett clambered aboard and plopped down on the wooden plank seat.

"Ho, Beulah, Ho, Jocko. Let's go!" Hadley guided the mules toward the river landing.

Breaking through the trees, swaying from side to side in the lumbering wagon, Jarrett caught his first view of a steamboat. He whistled.

Rising three stories above water, she glistened white against the blue river and the green trees. Her bell jangled. Gray smoke puffed from her chimneys. Scores of windows punctuated her white planking.

A sailor on board threw a line to a soldier waiting on a shelving rock. Another threw a plank from the ship to the rock. Sailors scrambled ashore, carrying baggage and cargo.

Someone from the ship tossed down a bundle of newspapers. A swarm of cheering Union soldiers surrounded the papers.

Union officers strolled down the gangplank.

"They hail from West Point. Going to confer with

Colonel Weer." A grin cracked Quartermaster Hadley's wrinkled, sunburned face. "Ain't she somethin', tho? Ain't she just somethin'?"

"She is that!"

Two sailors carried a bulky mail bag down the gangplank. Eager, uniformed men pounced on the bag. Deck hands unloaded boxes and crates.

"Ross, Captain wants you!"

"Me?" *What did I do wrong?* Jarrett vaulted from the supply wagon seat.

The soldier dropped a heavy barrel into the back of the Conestoga, making the wagon bounce.

High above Jarrett's head, the words *The Prairie Bird,* painted in bright blue letters across the upper deck contrasted with the alabaster of her gleaming sides. He found Captain Good standing beside the boarding plank. Should he salute?

"Come aboard with me, Ross. Stick close."

"Yes, sir!" Jarrett followed Good up the long plank, sidestepped soldiers working their way down the gangplank, toting boxes on their shoulders, and stepped off on the undulating deck.

The Prairie Bird's captain walked up. "Captain Hammerlock here. Be happy to give you a tour of my ship, Captain Good."

The boat rocked pleasantly beneath their feet as Jarrett followed the two captains across the deck and down a narrow staircase into the interior.

A steward invited them to inspect a spotless galley where perspiration-soaked men toiled over a cook stove.

Jarrett's stomach rumbled, reminding him he hadn't eaten since dawn. His mouth watered as he passed trays of fried chicken and mounds of mashed potatoes. The scent of food followed them as they walked into a large room.

"This is for poor passengers to sleep on the floor."

Captain Good nodded.

Jarrett trailed after the two captains as they clattered up a flight of wooden steps to the middle deck. "This is the promenade."

Jarrett wanted to linger, but his captain hurried Captain Hammerlock on.

"The gents and ladies' staterooms."

Jarrett stuck his head in and glanced around. A small room furnished with a washstand, blue-patterned wash bowl and pitcher, a mirror, a chamber pot, and two narrow berths, one above the other. The staterooms were hot and dark. A single candle could have illuminated them, but each had an elaborate gas light attached to the wall.

They trooped up an outside staircase onto the top deck. Captain Good strode to the rail.

Jarrett followed. The trees and riverbanks far below looked a verdant mass in the twilight. A strip of river rippled between the shore and the boat.

The Prairie Bird's Captain Hammerlock said, "I've things to look after. Nice to meet you, Captain Good."

"And you, sir." Good nodded.

The master of the ship strode off and descended the stairs.

Jarrett swallowed. He and Captain Good stood alone, facing one another.

"Ross, I brought you aboard to take your measure. I must have absolute confidence in my scouts. I need to know your capabilities. Rusty took a shine to you." Good's voice was stern. His intense black eyes ranged over Jarrett.

"Yes, sir." Jarrett met his gaze.

"Rusty's been on the lookout for my new scout for several months now. He's not an easy man to please." Good smoothed his gray mustache, his weathered face so tense, his nose jutted like the prow of a ship. "Tell me about yourself."

"Sir, I rode for the Pony Express until the telegraph was completed."

Good grunted, nodded, and leaned back against the railing.

Sweat trickled between Jarrett's shoulders, and down his back. His skin itched under the wool uniform. He ran a finger beneath the high leather collar. Good's unwavering gaze made him stiffen his back. "My father's the doctor at Tahlequah. We have a farm a few miles from town, and …"

"Yes, go on," Good's gaze knifed into Jarrett.

"My older brother's a Confederate soldier with Captain Drew's First Regiment Cherokee Mounted Rifles."

Captain Jubal Good's weathered face softened. He turned and stared across the dark river. A muscle quivered along the strong line of his jaw. Finally, he slapped a hand against the railing and faced Jarrett. "Because of what you've said, and because I trust Rusty's judgment, I'll lay my plans on the line for you."

Jarrett swallowed. Oh man, did he owe Rusty.

"We are on our way to join forces with Colonel Weer's four companies of North Kansas Parrot Guns and the First and Second Indian Regiments under Major Phillips. Our orders are to take Tahlequah and headquarter inside Fort Gibson."

"What!" Jarrett jerked forward.

Captain Good held up a hand, palm outward. "Just listen. We have secret information that Captain Drew and his regiment are ready to join forces with us."

Jarrett's stomach unknotted. His anger drained, leaving his legs weak.

"You and your brother will soon be fighting on the same side." Good clapped a hand on Jarrett's shoulder.

"Our enemy is General Stand Watie and his guerrillas. Is that a problem for you?"

Jarrett gazed into the water. "No, sir. Same old battle lines. The Watie Treaty Party against the Ross government." Jarrett's shoulders slumped. What chance did he and Delight have to be together?

"Explain," Good ordered.

Jarrett rubbed the back of his neck. He glanced at the sailors loading on a supply of coal. Could an outsider understand? "Back in '38 the Watie Treaty Party illegally signed away our Cherokee homeland to the Georgia government. That action tore our nation apart. Because of the treaty, the US government herded our people over the *'Trail of Tears'* to Indian Territory. My father lost his father, mother, and baby sister as well as his plantation, his slaves, his horses—everything."

"I see," Captain Good nodded.

Jarrett passed a hand through his damp hair. "All these years my great-uncle, Chief Ross, has tried to keep our nation unified. Stand Watie and his cronies have worked to split the Cherokees and be recognized as chief of those who hold the same view as he. Now this war has given him his best opportunity."

"I fail to understand why you're not pleased about

fighting this renegade if he is the party causing the disunity of your people."

Jarrett straightened. "Sir, the matter's more complex. Watie and his group have some truth on their side, too. These men are Cherokee too. They are people I've known all my life. I believe we can settle our problems without bloodshed. And I … I, well that is, uhh … about ten months ago I met someone. And, well."

"Go on."

"Sir, there are bitter feelings on both sides, but some of us are friends, and given time, I think we could overcome the past."

"Friends?"

Jarrett swiped the back of his hand across his wet forehead.

"Hmm. So, a girl must be involved. But you look young, certainly you don't take a razor to your face more than once a week."

Jarrett straightened. "I'm older than I look, sir."

Good smiled. "Ah, my mind flows unbidden to my own youth." He extended his hand. "Welcome, Ghost Rider. You are Ghost Rider, aren't you? Everyone's heard of the Pony Express rider from Indian Territory who saved several men from the Paiutes."

Jarrett grunted. "Sir, I'd rather you not mention that to anyone. I just did my job like everyone else."

"As you wish, Ross. Rusty will show you the ropes. He's senior scout. If you do as well as he, you'll earn my gratitude … and my trust."

"I'll do my best."

Quartermaster Hadley met them as he followed Captain

Good down the *Bird's* gangplank. Hadley led a black gelding, whose arched neck, raised tail, and proud step revealed Arabian blood.

Jarrett couldn't keep a grin off his face. *Love that horse.*

"I reckon you better change your forage cap for this here dress hat." Hadley handed Jarrett a tall, blue hat with a red plume, much like the Fort Gibson band wore.

Jarrett stuffed the forage cap into a pocket, placed the ornate plumed parade hat on his head, and mumbled, "Hope we don't wear this show-off hat very often."

He stroked his new mount and spoke in a low, caressing tone. "Hello, boy. Aren't you a beauty? We'll be great buddies, you and me. I like your spirit."

The gelding lifted his hooves high and danced. A pang shot through Jarrett's heart. What would happen to Sampson, still stabled at Fort Gibson?

Gathering the reins, Jarrett vaulted aboard as though the black horse were an express pony on the run.

Whistles and catcalls sounded from the lines of watching cavalry riders.

Jarrett ducked his head. His face heated. He lifted a hand and straightened the plumed hat, which had tilted over his right ear. He found his hands on the reins got results at the slightest pressure. This horse was pure joy. "Everything you do is right, boy. The only man I ever heard of who did almost everything right was Daniel. That's your name, boy— Daniel. Ho, Daniel let's go."

As if they had waited for him, the Tenth Kansas mounted. Captain Good's cavalry unit all sat astride black, high-stepping horses. Each man wore a handlebar mustache and long hair. They looked like a crack company of dragoons. Were cavalry dragoons the only army personnel permitted to wear long hair and mustaches? He fingered his upper lip. Would he be able to grow one of those handlebars?

"Move out!" sang Captain Good. He motioned for Jarrett to ride beside him to review the troops as they trotted past in formation.

The men rode past. Their black, matching horses stepped high, two abreast. Blue-coated men sat tall in their saddles, their plumed hats making them look taller. The men's long hair and handlebar mustaches gave them a look of jaunty arrogance. Their bearing proclaimed they considered themselves the best cavalry unit in the Federal Army.

The oaken butt of a carbine protruded from each rider's saddle. Polished spurs and sabers rattled and sent lightning reflections through the twilight. The men, uniforms, and horses gave the troops an aura of invincibility.

A dose of *esprit de corps* doused his stomach. If he had to be in the army, this was the best place for him. And he wasn't expected to kill. So that had to be exactly why Captain Good ordered him to review the troops. *Thank you, Father God for showing me my place in this war. I know you'll provide for my family.*

Jarrett fingered his hairless upper lip. Soon Jordie and he would be fighting on the same side.

He took a deep breath, sat tall in his saddle, straightened his hat, and swung his horse smartly beside his captain. They skirted the trotting soldiers and took places in front of the line.

Rusty rode behind Captain Good—so tall he dwarfed the large black horse he rode. Jarrett rode in the vacant spot beside Rusty.

Soon Jordie would be part of the Union Army.
Yet, Delight was still on the other side.

CHAPTER 23

July 1862

Jarrett and the Tenth Kansas Regiment rendezvoused with Colonel William Weer's forces.

A long procession of wagons crammed with Indian women, children, and old men, followed Weer's Union troops. The refugees were Opotheleyahola's Creeks and Seminoles who planned to return to their homeland after the troops drove the Rebels out.

~

That afternoon Jarrett stood in front of his own small tent.

A soldier galloped up. "Orders for you." He rode off.

Jarrett patted Daniel's neck and headed him through camp toward Captain Good's tent. He found Captain Good sitting at a makeshift desk in front of his tent. He dismounted and saluted.

Captain Good returned the salute, then lit a home-made cigarette and gazed at Jarrett, his sharp, black eyes unblinking. "Captain Drew and Watie's Confederate Indians are camped at Locust Grove. Watie's horsemen scout up and down the dirt roads in the vicinity of Cowskin Prairie. Head to Locust Grove and scout out the country between the Arkansas border and the Military Road. I need to know how many men ride with Watie, and what their plans are."

"Yes, sir."

Good motioned to his lieutenants to huddle close over some maps spread out on his makeshift desk. He glanced over his shoulder. "Get some equipment from Hadley."

"Yes, sir!" Jarrett mounted Daniel, rode back to his tent, stooped, and entered. His mouth went dry as he pulled off his riding boots, and his hands shook as he stripped off the hot uniform and rubbed his back against a tent pole to ease his prickly heat. He left his drawers lying on the ground.

The freedom of his buckskins lightened his heart, but the responsibility of his scouting assignment had the morning's hotcakes knotting his stomach. He stepped into his moccasins, then strode to find Hadley.

The squat quartermaster handed him a horseshoe kit. "Attach this to your belt. At times on a scout, you ride two hundred miles, often behind enemy lines, before returning to camp. If your horse throws a shoe, you'll be staring death in the face. That's why you need this."

Jarrett's stomach dropped. He flipped open the penknife Hadley handed him and examined the bore.

"To cut holes in your horse's hoof."

Jarrett slipped the penknife closed and checked the pliers.

"Use them to wire a loose shoe onto your horse until you make it back to camp."

"Thanks." Jarrett eyed the long prong to pick out stones. The terrain would be rocky, with hills and gorges, and hidden streams. So many places Daniel could throw a shoe.

Jarrett straightened. Emptiness replaced the knot in his stomach. If he were caught out of uniform, and the Rebs discovered who he was, they had authority to shoot him as a spy.

Daniel's familiar presence beneath the saddle steadied him. He swallowed, glanced around the security of camp, and set his jaw.

Off-duty soldiers clustered in groups and sang or joked. They took little notice of him as he rode past. The scent of coffee, fresh and strong, reminded him he would miss chow time. Away from camp, he urged Daniel into a trot through a growth of trees toward Locust Grove.

He sat forward in his saddle, so the sensitive horse broke into a gallop. Jarrett held him back and forced himself to relax and loosen his tense leg muscles. His hand trembled on the reins, causing Daniel to prance like a skittish colt.

Jarrett wiped wet palms against his buckskins and headed south with the low-slanting sun beating hot on his right side. The further south he rode, the more often he patted the Colt holstered at his side.

His golden buckskin shirt clung to his shoulders, and Daniel's shiny black hide foamed around his saddle. The western prairie, carpeted with tiny white flowers under a blasting sun, moved out to greet him. He felt naked, exposed to all lookers as a scout of the Union Army, as if the words were blazed on his forehead.

As he rode, he studied the landscape for prints of recent riders, searched for any movement in the wildlife. Nothing.

He was reasonably sure Watie and his band hadn't been in this vicinity. As the sun sloped to the western horizon, he sniffed the air for tobacco smoke or odor from campfires. Only the musky smell from his own perspiring body filled his nostrils.

Often, he dismounted to rest and water Daniel, walking the spirited animal so, if trouble came, the horse would have enough energy to make a mad dash getaway.

With darkness, hordes of mosquitoes swarmed him. Nerves jittery, he tethered Daniel in a clump of trees near a shallow stream and ate a cold meal of hardtack washed down with water. While Daniel cropped grass, Jarrett kicked off his moccasins and dangled his feet in the river,

"We'll sit tight until midnight and then we'll sneak as close as we can to Locust Grove and see what's happening," Jarrett whispered to Daniel.

Daniel switched his black tail at the large, green-headed flies that clustered on his smooth hide.

The heat was an enormous, humid hand wrapped around him. Fully clothed, he slipped into the stream, and the cool water washed away the heat, the flies, and the mosquitoes. He stretched flat on the rocky stream bed with only his nose above water.

Later, leaning against a tree, his feet dangling in the cool stream, he mentally sketched the majestic steamboat, *Prairie Bird.* He would assemble the carving by attaching three pieces of wood with notches and pins. This promised to be one of his most challenging carvings.

"Pesky mosquitoes." He brushed a biting female from his neck, kicked another, bloated with his blood, from his ankle, and crushed a third on his thigh.

I need a place to conceal intelligence about Rebel positions and numbers. I'll carve a hollow interior inside the Prairie Bird where Rebs won't think to search for stolen information that will get me shot.

Jarrett shrugged off the fact he would have to be captured in order for Rebels to rummage through his things. He would face that horror if the time came.

He stood and stretched. Midnight must be near. He crept from his hiding place.

Walking south, he led Daniel. He stayed close to the Military Road leading to Locust Grove but near the line of trees along the creek paralleling the road.

The moon lit the fields too well to give him any sense of security. Noticing his hands gleamed in the moonlight, he plastered them and his face with a coat of mud. He was still kneeling by the stream when a band of men thundered down the dirt road.

The horsemen rode recklessly, apparently expecting no enemy presence in the vicinity.

The hair on the back of his neck stood on end as he knelt among the thin line of trees separating him from the riders. They had to be Watie's men. He counted forty.

Minutes passed. Finally, he rose. Leading Daniel through the trees, he continued in the direction the riders had gone.

Daniel snorted. The saddle creaked as the leather scrapped against a tree. Jarrett froze. Moving at last, he tied Daniel to a limb and tiptoed on moccasin-silent feet toward the Rebel camp.

He stole from tree to tree to a small hill. A breeze wafted the smell of campfires. His heart drummed into his throat.

Once atop the rise he stopped. Below, spread across the entire valley, the Confederates camped, their fires dotting the meadow like fireflies. Now the odor of smoke hung heavy on the still air.

Yahola, how many were there? He crawled closer, the tall grass parting as he edged forward, the earthy scent filling his nostrils. Tiny bugs scampered into his eyes and face and stuck into the mud coated there.

Had to get nearer.

Thank God, he wore moccasins rather than his new leather riding boots.

As he inched closer, above the concert of insects, the sound of men's voices grew clearer.

Suddenly, the insects grew silent.

Jarrett froze. He heard a dull thud. Oddly familiar. What was it? His mouth went dry. Holding his breath, he searched the darkness. That noise could only be the butt of a rifle being rested on the ground. The alert was too close. Yet he saw nothing.

But he smelled fresh coffee and bacon. His stomach rumbled.

From the other side of the tree behind which he hid, a voice sang out, "All's well!"

A cold chill stole over his body.

Periodically, other sentries echoed the first voice.

Jarrett held each muscle tense, afraid if he moved an inch he would be discovered. Could the sentry standing on the other side of the tree smell his fear … or hear his stomach churn?

Seconds passed into minutes. Insects took up their chorus again. The soldier cleared his throat and spit. He paced a few feet, then returned.

Jarrett held his hand over his mouth to muffle his breathing. If only he could still the loud beating of his heart. Why hadn't he thought about sentries? What kind of scout overlooked such an obvious fact of military life?

If I'm caught here with mud on my face, the Rebs won't even question me. I will face a firing squad.

CHAPTER 24

Minutes ticked by. Behind the scant protection of the tree, Jarrett froze into a statue. He prayed.

For two long, torturous hours, the sentry stood—only a few feet away. The guard shuffled his feet restlessly. At times, he shouldered his rifle, then rested the weapon butt on the ground. Now and then, he sighed. Coughing and spitting must have kept him awake. He did a lot of both.

Mosquitoes feasted on Jarrett. His legs cramped.

From the direction of camp, footsteps approached through the underbrush.

Jarrett unholstered his gun.

The sentry's voice sounded loud in Jarrett's ear. "Finally! What kept you? You should have been here five minutes ago."

"Ah, I had to have another cup of coffee to keep me awake. Quit your grousing. Anything going tonight?"

"Nope. Not a thing. Quiet as a graveyard. Ain't no Feds around from here to Kansas City. I'm fer hitting the hay." The sentry lumbered through the underbrush like a Saint Bernard puppy, leaving a trail of broken twigs and snapped branches.

Taking advantage of the noise, Jarrett backed out of hearing range.

For a long time, he sat on the ground, hidden by bushes, jacking up his nerve. Then he crawled flat on his stomach through scrub and small trees, alert for sentries.

He followed the creek down below the hill. Hundreds of cavalry and artillery horses stood corralled near the water. Hiding behind a hedge, he counted two hundred fifty large tents. Figuring four men to a tent worked out to a thousand soldiers.

His heart lightened. *We outnumber them two to one.*

Around a campfire near the corral, coffee boiled in a camp kettle. A gray-uniformed man poured liquid into a tin cup and sweetened the brew. Probably with brown sugar.

Jarrett swallowed. A cup of coffee would taste like heaven on earth.

Tin grated against tin as the soldier stirred his drink.

Most of the other soldiers slept inside their tents. The few men still squatting by the campfires wore the shirts and trousers of farmers, trappers, hunters, and a few even flaunted city clothes.

Legs cramped and bone-tired, Jarrett crawled back through the trees. At the top of the rise, he stood and stole from tree to tree until he found Daniel. He led his horse over a mile before he mounted, then walked Daniel another mile before urging him into a mile-devouring canter.

The sun was rising when he arrived at camp. He slid off Daniel and made his report to Captain Good.

Good immediately called for his officers.

Jarrett washed and changed back into his hot, wool uniform. He rustled up a bite of food at the mess wagon, wedged himself between two saddles, and leaned his back against a tree. Wolfing cold beans, he noticed Rusty leave the captain's tent.

The red-head's six-foot-four frame clad in buckskin hunting shirt and leggings ambled nearer.

Jarrett dropped his fork and shoved his plate to the ground. What the …?

Rusty lumbered over. "What's the matter son, something got your goat?" He towered above Jarrett, his tree-stump legs spread, hands on his hips, his voice loud enough to carry through camp.

Jarrett jumped to his feet to face Rusty. "You followed me! You spied on me. Didn't Captain Good think I could do the job? Or was it you? You thought you had to drag along and protect me! You … you had—"

"Slow down, son, slow down." Rusty laid a heavy hand on Jarrett's shoulder.

Jarrett sprang away. "Don't *son* me, you big grapeshot! You spied on me. Don't deny it. Because you dragged me in from the river doesn't give you the right to shadow me. Get this straight, you big ape, I can handle any trouble that comes my way. I don't need a guardian!" Jarrett balled his fists and aimed a hard right at the grinning giant.

With surprisingly quick moves for such a muscular man, Rusty grabbed Jarrett's arm, twisted it behind his back, and applied pressure.

Jarrett dropped to his knee.

"Now listen, hothead." Rusty tightened the force on Jarrett's arm.

Jarrett grunted.

"Ready to hear what I've got to say?"

Jarrett nodded.

Rusty released his arm.

Jarrett rose slowly, working his arm, and rubbing his shoulder.

"Think, son. Cap'n Good conscripts a new man, one with a brother serving in the Rebel army, and he's supposed to trust this untried scout?" Rusty raised a thick red brow. "Does Cap'n look like a fool? What reason does he have to believe you won't cross over to the enemy once you hightail it from camp? Maybe you decide to desert, trot back to Tah-lah-ker or whatever the name of that place is, you let the Rebs know we're comin', and they're sittin' there waitin' for us, all dug in and ready to fight."

Jarrett's face burned. "So, you followed me to see what I would do? And what would you have done if I *had* deserted? Shot me in the back?"

Rusty's mouth tightened. "I wouldn't have had to shoot you, you hotheaded dandy. Wouldn't a been nothin' to tie you up in a knot and fetch you to the Cap'n for whatever he wanted to do with you." A frown darkened Rusty's usually friendly expression. "Only reason I made you a scout's because I don't like to see young'uns clapped into prison!"

Jarrett's ears burned. "Yahola." He turned from Rusty's gaze.

Rusty jabbed. "You just about got yourself killed and me too, seeing as I couldn't leave you there to them Rebs."

The muscles along Jarrett's jaw clenched. He tensed.

Rusty goaded, "You want to fight?"

Let no one look down upon your youth, but give an example by your conduct, speech, love ... Rusty is not a believer. The words flashed to Jarrett's mind. He swallowed hard and forced himself to extend his hand toward Rusty. "Sorry. If my brain had been working, I would have figured out why you followed me. Let's forget it."

Beneath his red mustache, Rusty's mouth dropped open. His hazel eyes gazed at Jarret's extended hand long seconds before crunching his palm in an iron grip.

Jarrett winced.

"Okay, son," Rusty lisped, emphasizing *son*.

His mouth turned up as the mess cook approached him with a hot plate of beans, bacon, and a steaming cup of coffee. He settled in Jarrett's spot between the saddles, a grin spread across his freckled face. "Thanks, Jeb. I sure appreciate you rustling up this grub for me."

Jarrett scowled at the cook. "You didn't help me find something to eat." He turned on his heel and headed toward his tent.

Rusty bellowed, "Just a minute, son. I want to talk to you."

Jarrett grimaced and continued striding. Abruptly he spun and strode back to stand above the giant sprawled on the ground, enjoying his food.

"Don't stand there, you give me a crick in my neck lookin' up at you," Rusty's voice sounded friendly.

"I always get a crick in my neck when I have to look at you," Jarrett kept his voice neither friendly nor distant.

Rusty laughed. His belly shook. His hazel eyes crinkled his sunburned face, and his muscled frame rocked. Tears glistened in his eyes before he stopped. "Fair enough."

He laid his empty plate on the ground at Jarrett's feet. "I think it wise that I point out a few," Rusty emphasized the word *few*, "of the mistakes you made on this scout."

Jarrett crossed his arms over his chest, lips tight.

"Number one," Rusty bellowed loud enough to attract the attention of soldiers playing cards yards away. They looked up as they had when Rusty baited Jarrett, ready to fling their cards down at the first sign of a fight.

"You rode in too close to where the enemy camped." Rusty took a long swig of coffee and slammed the empty tin cup on the ground.

Jarrett's ears burned. He curled his hands into fists.

"Number two, you didn't make certain you knew where the sentries were *before* you approached camp."

The watching soldiers lowered their cards and stood. Soon, grinning soldiers surrounded Rusty and him.

"Number three, you didn't …"

"Hold it!" Jarrett glowered down at Rusty and spoke through clenched teeth. "I don't remember anyone telling me I had to take lessons from you."

Rusty jumped to his feet to tower above Jarrett. He balled his great hands and stuck his face close. "Son, somebody's got to teach you to scout. If you're going out with me, I don't want no tenderfoot getting me caught by Johnny Reb."

Blood rushed to Jarrett's head. "I'm not going out with you. I don't have to ride scout with a big blunderbuss. Likely your massive feet make sufficient noise to wake a deaf Reb."

Rusty grinned. "You don't think Cap'n Good would let a boy do a man's job, do you? Why, the only way you're going to support a mustache is to cut the hair off your horse's tail and glue that horsehair on your lip."

Jarrett glared. "I think Captain Good sent a man to do a man's job and got a man's report."

In the silence, green-headed flies buzzed, sounding loud.

A rough voice called, "Come on, Rusty, teach him a lesson!"

"Well son, looks like you're in for a thrashing. Go ahead, you get first crack!" Rusty lowered his fists.

"You're the one wants this fight. You take the first shot." Jarrett held his fists stiffly against his thighs.

Rusty flushed, wiped sweat from his brow, and glanced at the surrounding men.

"Go on, Rusty, he asked for it," one soldier urged.

"Curses!" Rusty roared. "Who's givin' who a lesson?" He spun, shouldered through the circle of sweating men and stomped toward Captain Good's tent.

Jarrett faced the soldiers circling him. "The fun's over." He turned toward his tent.

The bugler blowing *Assembly* startled them all.

They all ran for the corral. Within minutes, long rows of cavalrymen stood, reins in left hand, waiting. The bugler blew *Prepare to Mount.* Each man hoisted a foot into the stirrup. The bugler blew *Mount.* The sound of scores of reins slapping and tail ends hitting leather simultaneously was muted thunder.

Jarrett rode tight-lipped and silent beside Rusty.

All afternoon the cavalry rode through the blazing hot July day. Red dust settled like another coat on Jarrett's uniform. The tepid water in his canteen was soon empty. Grit coated his perspiring face.

The entire division was on the move.

The cavalry walked their horses so the infantry could keep up, giving no relief from the pesky flies clustering on Jarrett's neck and face. Flies delighted to bite the tender flesh just above his high leather collar. He slapped at insects, tried to cool his temper, thought about his mistakes, and dreamed of Delight.

CHAPTER 25

Jarrett threw a cramped leg over the saddle and dismounted. Tired enough to drop, he uncinched his saddle. He rubbed his stinging eyes. He'd been riding for thirty hours and missed a night of sleep.

So had Rusty.

"I'll set up the tent." Rusty unbridled his horse. "You look bushed."

"I'll handle my own work." Jarrett wiped Daniel with the saddle blanket.

Rusty shrugged wide shoulders. "Suit yourself."

He and Rusty didn't speak as they erected the tent, laid out bedrolls, and concocted a cold supper.

Dusk turned black with little abatement of the blasting heat but bringing fresh hordes of mosquitoes.

Jarrett plopped on the ground beside his saddle, removed his spurs and riding boots, and deposited them near his hat and saber.

Rusty dropped his clothes where he stood. "Grow them mosquitoes big as toads around here, don't they?"

"Umm." Jarrett rested his head against his saddle almost asleep, wiggling his bare feet besieged with mosquitoes.

Rusty's big arms flailed as he shooed the insects. "Huh,

you don't need no one to take care of you. Just about got yourself shot last night—that's all." He shook his big head. "What are you youngsters doing fighting a war? You ought to be home until you have yourselves a chance to grow up."

"Not so young," Jarrett murmured, working hard to keep his eyelids open.

Rusty rustled around putting the cold food on a tin plate. "Cap'n Good ordered me to get your goat whilst you was tired, so as to know how you handle yourself. Reckon we found out." He glanced at Jarrett. "Would you a hit me back if I'd given you a crack?"

"Yep."

"I told Cap'n you was in control the whole time." Rusty grinned. "Not bad for a kid."

"Not a kid. Be twenty-one soon." Jarrett closed his eyes.

The big hand reached over and shook his shoulder.

Jarrett blinked bleary eyes.

Rusty handed him his supper. "You awake or sleep eating?"

Jarrett's vision was unfocused, but he ate. When his fork dropped into his tin plate and his eyes closed, Rusty prodded him into the tent, covered his feet with the rubber blanket to keep off the bugs, and shut the flap.

~

A shadow jostled Jarrett. He rubbed sleep-clogged eyes. Through the open tent flap he saw it was still dark outside. Sun wouldn't be up for an hour or so, by the look of the lightening sky.

Thomas from the next tent squatted beside him and

whispered, "No bugle this morning. We got to surprise Drew and Watie's men." He backed out the tent flap, and his footsteps rustled as he moved to the next tent.

Jarrett reached across to shake Rusty. No easy task rousing the conked-out giant.

Rusty woke, muttering and grumbling, his morning voice as rusty as his hair. After he untangled himself from his bedroll and crawled out of the tent, Jarrett handed him a plate of hardtack and cold beans.

Rusty grunted and silently shoved food into his mouth.

"Rusty, uh look, I'm sorry about yesterday." Jarrett shifted his feet, then bent to fasten his spurs onto his boots. "I'm willing to forget, if you are."

Rusty cleared his throat, pushed a big hand through his unruly hair and blinked, his eyes puffy with sleep.

"Come on, men," Thomas whispered from the next tent. "Assembly's in ten minutes."

Jarrett pulled up the tent pegs, folded, then packed the heavy canvas with the other supplies in their saddlebags, while Rusty lumbered in the dark, groping for socks.

Jarrett saddled Daniel before Rusty had his saber buckled.

Rusty's gear lay scattered about the trampled clearing, so Jarrett saddled the other scout's great black horse.

Then Rusty, wild hair awry, walrus mustache bushy and speckled with beans, strode over, and whispered, "That's all right, son. I reckon I was riding you hard yesterday and had it coming." Rusty's wide grin lit his face.

A low-voiced command passed from group to group.

In the darkness, Jarrett joined the other silent men who rode toward the Confederate camp. Wrapped in a cocoon of thought, he fought his own demons as he faced combat for the first time.

As his mind struggled with what he was about to do, a vivid image filled his brain—two ruined bodies lying in pools of blood, lives cut violently short. He'd never be able to erase those pictures of his murdered friends. He set his mouth.

As darkness lightened, Rusty moved his horse so close his black belly touched Daniel's. He leaned across his saddle. "Don't be scared, son. We outnumber them, and we've got them by surprise. Won't none of us get hurt!" Rusty whispered.

"It's not us I'm thinking of." Jarrett twisted the reins until his knuckles throbbed. "My brother might be in that camp. Captain Good said they planned to join us. Do they have any idea we're coming?"

"Darned if I know. Cap'n don't tell me what he's goin' to do. But I know one thing, he don't lie."

The sun reached the horizon, glittered across the dew on the meadows, and brought flies.

Jarrett recognized the rise beyond the camp. The hair on the nape of his neck bristled.

The bugle sounded *Charge.*

Black horses instantly broke into a gallop. The infantry followed at a run, bayonets fixed on their rifles.

Each cavalry soldier—except for Jarrett—brandished his Colt six-shooter. *Thank you, God, I'm only a messenger.*

Shots exploded from three Rebel sentries. Men clad in underwear and others, half-dressed, crawled out of tents with guns drawn.

As Jarrett followed the riders, gunfire from the cavalry

riddled the tents, leaving men sprawled on the ground. On and on through lines of tents they rode. Their Colts empty, the cavalry grabbed carbines from their saddles.

Jarrett turned in the saddle to look behind them. He narrowed his eyes against the smoke, flattened tents, and answering gunfire.

At the river, the cavalry turned their horses and galloped back through the camp.

Jarrett followed Captain Good. Not an easy task.

Good galloped through the bivouac area shouting orders, encouraging men, shooting, and waving his saber. Smoke and noise, cries of men and horses, and burning canvas added to the confusion.

Jarrett's eardrums throbbed from the explosions, and sulfur filled his lungs. Daniel danced skittishly.

"Ross!" Captain Good shouted.

"Here, sir!"

Jarrett recognized Confederate Captain John Drew standing unarmed next to Captain Good's horse. Even in defeat, the dashing commander looked resolute and sure of himself. Surprise registered on his face as he recognized Jarrett.

Captain Goode yelled above the flash and roar of battle, "Ross, find Captain Russell and inform him Captain Drew has surrendered!"

Jarrett galloped Daniel through the smoke, crackling rifles, and ping of bullets, toward Captain Russell's infantry. As he rode, he bellowed news of Drew's surrender. Behind him, the sounds of gunfire ceased.

Jarrett found Captain Russell sequestered behind a clump of bullet-riddled trees, giving instructions to several sergeants.

Jarrett yelled, "The enemy has surrendered!"

Swinging down from Daniel, he grabbed Captain Russell's arm and screamed, "Stop!" Exploding shots drowned his voice.

The sergeant turned, striding back to the battle.

"Captain Russell, Captain Good said the Rebels have surrendered!"

The infantry captain's expression relaxed. His eyes gleamed amid his soot-blackened face. "Catch those sergeants and order them to cease fire!" Russell roared.

Vaulting onto Daniel, Jarrett rode into the midst of infantry fighting and soon felt like a toy soldier in a shooting gallery, an excellent target for the prone soldiers. He pressed on to relay the news of the surrender.

One after another, he caught each sergeant, and the clamor of battle diminished.

Daniel crashed over a clump of bushes. A hidden Rebel soldier got off a quick shot that knocked Jarrett's forage cap off and sent it spinning into the air.

Then silence. That was the last shot fired in the battle of Locust Grove. Jarrett slouched in the saddle. He hadn't touched his carbine or Colt.

After the smoke cleared, and the prisoners were given the opportunity to change sides, just as Union intelligence predicted, Captain Drew and his Indian Guard joined the Union forces. Sixty-four mule teams, plus a Confederate supply wagon train, also turned Union.

However, Stand Watie and his group of guerrillas escaped.

Jarrett fed and watered Daniel, then set out on foot to

search the tents for Jordan. His heart lifted. There he was safe and unharmed lounging among a group of Rebel soldiers near one of the Confederate supply wagons.

Jarrett yelled, "Ho, Jordie, thought I'd find you where there is food. Should have looked here in these wagons first. At least you got a good breakfast!"

Jordan jerked to his feet, spilling molasses down his half-buttoned gray blouse, his blue eyes wide. "Jer, how in the name of—you're in the Union Army?" Then his eyes darkened. The cords in his neck bulged. He grabbed Jarrett's arm in a viselike grip. "How did you get here? What are you doing in uniform?"

Jarrett explained, understating his job under Captain Good and ended with, "Now we're both on the same side."

Tears glinted at the corners of Jordan's eyes. "I thought you were home taking care of the farm and out of danger. One of us in this war is enough. I was glad to be that one."

A messenger approached.

"Lieutenant Jordan Ross, Captain Drew needs you to take fifty soldiers to accompany the Cherokee refugees to the Tahlequah area."

"Jarrett, I'll get word to Mother and Father you're here with Drew and Good. They must be worried sick. Ironic how life is. Now, I'll be near home to look after things, and you'll be off serving in the army."

"Yeah, Jordie, real strange. I'm glad you're going." Jarrett pulled at his ear, a frown on his face. "I wonder, does Captain Good plan to push on to Tahlequah?"

~

Jarrett didn't wonder long. A week after Jordan and his men left to escort the refugees to Tahlequah, Weer's two divisions struck out across the countryside toward Tahlequah.

A week later Jarrett slumped in the saddle. They were riding deeper into Cherokee country and further and further from a supply base. General Weer was a nincompoop.

Jarrett wiped sweat from his forehead. What would happen to Runninghorse and Mist Over The Water if the war spread to their land? He gazed behind him at the long columns of Union Army soldiers marching toward Tahlequah. Would Delight's family evacuate? At least he would see Mother and Dad.

~

Watie's guerrillas cut Jarrett's Union divisions and calvary off from the river. The Union men now had limited water and food.

A few days later Jarrett's stomach felt the scarcity of supplies. Hunger gnawed on his insides.

Each soldier now received only a few ounces of hardtack and beans, eighteen ounces of flour, four ounces of bacon, and boiled coffee for a full day's rations.

That barely filled Jarrett's stomach at breakfast.

His mouth was continually dry. Lack of water in the blazing heat became a severe hardship. What water he obtained from muddy ponds and carried in his canteen was often contaminated. He boiled his before he drank.

But he didn't complain. He had life easier than the infantry.

Marching soldiers keeled over and lay on the dirt road until picked up and loaded onto one of the artillery wagons. Each day, more men fell.

Heat, mosquitoes, thirst, and sickness badgered him and the other soldiers. Jarrett had accompanied his father often enough to diagnose the men's illness. First, a man complained of exhaustion and lost his appetite. Next, he carried his six-shooter over his shoulder because his painful abdomen could not tolerate the pressure. Then a high fever sent him into a muttering delirium.

"Typhoid." Jarrett picked up a fallen soldier's shoulders. Rusty took his legs. Together they heaved the unconscious man into a wagon already loaded with sick men.

"What ya do for it?" Rusty slipped the soldier's forage hat over his eyes to shield him from the scorching sun.

"Only thing a person can do is try to keep the fever down and the patient comfortable." He mounted Daniel.

"That's impossible on the march. Maybe we should turn back." Rusty licked his dry lips.

"Weer made some bad decisions, but there's no turning back now to our supply lines." Jarrett shifted in his saddle.

"Closer to Tahlequah?"

"Yeah." Jarrett waved an arm at the surrounding countryside. "Rusty, can you believe these farms used to be well-kept? Look at them now, neglected with no one to lay in the crops."

"Yup, they look awful sad. Houses need repair, fences broken, no hay for the livestock."

"Looks like the Confederate Army conscripted all the local farmers. I've only seen women, children, and a few old men left on the farms now. Appears most women managed to put in a little garden for themselves, but there's nothing for the animals."

"Yep, son. Sure bad all right."

"I hate farm work, but I'm itching to help those people. Makes me want a leave so I can go home and get *our* crops in."

Rusty pointed to animals wandering outside a fence. "I'll lay you odds someone gets sent out after those cows. Rations walking around big as a mess hall."

Sure enough, as Rusty finished speaking, a forage party went after the cows.

A few hours later, Jarrett smothered guilt when he ate the beef, knowing the cow belonged to some farmer.

At night, Jarrett slid his tired body off his horse. He made camp while Rusty took care of the horses. Then he walked to the surgery wagons. Well into the evening, he sponged the men with typhoid whose temperatures soared. Then he fell on his bedroll for a few hours' sleep before the next day's march.

Rusty shook a finger in his face. "You'll come down with the typhoid or drop dead from exhaustion if you don't stop taking care of those sick men."

"Someone has to do it. I'll be fine."

Jarrett heaved a sigh of relief when their expedition, followed by a line of open wagons filled with hot, thirsty, delirious men, passed into Indian Territory.

At unexpected times during the day or night, Stand Watie's guerrillas ambushed them. Watie's fifteen-year-old son often led the attacks. Saladin had a reputation for being vicious and had once killed a soldier rather than take him prisoner.

From a hundred yards away, Watie's sharpshooters picked off Union men. Before the cavalry could swing into action, the Rebs disappeared in a cloud of red dust.

Captain Goode summoned Jarrett and Rusty to his tent. "Nolan, Ross, I need you to deliver a communiqué to Chief John Ross at Park Hill. Colonel Weer wants an interview. We'll camp here on Wolf Creek until we get an answer."

"Yes, sir!" Rusty and Jarrett answered in unison.

Jarrett carried ta white flag of truce under which he and Rusty rode.

They clattered into Park Hill, and Jarrett found the town little changed from that day in May when he had fallen in love.

"Must be a girl makes you look so perky," Rusty joked.

"Only the most beautiful girl in the world, and she's in love with me!"

"Hold on, son. Are you telling me you fell for a Rebel gal?" Rusty's face, caked with red dust cut by rivulets of sweat, took on a mock expression of gloom. "I knew you were a dandy the first time I laid eyes on you drowning in the Arkansas River. How about fixing me up with one of those pretty little southern belles? That is, if Cap'n don't call loving a Rebel gal treason."

Jarrett tugged on the reins. "Whoa, Daniel." He turned to Rusty. "Hold it. Here come some of my great-uncle's men. They recognize me."

"I'm sure glad they do. Twenty to two ain't good odds. They look like *they* been eating good."

Surrounded by Chief Ross's armed escort, he and Rusty trotted to Rose Cottage.

"Some *cottage*! That's just what I pictured a southern

plantation home would look like. That driveway must be half a mile long," Rusty murmured.

Jarrett pulled Daniel to a slower walk as they approached the two-story mansion.

Armed men ushered him and Rusty inside to face a white-haired elderly man, with bushy white eyebrows, baggy eyes, and a weary look, sitting behind a large mahogany desk. Jarrett cleared his throat. He always felt awed talking with his great-uncle.

"Hello, Jarrett. Good to see you."

"Hi, Uncle John."

"I'm surprised to see you wearing blue."

"No more surprised than I am to be wearing a uniform."

Three armed men rushed through the library doors and stopped short. One stepped forward. "Sorry to interrupt, but …" he walked forward, bent, and whispered in Uncle John's ear.

A stricken expression flashed over Great-uncle John's face. He rose and placed his hands flat on the top surface of his desk. "Forgive me, Jarrett, I have no time to talk. I know why you've come and have sad news for you. Tell Colonel Weer that, contrary to what Captain Drew told the Colonel, our Cherokee Nation has a treaty with the Confederate government which we feel honor-bound to keep. Though our Nation suffers for my actions, I must keep my word to the Confederacy."

A sickening feeling lurched in Jarrett's stomach.

"I wish we could have met under better circumstances, Jarrett. It's a sorrowful war that pits a great-uncle and his nephew on different sides. We do what we must. It was my hope that by joining the Confederacy, we could preserve our nation's unity. My allegiance is with the Union, but fate decreed we side with the Confederacy. We shall not switch to the Union side." His Uncle mustered a smile. "God bless you and keep you safe."

"Yes, sir. You too, sir." The lump in Jarrett's throat strangled further words.

As they rode back to their camp at Wolf Creek, Rusty halted his horse. "Somebody stomp on your grave?"

"Don't you understand? We're going to fight my own people right here in my territory. Jordie and I are on the wrong side."

"Hard luck."

"I'm about to lose everything important to me."

"Yup, and you with a Rebel sweetheart. I wouldn't want to be in your place."

CHAPTER 26

August 1862

*M*y dearest Delight,

    I know this letter may never reach you, but I must write in the hope that you will receive my news. I miss you. You are my sanity during these unreal days. You are my lifeline.

Since I don't know how much you've already heard about what happened to change the course of this crazy war, I'll explain what I lived through, and where we stand on our different sides.

I've met your friend, Captain Drew, on the battlefield. He's a good man.

Bewildered by Chief Ross's negative reply to join the Union, General Blunt ordered Captain Drew, along with fifty of our men, to Tahlequah. I remained in camp.

Without a shot being fired, our men marched on Rose Cottage, captured the two-hundred-armed Confederates body-guarding Chief Ross, and took them as Union prisoners of war. They transported Chief Ross to Washington.

President Lincoln pardoned Chief Ross, who took up

residence in Philadelphia.

Captain Drew and his men, including my brother, Jordan now in the Union Army, stayed at Park Hill to protect Chief Ross's holdings.

Fort Gibson, Tahlequah, and the Cherokee country north to the Moravian Mission are all in Confederate control, except for our one Union detachment at Park Hill under Captain Drew's command. This means Jordie and your friend Drew are surrounded by Rebels, and Stand Watie now has a free hand. So, you see, I'm much concerned for my brother. I ask you to pray for Jordan's safety.

I so pray you are safe at your father's home. I know how men who have been away from the civilizing influence of women sometime commit wild actions they would not otherwise do. I encourage you with all my heart to carry a gun for your protection.

Please stay safe. Take care, my precious love. You are my hope. My home. My future.

Jarrett

~

Fall tiptoed in with golden beauty. Late one afternoon as sun dappled autumn leaves sparkled on the clear waters of Wolf Creek, Jarrett received a message from home. His hand trembled as he opened the letter.

My dearest son,

These are grim days for us. Captain Drew's men have almost all been captured and either forced to swear allegiance to the Confederacy or taken prisoner. The last word I received from Jordan was not reassuring.

Now I hear from various sources that Jordan is hiding in the woods!

Yesterday, Stand Watie's sharpshooters killed two of our men in the Murrell orchard, and today several more are reported dead. How I pray constantly that Jordan is safe. If you should hear some word from him, you must let me know at once. A mother's heart cannot bear such agony.

The news from here is not all bad. Your father and I had decided to leave our farm and travel north to Kansas for safety when, thank God, that Confederate, Colonel Watie, took his men away from Tahlequah. I understand he is fighting in Missouri. So now, Fort Gibson is a ghost town. Your father and I are staying. It's lonely here with most of the civilians fled, but our situation is far better than we had with all the fighting and killing.

I can scarcely believe that Stand Watie has been elected Principal Chief by the Confederate Cherokees. Of course, most Cherokee repudiate him. But he is having his moment of glory. Your father tells me the old men who knew Watie as a youth are proud of him. It seems he is quite the commander. Enough of him.

Your father is well, although he has his hands full with war casualties. He cares for the wounded, whether wearing gray or blue. I see so many young men stumbling about with a crutch and one leg or lacking an arm. My heart cannot bear the sight. I pray for my sons constantly.

Men make war and fight. Women die daily, heartbroken.

Your friend, Claremont Flint, rides with Watie. He has some sort of command—he's a lieutenant, I think. Such a difficult war, friend fighting friend and, in some families, brother fighting brother. How I thank God my boys are on the same side.

Jerusha is fine, growing into a lovely lady. It is a mercy she is only eleven. I do not fear for her as the Wilsons fear for the safety of their thirteen-year-old daughter.

Jarrett tightened his grip on the letter. Murderous thoughts filled his mind. He shook his head and returned to reading.

I am not afraid here on the farm. We have a garden which will keep us through winter. The Confederates stole our mules and horses. I do not know what happened to Sampson, but I doubt you will ever see him again.

Jarrett swallowed hard. Sampson was a good horse, a loyal friend.

Paper is scarce. I had to use the back of these old ledger sheets. We hear little news of how the war goes, but rumors drift like thistles in the wind. As far as we can ascertain, the Confederacy is winning. What will become of my sons then?

We hear from Washington that Chief Ross spends time with President Lincoln. He explained how the Cherokee, except for Stand Watie and his men, now fight under the Union flag. I hope you get here in time to save Jordan. I fear for him. Since Watie is gone, I think Jordie will try to let me know where he is.

I am in good health and long to see you. Please send word of your condition. I have so much more to say, but my paper is used.

All my love, Mother

Head low, hands clasped behind his back, Jarrett strode the deep woods bordering Wolf Creek.

~

Rusty captured a Rebel courier before the soldier could deliver his communique. He brought it immediately to Captain Good.

To General Stand Watie.

Your regiment will return to Indian Territory. You will continue to harass the enemy's flanks and rear, stampede his animals, and destroy his foraging parties. If he should advance, join me here to defeat them.

I will not abandon you. You are my advance guard. I am sending four regiments of Texas Cavalry to aid you. This communiqué is entirely confidential.

I sympathize with you on your third son, Chumiskey's death.

G.C.

~

November 1862

Jarrett rode with Colonel Phillips and his cavalry to Fort Gibson to occupy the abandoned fort and to establish the southernmost outpost of the Union Army.

Once the horses were stabled and cared for, he raced

Rusty to their quarters. Jarrett reached the assigned room one step before Rusty.

He rushed through the wooden door, body wedged against Rusty's larger, broader body, to reach the bunks built into the side of the log wall. He reached them first.

Rusty shoved him aside and flung his bedroll on the bottom bunk. "Age before beauty, son."

Jarrett shrugged, slipped his bedroll onto the top bunk, and raised an eyebrow. "Top bunk's the one I wanted. You don't think I craved that bottom bunk, with four hundred pounds of heavyweight blubber sagging on my nose? To say nothing of finding a size fourteen foot in my face when you lumber down for assembly." Jarrett tossed a grin.

Rusty slung his heavy frame into the lower bunk. "So, we graduate from a tent to a room on Officers' Row right next door to the cap'n. I'd say that's a whole lot better than bunking in the wooden barracks with the other enlisted men." A smirk plastered his face.

Jarrett took a closer look at their new quarters. The walls were notched logs chinked with clay. He nodded. "You're right." Landing on Officers' Row, they now shared a twelve-by-fourteen room. Light flooded in from a glass paned window. A stone fireplace offered a homey touch. "Beats our canvas tent."

"Even with a dirt floor, this place is the best I've had in two long years." Rusty clasped his hands over his stomach and blew out a long sigh.

"Wonder where the ship anchor came from?" Jarrett ran his hand across the metal surface hanging above the stone mantle. "Gives our room a nautical flair." He glanced at Rusty spread across the lower bunk. "A room for an inflated dwarf should always have an anchor.”

Rusty chortled, his square, rugged face showing no displeasure.

“I recall hearing these rooms are blasted hot in the summer and cold and drafty in the winter.”

Rusty kicked off a boot. “Can’t be near as cold as a tent. Did I ever tell you about the time we was bivouacked in Kansas and the ice—”

“Hold that tale,” Jarrett picked up the boot and tossed it onto Rusty’s chest. “I’ll give you the cook’s tour of the fort.”

Rusty moaned, but he heaved his big frame off the cot, bumping his head on the upper bunk. “No sooner do I get comfortable than you want me to go somewhere. My backside is so sore from slapping that saddle I think I’m—”

“Fort Gibson is the oldest army post in Indian Territory.” Jarrett interrupted with a bored monotone, giving his impression of a tour guide.

“Cut the gab.” Rusty laughed with good-natured camaraderie. “Where’s the mess hall?”

Jarrett stepped to the open door and bowed.

Rusty clomped onto the walkway extending around the parade ground.

Jarrett followed. He squinted in the bright sunshine and pointed out the long building at the nearest corner of the square. “I attended a ball there last year.” *Hard to believe so much has happened since October. How upside-down the world has turned. Here I am a soldier.*

“No joshing.”

“The old fort sure looks good.” Jarrett’s shoulders relaxed for the first time in weeks. His boots clanked on the walk.

Behind him, Rusty's steps thudded a pleasant rhythm against the smooth stone path. "Let's grab some grub."

Jarrett pointed out some details of the buildings, parade grounds, and stockade. "Come on. This first." He led Rusty into the southern blockhouse and up a ladder. From the top they stared out through the openings in the logs from which guns could be fired.

Rusty leaned against the logs and peered out. "Quite a view."

Jarrett gazed around. Leafless oaks bordered the frothy Grand River. The countryside looked washed out in the November chill. Clouds gathered until only tiny fingers of sun touched the earth and glinted on the swift waters of both the Verdigris and the Grand Rivers.

He gazed through the square opening, his thoughts bright with memory. Delight had looked so …

Rusty gave Jarrett a poke. "Where's the Texas Road?"

"You can just make it out over the top of the officer's quarters." Jarrett straightened. "The road's the main highway from St. Louis to the Red River."

"Right. Let's eat."

They descended the ladder, passing sentries posted at the blockhouse.

Jarrett huffed as they stepped back outside onto the stone flagged walk. "Leave it to the army to build the hospital next to the river. Sometimes the Neosho floods." Jarrett pointed to a two-story wooden structure.

"Why build the hospital near the river?"

"Cooler and more breeze in the summer. This fort's nicknamed the *Graveyard of the Army* because the swamps surrounding us are full of disease." Jarrett strode north.

"Some people call the disease miasma. I read recently that one well-known doctor named it malaria. We know it as the Intermittent."

"You're a bundle of good news."

Jarrett pointed out the butcher shop, the new brick bakery, the carriage house near the stables, and the quartermaster's storehouse.

"The Rebs had their garden outside the stockade. If we're still here come spring, we'll have our turn working that garden."

"I didn't join no cavalry unit to farm. Come spring, my ma's counting on me to be home to lay in the crops. I'm itching to get back to Kansas. Just Ma and me left. She can't do much now, getting on in years. I've got to be home come spring."

Jarrett grimaced. "My folks need me too. We have a little money coming in from my father's practice, but mostly we live off what crops we bring in. It's going to be tough this spring though. Johnny Reb stole our mules." Jarrett glanced at the scores of mules corralled near the horse stables. "Never thought I'd miss those stubborn beasts."

Rusty pointed to a row of tiny rooms across the parade ground, each door and window barred. "I reckon that's the guardhouse."

The guardhouse brought back a startlingly clear memory—kissing Delight. Right there behind the jail. Once again, he felt her silky skin—smelled her sweet breath—held her warmth in his arms. His body tingled. Her blue-violet eyes looked up into his, wide with love and trust, dark with her answering promise as he vowed, "I love you, Delight. Someday, somehow, regardless of your family, regardless of the war, I'm going to marry you."

Rusty jerked his arm. "Come back to earth, son, and let's go get that grub."

Jarrett jolted back to the present and blinked. "Life here won't be so bad." A quiver ran down his spine. Except their men stood alone, surrounded by Johnny Reb.

"Ho, Jarrett! What's that whole slew of Indian women coming into the fort? Some of 'em are lookers. What's the deal?"

Jarrett stopped in a quiet spot beside the main well. "I'd guess they're here to do our laundry. But you best stay out of trouble."

Rusty laughed, his wide shoulders heaving. "No fun in that. I wouldn't mind sittin' in a jail cell a day or two for that kind of trouble. Don't tell me you let a little punishment scare you off!"

Jarrett placed a foot on the rail beneath the well's wooden canopy. Now, in this quiet place, might be the best opportunity he'd ever have. No soldiers milling nearby. "Look, Rusty, I have a certain code I live by, and trifling with women isn't part of it."

Rusty's hazel eyes rounded.

"Sometimes I've got to take a stand for the values I believe in. What I am and what I do are what I take with me into eternity."

"Wait a minute, wait a minute!" Rusty's voice grew agitated. "Are you saying you think what you do in this life is important in … in, um, heaven?" He ducked his head and glanced around.

"Yes." Jarrett perched on the edge of the brick well and braced his hands on the wooden cover.

Rusty thudded down on the ground below Jarrett.

"You've seen me work on that woodcarving of the steamboat, right? You might not believe me, but the carving's almost finished."

"Can't be. Don't look much like a steamboat. Anyway, what's your carving got to do with what we're talking about?"

"Right now, that wood doesn't look like much." He glanced to see if Rusty was listening. "But I need only cut a little here, a little there, and the steamboat emerges. It's rough now." Jarrett pulled in a deep breath. "That's the way I am—rough. God's not done carving me. But one day, when I see him, I'll no longer be rough." Jarrett shook his head.

"Sounds logical."

Jarrett traced the toe of his boot in the red dust. "Becoming what he wants me to be continues as long as I live."

Rusty huffed. "Captain Good says he finds his religion in nature. If that's good enough for him, that's good enough for me. Besides, I ain't done anything so very bad myself."

"Rusty. I couldn't even begin to let God change me until after I asked Christ into my life. He died so I could live. I only need to take his gift."

Rusty stroked his moustache. "Maybe so, but churches can't get along with each other. Nobody scraps as much as churches."

"You're right. Churches should be known by their love for one another."

"You're not joshing there." Rusty's voice grew more confident. "And as soon as they are, I'll become a pillar in a church."

"But." Jarrett stood up. "People being human, and churches being what they are doesn't change matters. There's a free gift to be taken."

A friend of Rusty's walked over to join them at the well.

Rusty frowned and shouldered Jarrett.

Jarrett nodded and shut his mouth. The three of them sauntered to the mess hall.

He slept that night in a bed for the first time in months. The air seemed stale. He missed the loamy scent of the earth. Missed seeing the brilliance of stars shining through the tent flap. Missed the whistle of wind through trees.

Outside the open window, an owl called a mournful hoot. A bad omen. If he believed in omens.

He rolled over, tangling his blanket around his knees and tossed in the narrow bunk. Sleep didn't come. He threw his legs over the edge and sat up. Who knew what was going to happen? *Our army has abandoned Fort Gibson except for the few hundred of us stationed inside. We're like prisoners.*

Jarrett cradled his head in his hands. *And I've heard nothing from Jordie.*

CHAPTER 27

With winter gaining a stronghold across the land, hundreds of homeless Indians camped outside Fort Gibson. Jarrett, scouting for the Union troops, shared his meager food with hungry Indians.

Even accustomed as he was to few comforts, he found life inside the fort harsh.

From the morning gun to dusk, he helped build stronger fortifications or dug earthworks or built brick walls to encircle the fort. He stopped often to blow on his hands and stamp his feet.

Stand Watie's guerrillas prowled the vicinity. At any moment, a soldier, shovel in hand, would cry out, fall, and lie bleeding across the embankment he had worked on.

Often the bugle called him into action.

Then, with the cavalry lured into the open, Watie's snipers riddled the ranks.

Jarrett and the other riders returned to the fort in defeat, bringing wounded and dead slung over their saddles.

Jarrett realized Fort Gibson was a prison, with General Watie and his men as the soldiers' deadly guards.

Watie intercepted food and ammunition trains.

Colonel Phillips ordered foraging parties sent into the

surrounding farms and towns.

Early one afternoon, with clouds hanging in the gray sky promising either sleet or snow, Jarrett stood outside the stockade with a group of other soldiers.

As a morale builder, men tried their skill at log rolling by the boat landing on the river. Bets rumbled through the off-duty soldiers as they guessed which man could stay on the log longest before tumbling into the cold Neosho River.

Dripping wet, shivering in the bone-chilling air, Rusty climbed up the mud bank, shook water from his long, red hair, and narrowed his hazel eyes. He pointed to a man riding toward them. "What kind of Indian is that?"

Jarrett turned.

The rider, with hair cropped close except for a center ridge like a cardinal's crest, trotted toward them. He looked half-starved.

"Osage." Jarrett lifted a friendly hand in greeting. Maybe the man had news of Runninghorse and Mist.

"Ross." The Indian's expression looked stern. "Him here?"

"I'm Jarrett Ross." His heart began pounding. His stomach knotted.

The Indian's voice was solemn. "Jordan Ross dead." He demonstrated a short measure with his hands. "Near Park Hill. Shot by gray suits."

Jarrett froze.

The Indian wheeled his skinny pony and trotted for the gate where he could beg food.

Rusty thrust a big arm around Jarrett's shoulders.

Jarrett shook him off. Pain sliced through his heart. He headed for the stables at a dead run, his sight blurred. He leaped onto Daniel's bare back and shot past Rusty and the other soldiers toward open country.

Rusty yelled, "Be careful!"

Pain twisted Jarrett's mind. His head throbbed. His face burned. No logical thought waded through the agony. Jordie dead. Jordie, bigger than life. So full of potential. Not to see him again. *Oh God, not Jordie!*

His heart sliced and bleeding, he galloped faster and faster.

Daniel broke stride, winded, lathered in the cold air.

Jarrett slid off and raced over rough ground, through bushes and brambles. He jumped ravines, rushing at breakneck speed. He fell. Sprang up and sprinted—where, he did not care. He raced until he dropped, his breath searing his chest. He sprawled where he lay.

Gloom turned to darkness. The temperature fell.

Frigid wind whistling through his clothes brought him to his feet. He stumbled back to find his horse.

And discovered Rusty waited there, rubbing Daniel with a piece of burlap. "You still in one piece?" He pulled a blanket from behind his saddle and draped the rough warmth around Jarrett's shoulders.

Head bowed, body hunched, he rode beside Rusty back to the fort.

~

January 1863

Jarrett stood at attention in front of Captain Good.

Good stood to his feet. "No supply train has made it

through Watie's blockade for months. I don't have the heart to seek more food from starving civilians." He slammed a palm against his scarred desk. "We have to raid Watie's camp. We'll starve if we don't get food." Captain Good's dark brows furrowed above his black eyes. "You're the only soldier familiar with the territory. Ross, I need you to guide us."

Jarrett nodded. *Brilliant idea.* His stomach agreed with Captain's plan. "Yes, sir. But there's a storm coming." His arm ached from the old wound he'd received while a Pony Express rider.

"How do you know the weather will change?" Captain Good's expression looked ambiguous, neither mocking nor challenging.

"Smoke from the campfires is staying close to the ground." Jarrett shrugged. "Fish are jumping out of the water to catch bugs, and what's left of the hickory leaves are curled. All reliable Osage signs that rain is on its way, and likely a bad storm."

Good laughed. "If it rains," and he pointed to the cloudless gray sky, "then we'll have better cover for our raid. That scoundrel Watie won't hear us coming."

And that had been the end of the discussion.

That night the men in the raiding party rode outside the fort's high wall, saddles creaking, no one speaking. The surrounding darkness was so black the soldiers near Jarrett were shadows.

He could see almost nothing, and the men trailing him in single file had to be blind as they followed the dark silhouette of the horseman riding in front.

Jarrett kneed Daniel, urging him into the river.

Soldiers followed. Iron shoes clinked on the slippery rock bottom. In the splashing current as icy water rose above boot tops, muttered curses splintered the ebony night.

The wind swooped in across the prairie, blew the men's forage caps off, and whipped their long hair into their eyes. The storm broke. Lightning flashed, spilling buckets of icy water. Jarrett shivered.

Daniel reared.

Behind him Jarrett heard other horses rearing, snorting, neighing, and prancing with nerves. Thunder roared and sleet slashed down in torrents. Jarrett's woolen uniform clung to his chilled flesh.

As jagged lightning cut the sky, for an instant turning darkness into light, he glimpsed faces of the miserable band of cavalry. He drove Daniel on through the night.

Fingers of rain slid down his neck, cold as naked steel. When he turned Daniel north toward Flat Rock where Watie camped, his reins slipped in his cold, stiffened fingers. He straightened his forage cap, but rain stung his face. Guided by intermittent lightning, he avoided the river's ford, always patrolled by Watie's soldiers.

Jarrett led the men into a wood.

As unseen branches whipped a rider's face, curses sounded

The ride was long, with the howling wind slowing their progress, and the freezing rain chilling their bones. Every few seconds, lightning arced through the sky. Thunder rocked the earth.

As they approached Flat Rock, the terrain roughened, with huge boulders and loose rock, small shrubs, and unseen ravines. Daniel tripped, and Jarrett almost pitched out of the saddle.

Watie had chosen his camp site well. Far above, on top of Flat Rock, his sentries could see the surrounding countryside from all four corners. There were no trees.

Jarrett felt naked and exposed, certain their small band would be seen during the vivid slashes of lightning. Above them, over the clinking of hooves against stone, he heard a familiar clank. He halted Daniel.

Captain Good edged close, signaling the men to halt.

What was that sound? Jarrett rubbed his dripping chin. As the noise and its meaning merged, he shivered. Bayonets being clamped to the stocks of rifles!

"They've seen us."

His hoarse whisper spurred Captain Good into action.

"After me, men!" Good roared as he charged up the hill toward Flat Rock.

A barrage of bullets shattered the night. A stab of wind startled Jarrett as a bullet whisked past his cheek.

Good grunted and swayed in his saddle.

A horse crashed to the ground. The Union soldier screamed in pain.

Another wall of fire bit into their streaking horses.

"Retreat!" Good yelled. "Retreat!"

Jarrett barely heard his command above the gunfire.

Desperate riders separated, seeking cover from the deadly bullets.

Watie's men did not follow.

A few miles south of Flat Rock, under the shelter of dense wood, Good reassembled his unnerved dragoons. He swayed in his saddle, cradling his left arm. "How many casualties?" he barked.

"One man dead and three wounded," someone answered.

Good sat in silence while he lit a shuck cigarette. The sweet odor from the homemade corn husk cigarette drifted on the wind.

With that tiny light, Jarrett watched rain slide down the peak of his captain's forage cap and drip down his cheeks.

As Good spoke, thunder crashed across the prairie, shutting out the sound of his voice. In the lightning flash that followed, his thick gray brows knifed into a frown of concentration above his long, hooked nose. His mustache dripped waterfalls onto his cupped hand as he drew on his cigarette.

"Ross," Good's voice sounded tight with pain, "after you lead us back to the fort, you have to come back and find out what Watie has on his side. He must have a whale of a lot more men than our intelligence reported. I need you to scout out what we're dealing with here. I'm sorry, but that's the only choice I have. We've got to have food, and we've got to find out what he's got up there. We don't have time to wait for a better opportunity. And you know the terrain."

Jarrett hid the fear churning inside. "Yes, sir."

"Good. Take us home."

After the long ride back to the fort, Jarrett rested his arms across Daniel's shoulders. He watched the cavalry unit trot past into the bleak night, listened as they splashed through the Neosho River, and hailed for the sentry to open the gate to Fort Gibson.

He hunched his back, dismounted, shucked off his drenched uniform and boots, and set his jaw as he pulled his buckskin shirt and leggings from his saddlebag. *If the Rebs catch me in civilian clothes ...*

He dragged his moccasins onto cold feet. "Daniel, looks as if we have a long wait until we get back to the fireside. And this downpour makes my arm hurt as much as it did the day I got wounded. My clothes are soaked. Why in this crazy world would any person in his right mind ride to Watie's camp on a wild night like this?" He swapped the army's recognizable McClellan saddle for his own.

Daniel stood with one hind leg drawn up to rest on the point of his hoof, his head drooping in the rain.

"Wish I could let you head for the stable. But our work's not done yet." He petted Daniel, hid his uniform beneath a stony outcrop, then checked himself and Daniel for any other sign they were part of the Union Army.

"Everything's square." He rubbed Daniel's neck. *If I'm discovered, what plausible reason can I give for being at Flat Rock?* He shook his head. *Well, I just won't be discovered.*

He mounted the slippery saddle and swiveled his horse back toward Flat Rock.

Thunder traveled farther and farther away across the prairie. As he approached Flat Rock, the rain slackened to drizzle, then the storm ended as quickly as the deluge had started.

The sky brightened. Dawn was not far off. The voice of a sentry echoed from the hilltop. Hair on the nape of Jarrett's neck bristled. The night had been a disaster. With a hollow feeling in his stomach, he listened as the sentry's cry was taken up one by one by other guards.

He whispered in Daniel's ear. "I'm cold, dog-tired, and soaked to the skin. You and I know I'm scared witless. Captain Good didn't do me any favor this time."

Somewhere, far to his left, an owl hooted. A bad omen.

Daylight would break soon. If he were going to ride into and out of that camp he'd have to go now.

"Daniel, right now I wish you were any color but black. Dumb idea having all our unit's horses the same color—a surefire way to recognize cavalry. Flat Rock, nobody goes to Flat Rock. Hunting's no good. Fish bite better down here. Nothing on that hill but rocks and boulders. No reason for a man to be there except for the purpose Watie's up there. A camp with a bird's eye view of the surrounding countryside. Yahola, I've got no choice."

He nudged Daniel in the ribs. They clattered out into the open just as a company of Confederate soldiers burst over the rim of the hill.

What timing! Cold fear shook his body. He trotted toward the band of armed men thundering toward him.

He rode as if he had expected to meet them.

They surrounded him, jostling his horse.

"Reach for the sky!" a voice commanded.

He laughed. "You're just the men I'm looking—"

A rifle barrel prodded his back. "Raise 'em, I said!"

He obeyed. "You're making a mistake, I—"

"Shut up! Any talking you do'll be to the gen'l." The rider took Daniel's reins and led Jarrett's horse up the steep hill.

Hooves slipped and clattered across the boulders, and before Jarrett could slow the pounding of his heart, he stood inside Stand Watie's large Sibley tent.

As he waited in the center of the candle-lit tent, hands raised so they touched the wet, sagging canvas roof, a pool of water collected at his feet.

He silently prayed. *Father, don't let anyone here recognize me.*

Watie slouched behind a crude wooden desk. He must have been up all night because his eyes, under bushy gray brows, looked alert. Those eyes stared at Jarrett for several long minutes. The man didn't speak.

Watie's black hair was streaked with white. Deep lines etched his forehead and flowed from his nose toward his stern mouth. He was a squat man, broad and short with pronounced Indian features. His physical appearance was unimposing. But the strength of his personality and the vibrancy of his spirit marked him as a person of power. He didn't need a general's uniform to make his presence felt.

"Well?" His gravelly voice made the question a command.

Jarrett forced a grin.

"We found this kid trotting up to camp below the south summit, sir." The respectful voice belonged to the soldier prodding his rifle into Jarrett's backbone.

Watie's face remained impassive, his eyes gazed into Jarrett as if he could, from Jarrett's expression, from his stance, and from his clothes, read his thoughts.

Never had he felt so vulnerable. A memory darted into his mind of the time when he was four years old, and his father caught him red-handed with a smoking, forbidden pistol, and an empty cartridge at his feet. Then, as now, he was certain guilt was scrawled across his face.

"So, you're a spy?" It was not a question.

"No, sir. I was looking for you, sir." Jarrett swallowed, throat suddenly dry. Tongue swollen. Heat stained his cheeks.

Watie cocked a skeptical eyebrow.

Jarrett spilled his words over each other in his best imitation of an excited kid standing in the presence of his hero. "I just rode in from Arkansas, sir. When I saw how the war was going with the Union taking all our country, I decided to hightail it over here and join up with you. All of us back home have heard of General Stand Watie, and I figured I'd rather fight with you than stick around home and see the Yankees take over and maybe get conscripted into their army. If I'd been a spy, wouldn't I have run from your men? I'm a good rider, and my horse is fast."

Watie leaned back in his camp chair. A smile creased his face, making him appear almost congenial. His stubby fingers unbuttoned his uniform coat, then he laced his hands behind his large head.

The tension loosened in Jarrett's shoulders.

But the general turned to a bunk in the corner of his tent where a tall, thin youth sprawled. He looked intelligent, but he had a hard mouth. Only his black eyes and heavy brows resembled his father's. The infamous Captain Saladin Watie, fifteen-year-old son of whom Jarrett had heard so many tales.

Saladin shook his head almost imperceptibly.

Jarrett's legs quivered.

"I think not, Father. Too coincidental. First the raid, now this kid. Sure, he looks young, but that doesn't keep him from being a spy. I don't trust him." The barely old-enough-to-sprout-whiskers captain's eyes sparkled like a happy devil.

General Watie ordered curtly, "Search him!"

Two of the soldiers searched Jarrett, even sifting hands

through his wet hair. They unbuckled his holster and handed his Colt and belt to the General.

Another soldier entered the tent holding Jarrett's carving of the Prairie Bird. "Found this in his saddle bag, sir."

"I live near the Arkansas River where it joins with the Grand. Boats steam up and down river every month. That is, they did until the war started." Jarrett tried to swallow the lump in his throat.

Two soldiers pulled off his wet moccasins in their search.

Watie inspected the carving, pressing and pulling various pieces.

Jarrett stood straighter, glad he'd not followed his plan of concealing a secret compartment inside.

The scowling general placed the boat on his desk. "Good work."

"My hobby, sir." Jarrett took charge of his fear. "I'm no spy. I came to join you against those Yankees! Quantrill rides in Kansas, and Watie rides in Indian Territory. I live closer to you, so I figured to join your men."

"Hogwash!" Saladin's high voice cut in. "The kid's a spy. I can feel his guilt in my bones."

"And what if his story is true? Would you have me shoot an innocent youth, my son? I feel you don't value life as you should. War hardens a man. I don't want him shot until I find out the truth. See to it, Sergeant Anderson. Make him talk!" Watie folded back into his camp chair and picked up some maps. Thrusting them toward the candle to see better, he muttered, "We can't take any chances. I want a report tomorrow morning."

Anderson answered, "Yes, sir!" Then he turned to a man standing behind Jarrett. "Get me some rope."

Footsteps scuttled behind him as the soldier left the tent.

Anderson shoved him toward the tent door. "You'll talk all right, spy. You'll be only too happy to spill your guts before I'm finished with you."

The soldier lunged back inside and tossed the rope to Anderson, who tied Jarrett's hands tight behind his back.

"General, please listen. You're making a mistake. I never would have come all this way to ride with you if I'd had any idea you'd think I was a spy. Do you arrest every true Southerner?" Jarrett tugged his wrists, but the rope didn't give.

For an instant, the great man appeared to relent.

But Saladin cut in. "Get on with the questioning, Sergeant."

Anderson tied a scarf across Jarrett's eyes. Two soldiers gripped his arms and shoved him out of the tent.

At least he would not be so recognizable with cloth covering half his face.

As Anderson marched him over slippery boulders, muttering spread through the camp.

Unable to see through the blindfold, Jarrett stumbled between the two soldiers shoving him. Once he fell, banging his knees against a rock.

"You two come with us," Anderson ordered. More footsteps thudded behind him, heavy boots clinking against stone.

They butted him forward until they reached the edge of Flat Rock.

He slipped.

They let him fall.

Sharp boulders bruised and tore his skin. At the bottom

he lay dazed until they hauled him to his feet. Jerking him between them, they forced him chest-deep into the frigid river. Two soldiers held his arms, and another gripped his legs.

He kicked and struggled, but the three soldiers plunged him beneath the suffocating water. The shock took his breath away. They held him under. He silently counted a full minute before they jacked him up.

"You here to spy on us?" Anderson's voice sounded faint over the roaring in his ears.

"No!" He gasped for air before they dunked him beneath the icy water again.

He lost count of time. His lungs burned and ached for air. His heart pounded. He spluttered and gulped, sucking in air when they wrenched him up.

Again, they shoved him under water. The suffocation was agonizing. Fighting mad, he struggled to free himself. But they held him down until his struggles grew weak and finally stopped as he slipped into thick nothingness.

CHAPTER 28

Faint words filtered through the darkness. Jarrett strained to hear.

"I think you left him under too long, Sergeant. He looks dead. He weren't that pale before, and his lips are blue. Is he breathing?"

Rocks poked into Jarrett's back. Must be lying on the riverbank. His limbs were heavy. He had no energy. His chest burned. Too spent to open his eyes. But he was alive.

A boot nudged his arm.

He stirred, sending his frame into spasms of coughing, choking, and heaving. Water streamed from his nose and mouth. Light swirled him in a whirlpool. He tried to lift his arm but couldn't. Realization trickled in. The tearing pain in his arms came from ropes around his wrists. Where was he?

Someone grabbed his hair and snapped his head back.

A voice screamed in his ear. "You're a spy, ain't ya!"

He tried to speak. Couldn't. Cleared his throat and swallowed. Tried again. "Me? A spy, never." His voice sounded like gravel crushed under buggy tires.

"Tarnation, Anderson, the kid's no spy. Let him go."

"Yeah, let him go, Sergeant. It's too cold out here to stand around in these wet clothes. I'm freezing."

"Build a fire. He'll confess before I'm done with him. Too many lives depend on our not making a mistake." Anderson's voice sounded deadly certain.

Two of the soldiers built a fire.

Another said, "I'm getting dry clothes and blankets."

"Bring breakfast too, Bob. We'll cook it here." Anderson ordered.

Jarrett twisted on the riverbank, but no matter how he moved, rocks poked fingers of pain into his body. The chill November wind cut to the bone.

The next he knew, the scent of bacon sizzling, coffee boiling, and beans heating cramped his empty stomach.

The sergeant everyone called Anderson stomped over to push his face next to Jarrett's. Pebbles stirred by his boots converted into tiny missiles that found their target in Jarrett's body and face. The man stooped, ripped off the wet, sagging blindfold and slapped a new blindfold over Jarrett's eyes. "No spy's gonna see our camp."

Someone else carried hot coffee, bacon, and beans over to sit beside him. The scent sent Jarrett's mouth salivating. "Come on, kid. Tell me why you're here, and you can have all the food your skinny belly can handle."

Jarrett cleared his dry throat. "I came to ride with General Watie."

"Not good enough. I'll badger you all day and all night until you admit you're a spy." Anderson chuckled.

Jarrett groaned.

Anderson's footsteps receded in the direction of the blaze. Sounds of men eating knotted Jarrett's stomach.

As the fire partially dried his clothes, he stopped shaking. Forks scraping on tin plates gradually stopped.

"What do you say, spy?" Anderson's voice again.

Jarrett didn't answer.

Someone knelt with a heavy knee on his chest, grabbed his hair, jerked his head back, and thrust the point of a sharp object at his throat.

Make it quick. Heaven will be so much better. And I'm ready.

Instead, the blade quit pricking.

"You're a spy, aren't you?"

"No." Jarrett's mouth was so dry he had to force the words. Sweat beaded his forehead. "I'm Jason Roberts from Arkansas."

"We'll see." Anderson answered grimly. "We got plenty of time to find out who you are. You best start talking."

"Came to join Watie."

"General gave us all day and all night. General Watie doesn't expect a report until tomorrow morning. Long before then, you'll decide you'd rather have a quick bullet instead of a slow, lingering death. You'll talk, spy."

Jarrett groaned. *How long can I withstand Anderson's torture?* Being blindfolded compounded his fear. He braced himself.

Anderson hauled him to his feet and forced him to walk.

Somewhere he'd lost his moccasins. He stumbled, his legs trembled, his chest burned, and he shivered so much, his teeth hurt. Jagged rocks lacerated his feet. He tripped in a ravine.

They dragged him on.

The crackle of campfires and the smell of sowbelly cooking alerted him they had returned to camp. Men muttered as they caught sight of him stumbling between his two guards. He heard the stamping and neighing of horses but lost all sense of direction.

They won't kill me unless they're sure. I've got to hold out.

The muttering voices, the sounds and smells of camp receded. He staggered on, with the soldiers half-dragging him. Brambles and rocks tore his knees.

Without warning, they shoved him to the ground, grabbed his ankles, and tied them tight. Then looped a rope around his neck and passed it through the ropes around his ankles, pulling the rope until his ankles were jerked toward his wrists. If he flexed his legs, the rope around his neck would choke him.

The sound of blankets spreading on the ground. The man with the baritone voice said, "I get first sleep. Wake me in a couple hours."

Jarrett moaned. Wind whipped through his clothes and sliced into his bones. The ropes cut into his flesh. Agonizing position. When he eased the pain in his legs and back, the rope around his neck shut off his air. If he couldn't hold his legs up high enough, long enough, he strangled.

Time crawled by. Would he go mad?

"How do you Kansas boys like our weather?" Anderson asked, his question innocent and congenial.

Jarrett gasped, "Not from Kansas. Arkansas."

Periodically Anderson questioned him, trying to get him to slip up, trying to get him to admit he knew something of Indian Territory or Fort Gibson or the Union Army.

The other soldiers didn't say much. One watched while the other two slept. From their different snores, Jarrett tried to picture what they looked like.

More and more often, the rope strangled him as his leg muscles spasmed. His body grew numb. At times, his mind went murky before he could move to relieve the rope's hold.

More time crept by. He counted second by second.

A heavy boot kicked him in his stomach. As his legs jerked, the noose cut off his air. Everything went dark. Frigid water splashed in his face brought him back.

"Jason Roberts, shall we continue interrogating?" Sergeant Anderson's voice sounded as cheerful as if he asked if Jarrett wanted a hot cup of coffee. "Or are you ready to confess?"

Pulling in a deep breath, Jarrett realized they had cut the rope around his neck. "No." His hoarse voice was barely a whisper.

Anderson dropped down to sit close. "How about it, Roberts, must we get rough?" He was chewing a piece of roast beef that wafted a mouth-watering scent.

Jarrett's stomach knotted. Tolerable. He'd been hungry before. That he could handle. But how much more torture could he take? If he weakened, he was dead. "Why are you so sure I'm a spy?" he croaked.

"A gut feeling. I said to myself, what would I do if I wanted to spy out General Watie's position on top of Flat Rock?" Anderson gave a huge burp. "Number one—I would choose the youngest, most vulnerable-looking man I had, but one with enough intelligence to take care of himself. That fits you to a fingernail." Anderson moved on the rocks, making himself comfortable. "Number two, I then asked myself, in the event that spy were caught, what excuse would he give for being in this remote spot." Anderson slapped his thigh as though an idea had suddenly occurred to him. "Of course, the only reason he could have, would be to join Watie's riders. Now isn't it a strange coincidence that's exactly the story you came up with?

"Besides, you're tough. Oh, yes, one other thing. That horse you rode in on hasn't been eating too well. He's thin, worn down with being grass-fed. No grain's been getting into Fort Gibson since we've captured all the wagon trains. And the gelding just happens to be black—like all the other horses in this particular Union cavalry." Anderson laughed, and the two other soldiers joined him as if they'd never heard anything so humorous.

"And number three, you arrived right after that shoot-out last night. Somebody at the fort wants to know what hit them!"

Jarrett struggled to sit. He swallowed. "What if I did ride up to join Watie?" His voice scratched his sore throat. "Other men have. What Yank leader in his right mind sends a spy immediately after a shoot-out? I had bad timing, that's all."

"Wrong time? I'll say it was the wrong time—for you."

Jarrett struggled to sit taller, trying to face Anderson's voice. "My horse is thin because he's eaten nothing but grass while we traveled cross country. Wish I hadn't come!"

"I'll bet you do. Make this easy for yourself. Your story doesn't hold water. A quick bullet now, and your suffering ends. Believe me, what I got in mind for you, you won't like!"

"I'm not a spy."

They untied his wrists, dragged him to a tree, and the sound of a rope thrown around a high limb caused his insides to quake. Were they going to hang him?

Instead, they tied each wrist to one end of a rope.

He lifted his groggy head and shook it, hoping to see over the blindfold.

"Jubal Good still smoke too much?" Anderson asked, his voice friendly.

"Don't know any Jubal Good." Despite his efforts, Jarrett's words slurred.

Two soldiers pulled the ropes.

His wrists jerked above his head, until he was forced to stand. Still, they hauled until his arms strained above his head.

"How's that feel?" Anderson asked as if he were concerned that position might be too uncomfortable.

"What do you think?"

The men dragged the rope tighter.

Stretched to full height, he stood on tiptoes. The ropes cut into his wrists. He could no longer feel his hands.

"I'll free you the minute you confess." Anderson patted him on the shoulder as if they were friends.

Jarrett shook his head.

"Hang him up, men." Anderson sounded tired, as if he no longer enjoyed the game.

Every muscle in Jarrett's upper body screamed. He gasped for breath. His feet dangled in thin air. He ground his teeth.

The soldiers tied their end of the rope around the trunk.

"If you want us, holler," one yelled.

His ears were ringing, his head drooping, and their footsteps were growing faint. Pain washed over him in waves. Surely his shoulders would separate, his arms be torn from their sockets. The old wound in his right arm shrieked.

"Stop," he screamed. "I've … I've got a friend riding

with Watie." He had to take a chance. Do anything. He couldn't take this pain. "Let me down. He'll tell you I'm no spy."

"You've got a friend. Hah! If you really had a buddy here, you would have said so long ago. You're lying." Someone yanked the rope, so his body swung in circles.

Jarrett screamed, "Claremont Flint." His breath came in sobs. "Flint will tell you I'm no spy!"

Desperate move. Flint doesn't know I'm a Union scout, but he knows I'd never ride with Watie.

"Aw, he's stalling. Let him hang here until we find Flint. Kid's a mite short. This little fun can lengthen him out." The speaker laughed.

"No. Lower him. Lieutenant Flint's on a raid. If this kid's Flint's cohort, he won't like how he's been treated. And if he isn't …" Anderson made a slashing sound.

As the rope loosened, the agony lessened. Jarrett slumped to the ground. They untied his hands. Then they hauled him to his feet, slammed his back against the tree, and tied him to the trunk.

All afternoon he sagged against the ropes binding him to the big tree. Wind lashed his numb body. His head ached wickedly, but he was alive.

Yahola, why'd I tell them about Flint? Stupid. Flint can't do anything for me without risking his own life. Dumb. Mistake. Dumb.

Time dragged. His numb body no longer felt pain. As the day wore on, his mind wandered until voices floated from soldiers walking yards away. Unintelligible at first, then …

"… seven-shot Spencer is just what the doctor ordered, and every dad-burned man has one now!"

A picture of a dark steel barrel with a walnut stock—a long sleek carbine that loaded shells with lever load through the butt—flashed through his mind. Seven shots, pumping out the empty brass cartridges. That's what he'd been sent to find out.

He sighed. No way he could relay the news to Good. Watie didn't have more men, he had repeating rifles. From where? Only factory was in the North. Who in the North was selling out?

Jarrett squirmed, but each movement tugged the ropes tighter. Had to escape. No wonder their cavalry ran into a hail of bullets last night. Repeating rifles!

The temperature dropped. Shivers started. Must be night.

Footsteps coming toward him. His heart beat way too fast.

"Here he is."

Anderson's hated voice was so close Jarrett snapped his head back and hit the tree trunk.

"You know this spy?"

Silence. Claremont finally answered. "Remove the blindfold so I can see his face. He does look familiar."

Before Anderson could move, Jarrett burst out, "Jason Roberts from Arkansas, you remember me, don't you, Mr. Flint? We met when you came over to Fort Smith to trade."

"Shut up, you fool!" Sergeant Anderson roared. He tore off the blindfold.

Jarrett blinked, dazzled by the moonlight sifting through the trees.

For the barest second, shock registered on Claremont's face. His hand pulled at his ear lobe. "Well, yes. I do remember you, Roberts. We did some trading and a little yarn swapping, as I recall." He stroked his broken nose. "Sergeant, this is the upstart who broke my nose. Not surprising he didn't mention me sooner. I wouldn't say we're friends." He chuckled. "But this fellow's no spy. Probably here to find excitement and make a name for himself."

Jarrett strained to keep his face from betraying relief.

Anderson's shrewd eyes narrowed. He rubbed a hand under his nose as though he smelled a skunk. "You vouch for him then, Lieutenant? You know the penalty for aiding spies?" The sergeant drew his heavy brows together.

Claremont scanned Jarrett as if he were as unimportant as a worn-out horse judged to go to the meat market. "I doubt this man's a spy. His pappy owns a passel of slaves over by Fort Smith, and he'd be red-rage angry if we shot his son. But don't take my word for it. Ride on over to Fort Smith and verify."

"Ha! Not likely with Arkansas in Union hands, and the rivers patrolled by Northern gunboats. If the general frees him, it's on your say-so!"

Claremont frowned. "I'm tired and hungry. Not my business if you shoot him. I'm not sticking my neck out for him. Do whatever you want. I'm getting some grub and shut-eye." He turned and strode toward camp.

Anderson punched Jarrett's arm. "Thought you said he was a friend."

"You know my name and where I hail from. You know I'm not a spy."

"Do I indeed? I've just enough doubt to keep you from being shot."

Jarrett's stomach dropped. If the ropes hadn't held him up, he would have fallen. "Yah—iipes!" he mumbled, almost betraying his Indian ancestry with his usual frustration word. "How do I prove I'm no spy?"

"Confess." Anderson walked fifteen feet from the tree and sat down with his back resting against an oak. "Bates, build a fire over here. There'll be frost tonight. Hanover, bring my grub and some of that hot coffee. We're staying the night. Maybe our spy will have something to tell me before morning."

Jarrett sagged against the ropes. If he made it through the next eight or ten hours without confessing, he might be set free in the morning. He shook his head. Even if he were released, for sure someone in camp would recognize him. Then he *and Claremont* would be shot.

Hanover returned with the sergeant's food. Then he stomped over to glare at Jarrett.

The tall man had massive muscles and mean little eyes. He grabbed a fist full of Jarrett's hair as he pulled the butt of his gun from its holster and smashed Jarrett in the ribs. There was a distinct crack.

Sudden, piercing pain. Jarrett groaned.

"That's for busting Lieutenant Flint's nose."

"Hold it!" Anderson cut in. "Who gave you orders to pistol-whip the prisoner? You're relieved of duty. I'm in command here."

Hanover's eyes blazed, but the gun descended into his holster. He turned on his heel and crunched through the frosting grass.

Anderson ate his supper.

Jarrett no longer cared. His tongue clung to the roof of his mouth. From far away, over the ringing in his head, he heard Anderson's order. "Bates, I've got something I need to attend to. Don't let the prisoner out of your sight. Tomorrow after chow I'll take him to the general."

Jarrett grimaced. *Watie. If the freeze doesn't finish me, he will.*

Saladin's face flashed into his memory. *Or his son.*

CHAPTER 29

Cold dug nails into Jarrett's flesh. His hands and feet were ice, his mind numb, working slow. Every breath brought pain.

For hours his guard, burrowed in blankets, had fed the campfire and not taken his eyes off Jarrett. Now the fire burned low, and the soldier's head often dropped to his chest, then jerked up, only to sink down to rest on his body again.

Beyond the fire's glow, the night, inky enough to feel, slept. Frost layered the meager brown grass and lay slippery on the rocks.

A twig snapped behind Jarrett. A tug on the tight ropes around his chest caused his rib to radiate pain. Somebody tugged and pulled at the ropes cutting into his body.

"Jer, you've got to escape. Too many soldiers here will recognize you without the blindfold. One look and the game's over," Claremont whispered.

Jarrett shook his head. Was his tired brain playing tricks?

Claremont kept working with the ropes.

Why doesn't he cut them? Get them off. Oh. Jarrett pulled in as deep a breath as he could. *Claremont must make this escape appear as if I had been able to free myself. Otherwise, he'll be shot for helping me.*

After what seemed like way too long, the rope around his chest loosened and with a quiet thud, fell to the ground. Claremont worked on the ropes around his wrists.

Jarrett clamped his jaw and stared at his prostrate guard. Snoring like a boar on the warpath. The man might be shot for falling asleep on duty.

Ropes fell from his ankles. He took a step and almost fell. He had to concentrate to stand.

"Let's go." Claremont grabbed his left arm and half-carried him through the rocks toward the east descent. Jarrett kept falling.

Claremont picked him up and slung him over his back. Jarrett clamped his lips against the pain in his chest.

Claremont struggled down the rocks toward the bottom of the summit, Jarrett bouncing on his shoulders. Panting like a steam engine, Claremont slid him to the ground. "I couldn't chance bringing a horse. Think you can make it back to the fort on foot?"

So, Claremont does know I'm a spy. Jarrett struggled to make his feet and legs hold him upright.

"Are you hurt?"

"Not bad. They broke a rib. But I've been tied up so long my feet and legs are numb."

Claremont shucked off his gray greatcoat and shoved Jarrett's arms into the sleeves. "Your teeth are chattering so loud we're sure to be heard." He sighed. "Sit a minute. When you get your feeling back, you'll be able to walk. Here, let me get these boots on you. Blazes, your feet are ice!"

"I owe you my life." Jarrett tugged to get the boots over his feet. "Glad you thought to bring these."

"Don't thank me yet. Soon as they find you gone, they'll

be out in force searching. We got to get you to the fort."

"Eleven miles. I'm not sure I can make it."

"You've got to. I'll go part way—until you get your strength back. Let's get started."

Jarrett forced his legs to move. He couldn't feel his feet. They slammed like two stiff boards against the rocks, sending shocks of pain to his chest with every step.

But he was too slow.

Claremont eased Jarrett's arm over his shoulder and half-carried, half-dragged him through the dismal night.

What seemed like hours later, Claremont stopped to rest. "I wish I had taken the chance of getting that horse, but it seemed too risky. I thought you'd be in better shape and could slip out of here on your own." Nervousness edged his voice.

"I can make the fort from here. You'd better get back to your camp before you're missed."

"Not hardly. You'll drop in your tracks."

They struggled through the night, panting and grunting. With an occasional moan Jarrett stumbled as they half-walked, half-ran toward the safety of Fort Gibson.

Only the jolting of the frozen ground told Jarrett his feet hit the earth.

A memory spurred him on. The race in the Osage village with Runninghorse when he had sprained his ankle. He'd finished last, much to Runninghorse's disgust. He remembered his friend's words, "*Much bad race. If Pawnee chase Woodcarver, he be dead. Pain no reason lose race. Lose life.*"

Knowing Claremont, he wouldn't leave him by the roadside if he quit. Then the Rebs would find them both.

Jarrett set his jaw, forced his mind above his agony, and ran. This time he could not quit.

"You can make it, Jer, we're halfway. I can't let you rest. You'd never get up. We've got to hurry, or I won't make it back to camp before sunrise."

"This is getting to be a habit—next time, I get to help you home."

Claremont chuckled.

Jarrett stopped and faced his friend, his shadow too dark to make out his features. "Sun will rise in another hour. You've got to get back to your camp. I can carry on from here."

Claremont shuffled his feet. "You sure? I hate to leave you here, but I can just make my way back to Flat Rock before sunrise." He laid a heavy hand on Jarrett's shoulder. "I'll see you when this insanity's over."

Jarrett struggled out of Claremont's coat, gripped his arm, and gave him a man hug.

Claremont patted Jarrett's back and melted into the shadows.

Jarrett struggled on toward Fort Gibson, praising God at every step for sending Claremont to save him.

As dawn broke, he stumbled in through the fort's gates.

As soon as he could drag himself to Captain Good's tent, he stood, hands braced behind his back, facing a man roused from his bed, hair tousled, eyes red, but widened after the report Jarrett provided.

"Good work, Ross! You'll be decorated for your service to the United States." Captain Good's tight mouth loosened in a rare smile.

"Thank you, sir." Jarrett shuffled his feet, his thoughts

revolving around food, rest, and getting his broken rib taped.

Good's expression returned to its habitual grim compression. "I'll ferret out the source of who is supplying repeating rifles to General Watie. Someone in the North is selling out our country. Committing treason."

Jarrett nodded.

"Unfortunately, I won't be able to use you as scout now."

"Sir?" Not scout!

"I still need you. But you understand that if the Rebs capture you now, they will have no compunction about shooting you as a spy. You'll be safer inside the fort." Good rubbed a bristled chin, his eyes thoughtful. "I understand you know some about surgery. The post surgeon needs an assistant."

Ugh. Jarrett's stomach knotted. "Yes, sir."

"That plan doesn't seem to appeal to you."

"No, sir. Not in the surgery, sir. I'd rather take my chances with the dragoons."

"You'd rather ride with the cavalry?"

"Yes, sir!"

"But you object to killing?"

"Yes, sir. But I can be useful as a courier."

"So be it." Captain Good held a finger in the air. "I hope your friend Flint wasn't discovered. He could have joined our side and received immunity."

"I know, sir, but his sympathies are with the South. He wouldn't have changed allegiance."

Captain Good's iron gray brows furrowed above his hooked nose. "And yet he helped an enemy escape."

Jarrett smiled. "After this war's over, he'll be my brother-in-law."

"Ah. Blood's thicker than politics. I'd say he's a brother now."

"Yes, sir. Our Cherokee motto is *As brothers live, as brothers die.* I wish we were all on the same side."

CHAPTER 30

April 1863

Jarrett burst into the quarters he shared with Rusty and shoved the newspaper in front of his friend's nose.

Rusty rolled out of his bunk, sat on the edge of the bed, and yawned. "What's this? The war's over?"

"No, but this is the best news I've had in a long time." Jarrett shook the paper straight and read:

"The Cherokee Nation Changes Sides. The Cherokee National Council met at Cowskin Prairie, deposed Stand Watie as principal chief, and reinstated John R. Ross. The council dissolved their treaty with the Confederacy and voted to remove all Cherokee officials who are not loyal to the Union. They abolished slavery."

"Does that mean Watie's on our side now?" Hazel eyes wide, Rusty stood and stretched, his large frame filling the small room.

"Unfortunately, no. It means we're back to the same old Cherokee feud we had in 1838. The Treaty Party, of which Watie is principal chief, and our own Ross Party."

Rusty grabbed a shirt off the floor and stuffed it over his head. "Why change sides then?"

"After we win this war, rather than punishing us as rebels, President Lincoln will reward our Cherokee Nation for service." Jarrett folded the newspaper and shook it at Rusty. "And we *will* win this war."

"Sounds good for you." Rusty frowned and tilted his head. "But does the Cherokee changing sides cause an about-face out here in the West?"

"Not exactly. But since General Stand Watie's Cherokee faction now stands alone with the Confederacy, this news might cool Watie's fervor. He might quit raiding and killing Yankees."

"Doesn't appear like Watie's doing any allegiance-changing, the way he's harassing us. We still don't get supplies through his barricade." Rusty patted his flat stomach.

"I didn't expect Watie to jump the fence. But I hoped he might. Since General Grant laid siege to Vicksburg, I'd guess the war's winding down."

"Don't count your chickens …" Rusty gathered his footwear from where he had tossed them last night, plunked down on the edge of his bunk, and tugged on his boots. He stood and shoved his face next to Jarrett. "Ho! Looks to me like you're working on something! You trying to groom a dragoon's moustache?"

Jarrett fingered the fuzz above his upper lip. "Mine won't be a giant red mustache like yours, but this sad beginning will grow. Soon it'll be fine enough to make me part of this unit!"

"You don't need that wisp to make you part of this

Cavalry. You've earned your way."

Jarrett straightened his shoulders.

Together they tramped through the door, slammed it behind them, and strolled the stone walkway.

~

Jarrett stepped outside his room at Fort Gibson and inhaled the sweet air. "Spring came late this year. Our people say one should walk softly because Mother Earth is pregnant."

Rusty's heavy tread resounded beside him. "Sun will be up soon. Let's see what daylight brings."

They entered the mess hall and joined the line waiting to be served.

"Hope we get more vittles this morning. My backbone's rubbing my stomach." Rusty rose on tiptoes to see above the heads in front.

"No such luck." The mess cook ladled gravy over two small biscuits on their plates.

Didn't take long to finish eating. Jarrett frowned. Still hungry.

Morning bugle blared. He and Rusty jumped up, joined the other troopers, and trekked outside in time to see the sun rise.

Rusty raised his copper brows. "Looks hazy today. Blasted heavy haze. What happened to the fresh air we had before we went to mess?"

Jarrett sniffed. "Not haze. Smoke."

The bugle blared *Stand to Horse*.

Jarrett raced behind Rusty's long strides to the stable.

Mount.

Already waiting on his horse, Captain Good pulled his gelding into a turn. "You men follow me."

Jarrett secured his cap. He joined the other men, and they trotted out the gate in two jaunty lines, the stars and stripes fluttering in the breeze beneath the lead horseman.

With his horse fresh and eager to run, Jarrett welcomed the opportunity to leave the confines of the fort. He sat astride a new mount, just as black and beautiful as Daniel, but this one was a mare. Her quiet temperament didn't suit him as Daniel's spirit had, but she was a good horse.

Jarrett raised his voice to be heard over the hooves clattering on the hard-packed dirt. "I'll wager Sergeant Anderson rides Daniel now, Rusty."

"Let's hope we don't find out. You don't want to meet up with that group again."

"Not in this lifetime."

As they thundered toward Park Hill, smoke billowed toward them. Jarrett's shoulders tensed. The horses galloped into falling ashes and heated air. Around him, men unsheathed their carbines and held them ready.

Hooves rattled on Park Hill's main street.

No, not the Female Seminar! Jarrett leaned forward and touched his heels into his mare's sides.

Rusty yelled, "What's on fire?"

"Just the pride of the Cherokee Nation!"

Stench of blazing wood permeated the air. Cavalry horses, shoulder to shoulder, Jarrett thundered past the charred remains of both churches. Blackened timbers loomed through the smoking ruins like seeking fingers. The new bell from the Presbyterian Church lay cracked among smoking ashes.

Jarrett directed his mare around the curve in the brick road. His stomach twisted.

Barefoot, half-dressed young ladies carried sloshing pails of water.

Suffocating smoke rolled from the lower windows of the school, across the long veranda, and scorched the brick pillars. A sheet of flames erupted through the roof. Along the upper stories, crimson tongues licked out the windows. They were too late.

In the meadow surrounding the seminary, groups of girls clustered in nightdresses, their long hair flowing unbound to their waists, gazing at the blaze devouring the structure.

A roar and crash of timbers and the second story fell. A weight crushed Jarrett's chest. Watie and his men had gone too far.

Captain Good's grizzled brows drew into a frown. He stared at the schoolgirls as though he feared they would faint or dissolve into hysteria. "Ross, you know this town. Where can we find suitable quarters for the ladies?"

Jarrett patted his skittish mare's neck. "There's Chief Ross's Cottage or the Murrell Home down the road. Either would be large enough to house the girls until their parents can come for them."

"Fine. You ride over there and secure permission. In the meantime, we'll do what we can to douse the fire. Who is in charge of those girls?"

Jarrett pointed toward an older woman whose graying hair was pulled back into a tight bun. "I think she's the matron."

The woman's wide eyes and wringing hands announced

she was in no condition to take care of anyone.

For the first time since Jarrett had known his captain, Good looked uncertain.

Jarrett glanced at the scattered girls and the distressed woman.

"I'll be glad to take care of the young ladies, Cap'n." Rusty grinned and turned his gelding toward the huddled girls.

"I'm sure you would. Okay, you ride with Ross."

"I know a shortcut to Rose Cottage." Jarrett trotted toward the woods. Rusty followed. Before they'd cleared the woods, Jarrett's stomach churned. Smoke darkened the sweet spring sunshine.

At the entrance to Rose Cottage's long driveway, Jarrett pulled his mare to a standstill. The home had not been spared. Memories of his annual Christmas visits to Rose Cottage with its red and green festivity were overcome by the pall of gray smoke smothering his senses.

Outbuildings sprinkled about the grounds spouted smoke and fire. They were too late to save anything. Jarrett hunched his shoulders.

"Look!" Rusty pointed.

A shadow caught Jarrett's eye. "Horses in the orchard. Watie's men are still here."

"I count four, five! Let's get 'em!" Rusty held his pistol in one hand, thrust his reins in his teeth, and pulled his carbine from the saddle.

"Hold on! There's probably a dozen more hidden in that orchard. You know how I feel about killing."

"Come on! One race through, and we'll head back to the unit!" Rusty kicked his black horse into a gallop.

Jarrett grunted. *Can't let Rusty ride alone!* Pulling the pistol from his holster, he kneed his mare into a gallop and followed.

Shadows moved behind the trees.

Rusty shot a gray-clad soldier.

The man tumbled to the ground like a rag doll. Rusty got off several more shots. Rebs scurried behind bushes and trees. Two ran for shelter on the far side of the burning smoke house.

Rusty winged a soldier who waited an instant too long to take aim. He tried to get off another shot, but his Colt was empty. He thrust the weapon into its holster, held his carbine in the air, and yelled like a madman.

Jarrett raced up beside him, his horse rearing. "Let's get out of here! There are more than a dozen Rebs!"

Less than twenty-five yards away, men darted from tree to tree.

"Right. Come on!" Rusty galloped away.

Jarrett's horse staggered and stumbled. Blood spurted from a bullet wound in her shoulder.

She fell. He jumped free.

She landed on the side that held his carbine. The mare screamed and writhed, her hooves beating the air. He ended her pain with a shot to her head. Tried to wrench his carbine from its saddle sheath, but the horse was too heavy.

Rusty doesn't know my horse is down. Bullets whined. Jarrett lay flat hiding behind his dead mare. Bullets slammed into the horse. Bloody flesh flew into his face and hair. All around him bullets kicked up grass and dirt.

These men have only to pin me here, surround me, and either shoot me or take me prisoner. I'm a sitting duck! With his forearm, he swiped at the sweat dripping into his eyes. If the Rebs took him prisoner, at Watie's camp they would recognize him. Shot or captured, he was a dead man. His heart pounded. His vision blurred. He counted his bullets. Only five left. He buried his forehead in the mare's side.

Rocks scraping, bushes bending, the Rebs advanced on foot.

A storm of bullets riddled his dead mare. A ricocheting bullet tore his uniform. Nose against his mare's side, glossy black coat red with blood, her good, horse odor turned sour.

A Reb raced to outflank him.

Jarrett slid his weapon along the mare's bloody back and pointed his gun at the Reb. Blood and bullets spattered around him. His pistol wavered, his hands slippery with the mare's blood. The Reb crept to a spot behind the dead mare where he could take a better shot.

From behind, the clatter of hooves broke into Jarrett's concentration.

Rusty shouted, "Grab on!"

Rusty's horse slowed. Jarrett leaped but missed. He grasped the back of Rusty's saddle and hung on.

Rusty's big hand grabbed him by his uniform and hauled him astride the horse's rump. They thundered away. Bullets whizzed close to their ears.

They reached the deeper woods.

"There're not chasing us." Rusty stopped his big horse.

Jarrett wiggled off and stood, legs shaking. He hung onto the saddle with both hands. *I am not going to die.*

"Where'd you get hit?" Rusty's booming voice sounded far away.

"I'm fine."

Rusty's big hands probed him.

"I'm not hurt. Take your hands off me!"

"You've covered with blood. You're hit and don't even know it."

Jarrett felt his head. Blood lathered his forehead. His hair and forehead were matted with blood. Suddenly he laughed.

"Did a bullet rattle your brain?"

"Don't look at me like that, you Kansas bushwhacker. This isn't my blood, it's my horse's."

They leaned against Rusty's gelding and laughed until tears flowed down their faces.

CHAPTER 31

Jarrett hopped off Rusty's horse's rump. "Thanks for the ride." He grinned up at his friend. "And for saving my life."

"Anytime, Ross. My pleasure."

~

Four days later, Jarrett rode back into camp on his new mount, dismounted, and strode directly to Captain Good's command tent.

Good turned from his water pitcher, shaving cream lathering his cheeks. "From the look on your face, I see the news you bring isn't what we hoped." Good wiped his face, moved to his desk, and sat behind the makeshift table. "Pull up that camp chair and give me a detailed report."

Jarrett shoved the chair over and sank down. He'd been out for two days with no rest, but he relaxed on its canvas seat. He leaned forward and cleared his throat. "Rusty overheard several of Watie's men talking. General Watie plans an extended campaign to burn and destroy everything that belongs to Union sympathizers in our Cherokee Nation. I've seen firsthand his diabolical work."

Good winced.

"Watie killed livestock and burned the Council House. I watched private homes emptied and furniture ripped open as the Rebs searched for jewels, silver, and whatever else they could find. They destroyed fields and gardens and torched homes. Watie plans to leave Cherokee Union sympathizers with nothing."

"Are you sure the situation's that bad?" The captain sipped water from a tin cup.

"Watie's strategy is to drive every Union family to Fort Gibson for protection, so we will be obligated to feed them. Since our supply wagons can't get through Watie's blockade, the Rebs can force General Phillips to evacuate the fort."

Good stood and paced his tent. "Which leaves the entire Cherokee Nation belonging to the Rebels. We must stop them."

~

Jarrett rubbed his growling stomach. "Watie's strategy is working." He unsaddled his horse.

Rusty wiped a blanket over his gelding's sweating back. "Don't know how much longer we can take this siege." He massaged a tender spot on his horse's back. "If we surrender the fort, we'll be taken prisoner."

Jarrett groaned. "Pray we don't."

"Maybe we'll evacuate. Live to fight another day."

General Phillips refused to evacuate. Instead, he again cut rations and increased the forages into the devastated countryside. He ordered the troopers, "Flush out and fight the guerrillas. Show them no more mercy than they give us."

Jarrett found guard duty impossible. Rather than stop the people streaming in from the countryside, he and the other guards opened the gates to them.

Jarrett could barely make his way through the crowded fort. The place burst at the seams with women and children.

He and Rusty gave up their quarters to a large family and slept on the parade ground.

Each day when Jarrett rode out to flush out Watie's men or to forage, more gloom hung over the devastated land.

One dull rainy day as he and Rusty sat by the well eating the few pieces of hard tack they had for lunch, an Indian on a pinto with his ribs jutting out, rode up to him. "Ross, letter." He handed a crumpled ball to Jarrett.

Jarrett's heart pounded. He straightened the crushed ball.

My dearest son,

Watie burned our farm. Grandfather Worchester, Jerusha, your dad, and I are safe. Today, we are travelling north to live in Kansas with friends. We plan to return after the war. Please stay safe. We pray for you constantly. I must go.

Love you so very much,
Mother

Jarrett refolded the crumbled half-ledger sheet. *Thank you, Father God, my parents are safe.*

"Good news from your folks?" Rusty stood and stretched.

"Yeah. My family have gone north to escape the war."

"Better than coming here. These refugees inside our fort

are as good as prisoners of the Confederates."

"Right. I've counted over twelve hundred."

"We will all starve." Rusty made a one-eighty circle and gazed around the fort. "Say, Ross, I got an idea. Someone should know how conditions are here." He dug into his pants pocket. "I found this little book full of empty pages on our last forage. Thought it might come in handy. How about you write what's going on around here." Rusty shook his head. "I thought I might, but I'm not handy with words." He extended a small black leather-bound book. "Here, take it. Write what you see."

Jarrett gazed at the parade ground overflowing with makeshift tents and beds. "I don't know. It's dreary stuff." Yet a tiny glow burned in his heart.

"Come on. Do it."

~

June 1863

The words flowed easier than Jarrett imagined.

Bloody skirmish with Watie today. They killed about thirty men. Am hungry all the time, but we still have fake coffee three times a week.

Often, I lie under the stars and pray for the war to end. I long to hear cows lowing and hogs squealing, see fields of wheat and corn growing, and know no one is hungry or hurt.

~

July 2, 1863—Federal commissary train got through

from Fort Scott, but not without a battle. We fought for two days on Cabin Creek, and if the creek hadn't been flooded, Watie would have taken the train. Lost quite a few men, but now we have more food. I missed the fight because of another problem.

I've been sick. Illness hit me suddenly. It's the Intermittent. We had just finished distributing food to the civilians, and I had been sweating so my uniform was damp. Suddenly I got a chill. Pretty soon I was shaking so violently Rusty took me to the hospital. While I lay there in a bunk, Rusty and the surgeon piled on the blankets, but they didn't help. I got the worst headache I've ever had. My eyes ached so I thought the sockets would rot. Rusty said I was out of my head. When the fever broke, my uniform was soaked. My bunk was soaked, and Rusty was so scared he called the chaplain.

This process repeated itself every day for the next six days. The surgeon says the worst is over, but I can expect to have these attacks every other day or so for the next six months, or a year or ten years, depending on when my body can shake off the sickness. When the attack first comes on, I take enough quinine to stick on the end of a knife. Is it bitter! But the quinine helps.

I don't like to admit how much time I spend dreaming of Delight since I'm in no fit condition to do anything else. I long to see her. One glimpse of her would do me more good than all the medicine in Indian Territory. I dream of her eyes framed in those thick lashes looking at me. I see the sun shining on her hair as it falls around her face. And long to touch her. I miss her warm, sweet presence. I hate not knowing where she is or if she is safe. I'm almost glad the whole territory is in Confederate hands because then I feel she is safe. I know she is waiting for me. I trust her love. Memories of her fill me with longing such as I have never known. Perhaps Claremont saw her and told her of our adventure.

I just received word I must move out. The hospital is overcrowded. I'll give my place to those in more serious condition. So, it's back to a blanket on the parade ground.

I keep quinine with me at all times. The shakes occur every other day and drain my strength. Now that I'm better, hunger plagues me. Rusty has an even harder time. A big man like him has the same rations I do. He's lost a lot of weight. We all have.

~

July 16, 1863—Tomorrow is the big day. The Rebel Colonel Cooper has gathered an army of Creek, Choctaw, Chickasaw, and Watie Cherokee forces with two squadrons of Texas Cavalry. They plan to march up the Texas road and capture Fort Gibson. At present, they are camped along Honey Springs, awaiting reinforcements from Fort Smith. Good old Rusty got this intelligence a week past.

Thank God General Blunt made a forced march down from Kansas and arrived here to reinforce us a few hours ago. Blunt brought supply trains. Enough food so everyone eats!

Tomorrow, we attack Cooper at Honey Springs. We must defeat the Rebs before they join forces against us.

I should be sleeping but am too unnerved. We are all lying crowded together around the Neosho River outside the stockade. My light is a candle sitting in the round end of my bayonet which is stuck into the earth. All around me are men trying to sleep, but I doubt many can. We are all too busy thinking our thoughts and remembering our loved ones. The heat and mosquitoes are unrelenting.

My sickness has improved to the point where I suffer an attack only about every fourth day, and the attack only lasts about three hours, during which time I have learned to keep going. I should be fit for duty tomorrow.

If we win the battle and route the Rebels, what will happen to Delight? This thought torments me so I scarcely remain sane. I know our side has committed atrocities against civilians. Somehow, I must get leave and find her. If we win, she will be safer here with me, even though the fort is crowded. I'm sure Captain Good can find room for her. But I pray she and her family have already gone south to Texas. I cannot rest until I find out.

~

The bugle sounded.

Jarrett opened heavy eyes. Good, he'd slept after all. In the darkness men fastened on sabers, holsters, and guns.

He felt his way for his empty grub sack, his saddlebags, and his mare.

There was little talk—just the rustling of feet, clinking of weapons and gleaming of eyes.

Then he stood in a long line of cavalry, every nerve alert, waiting.

The bugler blew *Stand to Horse.*

Jarrett's foot hit the stirrup with a slap.

Then came the call *Mount.*

Jarrett's reins slapped, and his tail end landed in his saddle, along with scores of others, sounding like welcome thunder in a drought.

Excitement twinged through him as the cavalry trotted two abreast in precise rows, plumes and moustaches waving in the pre-dawn coolness. He sat ramrod straight in his saddle, swung his horse in at the head of his unit to ride beside Rusty, and followed Captain Good.

Today, they faced the enemy. *I pray this is our final battle.*

He raised his chin. General Blunt's reinforcements tripled their ranks. Behind them marched four thousand infantrymen, and behind them horse teams pulled cannon. Horse-drawn ambulances and supply wagons followed in the rear.

When he rode through the fort's gates, a multitude of women and children crowded the area, waving. No doubt praying husbands and fathers would return.

As Jarrett neared Honey Springs, the sun rose to their left, treating him to a glorious sunrise.

All nature signs pointed to rain tomorrow. Would he be alive to see it?

Thank you, Father God, my family is safe with friends somewhere up north. Please keep Delight safe wherever she is.

Would he ever see her lovely face again?

CHAPTER 32

August 30, 1863

I write this for my loved ones should they ask how I *fought in the War Between the States. I feel no desire to speak of my experience. Rather, after writing this, I wish to bury my memories.*

On July 17, we found the Rebels well dug in behind tree-studded ravines and earthworks. Our unit was ordered to stand by, so we waited in a small wood. Some men grumbled. I felt relief.

I heard the battle but could see little. I could only guess what was happening. To my right, guns fired. Sulfuric smoke hung over the area. With thunderous hooves, a six-horse team roared past. A rider rode one horse of each pair, and the horses dragged a caisson and a twelve-pound cannon.

Three more caissons arrived. They stopped about a hundred yards in front of our company. The gunners loaded, then held up his hand. Someone pulled the lanyard, and the cannon roared. Smoke billowed, the ground trembled.

My mare lunged, so I was almost unseated. I felt as tense and wild as my horse. Smoke filled my nostrils. The great guns roared again. Holes gaped in trees. Heavy branches crashed. Screams rose from within the smoking woods.

Beside me, Rusty's face went white. I suspect mine did too.

Then our bugle blew. We galloped double-time after Captain Good, straight into the smoke-shrouded gully. As we thundered in, I saw dead men lying in grotesque positions.

"Fix bayonets!" Captain Good shouted.

A spasm shook me. My eyes streamed tears from the smoke and from the sight. Then, alongside my buddies, at a dead gallop we pulled our rifles from their scabbards, slipped our bayonets from our belt, hooked them over the muzzles and twisted. We put our reins in our teeth and grabbed our Colts. As courier, I had no intention of using my weapons, but I had to be in battle readiness. I set my jaw so hard it ached.

We swept past General Blunt, who was surrounded by a group of officers on horseback. I fixed his location in my mind as we surged forward into a blast of gunfire. Bullets slammed into our dragoons. Some men fell.

Anger—sudden and intense—filled me. I could not recognize who dropped, but they were friends. Men I knew well. Grief, still raw from losing my brother, churned again. I strove to keep my wits about me. Captain Good counted on me.

Bark flew off trees. The horses plunged nervously, eyes protruding, but kept going forward. Another blast and a bullet stung my cheek.

The forest in front of us spewed fire. Men and horses fell all around me. I experienced no fear. I felt more alive than I had ever been, as if all of life up to now had been a rehearsal and this was the play. I hated the death and destruction, but I would do my duty and not let my comrades down.

With a deafening roar, grapeshot smashed through the air. The ground trembled. My ears rang so I could barely hear the bugle blow Retreat. Our men turned in their saddles and fired until their carbines were empty. We retreated deliberately, in good order.

I rode close to Captain Good's side. Throughout the woods, on the churned grass, bodies sprawled in scattered heaps. They looked unnatural and incongruous among the broken trees—and they wore blue uniforms.

I cannot rid myself of that sight.

Then I saw Rusty. He lay behind a scrubby bush, his rifle in one hand, his other arm spurting blood. His hat was gone, and his red hair shone in the smoke like a target.

The Rebs were advancing, stealing from tree to tree.

Rusty's mouth opened, but I couldn't hear him over the ringing in my ears.

I wheeled my mare and galloped toward Rusty. Something hit my leather cross belt and knocked the wind out of me. I almost toppled from the saddle but hung on to my trusty girl.

As I stretched down for Rusty, fire cracked from beyond the bush. He couldn't reach me. I slid off my horse. But before I could hoist Rusty onto the saddle, I had to stop those advancing Rebs.

I aimed and fired until my carbine emptied. I saw men collapse but felt only relief. Then a Reb broke through to where Rusty hid behind his fallen horse.

The Reb aimed his rifle.

I thrust him through with my bayonet.

He looked at me, eyes wide, brows raised.

I watched as blood dripped from his mouth to his beardless chin. Then he folded in on himself and fell to the ground. I snagged Rusty's arms and tried to hoist him to the saddle. He was heavy, almost unconscious. I seemed to have superhuman strength as I wedged him over my saddle. Dropping my empty carbine, I clutched the back of my saddle and swung up to my horse's rump, kicking her to a gallop before I was fully on.

Rusty whispered, "Thank you" in my ear.

After I deposited Rusty into an ambulance, I noticed my hands were not trembling, nor was I frightened. But the young soldier I had bayoneted remained vividly behind my eyes. Fleeing the memory of his face, I galloped to Captain Good.

I found our company riddled by the enemy's fire. Captain Good ordered the remaining men to take the hollow from which we had just retreated. First, we must recross that open field and face the Reb's deadly fire again.

Captain turned his soot-blackened face to me. "Find General Blunt and ask for cannon to clear our way."

I obeyed, then returned from my mission shortly before the caissons moved in.

I dragged in the saddle now, barely able to think. War is chaos. Peace a dream. I scarcely remember peace.

Then the battery bombarded the hollow again.

Alert again, I charged with our men across the open meadow, dismounted, and took cover behind the trees on the other side where we fought on foot like infantry.

Captain Good ordered, "Ross, find Lieutenant Grayson. Tell him to protect our flanks and reinforce our dragoons."

I leaped on my mare, but in the smoke and confusion, it took some time for me to locate Lieutenant Grayson.

I turned in the direction I thought our lines were. Smoke made the air difficult to breathe. I had a fit of coughing before I could convey my message to Lieutenant Grayson. Immediately, he ordered his company to follow me.

On foot, his dirty, exhausted men followed my horse.

This time, the field artillery did their job. We ran over that open meadow and charged through the trees in time to back Captain Good's Dragoons. They fought with bayonets, not having time to reload their rifles. Lieutenant Grayson's men routed the Rebels from the hollow.

Captain Good's hand trembled as he lit his homemade shuck cigarette. "Ross, find General Blunt and report our position. Ask what we should do next—sit tight and hold the hollow, or advance."

The wavering lines of battle confused me. In one clump of trees, the Rebs advanced. Down the next hollow, our men strode forward, while behind them, more Rebs cut off our men at their flank. There were no clear-cut lines. Here a Union flag flew and close beside it a Rebel flag waved.

Just then the Intermittent struck. I shivered but pressed on.

I had to find General Blunt.

That is the last thing I remember.

~

September 1, 1863

I continue my narrative today, having earlier become too

weary to finish.

I was never aware I had been hit, but obviously I had. I lay on my back beneath a great old oak. Twigs and grass were strewn across my face and body. I tried to sit but found I couldn't. Pain radiated from my forehead and behind my left eye. I raised my hand to my head and felt warm blood oozing down the side of my head. Not far from where I lay, the battle still thundered. I blacked out.

When I awoke, the battle had moved away, but men walked around me. They were not in uniform, so they had to be Rebs.

My head stopped bleeding. I felt grateful, but pain racked me so I couldn't sit. My vision was blurred, and I could barely see.

I must have lost consciousness again because when I opened my eyes, there was no sound of battle and no one walking. Moans sounded around me from the wounded. Darkness came.

A man prayed and cried.

The sound of men in agony is heartbreaking. But worse still is when their groans stop. We lay there together, men in blue and men in gray. No longer enemies, but human beings in pain. My thoughts tormented me about the men I had killed. I had disobeyed my God and taken life. In war, yes. In self-defense, yes. But that didn't bring me peace. I had sent men into eternity—young men in the prime of life, who may not have known my Savior. The anguish in my heart tore me more than the stabbing in my head. I prayed for the men I killed—and for their families. I prayed for forgiveness, but the young soldier's face lingered in my mind. I could not forget the blame in his eyes. Against my deepest principles,

I had taken life. With the ground hard beneath me, I searched into the blackness of my soul.

Something Uncle Jeremy told me filtered into my pain-racked mind. I remembered the overwhelming intensity of his green eyes. Uncle Jeremy said, "God designs problems for your life so you can experience need. You begin to really know God according to the measure of the difficulty he meets in your life. Perhaps this is one answer to the mystery of suffering."

I prayed for forgiveness and knew, somehow God forgave me for taking those lives.

We lay on the battlefield all night. It didn't seem long, so I must have blacked out again. With sunrise a horrible weariness filled me. I felt certain I would die. I would never see Delight again. Never see my family again. Never know if Rusty was alive.

Rain fell. My mouth and throat were so dry I sucked moisture from my uniform sleeve. The uniform that bestowed on me the right to kill.

Two men found me, lifted me to a stretcher, and carried me to where an ambulance waited. Whether I was in Union or Rebel hands, I did not know. Nor did I know who had won the battle.

The ambulance jolted, and I blacked out.

~

September 7, 1863

When I woke, it was morning. I lay in a hospital bed at Fort Gibson, relieved to find myself in Union hands. My filthy uniform was gone. I wore a nightshirt and had been washed and bandaged. The pain in my head was still severe. My left eye was bandaged, and my sight blurred in my right eye. People were shadows.

Rusty sat beside me. I recognized his voice and big form. When he saw I stirred, he spooned warm broth into my mouth. I could barely swallow at first, but soon I was able to eat enough to satisfy him.

Around me, wounded men filled the hospital. Those who could walk helped the surgeon with those who could not. I was under strict orders to lie flat on my cot, which was easy to do as the pain became excruciating if I attempted to lift my head.

Days passed in rugged slowness. Rusty was the one cheerful presence in the crowded room filled with moaning men. When my vision finally began to clear, I was shocked to find Rusty sitting by my bunk, his arm swathed in bandages from the elbow up. From the elbow down, he had no arm. Since he was caring for me, I had figured him not to be badly wounded.

He grinned his wide, happy grin. "Could have been worse. If some kid who can't even grow a respectable mustache hadn't saved me, I would have died."

Even with Rusty there, the days were long and tedious as I mended. Other men either died or left. When could I go?

Finally, the day arrived when I could sit. The surgeon removed my bandage.

Rusty nudged my shoulder. "You look great. The scar isn't so bad."

Except I had completely lost sight in my left eye.

"Your eye looks as good as your right one. Are you

certain you can't see?"

I held my hand over my right eye, and with my left eye wide open, stared toward the sun shining through the window. "Nothing. Black." And yet I felt so grateful to be alive.

I had long since been told that our forces drove the Confederates out. Their defeated troops withdrew to camps in the South, leaving Cherokee Territory in Union hands.

With the war over in this area, some friends got tired of me moping about Delight and searched the countryside for her. But they learned nothing, and I still have no knowledge of her whereabouts. I'm in a fever to get well enough to look for her.

It's ironic that the battle of Gettysburg occurred at about the same time in the East as the battle of Honey Springs in the West. In Gettysburg with Lee's defeat, the Union struck a deep wound to the Confederacy. In Honey Springs, with Cooper's defeat, the Union broke the Confederate resistance in the West. How much longer before Lee surrenders?

I find I need more courage after the battle to face the reasons why so much slaughter was necessary than I needed courage on the battlefield. Are the reasons for war ever as awful as the results?

I have one consolation. In his own frank way, Rusty told me God has begun to make a woodcarving of him. That information gave me great joy.

I'm a different man now. I have nightmares every night. I see men's twisted bodies lying on wooded hills. I see an army of ghosts rising from the bloated bodies with empty, staring eyes. They wander through blackened countryside. And I rouse, sweat-drenched. I, who vowed never to send a soul into eternity.

It was a shocking journey to discover life can be lost in a blink. There are no guarantees and for many, no second chances. I find life is a precious gift.

Rusty read a newspaper article about the tombstone Abraham Lincoln recently raised over the grave of a young man killed in the battle of Gettysburg.

The tombstone was inscribed HE DIED FOR ME. In just the way the man died for those not in the war, Christ died for all men, giving freely to all who will receive the gift of eternal life. This gift of salvation is the most precious thing I possess and the only one I cannot lose.

CHAPTER 33

October 15, 1863

Jarrett saluted. "Thank you for the furlough, Captain."

Captain Good rose from his seat, walked around his desk, and shook Jarrett's hand. "I've never been prouder to promote a man to first lieutenant. I'm sorry to assign you permanently to the fort."

"I'm happy with my new duty, sir. Training those glorious black horses is a treat for me. I'll take charge as soon as I return." *If I make it back from Texas alive.*

"You deserve it, Ross. Glad your wound is healed. I assume you're going to search for your Rebel sweetheart."

"Yes, sir!"

"Good luck. I reckon you think after the Rebs' defeat at Honey Springs, her family fled to Texas for sanctuary. Be careful there. Place is Rebel territory. Dangerous for any young man not wearing gray." Good offered one of his rare smiles. "Go find her."

"I will, sir." Jarrett turned, ducked out the tent door, and sprang on his waiting horse.

Once outside Fort Gibson, he halted his latest military-supplied steed and gazed back at the busy activity inside the gates. "Well, Onyx," he patted the glossy black neck. "Without Watie's bushwhackers, feels free out here." Except he couldn't help keeping a lookout for Rebs even though they had evacuated the area and moved south. "I pray Delight hasn't gone to Texas, but if she has, I'll go after her." Beneath the freedom of his buckskin, he straightened his shoulders, then tipped his hat to the fort. "When I return, I won't be alone, even if I have to search Texas, Arkansas, and Missouri to find her."

Jarrett inhaled the crisp morning air, turned in the saddle, and checked the straps on his saddlebags. He ran his fingers over the army-issue carbine in its saddle sheath and tightened the belt holding the holster of his Colt. Then he patted his shirt pocket containing all his back pay.

He'd shaved that morning, leaving the sandy-blond mustache struggling above his upper lip. The mirror hanging on a post above his water pitcher had shown a raw, livid scar slashed across his left brow. But his two blue eyes looked identical. So, the loss of sight in his left eye was undetectable. Would Delight still love him the way he looked now? He clicked to Onyx. "Come on, boy. We've twenty miles to go."

As if happy to be on the road, Onyx broke into a trot.

The first jolts of the hooves on the road started a pounding in his head. Occasionally he still suffered severe headaches from his wound, so he shouldn't be surprised to get one now. But no signs of his periodic bouts of the Intermittent. He smiled. Today started a new chapter in his life.

As his black gelding raised his legs high and trotted through the sunlit October morning, his headache lessened.

His heart leaped with the beauty of rust and gold leaves contrasting with the blue cloudless sky.

He inhaled the nippy air, feeling young again for the first time in months. He settled his broad-brimmed hat securely and let Onyx lope.

Some time later, at a pleasant bend in the road, he rested Onyx and ate hardtack for lunch.

In the saddle again, he turned Onyx off the Texas Road where the dirt road forked and headed for the Flint Ranch.

He reached forward and patted Onyx's neck. "Their ranch house has been burned to the ground, but I have to ride by before we turn south."

He fingered the raw scar on his forehead. "I'm not going to worry that the post surgeon warned me another blow to my head might blind me. I've got to find Delight."

Onyx flicked his ears and broke into a gallop.

Jarrett rode easy in the saddle. Three days to ride down to the Texas border. Three days to search the refugee camps. If Delight wasn't there … then on to Texas.

Onyx cantered past the woods. The land grew more desolate. No livestock grazed. No living thing in sight. Eerie. The spookiness increased as he slowed to a trot approaching the Flint Ranch. The split rail fence still surrounded the grounds. The gravel path still followed its curve up to the house. But the house was gone. Instead, blackened timbers and a half-burned fieldstone fireplace reached crippled fingers to the sky. The nearby trees stood barren, bark burned, leaves gone.

Jarrett slumped in the saddle and gazed at the ruins. The meadows were weed-choked and untended. Looked as if the Flints had lost everything. Rusty had reported that both Flint men were still alive and still rode with General Watie far in the South, fighting for what they believed was right. Fantastic to know Claremont was alive.

Jarrett sighed, picked up his reins, turned Onyx, and headed south. Texas would be a long, hard ride.

His side vision picked up a flutter. He stared with his good eye, then urged Onyx back to the fence.

Tied to the broken gatepost, dancing in the breeze, waved a faded blue ribbon.

Their secret message.

His pulse pounded. The world swayed as his heart found a place to hope.

He sprang off Onyx, let the reins fall, and touched the rough crevice in the rail fence. Prodding and tugging, he extracted a tiny oilskin packet and with fumbling fingers opened the packet.

A note from Delight. His hands trembled.

Dearest Jarrett,

I know someday, if you live, you will come for me. I refused to go to Texas with my mother because I feared if I did, I would never see you again. Instead, I asserted my will for the first time in my life—I am nineteen now. After several bad scenes, Mother relented.

I am staying in the Murrell Home. Grandmother Murrell kindly consented to take me in so that I might help her care for the orphaned children living here. No one else knows where I am.

I cannot leave until I see you. How I long to go to you but seeking you is too dangerous since every Union soldier knows my father and brother. I fear I will be killed in revenge.

I heard rumors you were wounded. Even if you have lost both legs or both arms, my love is still yours. I have waited three long years for you. I shall wait three more if I must, but I shall be here when you are free to come for me.

I pray you will come soon.
Yours until death,
Delight

His throat closed. Tears blinded his eyes. He folded the note, pressed the crumpled paper to his lips, then tucked the precious words inside his breast pocket. He leaped onto Onyx and galloped back in the direction of Park Hill and the Murrell home. Delight had not been there when the fire burned the Women's Seminary. He'd searched for her, thinking there might be the slightest chance of finding her.

Onyx broke into a sweat.

He slowed his gelding to a canter.

Almost a half hour later he pulled Onyx to a stop in a secluded area on the outskirts of Park Hill. His shoulders relaxed. He could breathe again. Except for the grounds' unkept appearance, the Murrell house looked untouched by the war.

Working to steady his trembling hands, he tied his horse to the hitching post. In front of the gate leading to an overgrown flower garden, he paused and gazed at the large two-storied home.

A shiver shook him. Definitely not from the Intermittent. He whipped off his hat, brushed cold fingers through his hair, then dusted his boots against the backs of his buckskin-clad legs.

He exhaled a silent prayer and pushed open the gate.

The metal screeched.

He strode up the unkept walkway and banged on the wooden door.

No answer.

He pressed his ear to the wood and heard muted voices inside. He shifted his weight from one foot to another, bracing his weak knees. He knocked again. *Oh please, Lord, let Delight still be here.*

The door burst open, and a tousled, brown-haired head peaked out. An impudent voice asked, "What do you want?" Brown eyes flashed fire.

"Miss Delight Flint."

"Why do you want her?" Narrow shoulders squared. The child stared up, inspecting Jarrett from head to toe.

"I'm a friend. I must see her. She's expecting me." Jarrett pulled in deep breaths and unable to stand still, paced the veranda.

The boy continued to stare, his brows drawn tight, and his lips compressed.

"Well, tell her I'm here."

A voice floated from inside the house. "Who is it, Noah?"

Noah yelled loud enough to alert the household and anyone who might be on the far reaches of the grounds. "A man. Wants to see Miss Delight."

"I'm coming!"

"He's wearing a gun. He don't look so tough 'cept his eyes. We'd better not let him see her." The child pulled his head back inside the house and slammed the door.

Jarrett smashed a fist against the wood.

The door reopened. Holding the door as if she feared he might force his way into her home, an elderly woman peeked out. She was delicately boned and wore her white hair pulled into a bun. Her head barely reached Jarrett's shoulders.

Jarrett softened his voice. "Good morning, ma'am. I would like to see Miss Delight. Would you tell her Jarrett Ross is calling?"

Her gray eyes looked him over as thoroughly as the small boy's dark ones had. She stepped out onto the veranda and closed the door behind her. Tilting her head to one side like a bird seeking worms, she continued her inspection.

Jarrett waited.

Finally, a twinkle appeared in her faded eyes, and a smile smoothed her wrinkled lips. "How did you know Miss Flint was staying here?"

"She left a note for me. May I see her?"

A cluster of children pushed their way out the door and onto the veranda. Frowning and murmuring, children with hair and skin of various shades oogled him with suspicious eyes.

The fragile-looking lady gathered the gawking children and herded them back inside the house. "Shush. Go inside." She lifted her face to the sky. "The Lord's telling me you're the one."

Jarrett's heart pounded.

The lady's voice quivered. "Delight is in the orchard, picking apples. I expect if you walk around back there, you'll surprise her, Mr. Ross. I expect you'll surprise her a good bit."

Jarrett mumbled a quick, "Thank you, ma'am." He pivoted so fast he almost stumbled off the veranda, leaped down the steps, and raced to the orchard.

He saw her. In the orchard under the branches of a stunted apple tree.

She turned her head, saw him coming. Her expression transformed from calm to ecstatic. Delight, blonde hair streaming behind, raced toward him her long skirts bellowing behind.

He opened his arms and folded her to his chest. Her beautiful frame pressed against him, and her fresh scent filled his senses. He'd longed to have his arms around her for more than two war-torn years. Now, he'd hold her forever. Never let her go.

The world faded. Happiness, joy, love, completeness, and a hundred other emotions nailed him to the spot.

She buried her delightful face in his shoulder.

Her sweet, full lips were warm and responsive beneath him. He lifted her and molded her body to his. Pent-up yearning and loneliness stored from long months apart burned strong in his kiss.

She broke away. "Jarrett, you must stop." Her breathless voice and the pulse pounding in her delicate neck made his heart soar.

In her simple, dark cotton dress, she looked more beautiful than he remembered. He caressed the silvery-blonde hair falling around her face.

Her lips trembled. With a gentle finger, she traced the raw scar across his left brow. Her touch sent currents through his body.

She smiled. Deep dimples appeared in her cheeks.

Tremors send currants of joy through his body. There was nothing he would not do for this girl. He loved her more than his own life.

Delight caressed his cheek. "You've changed, my love. You've something inside now that you didn't have before." Her finger traced his mouth. "You've always had strength, moral and physical. I think that's why I fell in love with you. But now you have something new. Compassion, I think. Compassion and understanding. I can see those things in your eyes. And pain."

"I thought you fell in love with my dashing personality."

Delight laughed. "Yes, that too." She cupped his face with her warm hands.

Jarrett kept her close. "You are the love of my life. Come with me," he whispered into her ear, his cheek against her soft hair.

She pulled back to look into his eyes. "Where?"

"To Fort Gibson. Uncle Jeremy's there again for a few days. We can get married this afternoon!"

"But …" her hand brushed at her tousled hair. She gazed down at her drab dress. "I look—"

"Beautiful! You are the most glorious woman alive." He traced her lips with his finger. "Inside and out. Thinking of you has kept me sane during the worst times of my life. I cannot live without you."

"Yes, my love, yes. I cannot believe you've finally come for me."

"And I've stashed enough money that we can start a horse farm when the war's over. You do like horses?"

She nodded, her blue-violet eyes sparkling.

"I'll buy the best mares the army will sell me."

She pulled back to gaze up at him. "Really?"

He tugged her close again. "And for now, you'll be safer

at the fort with me."

She tipped her head to gaze into his eyes, her own anxious. "But the children? I can't abandon Mrs. Murrell."

"I'll have soldiers from the fort come and fetch them all. We'll see they are taken care of." He pulled her to him, kissing her hair, her face, her lips.

Delight, eyes dreamy and lips smiling touched his mouth with a tender finger. "What about Father?"

"I'll take my chances." Jarrett grasped her hand and tugged her along as he ran toward his horse. "We'll be married before I see your father again."

She stopped midstride. "Married? After all this time? Tonight?"

"Absolutely tonight. We've been apart way too long. The Lord has preserved us for this day, my love! We were born for such a time as this. With our love, you and I will end this fifty-year-feud."

Delight twined her arms around his neck and kissed him, long and sweet. When she pulled back and gazed up at him, her astonishing eyes sparkled. "The war has mellowed Father. Though he didn't accept you before, he certainly will when we lay his first grandbaby in his arms. My father adores children."

"Who would have thought?" Jarrett took her hand, and they raced through the forlorn meadow that would someday be beautiful and serene again, just like their lives together.

EPILOGUE

In other parts of the United States, the Civil War continued its bloody destruction for another year and eight months. In Tennessee, the costly battles of Chickamauga and Chattanooga were fought at the site of the old Cherokee Nation where Cherokees were removed from their homeland to travel the Trail of Tears. You can read of that event in my book, *Trail of Tears: the Story of John Ross*.

In Indian Territory, Stand Watie retreated to the far south into winter quarters in the Choctaw Nation near Boggy Depot. His men were worn out, often without sufficient food or ammunition, and rode poor, thin horses. But he made every effort to feed starving Confederate refugees along the Red River and Texas border.

Early in the spring, Stand Watie took to the field again. But Union soldiers brought in from across the Mississippi overwhelmingly outnumbered his scanty force. After the fall of Vicksburg and the victory at Gettysburg, these Union Soldiers were no longer needed east of the Mississippi.

On May 10, 1864, President Jefferson Davis made Stand Watie a brigadier general. He was the only Indian to become a brigadier general during the Civil War.

Ten weeks after General Lee's surrender at Appomattox

on April 9, 1865, and a month after General Kirby Smith surrendered in Texas, Brigadier General Stand Watie, on June 23, 1865, went down in history as the last Confederate general to surrender his sword.

After his capture, Chief John R. Ross lived in Philadelphia for the duration of the war. President Lincoln and his cabinet treated Chief Ross, as principal chief of the Cherokees, with respect. During the winter of 1863, President Lincoln promised Chief Ross that the United States would not hold the Cherokee treaty with the Confederacy against the nation. He would give them a full pardon.

Chief Ross enjoyed a close personal friendship with President Lincoln. But, following the war Chief Ross suffered ruined health. He was grief-stricken by his young wife's death in Philadelphia, his eldest son's death in a Confederate prison camp, and by the devastation of the Cherokee Nation.

Chief Ross was so old and ill he was unable to attend any of the peace treaty negotiations between the Cherokee Nation and the United States. Had President Lincoln not been assassinated, Lincoln would have given the Cherokee Nation a full pardon for joining the Confederacy.

Stand Watie's faction sought permission to divide the nation into two separate nations. The U.S. rejected that solution for securing peace between Union and Confederate Cherokees.

The peace treaty signed July 17, 1866, was a hard blow to the Cherokee Nation. The US required them to grant a right-of-way to railroads to cross their country. The Cherokee rightly feared this would encourage white settlement within their nation. The US also required the Cherokee to give up all their neutral lands in Kansas to allow the United States to locate friendly Indians in the Cherokee Outlet. The treaty gave the United States the right to erect military posts within the nation to police it. All this as reprisal for joining the Confederacy, even though two Cherokee regiments fought most of the Civil War on the Union side.

But the United States did give the Cherokee the right to remain an independent republic.

Two weeks after signing the peace treaty, August 1, 1866, Chief John Ross died. He had served his nation for nearly half a century.

Stand Watie was destitute after the war. His son, Saladin, died in 1868, and in 1869, his youngest son, Watica, died. Stand Watie died on September 9, 1871, soon followed by his two daughters in 1873. When Sarah Watie died in 1880, Stand Watie's family ceased with no descendants.

Following the deaths of Stand Watie and John R. Ross, the division that had torn the Cherokee Nation from 1830 until 1871 began to heal.

Would history have been different if these two great men—one a political genius, the other a military genius, both claiming to be Christians—had buried their differing philosophical views, and united as Christian brothers for the best interests of the Cherokee Nation?

Dear Reader,

I hope you enjoyed *For Such a Time* as much as I loved writing about Jarrett, Delight, and the Ross and Flint families. Thank you for joining me on this journey of love, adventure, and faith.

For Such A Time is one of my favorite stories because the novel is based on history. Almost everything that happened to Jarrett occurred in history.

This is a story of ordinary people who do extraordinary things, a theme that often occurs in my books. I pray you will join me as I continue the Ross Saga, with stories of Jerusha Ross and Jeremy Worchester.

I find it such a pleasure to speak with my readers. Please visit with me at www.AnneGreeneAuthor.com, and www.facebook.com/AnneWGreeneAuthor. You can also subscribe to my newsletter so we can keep in touch. I enjoy discovering what you think about my books.

Thank you for reading *For Such a Time*. Please consider telling your friends how much you enjoyed this book and post a short review on Amazon or Good Reads. Word of mouth is an author's best friend and much appreciated.

Hugs,
Anne

BOOK CLUB DISCUSSION

1. What lessons did Jarrett learn during the buffalo hunt?

2. What did you discover from Jarrett's experience with the Pony Express?

3. Do you believe a man and a woman could remain in love when separated for such a long period? Why or why not?

4. The faith element was important to the story. How did Jarrett's growth in faith speak to you?

5. What did you learn from the real-life events of the buffalo hunt, the Pony Express, and the Civil War as fought in the West?

6. What was your reaction to Jarrett and Delight's romance?

7. What do you think was the author's purpose in writing this book?

8. What parts of the book did you find thought-provoking or disturbing?

9. What themes did you detect in the story?

10. Did the book give you any new insights?

Feel free to email me at: <u>annewgreene@gmail.com</u> with your thoughts.

Enjoy an **excerpt** from Book 1 of the Ross Family Saga.

TRAIL OF TEARS, THE STORY OF JOHN ROSS

CHAPTER 1
June 1838

John Ross walked with a confident stride, sure of his place in the world. He swung his arms, relishing the freedom of his buckskin shirt, so different from the confining claw-hammer coat dictated by his aristocratic status. His long steps covered ground fast. He wiped perspiration from his forehead and couldn't wait to strip and dive into the cool lake.

Today, Father had released him from his responsibilities.

Father would not admit to giving John a day off because he needed one. But Father wasn't blind. Last night, John dragged one foot after another when he trudged up to his bedroom. Learning to oversee the Ross plantation hadn't been easy. Without resorting to whips, he used sweat and guile to motivate their slaves.

"Gain their respect. Show them you can do any job better than the best of them." Father's hand had been warm on John's shoulder. "Make them hustle to keep up with you."

John hadn't been certain he could obey Father's orders. But he stood in line beneath the blistering sun for hours loading wagons with heavy bales of cotton to be driven north from their plantation to what had been called Ross's Landing, last year renamed Chattanooga.

Many times, only his pride kept him working. He couldn't quit with the slaves watching. If he gave up, they would dub him a lily-livered silk stocking and wouldn't work.

He flexed his calloused hands. All the suffering had paid off. He was in top shape, his muscles toned … lean and hard, and his pale skin tanned golden.

A strange rustle disturbed the leaves ahead. What? His moccasins skidded as he slid to a stop on the dewy grass. A huge fallen oak blocked his path, and the scent of fresh sawdust filled the air. He touched the still-living end of the hewn-down tree. Who dared remove their boundary oak?

Every nerve prickled. He rubbed a hand across the back of his neck where short hairs bristled.

He had been born here where the wind blew free, his father before him, and his father before him. John knew every stream and every wood. The land would one day be his, and he would never let anyone steal this property.

He glanced around, scanning the countryside. The small lake sparkled, serene in the early morning sunlight. Across the water, familiar farmland rolled toward foothills. Mountains rose above the hills, following each other in stately procession, peaks shadowed with smoky haze. No movement. No enemy.

He shifted his feet. What should he do? In the distance, a horse neighed—answered by another. He stiffened and clenched his fists. He had to get home. Something was wrong.

He spun back the way he had come and ran. In the still, muggy air, his moccasins made no sound as he bolted down a path beneath trees festooned with ivy. Hearing sharpened for danger, but only the shrill chirp of an occasional bird, bees buzzing among wildflowers, and the whisper of squirrels foraging for nuts broke the silence.

Humid air hung a damp coat of perspiration, wetting the buckskin on his shoulders and chest. Swiping a sweaty arm across his brow, he raced on. He leaped a clump of wild raspberry branches reaching across the trail to rip at his buckskins.

Suddenly, gunfire rattled from the direction of the house.

He veered into a shortcut, pounding off the narrow path, shielding his face as he plowed through tangled briars and bushes. Shot after shot crackled through the still morning. He bounded into a sprint. Must be an army. Why hadn't he carried his rifle? The woods thinned and acrid smoke floated in to sting his nostrils. Fear iced his heart. Gasping for breath, dull pain racked his side as he broke free of the woods and dropped behind a large magnolia tree.

High on a hill at the end of an avenue of oaks, puffs of smoke erupted from rifles dotting the perimeter of the lawn surrounding his parents' white-pillared mansion. Flames licked through two of the downstairs windows.

John's stomach cramped into a hard knot.

Bands of men concealed themselves behind the trimmed hedges. Judging by the baggy broadcloth trousers, the attackers resembled bandits rather than an army of trained soldiers. Their heavy boots crushed Mother's summer flowers.

He set his jaw and gripped the rough trunk. How could he rescue his family? Gulping in deep breaths, he hunched over and crept up the hill, darting behind trees. When he reached the huge tree fifty yards from the wide veranda encircling the house, he crouched and poked his head around.

Barricaded behind a dozen shade trees, attackers peppered gunfire at an upstairs window. One shooter hid behind the nymph in their fountain. Another ruffian stooped on the veranda below the parlor window. A spark flickered as the assailant ignited a bundle of twisted straw.

Glass tinkled and the blazing straw arched inside the parlor.

John swallowed the lump clogging his throat. How could he stop so many invaders? He gritted his teeth and dug his fingers into the rough tree trunk. Suicide to go out there.

Thick smoke billowed from the lower windows, blackening the white boards of their home. Just above the blazing parlor, from an upstairs window, shots thundered down on the bandits swarming the house. Through the smoky haze, a lone gunman faced the open window and tried to reload.

Father!

He stood framed against the window, his grim,

determined face pallid through the smoke. Fire spurted from half a dozen guns below. Father dropped his rifle, clutched his head with both hands, fell against the high chest behind him, and then his body hurtled through the open window. He plunged through space and thudded on the grass.

Blast the danger! John bolted across the lawn to his father's side, dove to his knees, and cradled his father's gray head. Blood dripped, spreading a warm pool over John's cold hands.

"Father, can you hear me?" John forced the words through his tight throat. This nightmare couldn't be real. He stared at his father's blood-spattered face. The man who had loved him and guided him as long as he could remember had a frozen look of surprise. John closed his eyes, the sight too horrible to accept. Warm, sticky liquid leaked on his hands. Hot tears forced their way down his cheeks. He'd make Father's killer pay. He'd exact vengeance.

Footsteps clumped through the grass. Father's body limp in his arms, he glanced up.

A stocky man with a crooked nose raced from the shadow of the veranda, and a rifle butt descended. John raised his arms to protect his head, but pain exploded in his skull … darkness threatened to close over him. He fell to his hands and knees almost on top of his father's body and fought to clear his vision.

This couldn't happen. He had to rescue Mother and Pris. Stop these insane men.

Flames jumped through the windows, singed his shirt, and set fire to the grass. A burning timber fell across his father's body. Violent hands grabbed John's arms and dragged him away from the blazing building. Gravel tore his knees. Rough hands jerked his wrists behind his back and rawhide bit into his flesh. He blinked hard and glared up at the man who rifle-butted him. John shook his head, too groggy to fight the soldier tying his wrists together. Another ruffian shoved John, and he landed on his back.

Drifting on the edge of consciousness, head exploding with pain, John caught scattered glimpses of the marauders' relentless work. Looters smashed in the windows with their weapons and squirmed through jagged glass to crawl into the unburned portion of his home. Soot-faced thugs, armed with muskets, pistols, and knives, made repeated trips into the flaming house. They emerged, booty loaded on their backs and straining their arms. The raiders grabbed everything from family heirlooms to copper spittoons. One fat man carried a bronze chamber pot on his head. John tried to squirm into a sitting position. He had to save Mother and Pris. Dizziness forced him to slide down to his side and lower his head. Through tear-blurred eyes, he recognized two of the robbers as neighbors.

Three husky marauders, their calico shirts dark with sweat, strained to steal Mother's rosewood spinet but jammed the beautiful piece in the open front door. As flames devoured the polished wood, the thieves scrambled outside.

Tremors spiked inside John's chest and burst firebrands through the pounding in his head.

Where were Mother and Pris? How could he get to them? When he left this morning, Mother had been sleeping. He hadn't seen her or his baby sister escape. Could she have grabbed Pris and slipped out the back door while Father held off the looters? Or were they still trapped inside their flaming home?

He must help them. Must get them out. He jerked his arms, struggling with the rawhide, but the thongs cut into his wrists and pinned his arms behind his back.

"Dang it. I sure did hanker for thet big house of yourn, but this riffraff they call the Georgia Militia don't obey orders." The man with the crooked nose stood over John. He scowled, seized John's arms, yanked him to his feet, and shook him until John's teeth snapped together. "Your stupid old man put up a fight. He'd still be alive if he'd a come along peaceable." He shoved John hard.

John fell and cracked his left knee against one of the rocks lining the drive. Sharp pain streaked from his knee to his ankle. He grunted.

The man shook his fist at the pillaging troops and kicked the gravel in the driveway. "Dang it! You sorry excuses for soldiers owe me a mansion."

John struggled to his knees, but the world dissolved into blackness. When the darkness receded, intense heat from the inferno scorched his view—or was the fog thick smoke?

He didn't know. Nightmarish figures scattered from the house and headed toward the stables.

John felt detached, as though he were somebody else, standing remote above the body lying in the drive. Was he dead? Had his spirit escaped his body? A sense of duty compelled him to mentally record what the soldiers inflicted on the Ross family. He no longer saw the invaders but heard them even above the crackling fire and falling timbers.

"I git that there Jasper. Never did see no horse flesh could beat thatun!" howled a voice rising above the tumult.

Frightened horses neighed and pranced. Then they were loose, galloping down the drive toward where John lay. Eyes wild, they stampeded from the hooting men. The ground trembled beneath John's head with the roar of their escape.

In the lead, the Ross's high-strung chestnut broodmare fell. A loud snap and he knew her leg had broken. She landed so close the bone protruding at an angle almost caught him in the eye. She squirmed, screaming, pawing the earth, unable to regain her feet. One hoof struck John's shoulder and the next few horses sailed over her, but one that followed too closely trampled her. The chestnut's screams echoed in his ears. With a sudden rush of wind, two other animals jumped him.

Sharp pebbles struck his chest and cheeks. Sweat trickled down other horses' legs as they vaulted over him or galloped by. Greedy men risked being trampled as each tried to rope a blooded horse, some of the fastest in Georgia. Two rough-looking thieves fought for Jasper, John's black stallion.

Lord, please let them fail. Much better to see his horse run wild than belong to bushwhackers.

Rolling together in the gravel, the bandits bit, kicked, and gouged each other.

John tried to whistle for Jasper. If his horse stopped near enough, he might get a leg over Jasper's bare back. But his lips were dried prunes, his tongue plastered to the roof of his mouth. Even as the two brutes tussled on the path, clawing at each other's eyes, a third man leaped upon John's quarter horse and headed for the woods.

John groaned. He loved that horse.

A flying ember landed on his neck, searing his flesh. Each time he inhaled, hot air scorched his lungs. More sparks branded exposed skin. He jerked his hands, but the thongs only cut deeper into his wrists. He struggled to his knees, but the dizzy blackness returned. Collapsing onto his chest, he wormed over the sharp gravel and reached singed grass, hard and prickly against his body. He rolled over and over until the pressure of a tree against his back stopped him. Here the grass felt soft, the shade cool. He rested his aching head against the lush green carpet, his eyes streaming water.

Shoving each other, the thieving mob broke open the doors of the wooden structures housing the Ross slaves.

Looters dragged screaming, fighting, and cringing black women and children outside. A babble of voices merged, with one loud enough to challenge. "I'm gittin' me a slave gal. Take yer hands off her. I had her first. I git her if I got to rip her arm clean off! Leggo, 'fore I shoot you!"

A fox-faced man, greasy hair straggling to his shoulders, tore a crying infant from his mother's arms as another thief dragged the woman onto his horse.

"Hey, Jake, what you want that chile fer?" A nasal Southern voice rose above the tumult.

"My ole lady hankers fer a slave, even iffin she gotta hand raise it." The man cradled the screaming child to his chest and ran for the woods.

Old Mammy Jolene attempted to stand against the mob. "If my man was here, you wouldn't be takin' me nowheres."

"We got them husky field hands 'fore we came here. Surprised 'em. They's tied up safe in them trees yonder. We done put our names on 'em with our knives," a gleeful voice declared. "Hollingshead, you git these here slaves housed up real good, so's we can pick 'em up when we git back. Rest of you men, c'mon, we cain't play here all day," ordered the crooked-nose man who seemed to be in charge. He and another man strode past the flaming ruins of John's home.

Smoke cast a heavy shadow, turning the sky dirty brown and shutting out the sun. The stench of charred wood seared John's nostrils and every breath hurt. Flakes of soot floated thick as rain, to settle in a thin layer over the grass, over the trees, over everything that didn't move.

As though separated from him by a long tunnel, voices echoed strangely before they penetrated his mind.

"Ho, Sergeant. What are we going to do with the lad?"

The rogue turned toward John. "Huh, he still alive? Git him on his feet. He'll be shipped to Indian Territory with the rest of 'em."

The smaller man squatted in front of John. "He don't look any too chipper."

"Dump some water on him an let's git goin'. If he don't git up, shoot him," snarled the man in charge. "Won't git no medals from Gen'l Scott iffen we're late."

"Won't get no medals from Gen'l Scott anyways 'cause of this day's work." The other man muttered and prodded John with a booted foot. "You better git up, kid."

The shock of water drenching his head and face cleared away wisps of the fog. Looking up through a wet film, John shook his head. Pain wrenched a moan from his dry lips.

Through the brilliant sparkle of a million spots dancing before his eyes, he strained to see the two men.

"Listen, boy, I want you to hear this. This is from Gov'nor Gilmer, Georgia's finest." The looter pulled a folded paper from inside his butternut linsey-woolsey shirt and unfolded the sheet as formally as an orator. "To Thomas J. Worthington." He patted his broad chest. "That's me, boy. 'For meritorious service in the Georgia Guard: the plantation, Pleasant Acres, now owned by one Elias A. Ross, consisting of 700 acres of tillable plantation land and forest. Signed, Governor George Gilmer, Georgia.'" He waved the paper in front of John's nose. "Deed's all legal and proper, boy."

"Legal? You thieves." John tried to bellow, but his voice rasped. "You're stealing our plantation." He tugged against his ropes.

Sergeant Worthington assumed a brisk, businesslike manner. "Up on your hind legs!"

When John made no move to obey, the sergeant seized John's arm and dragged him upright.

The ground whirled beneath John's moccasins, and he would have fallen without the support of Sergeant Worthington's sweaty arm. John fought bile rising into his throat, hating his weakness in front of these plunderers.

The sergeant shoved him toward the line of trees marking the gravel drive descending to the road. "Git movin', kid."

An acid hole formed inside John's chest as he gazed back over his shoulder. Water dripped from his hair, and his eyes smarted. He'd failed to get Mother and Pris out of the house.

The Militia murdered Father, and the US Government stole their land.

A wave of grief slipped through John's anger shield. He gazed at the smoldering gash between two ghostly chimneys where wisps of smoke spiraled from glowing ashes. The black hole had been home these nineteen years and yet, he would not give way to anguish. John stiffened his spine, jutted his chin, and glared at Sergeant Worthington.

"I'll make the Governor of Georgia sorry for this day's work! He'll pay for my father's murder. And you'll hand me back the deed to our property."

ANNE GREENE BIO

Anne Greene's home is in Allen, Texas, just a few miles north of Dallas. Her husband is a retired Colonel, Army Special Forces. Her blonde and white Shih Tzu, Lily Valentine, shares her writing space, curled at her feet. She has four beautiful, talented children, and eight grandchildren.

Besides her first love, writing, she enjoys travel, art, reading, and movies. Life is good. Jesus said, "I am come that you might have life and that you might have it more abundantly." Whether writing contemporary or historical, her books celebrate the abundant life.

If you're an electronic reader, CLICK ON THE FOLLOWING LINKS to learn about Anne's other books. If you are a print book reader, you will find all her books listed on her website, http://www.AnneGreeneAuthor.com or on Amazon.com.

Anne Greene writes about ordinary people who do extraordinary things. She delights in writing about alpha heroes who aren't afraid to fall on their knees in prayer and about gutsy heroines. She writes both historical and suspense novels.

For Such A Time, The Story of Jarrett Ross is Anne's 40th novel. The first book of her Ross Family Saga is titled *Trail of Tears, the Story of John Ross. Angel With Steel Wings* is the first book in Anne's WWII Women of Courage series. A visit to

Scotland resulted in Anne's award-winning Scottish historicals, *Masquerade Marriage* and its sequel, *Marriage By Arrangement*. Anne's Holly Garden Detective series blasts off with *Red Is For Rookie*. *Shadow of the Dagger* is a contemporary suspense. Plus Anne's 34 exciting novellas. Anne and her hero husband, Army Special Forces Colonel Larry Greene, live in McKinney, Texas. Tim LaHaye led Anne to the Lord when she was twenty-one, and Chuck Swindoll is her Pastor. Anne's highest hope is that her stories transport you to awesome new worlds and touch your heart to seek a deeper spiritual relationship with the Lord Jesus. Anne is a multi-award-winning author.

BOOKS BY ANNE GREENE
Angel With Steel Wings, Book I of World War II series, Women of Courage
Red Is For Rookie, Book I of Holly Garden Detective series
Shadow of The Dagger, Book I of CIA Operatives series
Trail of Tears, The Story of John Ross, Book 1 of the Ross Family Saga
Masquerade Marriage
Marriage By Arrangement

NOVELLAS BY ANNE GREENE

A Christmas Belle
A Crazy Optimist
A Groom for Christmas
A Rebel Spy
A Small Voice
A Texas Christmas Mystery
A Williamsburg Christmas
Angel with Steel Wings
Avoiding the Mistletoe
Brides of the Wild West
Daredevils
Dollar Brides
Hatteras Island Mystery
Her Reluctant Hero
Holly Garden, PI: Red Is for Rookie
Keara's Escape
Lacey and the Law
Lord Bentley Needs A Bride
Love At Christmas
Marriage By Arrangement
Masquerade Marriage
Mystery at Dead Broke Ranch
One Groom Is Not Enough
Recipe For A Husband
Shadow of The Dagger
Spur of the Moment Bride
Texas Law
The Choice
Tipsy in Love
Trail of Tears, The Story of John Ross

<u>Anne Greene Author Home Page</u>

<u>Anne Greene's Books on Amazon</u>

www.ingramcontent.com/pod-product-compliance
Lightning Source LLC
Chambersburg PA
CBHW070556300726
48975CB00006B/1599